SINS

OF OUR

FATHERS

SINS OF OUR FATHERS

A novel

SHAWN LAWRENCE OTTO

MILKWEED EDITIONS

Published 2014 by Milkweed Editions
Printed in Canada
Cover design by Mary Austin Speaker
Cover photo/illustration is in the public domain.
Author photo by Jeff Johnson
14 15 16 17 18   5 4 3 2 1
First Edition

Milkweed Editions, an independent nonprofit publisher, gratefully acknowledges sustaining support from the Bush Foundation; the Patrick and Aimee Butler Foundation; the Driscoll Foundation; the Jerome Foundation; the Lindquist & Vennum Foundation; the McKnight Foundation; the National Endowment for the Arts; the Target Foundation; and other generous contributions from foundations, corporations, and individuals. Also, this activity is made possible by the voters of Minnesota through a Minnesota State Arts Board Operating Support grant, thanks to a legislative appropriation from the arts and cultural heritage fund, and a grant from the Wells Fargo Foundation Minnesota. For a full listing of Milkweed Editions supporters, please visit www.milkweed.org.

Library of Congress Cataloging-in-Publication Data

Otto, Shawn Lawrence.
Sins of our fathers / Shawn Lawrence Otto.
p. cm.
ISBN 978-1-57131-109-2
Summary: "After embezzling funds to support his gambling addiction, an unscrupulous white banker in Minnesota is blackmailed by his boss into sabotaging the creation of a competing, Native American-owned bank. As the banker befriends the people he's trying to frame, he struggles to escape from his past and do the right thing"-- Provided by publisher.
1. Banks and banking--Fiction. 2. Extortion--Fiction. 3. Whites--Relations with Indians--Fiction. 4. Compulsive gamblers--Fiction. 5. Self-realization--Fiction. I. Title.
PS3615.T95S56 2014
813'.6—dc23   2014024589

Milkweed Editions is committed to ecological stewardship. We strive to align our book production practices with this principle, and to reduce the impact of our operations in the environment. We are a member of the Green Press Initiative, a nonprofit coalition of publishers, manufacturers, and authors working to protect the world's endangered forests and conserve natural resources. *Sins of Our Fathers* was printed on acid-free 100% postconsumer-waste paper by the Friesens Corporation.

To the underdogs

SINS

OF OUR

FATHERS

I

THE DEAL

I

The first thing JW noticed when he walked into the Hiawatha room was how different it was from what he had expected. Its low-rise tiers of seating resembled an upscale college lecture hall more than a hotel conference room. And it was surprisingly full. The air was rich with the colognes and perfumes of suited bankers. They moved up the floral-swirled tiers like a herd of mountain sheep. Clumps of them murmured in side eddies, and others sat to open laptops or check cell phones. A pretty brown-haired woman in the front row smiled encouragingly at him. He thought he might remember her from the Bemidji branch.

The setting was actually quite good, he decided, as he navigated between the long front table and the whiteboard. He was here to teach, after all, though his subject was a little different than the usual product introductions and regulatory claptrap people dozed through at these conferences: crashing on donut frosting and waiting for the next coffee break, then cordial and chummy at the lunch buffets before finally coming alive with free-flowing alcohol and the grind music of the last decade in the evenings. Unlike their more-buttoned-up CPA brethren, bankers tended to be party animals—not like the crazy excesses of the investment community, of course; no cocaine-tinged threesomes, no strippers—but edgy enough to be shocking to their customers nonetheless, were they to see them in the evenings at one of these conferences.

In many ways, JW's presentation appealed to this racier side of banking, because it dealt with danger, and not danger in the traditional sense, but existential danger, and its dramatic companion—opportunity. Instead of delivering the usual boring drone on the security features of the new hundred-dollar bill, he was here to talk about crime—specifically, redlining, and how to avoid being accused of it while still maximizing returns.

The room was packed and abuzz with an expectant air. Bankers stole glances at him and then went back to their huddled conversations, their leaned-in, best-new-friends-since-last-night joke-telling, their texts and e-mails about how boring it all was to their honeys back home.

He found a limp dongle of black cords emerging from a hole in the center of the table. He opened his briefcase and pulled out his laptop, unspooled and connected its cables. At forty, he was still in decent shape. He still had his hair, and it was still brown. He wore it swept back and a little to the side, though a few boyish sprigs always seemed to flop over the left edge of his forehead. He had a slight scar above his right eyebrow: a reminder of his teenage years training horses. It gave him a rugged air of adventure that contrasted nicely with his well-tailored banker's suit and his crisp white shirt. An air of mystery, his wife Carol called it, which was appropriate for talking about crime and its avoidance, something she found sexy. He was quite presentable, all things considered, and to the extent that being a leader creates charisma, he had a special magic about him when he was on the circuit doing presentations. He stuck a USB clicker into the slot on his laptop, touched the room control screen to light the hotel projector, and brought up his presentation:

BANKING IN INDIAN COUNTRY
Presented by John White
North Lake Bank, North Lake, Minnesota
Midwest Community Banking Conference
Dakota Grand Hotel, Minneapolis

He glanced at the clock. It was still a minute early, and more bankers were shuffling in. He had forty minutes. He pulled out his cell phone and checked his e-mail, but his inbox held nothing new apart from the usual junk mail for online gaming sites and reduced-rate mortgages. He set the phone down and cast his blue-gray eyes—Finnish eyes, his mother had called them—out over the audience, waiting patiently and silently as the stragglers found the few remaining seats. It was a full house.

He noted the bankers' suits from last season. Their briefcases' pale worn edges. Their creased shoes. How some of the women—late thirties (mojito-drinking karaoke singers, no doubt)—unexpectedly carried needlepoint handbags against their polyester skirts, done in Norwegian or German designs. They were mostly small-town bankers, these clues told him. Rotarians. Lions. Deacons. Community leaders. He saw Charlie Weston from New Ulm, and Bill Heimlich from Redwood Falls, and Ann Wilson from Detroit Lakes, all presidents of small-town community banks. He had once capsized a fishing boat on Rainy Lake with Ken Iverson and his boss, Frank Jorgenson. The three of them were drunk silly on vodka gimlets, and laughed as they found their footing in chest-deep water next to the dock. But those days were long past. He waited until the last of the bankers settled into their seats before he began to speak.

"When I first started in community banking, the only

reason for people to visit an Indian reservation was to buy moccasins and blankets. Now, people flock to their casinos in droves, and they make money hand over fist. The playing field has changed, and we community bankers need to up our game. I know many of you have banks in communities near Indian reservations, so today I will show you some tools to help you up that game, while avoiding some of the most common legal pitfalls. But I'm also going to warn you: things are not always as they seem."

Over the years, JW had honed the drama of this opening with the air of a magician. When he did it well, it grabbed his audience's attention from the first sentence. He sometimes felt he should have been a teacher, or perhaps a stage actor. He enjoyed playing an audience: reading them and molding the shape and rise of their emotions—these things came to him naturally, as if he were conducting a symphony. He walked along the whiteboard, stepping in and out of the Powerpoint with the confidence of a showman, one hand in his pocket as he changed it to a new slide:

MANAGING RISK ON A RESERVATION

He turned up the front lights enough to bathe himself in a milky wash, highlighting the whiteness of his shirt, his close shave, his shining eyes. The sun was brilliant outside, and it seeped in through the dark vertical blinds. With the audience in shadow, he felt as if he were a thespian under stage lights.

"So who can tell me the biggest risk banks have when lending to Native Americans on a reservation?" As he waited for an answer he took a Styrofoam cup from a stack and poured coffee. Audiences always took their time with this one, which was an important part of his build. For all their raucous private partying, bankers were terrified of the discussion he was proposing, because it was public. They were happy to talk about race—guardedly, with known entities, and in small groups—but they didn't know how to deal with it in a public forum. He tipped in some creamer and stirred, the black of his coffee going tan. He sipped and watched them adjust to the unnerving idea of discussing it in the open.

One of the bankers in the second row finally shifted and looked around with a sort of cocksure grin. He had reddish tanned skin, gold chains, spiky hair, and a party-ready attitude. He reminded JW of a former high-school football star who had faded to pudge. His demeanor seemed to say "what the hell": a monkey who found the cage door standing open and decided to plunge through.

"They're deadbeats?" he volunteered. He grinned and bobbed his head as he looked around for supporters. JW imagined him leading a conga line later, Hawaiian shirt open, his drink raised like a baton. A few of the bankers chuckled noncommittally as they glanced at JW to see how far he would let them go. This was code, a way of asking whether this sort of good-old-boy racism would be tolerated. The woman in the front row shot him an angry glare for even letting it get this far, then rolled her eyes and shook her head to signal her displeasure at the inappropriate remark.

He set his coffee down. It always amazed him how this one question touched things off. Race was still a powder keg, and its frank discussion divided audiences with powerful, emotional reactions, which is of course why he used it. He had once read, when researching for a discussion with his daughter, Julie, who loved science, that much like humans, primates ostracize one another and commit violence and murder, particularly against other tribes. Exploring that impulse was his intent: to stir up these primal feelings and to present people with their own racism (for they all had it), and then to dig deeper and get past it. People didn't know how to talk about race; there was no safe territory. It was buried under political correctness, as untouchable as a dead pharaoh, its brains pulled out and its body wrapped in cloth and then gold and then stone. Buried away. Long gone and desiccated under a pyramid of laws and regulations and social mores, brick by brick, that now generally forbade its discussion. But it lived still, underground, in small-group conversations, and even more openly now in Tea Party politics. Truth be told, many laws and regulations did go too far, and they created resentments, he thought, because they gave unfair advantages that could sometimes be dangerous to businesses, and to banks in particular. That's why they were all here today. To work through all that. To separate race from business. To get their heads straight and to clarify *intent*, a word that contained a universe. He gestured toward the man and began to unwind the mummy.

"That," he told the audience, "is exactly the kind of thinking they use to outsmart us."

No one moved. The air conditioning came on, and the window blinds began to shift and clatter, letting in streaks of light that shot over him, then faded like an old movie. "We can no longer afford to underestimate these people," he said. "They're making way too much money. Let me give you an example." He walked around to the front of the table. "I had this customer, a builder, who said to the Potawatomi band in Wisconsin, a hundred and fifty miles away, he said, 'I will build you a bingo hall, for free. You don't have to pay me a red cent. You just pay me out of cash flow when you get it up and running. I will finance it for ten percent annually on the outstanding balance and give you a ten-year loan. I will take all the risk. All of it.' Well, we lent him the money to do it, and we lent it to him at eight percent. Going rate for commercial loans was six. So everybody's set up to make good money. Right?" He surveyed the room. "Potawatomi win, builder wins, bank wins."

He studied them, a hand in his pocket, and went on to describe how hard the builder had to fight to get the permit because the local community was up in arms over the idea of Indians and gambling. There were political battles at the planning commission over a variance they needed for a new access road. The builder went through real heartache—expensive delays, his windshield damaged, his tires slashed—but the resort owners came to the rescue after JW visited the town. He simply made the point that the band wasn't building a hotel, just a bingo hall, and people would need places to stay.

JW pushed off the desk and watched his audience's reaction. "So a year later, he finally got it built. Band had a grand opening, and you know how long it took them to pay it off? Three months. Three months to pay off the entire construction loan. Potawatomi won on that one. Now they got a hundred-and-forty room hotel."

He stood silently, watching them. Sipped his coffee. "Do they sound like deadbeats?" He paused and looked at the pudgy playboy, who shrugged. "Please avoid all the old chestnuts about race. I'm not interested in grinding whatever prejudices or opinions people may have about Native Americans, however valid or invalid they may be. This is about business. I'm strictly looking at banking risk, specific to lending to Native Americans living on a reservation."

He walked back to his laptop, where he underlined the

words *risk* and *on a reservation* with his forefinger. Two yellow streaks arched across the projected slide behind him. He waited, but no one else seemed ready to engage.

"The risk," he said, "is the reservation itself. Let me give you another example." He began walking, and then he looked up at his audience. "About a year ago, a fellow walked into my bank in North Lake, a Native fellow, Ojibwe, named Johnny Eagle. Tall, thin guy, good shape. Clean, well put together. Italian shoes, thousand-dollar suit. Turns out he'd been in there before to see my loan officer, Sam Schmeaker. Sam had turned him down for a loan, so he asked to see me. Ordinarily I don't second-guess my loan officers' decisions, you know how that goes, but he was Native. So it's a riskier situation. Right? You know this."

Several bankers nodded and some shifted. Many of them managed banks near Indian reservations, and they knew the risks he was describing. EEOC risk. Compliance risk. The story was beginning to work its magic.

"Receptionist showed him in, we shook hands, he sat down, and right off the bat, as I open the file, he says, 'It's a creditworthy application.' So I knew he had some sort of banking knowledge, right? I found his credit report, high seven hundreds. He had good credit. This was starting to look like a problem for us. Then he told me, 'I happen to know that my band has several million dollars on deposit with your bank, and yet you barely make any loans to us. Why is that?' He was watching me closely, and suddenly I felt like I was in a chess game. This was getting dangerous from a regulatory point of view, I thought, and this guy could be setting me up, so I had to be careful. He might be accusing me of a crime."

"I looked him straight in the eye and I told him we love to make loans to his band. Love them. That's how a bank makes money, I said, is on the spread between loan interest and deposit interest. He held up a hand and sat back in his chair. He told me I didn't need to educate him about banking. He was talking about loans to his *people*, he said, not the band."

JW walked back along the front of the table. He leaned back against the desk.

"He said to me, 'Look, Mr. White, I'll give it to you straight. Have you ever heard of an Indian car competition?' And so I'll ask you now. Have you?" JW paused and watched the audience, the sudden silence a sound all its own. No one raised a hand. "Come on, you people bank in Indian country!" He looked at the woman in front. "You?" She shook her head and looked down.

He launched off the soapstone counter and walked back around the desk, clicking the slide advancer. "I hadn't either," he said. Towering over him was a slide of a jalopy cobbled together from different cars of different sizes, makes, and colors. Its front fender was blue, a door was red, and the hood green. A supercharger emerged through a hole in the hood, its air scoop made out of an old tuba. It had a spoked wheel in front and a truck wheel in back, and a rear spoiler made out of two-by-sixes. An Indian in glasses was grinning from the driver's seat and waving a trophy out the window. The overall effect was comical, and some of the audience laughed. Others sat back in their chairs, two fingers on their cheeks or their arms folded, unsure what was permitted or expected of them. Fifteen minutes in and he had them.

"This is the winner of an Indian car competition." He said this with a straight face, but his wry tone carried an expectation of mirth, and more people laughed. Even the woman in front was smiling up at the grin on the Native American's face. "Johnny Eagle told me they have them at powwows and on some of the reservations," he said. "An Indian car is a car that's been pieced together from the parts of other junked cars, and sometimes other stuff. They have competitions to see who can have the craziest, silliest-looking one that still runs. This guy obviously has a creative flair." The audience laughed again.

"So Eagle described some of them, smiling the whole time, but as soon as I laughed like you are he slapped his hand on my desk!" JW slapped his hand on the table loudly. Half of the audience jumped. He was scowling, feigning anger.

"'You don't have the right to laugh,' he told me, even though they're supposed to be funny. Imagine that. Here he had coaxed me into laughing at something even he thought was funny, then he criticized me for laughing at it because I'm white." He looked at them. "That's racist. Yet science tells us that there's no appreciable difference between the races, that the concept of race is a social construct." He looked at the woman in front again, pointed to her. "You laughed. Why do you think he wouldn't like that?"

She blanched. "I don't know," she said.

"Do you think you were being racist?"

"No."

He nodded. "You weren't. You were the victim of a setup, comedic or otherwise. He said that Indians do it to make light of a bad situation: They can't get loans because they have no credit, and they have no credit because they can't get loans, and that's wrong, wouldn't I agree? 'A bank that did that,' he said, 'that took Indian deposits and still refused to lend, should be put out of business,' would I not agree."

JW pointed an accusing finger at his audience, still in character. Then he calmed. The air conditioning turned off and the window blinds fell back. It was the halfway point, where the arguments turned and began to get complicated and dangerous. He walked again, and his Nordic bearing returned as their eyes followed him.

"So you can see the danger," he said. "The man wasn't there to plead his case, he was there to plead his people's case. He was on the verge of accusing me, my colleague Sam Schmeaker, and the whole bank, of racism and redlining—in short, of a crime. All because Schmeaker had rejected his loan app and I had laughed at a situation that he had portrayed as amusing. So now the customer isn't the customer anymore, is he? He's become the enemy. Let's be honest, we've all seen this." JW continued walking, and he began to gesture with each new example. "There's the woman, no offense to the women in the room, who left the bank claiming sexual harassment that nobody else had seen, and demanded six figures or she would sue. Or the minority employee who, when fired for a documented cause, filed an EEOC complaint, claiming discrimination, and demanded a six-figure settlement. The Muslim who sued because there was no special room set aside to pray five times a day at work. The custodian who faked a back injury and claimed permanent disability, then was seen out golfing. Right? You don't make it in business without spotting the predators who turn laws that are designed to level the playing field into tools of extortion. Because if you're not careful, they're going to get you. And if they do, it's going to drive up prices for your customers, if it doesn't put you out of business."

"The same kind of thing can happen in a lending situation. Federal laws designed to ensure equal opportunity can be abused by predators to put a bank at a legal disadvantage and to extort money. So in banking, if you're smart, what do you do? You have to use the law preemptively in order to keep the advantage and keep the playing field level so those bad actors can't get a foothold to build a case."

The bankers in the seminar room were riveted. JW's stories conjured up so many aspects of race, law, and economics that seemed fraught with peril—both personal and professional. This was his intent. For a student to learn, you first had to elevate their level of concern, he believed, and then you had to create cognitive dissonance. He did this by playing with their fears and prejudices, and setting them against their hopes.

As he moved back to the center he saw his boss, Frank Jorgenson, sneaking up the steps at the side of the room. Jorgenson was a co-sponsor of the conference this year. After a decade at North Lake, he had gone on to manage the bank chain's entire Greater Minnesota operations, and now people considered him CEO material. Several of the bankers sat up as he climbed the tiers. At fifty-five he had a round face and extremely close-cropped hair. He carried himself with the swaggering, faux-jolly demeanor of a cop, with a big white smile and a toothpick stuck in the corner of his mouth. He had cautious eyes that were constantly sizing people up. He leaned against the wall, his growing belly emerging from his suit coat like a sack of oats. He waved JW on.

"Okay. So a Native customer with decent credit asks why we don't lend more to his people. Almost a threat, but not quite. So the situation is delicate, to say the least." He watched them think it over. "One false move and you could wind up in a lawsuit. The most important thing for you to do at that moment is what?"

He scanned for hands and took another sip of coffee. It

had the faint flavor of burnt plastic, so he set it down. He checked his watch. He had ten minutes left. A balding banker near the window raised a hand.

"Yessir," said JW.

"I think your hands are tied."

"Why?"

"Well, we run from that stuff. Federal law prohibits redlining—"

"And the Community Reinvestment Act requires banks to apply the same lending criteria in all communities," said another banker in the center. He had a self-important moustache and blow-dried hair.

"If they escalate it to the branch president," said the first man, "and they can show income and collateral, you gotta approve or you expose the bank to a lawsuit."

JW nodded and waited for any further objections. This was the point where he would pivot the talk. He glanced up at Jorgenson and saw a twinkle in his eye.

"One word," he said. He advanced the slide to show a handshake between a white hand and a Native American one.

"Empathy."

He looked at them, then launched back into his story. "The surest defense against this sort of predator is a hand reached out in friendship. This makes clear that you are not doing what he is accusing you of. And it protects you in court later on."

He ran through a series of slides illustrating the bank's outreach to the Native community. "We donate to the Indian college fund. We sponsor the Native Night Out against crime on the reservation. We're a sponsor of the reservation high school sports teams. We try to be a good neighbor in the community. That kind of outreach, that empathy, was doubly important in this guy's case. He had been a banker himself, right here in Minneapolis, before moving back to the reservation. In fact, he probably had more CE credits than most people in this room. And make no mistake, a legally sophisticated opponent is by far the most dangerous. So. Preemptive community outreach. But there was still a question. Why would he accuse us of redlining if he was just trying to get a personal loan? The man must have successfully navigated the line between race and business for years in Minneapolis. He had to know that barking at me like that would set off red flags. So what do you think? Was he try-ing to entrap us?"

JW paused and scanned the room while they thought. "When you don't know the answer to a question like that," he said, "and most times you don't, there is still one good defense. More empathy. 'I really empathize with members of your band,' I told him. 'How frustrating it must be, deal-ing with people like Sam Schmeaker, and what can seem like a double standard.' He was disarmed. His whole pos-ture changed. 'Redlining is illegal,' I told him, 'and worse, it's wrong. I'm sorry if Sam offended you. For what it's worth,' I said, 'I do know that was definitely not his intent.' Those last four words are critical under Regulation B of the Equal Credit Opportunity Act. Repeat after me: 'definitely not our intent.'"

He conducted the audience in the recitation. "Good."

The slide changed to one showing the phrase. JW looked around the room at his audience. The balding banker by the window was confused.

"So you approved the loan?"

JW shook his head. "No. This is where the risk of the reservation we discussed earlier comes into play. It has noth-ing to do with him, or with race, okay, so forget all that. What matters is Regulation B, which says, and I quote, 'The act and regulation may prohibit a creditor practice that is discriminatory in effect because it has a disproportionately negative impact on a prohibited basis, even though the creditor has no intent to discriminate and the practice appears neutral on its face, unless the creditor practice meets a legitimate business need that cannot reasonably be achieved as well by means that are less disparate in their impact.' Okay? It's the 'legitimate business need' we are talking about. I'm not trying to discriminate, and I'm not racist. In fact, I help the Native community. I do outreach; I give them money. But my job is to protect my bank's assets. I have a legitimate business need to do that, or I can't continue banking. I can't assume someone can't pay, but I can point to the legal problems inherent in lending on an Indian reservation. So I told him, 'Your reservation is a domestically dependent sovereign nation, and as such it does not have to recognize certain federal laws with regard to foreclosures.' He immediately objected—"

JW shot up a strident finger, assuming Eagle's role again.

"But I cut him off. 'Of course I want to help you! We're in the business of making loans, right? Be silly not to. And frankly, we'd be absolutely crazy not to want to do business with a customer with your credit history. But,' I said. 'I need you to help me.' 'How can I do that?' he asked. And I said, 'Very simple. Very easy—'"

JW held his hands open as he reenacted the encounter. His eyes shone. "As a condition of the loan, you sign a waiver that prohibits you and your band from using their sovereign status as a shield to avoid legal disputes filed in United States courts. If you default, we have a right to acquire a portion of tribal land. Can I have Sam prepare that for us?"

JW strolled across the seminar room as they contemplated the legal maneuver he had just described.

Jorgenson watched from his place against the wall. JW knew that this is what Jorgenson had invited him to the conference to do. He had told JW he would make sure that every president and vice president from every Capitol Bank Holdings branch in Greater Minnesota was in this room. Jorgenson couldn't say these things himself, not in his position, but he wanted JW's methods to become wider practice as the chain expanded its holdings in communities near casinos. Reducing the downside was absolutely essential to his expansion plan. And improving the performance of the Greater Minnesota banks overall was the key to his campaign to be named CEO when the Old Man retired. It stood to reason that such a development would also be very good for his old protégé, JW.

"Typically," JW went on, "the Native customer will reject this condition for legal or, more often, emotional reasons. As you can understand. These structural legal conflicts are a sad part of our country's legacy, something none of us should be satisfied with. We have simply got to do better. But tribes are domestically dependent sovereign nations. They own reservation land collectively, not as individuals, and as bankers it's neither your fault that it is this way nor your responsibility to fix it. You can't change the legal system or the very unfortunate history of the United States when it comes to the treatment of Native Americans. You are required to work within it, and you have a legitimate business need to protect your customers' assets to the best of your ability. Now, I'll look for an answer from a brave soul." JW faced the audience, his hands in his pockets.

"Is this redlining? Is it a crime?"

His shirt was a brilliant white, his tie a lavender slash.

He was almost done, and on time. Just a few minutes left for them to understand, his lessons slipping into their thinking, their mental scales tilting. Finally the balding banker replied in a voice that was barely audible.

"No," he said. "It isn't."

His look admitted the truth of this, but nevertheless he seemed defeated by it. JW saw Jorgenson make a note in his cell phone as he watched the man's reticence. Jorgenson viewed anyone who wasn't adamantly in support as a bitter enemy, and someone to purge. It was his one major weakness.

JW gave a slow, gentle nod.

"No. The gentleman is right. He is absolutely correct. This is not redlining. This is business. You have left the choice up to the customer. Remember, this is the free market. You are using an inherent conflict in federal law to protect your assets, which you are obligated to do as a fiduciary. And, incidentally, any choice the customer makes, you win. You can protect your bank, which is your depositors' funds, your community's funds, and you can make money. You have reduced your exposure to risk, and hung onto your casino deposits."

The room was silent. A tone sounded and a female announcer's voice came on over the room's speakers.

"This concludes our afternoon breakout sessions," she said. "Please join us for a wine and cheese reception in the Pocahontas Room."

For a moment, the bankers remained in their chairs, mulling ethics, profits, and legality. It was, as JW had said, a new era. The buzzword at the conference was aggregation, which meant cobbling many small victories together into larger portfolio gains. It's what the big boys were doing, and it required intelligence and agility at the margins—the very qualities JW was talking about. The law was no longer a sim-

ple set of boundaries to the playing field; it was sports equipment to be used in the game. Community bankers needed to
get more aggressive or they were going to get eaten for lunch.
They had to remember their role. They weren't legislators or
social workers. They weren't there to right the greater wrongs
of society. They were bankers. And as the plenary speaker
had said in the morning keynote, "If you're not at the table,
you're on the menu."

Jorgenson shifted off the wall. He drew his hands from
his pockets and started to clap. The bankers glanced over
at him and then joined in. He walked down the steps along
the wall as the applause continued. The bankers gathered up
their briefcases and swag bags and began to mill out.

"John White," he said, stepping up to the table, "you are
a strategic genius."

JW smiled wryly and coiled his power cord. "I guess that's
why you made me branch president."

Jorgenson laughed. "Guilty as charged. You got time for
a Grain Belt?"

JW looked at the clock and winced. "I told Carol I'd
be home for dinner. It's a four-hour drive. Can I take a rain
check?"

He saw a cloud pass briefly across Jorgenson's face, then
it was gone. Jorgenson smiled and nodded. "Yeah, sure. How
is that beauty queen?"

"Oh, you know Carol. Always into something."

The two of them walked out onto the mezzanine, where
conference-goers were congregating in small groups or speaking with industry reps at display tables along the walls. Like
royals, they strolled toward the glass balcony and rode the
escalator to the vast atrium below.

They shook hands at the bottom, and then JW pushed

his way out into the afternoon sun. It was bright and hot, and as he turned he could still see Jorgenson, a ghost beyond the glare of the plate glass, standing there watching, with a hand in his pocket. For an instant, his expression seemed almost malevolent, but then the glare shifted and Jorgenson smiled and waved. JW waved back and stepped across Nicollet Mall, heading toward his parking ramp.

2

Jorgenson's expression stayed with JW as his dirty white Caprice made its way north and west into a purple-orange sunset. He had left the interstate just before Duluth and taken a four-lane, divided artery that angled off into the north country. After an hour it lost its median and came together, squeezing its way into a small town and finally ending at a flashing red light. JW turned onto a narrow, two-lane capillary that shot out past a Cenex station and a Dairy Queen (three people in line at the small yellow window—a handful of kids romping on a red picnic table—a girl crying over a dropped cone on the sidewalk, long light in her blonde curls) and then he was out into the rolling farm fields and sudden bluffs of Minnesota's Iron Range.

The region's iron and taconite mines had sprouted dozens of little towns full of Finns, Croats, Cornish, and Italians—all of them stout, resilient people who could cheerfully survive decades stooped in tunnels moiling with pickaxes, so long as they had beers and pasties and the love of friends and good women. An hour ahead, in one of those range towns with its little Victorian houses covered in asbestos shakes, his wife Carol and their thirteen-year-old daughter Julie were waiting for him.

The road plunged into an area of glacial moraines. The sun lit the tops of the domes and angled long brown fingers into the valleys. Columns of shadowed geese piled down onto shimmering lakes, forming dark squabbling islands. Wetlands grow damp beards of fog.

For the first part of the drive, JW had listened to an audiobook called *The Power of Habit,* about whether or not we have free will. It was a question that had come to occupy him recently. He had started listening to science books like this when Julie was eight or nine and he ordinarily loved them, but tonight he kept reaching up to turn the player off. The feral look in Jorgenson's eyes kept coming back to him. He wondered if he had imagined it, or if he had overlooked something important in their parting exchange about getting a beer. He hoped he hadn't missed a career opportunity. He and Carol were tight on money, and if a new opportunity to help Jorgenson had been in the offing he should have stayed and gotten the beer. Even though Carol was expecting him, she would have understood.

Each time he turned the player back on, the worry boiled back up, and he turned it off again to think things through. He finally unrolled the windows to let the grassy air fill the car and buffet his ears with noise. Jorgenson was going to make a play for CEO when the Old Man retired. Maybe this had been a chance for the upper executives to feel JW out, to see if he could fill Frank's shoes managing the Greater Minnesota branches.

If that was the case, Carol wouldn't want to move. She loved North Lake. He wondered if he could somehow manage things from there. After his dad was laid off from Reserve Steel, JW remembered, he had taken a job selling leases for cell phone towers. The job had him on the road a lot, but he had made it work. "How do you know when you're up North?" his dad used to ask farmers in order to loosen them up. "There's no sign announcing it, but you know you're there when the Dairy Queen sells bait." It always got a laugh.

On the other hand, maybe Frank had discovered the loan he had made to himself, and wanted to discuss it in private. A spike of anxiety shot through him. That would explain the predatory quality JW thought he had seen in his eyes. As he drove onward, his mind swung from one possibility to the other. He decided to call Jorgenson in the morning to apologize, and to see if the conversation led anywhere.

The stakes were high. North Lake was a torn-up town after the mines closed, and many of the workers, who lost their jobs and their pensions, still pined for the old days. There still wasn't as much opportunity as there had been. It was during this aftermath that he and Carol had first fallen in love—a love that was in many ways responsible for his working for Jorgenson now.

Carol Ingersoll was the daughter of one of the town's most respected families. With fine blonde hair swept over her low forehead, her round blue-gray eyes and knobby nose, her wide neck and button chin, she wasn't a classic beauty. But she had an angular jawline and plush lips, so she was thought of as the town beauty nonetheless. She was popular and personable, she was believed to be smart, and she was at the top of the social food chain. JW, on the other hand, was a scrappy seventeen-year-old horse trainer, a loner in school with middling grades, who worked to make extra money to support himself during the long stretches when his dad was away on the road.

He thought about the moment of their meeting. He was delivering a mare from Fredrickson's Barn to Olson's Stables, which was the more upscale horse barn that catered to lake people from the Twin Cities. Everybody was trying to figure out ways to make money off the lake people. The Main Street businesses had even started selling North Woods–themed kitsch and faux antiques to attract vacationers.

He remembered hauling Fredrickson's old blue horse trailer into Olson's gravel lot, the truck's rusted fenders flapping like an old person's jowls. He slowed to a stop in a cloud of yellow dust near the mouth of the red-and-white barn, by far the most suc- cessful boarding facility in the area. Its main door stood open to the sun, and its broad center aisle shone with the muted wood planking and bright silver bars of horse stalls. Bales of pine shav- ings were stacked on pallets just inside, and a delivery worker was loading his forklift back onto the end of his truck. JW turned to let the mare out and saw Carol and her friend Mary Beth walk- ing toward the barn.

"Hey," she said, with a little wave and a smile. Such per- sonal acknowledgment was unexpected. But in that one wave the notion that he could have this most desirable of girls shot through him. He could immediately imagine her smell, the feeling of her fine arms and hands, her hair on his face. His mind raced. Olson needed a younger trainer like JW, he told the stable owner when he checked in the horse. It would help bring in the girls.

"Where the girls go, the families go," JW said. Olson knew it was true. Horses had mostly become a girl thing in recent years, and so Olson took JW up on his offer to work a week for free to see what he could do. By July it had become a full-time summer job. He'd taken the girls off barn nags and put them on two of Olson's fancy show horses. He promised he wouldn't let the girls screw them up, and he worked with them in the riding ring out by the road, where two pretty girls bouncing on horseback brought in even more clients for the stable and its talented young trainer.

By August, when Mary Beth went on a family vacation

to the Wisconsin Dells, Carol came for private lessons. He took her on long trail rides through the thick grasses along the riverbed. They talked about life and their classmates as the water flowed by, thick and brown. Most of the time it was Carol doing the talking, and JW thrilled to feel her thigh brushing against him, or to direct her hand placement with his own.

By the beginning of the school year they had become a couple, throwing the town's social balance out of order. She told her friends that he was really smart, but despite what he would come to think of as her down-to-earthness, her crowd was one of speedboats, water skis, and downhill skiing trips to Spirit Mountain—or even Aspen—in the winters. Her friends were the children of the top executives from the paper mill and the former mine manager. JW had grown up in a four-room house, and the farthest he'd been was Fargo. Yet somehow—after a few weeks of gossip and consternation—he became cool, a token of their open-mindedness, and the social stratification of early high school began to fall away.

He and Carol continued riding. He loved her sleek blonde hair, her plush pink lips, and the strange gray-blue pools of her round eyes. At night they had exuberant sex—in the tack room, in an empty stall thick with pine shavings, in the changing rooms of horse trailers. He loved the sound of her gasping, rhythmic sighs.

In the spring he was invited to the Ingersoll home for dinner. Arguably the nicest house in town, it was a classic brick and clapboard two-story colonial with mini-mansion touches—the small, white-columned front portico, twelve-pane double-hung windows, and white painted shutters. The interior had an enormous wood-paneled family room hung with brass rubbings from England and a high trompe l'oeil ceiling painted like a summer sky. Mrs. Ingersoll kept fresh flowers in vases and plastic on the pale sofas in the living room.

Carol and her younger brother, Evan, who was twelve, sat opposite JW at the Queen Anne dining table, with Carol's parents, Bob and Mary, on either end. He remembered the light streaming through the lacy living-room curtains and falling across the ashen blue carpeting. Mary's knife clicked faintly against her china as she quizzed him, the expanse of the living room opening up behind her. "Have you given much thought to what you're going to do? For a career."

"A little bit," he replied. "Right now I'm thinking about training horses."

"He changes it weekly," added Carol.

He felt his face redden at this betrayal.

Mary smiled and went back to her carrots. "Well, sooner or later you'll have to pick one and stick with it, I suppose."

"I know," said JW.

"You could be a horse trainer," Bob said from the other end of the table. The French doors to the sunroom stood open behind him. "But there isn't much money in it."

"Yeah," said Evan, "Like loser money." Carol elbowed him.

"There's ten dollars an hour in it," JW said to the boy, suddenly defensive. He glanced toward Mr. Ingersoll. "Maybe that's not that much for a grown-up."

"Well, that's pretty good for a kid, especially these days," replied Bob, eyeing Evan. "But you can't do it forever. And you probably want a better lifestyle. Have you thought about that?"

"Not really." JW was adopting the aw-shucks air of a hayseed, something he did when he was nervous, but he kicked himself for it and sat higher, adjusting his grip on his silverware.

"The key to making real money is to do something that helps people control their destiny." Mr. Ingersoll poked the air with his fork for emphasis, then went in for another bite of chicken.

"I guess I can see that," said JW.

"Take your father," Mr. Ingersoll went on. "He puts up cell phone towers, right?"

"Sort of. He drives around and sells the leases."

"Even better! He helps people control their destiny by giving them power. He helps famers make money off those leases, and he gives people power to make their lives better by having the convenience and safety of a cell phone. Do you see?"

"I guess." JW had never really thought about his dad like that before, and he didn't think many other people did either. His dad was a traveling salesman who drank too much.

"You see?"

"You give people choices," offered JW agreeably. He felt like a rube being polished up for the fair.

"Exactly! Choice is freedom. You work in a business that expands their ability to better their own lives. Horses used to do that. Then it was cars. Now it's cell phones."

JW nodded and smiled "That's an interesting observation," he said. Carol crossed her eyes at him from behind her drumstick, as if to communicate that she'd heard these sorts of lectures many times. He was starting to forgive her.

"Maybe you should consider taking a job at the bank this coming summer," offered Mary. "That helps people control their lives. Bob could introduce you to the president." She glanced at Bob, who shrugged and nodded.

It wasn't like they had told him to do anything, JW thought as he drove home from Minneapolis. Yet in many ways the strange *keitos* of chance and emotion running through that dinner had laid the foundation for where he was now. The Ingersolls had set an expectation for the boy who was by chance dating their daughter, a certain standard he had to maintain. And so he took a summer job as a teller at the bank, letting his former life fall away like an old skin, with hardly a look back.

A lot of the girls who had been coming in for riding lessons on evenings and weekends instead began making small deposits and withdrawals during his shifts at the bank. Frank Jorgenson, who at thirty-three had recently been promoted to president, noticed the influx of femininity and took a liking to JW. He'd come over and goof around with him when the girls were in. JW soon realized this was a performance of sorts, but he enjoyed it too, and Frank was funny in a pudgy, self-deprecating sort of way. One day he even asked one of the girls out on a date. When her parents came into the bank to talk to him about it, he told them he had been joking. They couldn't be serious—"I mean, look at me"—and soon he had them laughing about the whole misunderstanding while their daughter sat red-faced in the reception area. Other times he would run for a six-pack of Grain Belt—JW was still seventeen—and they would sit in Frank's office after hours and drink while Frank lectured to him about banking and how the world was changing.

"There are too many people. There are going to be fights over resources," Frank said. He pointed his beer bottle at JW, his eyes glistening. "We bankers are in a position to control that, and it's going to make us immensely rich."

JW kicked himself again for not staying for a beer with

Jorgenson. The road dipped into another low vale that blocked the sun. The air flowed down cool and moist with a gathering fog, smelling richly of fresh-cut alfalfa. On the left the land rose to a hayfield that still looked dry and warm in the long sun. A farmer drove a red tractor over the short-cropped stems, pulling a dusty green hay baler and a fully stacked wagon. Two boys sat high atop the bales, pitching and rolling. He felt the congestion of the city falling away. He tuned the radio to the Power Loon, and soon he was singing along to an oldie about satisfaction, a hey hey hey.

Ten minutes later, he pulled into a Cenex station and got out under the yellow-white canopy. The red band on the pumps glowed in the beautifying light of what his high school photography teacher—a peripatetic man named Rolf Van Hoevel who wore a walrus mustache and clogs—had called the magic hour. He passed the pumps and went inside. It had become somewhat of a tradition, buying artificial flowers at this Cenex. They sold bouquets of them in a plastic bucket near the register, pale blues and reds and yellows and whites, all mixed together in a pop-music arrangement of pastel fireworks.

He set the bundle on the seat of his car and pulled back out into the sunset. Driving home reminded him of happier times, when he had driven the same road with Julie. On her birthdays he would take her out of school, and they went on elaborate field trips, to the Science Museum in Saint Paul, or the aquarium in Duluth, or the Cirrus Aircraft plant. These were natural interests of hers that her mother didn't respond to, but he believed you took a kid's natural interests and built the kid up into the world from there. The interest was the foundation. So he gave her options, and they would go on the field trip she was most excited about. They called these trips their dates, and they would talk about nature and science and biology. JW even made a point of studying up on these subjects so he could answer her questions. He bought her books. He started a subscription to *Scientific American.*

It was different with his son Chris. First it had been stamp collecting—the two of them had spent hours bent over the yellow kitchen table with duck-billed tweezers, surrounded by wax paper and fat, staticky books reeking of mastic, stamps flapping like gossamer insect wings as they turned the heavy pages. But the stamps' filigree soon faded into the hormone bath of early adolescence, and then it was all power and gas. Minibikes and small engines led to the homemade go-cart with the old Kohler he had salvaged from a broken wood splitter. Then it was on to hunting and gun safety classes—an interest that was abandoned, in turn, after Chris squatted next to the doe he shot at thirteen, looking into its dark eye, petting its fur as its organs steamed in an iridescent pile among the leaves and forest detritus. After that it was back to engines: first tuning the riding mower to achieve peak performance, and eventually the Mustang they bought for just seven hundred dollars. They spent long nights bent over it in the garage while JW's car sat outside in the weather, their hands coated with a gritty molasses of black oil and road dust, their knuckles skinned red in the engine's dark cubbies. What he wouldn't give to have just one of those long, sore nights back.

The air grew dusty and dry now despite the cooling. The purple-orange sky had faded to sapphire, and billboard lights flickered on. He was nearing the big prairie, where the rolling hills and dales of the glacial moraine began to flatten and stretch their legs westward for their run through the Dakotas. Here the billboards were smaller, made by locals from plywood on six-by-six posts. They hunkered close to the road, lit from below by fluorescent tubes that attracted fleets of dive-bombing insects. Spiders cast their nets into the night seas and sailed out on bands of silk. He passed a sign for the Many Lakes Casino:

WORK HARD.
PLAY HARD.
WIN BIG.

He was nearing home.

As JW drove, he watched closely for the roadside spot where it had happened; it was easy to miss, in spite of the fact that it held such life-changing prominence. Sometimes he had to turn around and go hunting for it, peering across the pavement as he drove, searching for the small white cross. But this time he saw it early, backlit by the low-angled sun, and he pulled over and got out. He walked around the car, took the bouquet out of the passenger door, and carried it over to the marker, which bore a single word: Chris. An older bundle of flowers was faded by the sun and covered with a patina of dust kicked up by a month of car traffic. He squatted and untwisted the wire that he used to hold them in place, then fastened the new bouquet and arranged it as fully and attractively as possible, fluffing the individual petals to broaden the flower heads.

"Goodnight, son," he said. He stood and carried the old bouquet to the car, throwing it into the passenger footwell, where it couldn't sully the upholstery.

The dusky rolling hills ran out behind him under darkening skies and the wind filled his ears as he drove on. Ahead the road climbed back out of the valley, and the dark planes of a building materialized from the shadows on the right. The fading light conjured parts of cars, and then fourteen massive searchlights shot up into the sky, their beams crossing to form a giant teepee of white light. Banks of neon splashed out, the colors bouncing over the roofs and glass parts of the cars like thrown watercolors. *Many Lakes Casino*, the roadside monument said, *Win Big!*

He passed the turnoff, the neon glow lighting his windshield and turning the backs of his hands red on the wheel. He thought of Chris's accident and the sudden shock of it—a ripping away when he hadn't been looking. The red fell from his hands like fading fingers as he climbed the hill, a new vista opening, and his thoughts returned to the dinner Carol had waiting, where he hoped to save his marriage and his relationship with Julie, his remaining child. Chris's death had sent him into a tailspin, futility crashing over him in swamping waves, spinning him in the undertow. Problems had cropped up in their marriage, cracks and fissures that grew into crevasses and canyons, over money, over his gambling. Carol always seemed angry, and Julie had stopped talking to him. But Carol had agreed to see him, and his heart sped a little now that the moment was imminent.

He adjusted his visor against the low blast of sun. He was going to find a way, starting tonight, to turn things around. A way to come together and move forward again—not as if nothing had happened, but acknowledging that it had, and then finding the forgiveness and the strength and the love to heal together. He didn't really know what he was going to say, but he was determined to make it happen.

His Caprice shot on into the sunset, becoming small and bright as a satellite. But even then he could feel gravity taking hold. The waves of the casino accreted weight and moment. The car reached a sort of apogee, and then he pulled over and turned around.

3

The Many Lakes Casino lot was awash in color and buzzing with sound. A charter bus disgorged senior citizens under the massive front portico, their silver hair running from green to red to blue in the shifting lights. One of them trailed an oxygen tank with aluminum wheels.

JW turned off his car. A breeze lifted in through the window. The dark leaves of sugar beet greens clattered on the edge of the lot. Several pairs of men and women were walking toward the casino, hand in hand.

Julie had given JW a plastic Jesus on the cross when she was nine or ten, and it dangled from his rearview mirror, swaying in the breeze, its clear plastic beads refracting the colored lights. He reached up and steadied it. He needed to get home, but the day had unsettled him.

"Okay," he said, closing his eyes, "if I open my eyes and see a man and a woman holding hands, I'll go in. Just for five minutes. Just send me a sign." Carol would have dinner in the oven by now. It would be out in half an hour. He needed to patch things up with her and Julie, to heal the rifts that had formed since the accident. He hadn't handled it well; he knew that.

She had been even more distant lately, not returning his calls, and the red heat of anger that had been in her voice this last year was fading into a cool reserve. It was fine. He could do what he wanted. Whatever he thought was best. All phrases to let him know that life, and Carol, were moving on, that they had become unhitched. If she would only wait, if he could just get through this, come out the other end with the big win, it would get better. Because with money came hope, and freedom. He could tell Carol about Frank wanting to have a beer. How it made him late and he'd been driving fast to make up the time. Just a half hour inside the casino. Just a short bump. It would give him time to bolster himself.

He opened his eyes, but no one was holding hands. He craned his neck to peer around the rear window stanchion. Not a single couple. He laughed and shook his head.

"All right, all right, I hear you," he said. He reached for his dangling keys, but then he saw two women join hands.

Close enough. He got out and locked the car. Just in and out. Five minutes, ten tops. A quick bang. It always improved his mood, energized him, made things somehow more manageable. He shot his cuffs and headed for the grand portico.

Most people would be crazy to go gambling like he did, he knew, but as a finance professional he had an advantage, and he used it. He understood margins and risk in a way casual gamblers did not. The senior citizens were clogging the entry foyer. They chattered and lurched about, trying to buy chips. He maneuvered his way through the irritable throng. A voice that sounded like Willie Nelson wafted out of the theater, singing *You are my sunshine*. He had sung that to Julie as a baby. He stepped into the enswathing maternal smell of stale cigarette smoke.

He spent three hundred dollars on chips and headed into a sonic cloud of silvery coin chinking. No wonder old people like casinos, he thought. He didn't care for the slots himself because there was no skill involved. He sometimes played poker, but most nights his game was blackjack. And tonight, something was going to happen, he could feel it. He was a dog on the hunt, yelping and straining at the leash, shedding his stiff banking persona and thrilled to be giving himself up to chance.

He passed Charlie and Maynard, two Native guards.

"Mr. White," Maynard nodded.

"Maynard. Charlie," he replied. A Native waitress named Stormy carried a tray of drinks. Wide high cheeks, a flat nose, small eyes with a laugh in them, big hoop earrings. They said she was Dakota, but she'd been living outside North Lake and working at the casino for years. She always seemed to find him. "Good evening, Mr. White," she said.

"Stormy, it is a great evening. You time me! I'll be in and out in five minutes, boom! A thousand dollars! Or ten!"

She laughed as he lifted a drink from her tray, feeling spry. She shook her head and walked on.

The chrome-and-green-glass escalator gleamed with the satisfying quality of 1950s science fiction, smooth as ice to the touch. It had seemed such a ridiculous thing the first time he saw it, going up a single floor, short in stature and full of grandeur, like the prized possession of a pygmy chieftain. But it had grown on him, his stairway to heaven. He stepped off and rounded the corner by the Moose Café Bar, heading for the blackjack section, where the smiling dealers waited behind their Kool-Aid-blue half-moon tables, always welcoming, always encouraging, but somewhat otherworldly.

"Welcome back, Mr. White!" They greeted him like a head of state. "Welcome back!"

The tables seemed somehow alive, their felt almost like a skin, warm and cool at once, and printed with zones to show where the cards went. The edges were padded for

comfort, and each table had four inviting chairs. The dealers stood inside the moons' curves, ready to play. JW picked
his luckiest table and sat down.

Gambling, like banking, was all about managing risk. JW
kept a tattered book on blackjack in the car. He had read it
cover to cover many times, seeking clues to bend the arc of
fate his way. The biggest thing to overcome was the house
advantage, which came from being able to play more than one
player at a time, tilting the odds slightly in the dealer's favor.
Teams of players secretly working together could overcome
this by playing at different tables, but the casinos banned
anyone caught doing it. An individual could overcome it by
counting cards: mentally adding one every time a small card
was played, and subtracting one every time an ace or ten-
card came up. When the count got high it meant the deck
was loaded with tens and you went in big. But there were
cameras over every table, trained on the players to watch for
this sort of too-convenient timing, so JW was cautious about
using this method. Still, there was something about trolling
the stormy ocean of chance, and pulling a big win back out of
it, that drew his obsessions to the surface.

Tonight, as it turned out, he didn't need to count. The
cards were all going his way naturally. The payout in blackjack is three to two, and on splits and double-downs a player
can double that. The goal is to hit twenty-one without going
over. The dealer stays on seventeen or above. JW's luck held,
and over the course of an hour he kept getting the cards, one
after another. His three hundred dollars multiplied until he
had twenty-seven thousand in stacks of multi-colored chips. A
crowd gathered—young, vibrant, alive in the moment, enjoying
his spectacular winning streak. The table felt glowed electric
blue and the cards had a satisfying slippery thwack.

He knew people tended to make mistakes under such pressure. The best thing you could do was to follow a system and forget about the money and the audience. Some players pulled ten, twenty, or even fifty percent back out of each hand as a policy decision, but in his mind this was foolish because over time the house had a slight statistical advantage. By holding back, he would not be fully putting his money to work against that advantage. Mathematically, it was better to have all his chips in play, and to play it up as fast as he could, then get out.

That's what he was about to do after another hand. It was time, he could feel it, but he was within spitting distance of paying off the second mortgage on his house. He felt in total control, reacting instantly. He saw the move, he felt it, he knew it was right, and he played it, over and over. Bam, bam, bam: Thor at the hammer, directing each slam of lightning—there, there, there. But that was a false sense. He knew it. He reminded himself to stay calm. He didn't have to hit twenty-one. He didn't even have to beat the other players. An old man in a rumpled suit—his ashen face was caving in on itself—presented no competition; neither did a younger one with earrings and a goatee and the cocky, puppy-dog air of some sort of media artist. He slouched in his paisley shirt and flung his dark greasy forelock aside, then let it fall again before flinging it back as if it had only just fallen for the first time. JW only had to beat the dealer. Bam! Another win! Yes! The old man pushed back from the table with a wave and a grim expression. JW watched him hobble off through the surrounding crowd. He took a sip from his drink and cautioned himself to use math, not to get sucked in by his emotions as the stakes rose. If he could stay technical, he could maximize his chances of finding a streak that would beat the house advantage in an even bigger way. He refocused on the game as the dealer began another round.

He had cleared nearly every ace in the shoe. He'd counted seven of them. Aces give players a lot of protection because they can be played as a one or as an eleven, so if you bust past twenty-one playing the ace high, you can fall back and use it as a one. Now that there was only one other player at the table, the odds were actually starting to tilt further in his favor.

"Hit me," he was about to say, but he held up to think it through, and goatee looked over at him, mildly amused, and took a slug of his cocktail.

"You doing okay, my man?"

JW nodded, giving him minimal attention. It was stupid to banter at a time like this. It was all about managing risk. He was at seventeen, and this was not the conservative move he'd been making all night long. His heart sped up just thinking about it. But he'd seen almost every face card played already, and the tens, too, so the chances of going bust were smaller than average; in fact, they were increasingly smaller than average. Still, it was crazy to take a chance with so much money riding on one bet, so this time he held back three thousand in chips, breaking his own policy. The crowd applauded as if he'd done something brilliant. A man came out of nowhere and pointed at him.

"You, sir, are a winner!"

Obviously drunk. He sipped the water from the bottom of his ice. Stormy swooped in with another round of free drinks. "No, I'm okay," said goatee. He lifted his hands up and leaned back, patting his paisley belly. "I gotta maintain my girlish figure." He laughed and flung his hair. "Gotta fit in a canoe tomorrow."

"JW, why don't you take a break?" whispered Stormy. He could feel her warm breath on his cheek as she clawed up his old cocktail napkin. "Have a drink and cool down," she said.

He glanced at her and saw her concern. Dave Anderson, the casino manager, was watching from behind the crowd. He had read that managers often sent a waitress like Stormy in to distract a player and break a winning streak.

"We need this," he told her. He thought about the relief, how happy Carol would be. "Hit me," he told the dealer.

It was a three. His instincts were verified, and the crowd applauded. He had an extremely formidable twenty. Stormy sighed and pulled away with her tray.

"I'll stay!" He laughed. Three to two on twenty-four grand. He'd hit the road with thirty-nine thousand dollars, enough to really turn things around.

Goatee busted out at twenty-four. "Dude, it's all yours," he conceded, pushing back from his chair, smiling around at the onlookers, his cheeks bright red. JW nodded and waved. Everything he had was riding on the next few cards. He should be nervous, he realized, but he felt good. Confident. The math was on his side. The probability of the dealer beating his twenty was very low. He was giddy. He was bouncing his knee under the table.

"Dealer has an ace in the hole, does the player want to buy insurance?"

It had to be the last ace. And even though he was a finance guy, JW hated insurance. He preferred to use risk management strategies that he could control. He quickly ran through the odds. If the dealer turned up an ace chances were about one in three that the next card would be a ten-card and the dealer would hit twenty-one. An insurance bet was like hedging in stocks. It paid two to one if the dealer got twenty-one,

helping mitigate the loss. But you lost it if not, which damp-
ened the win. He drummed his fingers. Because so many
face cards had already been played, the chances of the dealer
turning up a ten were lower than normal, and twenty-one
was the only score that could beat his hand. Plus, he only had
three thousand held out of play to bet with, so even if he won
the insurance bet, he'd walk away with a measly six thousand,
and if he won the main bet, he'd lose the three, reducing his
take to thirty-six thousand, which was short of the amount
he had decided he would walk away at. He could take a loan
from the casino, but he didn't really have any more money in
the bank to pay it back with.

"I'll pass." Just one card more.

The dealer's king of hearts. The blast of it obliterated all
other sound. Gone were the incessant chinking and bleep-
ing, the congratulatory encouragements of the slot machines.
Gone were the music and the cacophonous crowd applauding
his moves. Gone were the sibilant laughter of his children
and the raspy guffaws of his wife. Gone were the discussions,
the awards, the handshakes at the bank. The only sound in
life was the sound of a car crashing and thundering through
his chest.

"House wins," he faintly heard the dealer say.

He closed his eyes. It was gone. He struggled for logic.
Don't try to recapture it, he thought, just realize where you
are now. And yet a wall of grief rose up in him. All that money, just torn away. He opened his eyes and looked down at his
remaining chips. A measly three grand. The crowd of poor,
older people began to drift away.

It shouldn't have been. The odds had been with him.
But he had to play on, and put emotion behind him. In
fact, the odds were even better now, when he thought

about it. He held back his three-hundred-dollar nut and pushed the remaining twenty-seven hundred into the box. He could claw his way back up to into thirty and this time he'd walk away, no matter what. Even at thirty. He could imagine Carol's surprise, and her relieved happy smile, at thirty thousand dollars. He needed that happy smile. The money would solve so many problems, the silly mundanities that had been driving them apart.

Two new players joined him at the table—an excited blonde in her twenties and her obsequious boyfriend. The dealer replenished the shoe, and JW slid his cards over the magic blue felt. Turned them up to look. A five and a seven, so he was at twelve. The play cycled to the boyfriend, then the blonde, and no face cards came up, making his chance of getting one that much higher. Dealer could get one, too. So he had a choice. He could sit at twelve and probably lose the twenty-seven hundred, or he could take a hit. The odds were two to one he would survive, since face cards are only a third of the deck.

"Hit me," he said.

It was a jack.

"Sorry, JW," the dealer said as she raked in his chips.

He sipped his drink, then picked up his original three hundred dollars.

"No worries. All about the fun, right?"

She nodded and dealt a new hand as another player took his place.

He rode the glass-and-chrome escalator back down. Willie Nelson had gone and the lines were long at all the teller windows, so he used the cashier booth in the center of the slots area. The whir of colors and ringing bells made him feel like he was standing inside a toy. The machines emitted friendly voices, as if he were at a vast cocktail party of single robots on the prowl. The blue hairs sat staring at them, sipping their cocktails and their red wines and munching on pretzels as they pushed the spin buttons over and over. Spin, coin, spin, coin. Chink-chink.

As JW stepped up to the cashier he saw the woman across the aisle do something incredibly stupid: she left a dollar slot machine with a Top-Dollar Advisor feature and headed for the flashing-light slot machine near the front. He couldn't believe it. The Top-Dollar Advisor was one of only two machines like it in the entire casino. It was rumored to have the highest payout percentage in the state, and so it was almost never available. He knew he should be getting on the road, but he had time for a few quick spins. He traded his chips for tokens and hurried to the prized stool, slipping in ahead of a man who was pushing his walker in the same direction. Immediately, he hit a payout and collected twenty dollars.

"I think this round's on you!" the machine said in the voice of Cliff Clavin from the old TV show *Cheers,* and the chorus sang *where everybody knows your name.* He put the tokens in his keeper basket and played again.

"Congratulations!" Cliff said cheerfully, while the display advised him of the upcoming odds. If you paid attention, he knew, over time the Top-Dollar Advisor could help you beat the house.

After another hour or so he was still hanging in there. He was down to about a hundred and fifty dollars, but he still had the twenty-five in winnings off to the side, so he wasn't doing too bad. Plus he'd had a lot of fun and several more free drinks. The difference between guys like him and problem gamblers, he realized, was that he knew when to stop. He'd spent half his nut, so it was time to lock in his winnings and cash out. All in all, he was only down a hundred and twenty-five. It was a fair price for a night out having fun, and he'd had a couple free drinks and some food to boot, so it was less than a hundred bucks when you thought about it. Not bad for entertainment.

He cashed out at the VIP window.

"See you tomorrow," the teller said.

He shook his head. "I'm not in here that often," he replied.

"I know," she said, flushing. She smiled, wrinkling up her nose. "Just wanted to say something to you. Have a good night."

As he passed the Big Winner mirror he noticed how rounded his shoulders were. He stood up and pulled them back, stretching his shoulder blades—like angel wings, the chiropractor had told him after Chris's accident, back when his headaches were nonstop and he worried he had a brain tumor. He really needed to practice better posture. He used to have that naturally from training horses. It was probably the driving. He would exercise in the morning. That kind of self-discipline was something he'd always been good at. It had always been his secret weapon, in business and in life—his ability to pursue the goals he set with unwavering determination. He glanced at his watch. 10:57.

Fuck.

He hurried to the car.

4

Carol and JW's house was on a residential street opposite the city park. When he was a kid the park had been groomed like a golf course, but in the twenty-five years since the mine closed the city had gone longer and longer between mowings. As he pulled over, he saw dandelion heads glimmering like pale mold in the moonlight. It was the house of the fateful dinner, and now it was theirs. When Carol was pregnant with Chris, Bob and Mary announced that Bob had accepted a new job in Atlanta. They had purchased a condo there and were going to keep an apartment here in town. They were giving them the family home so that their grandchildren could grow up like Carol had: playing in the park until the squirrels scampered at dusk, and dreaming of England and being royal.

The house was dark now, except for their second floor bedroom window. The clock glowed dimly on his dash: 11:15. She was likely in bed reading, or watching the late show. Perhaps it wasn't too late. He stepped out of the car and eased the door shut. He crossed the street. He would apologize. He had been delayed, and he had forgotten to charge his cell phone, he would say. It had run out. How stupid of him. But as he headed up the walk the window darkened. He continued on to the doorstep, where he saw his mail lying in a small bundle. A sticky note flapped in the breeze:

John—
Went to bed.
Carol

He picked it up. He ran his fingers down the grooves of the doorframe's half-Roman column. Rousing her at this point would not end well. He stood quietly for a moment as his hopeful vision of the evening dissolved, wishing there were some way he could reverse time and power past the gravity of the casino. He turned back to his car. He sat there outside his darkened house, then finally drove off into the night.

Aside from a few bites at the casino, he hadn't eaten since breakfast. He stopped on the way home for gas and some food. He pulled a Chuckwagon sandwich from behind the glass cooler door and stuck it in a microwave on the orange counter by the window. Outside, the local sheriff's deputy, a big bearish guy named Bob Grossman, had his red and blue lights flashing as he talked to a car full of kids parked in front of the store. He didn't look happy.

The microwave dinged. JW pushed the greasy button and pulled out the hot plastic pillow, avoiding the steam emanating from the tear he had made in the corner. The police lights shone into the store as he made his way toward the counter, turning the customers faintly red, then blue. A bunch of Native American kids tumbled out of the car. He watched them jostle each other, laughing like they didn't care, as Grossman yelled at them. He set his sandwich on the counter.

He had seen Grossman do this before. The Lions' Club had even had him in to talk about what a hazard the reservation kids were, and his strategy of keeping pressure on them. The boys ran wild and drank and caused problems ranging from burglary to traffic accidents. The dysfunction, addiction, and poverty of the reservation was a regular point of contention at Chamber of Commerce events, where the more conservative members groaned about how the Native Americans lived in a welfare culture, while the liberal members said it was because of a cycle of poverty and broken families. Grossman was a member of the Rotary club, the Chamber, and the Lions, and was widely felt to be the best check they had on the problem. Some people were talking about supporting him for sheriff when Big Bill Donovan retired. JW grabbed a few paper napkins from the dispenser next to the register.

"Gas on three," he said.

The cashier typed in the gas and bleeped through his food with a bored affect as JW studied the rolls of lottery tickets under the scratched plastic fog of the countertop.

"Thirty-one forty-nine. Anything else?"

"Yeah, give me a hundred and fifty in scratch-offs. Loons."

He felt embarrassed, as if he were asking for a copy of *Penthouse*. She pulled out a long streamer of shiny-foiled tickets. The loons' backs glinted in the light.

"Thanks," he said, folding them accordion-style as he hurried out the door, forgetting his sandwich and drink inside.

He stuffed the remaining bills and coins into his pocket, then headed past the Native American boys, who were clearly drunk. He thought about the wreckage his ancestors had caused by introducing alcohol to the Native Americans, and they by giving tobacco to whites. He scratched his thumbnail across a glistening loon to reveal the number sets—it was a loser—and got into his car, thankful that he didn't have those kinds of problems.

His apartment building was just half a block farther up Sixth, behind the Food 'n' Fuel. It was on a narrow strip of land between Sixth and the highway, just beyond Sabo's Guns. The building was long and short, clad in rough plywood siding wavy from rain. Thin layers of it sloughed off like dead skin in the summer. The building had a crabgrass lawn and a gravel parking lot. A billboard loomed overhead, advertising Dr. Reed Orput, who could renew your confidence with a mouthful of dental implants. *Remake your life,* it said, *with Dr. Reed and the Smile Factory.* Orput's porcelain grin had become a navigation point for JW, indicating where to turn.

A much smaller sign at the parking lot entrance said *Whispering Pines Apartment's, Your new home!* Every time JW pulled past it he was irritated by the misplaced apostrophe, but he hadn't gotten around to scratching it out. There were no pine trees on the property, but someone had once planted juniper bushes amid wood chips that were crumbling to soil next to the building's foundation.

He approached the entrance carrying his briefcase, his bindered stack of mail, his keys, and his ribbon of spent lottery tickets. A large Walmart semi barreled past on the highway, buffeting him in its hot backwash. He twisted his key in the lock, pulled the glass open, and went inside.

His apartment was on the second floor, six steps up from the street. Second-floor units cost ten dollars a month more than first-floor apartments. JW stuck a small key in his dented brass mailbox, but there was nothing inside. He headed up the stairs, his shoes sticking to the yellowing plastic runner. The hall smelled of borscht. His door was halfway down the hall on the right, the highway side. A bright orange piece of paper was stuck to it:

EVICTION NOTICE.
You are hereby ordered to
VACATE YOUR PREMISES IMMEDIATELY
due to NON-PAYMENT OF RENT.
Move now! Save court costs!
—Whispering Pines Management

An artery pulsed hot in his neck as he peeled the notice off. He heard clattering dishes from somewhere, a TV, late-night laughter with some woman. He wondered how many of the tenants had seen it, and wished management had simply called him.

He went inside and tossed everything on the coffee table. The apartment was cheap anyway. That had been its advantage, and it came furnished, so when JW moved out of the house he didn't have to buy all-new furniture for a temporary separation while he and Carol worked on their marriage. Of course, tonight he may have blown that too, he thought.

He turned on the TV and headed into the kitchen, a small galley that sloped sharply downhill toward the highway. The announcer's voice boomed in the other room as he opened the fridge. "Baxter Pawn Baxter Pawn Baxter Pawn! Just three hours from almost anywhere and the largest selection in the upper Midwest!"

He stared into the fridge's yellow interior and shook his head to regain his focus. Pig's Eye pilsner, Red Owl milk, Swanson TV dinners. Some bologna gone green. He took out a beer and closed the door. He wasn't a slob, JW thought, but he should be cooking. The fridge should have real food. Perhaps that was part of the problem. Not enough self-care. He had been spending too much time at the casino. He was a well-respected banker with a beautiful family. And yet here he was, with no real sense of what he should do next.

He turned and walked back across the slanted floor. Road construction on the highway had caused the building's foundation to bow inward. He had examined it one day while doing laundry on the first floor. It explained why the windows along the highway side would not open and why the floor ran at a funhouse slant.

This flaw presented the need for special adjustments. The legs of his bed were propped up on the road side with chunks of two-by-fours. In the kitchen the fridge and the range both trudged uphill. The countertop tilted downhill. On his first day in the apartment JW had come home to find his brand-new Walmart toaster oven in pieces on the floor.

He returned to the living room. The pale-green brocaded sofa emitted a sharp, dusty odor when he sat down. He grabbed the remote and changed channels to the Home Shopping Network. He ran through his ribbon of scratched-off loon tickets until he found the two winners. He tore them at the perforations and tossed them on the coffee table. Six dollars each.

"Isn't it gorgeous?" the blonde saleswoman asked viewers as she modeled a cubic zirconium necklace. "What woman wouldn't fall in love with the man who gave her this?"

He opened his first letter, a bill from Connexus, the local rural electric cooperative.

DISCONNECTION NOTICE: *Your electricity will be DISCONNECTED for non-payment. You must call immediately.*

He set the mail down and rubbed his temples.

5

The following morning was fine and dry, and it felt warm as JW left the building. He pulled out onto Sixth, heading for the highway. The city of North Lake had a scenic rusticity that owed much to its proximity to the west end of the Boundary Waters Canoe Area Wilderness, a vast roadless expanse of hundreds of lakes along the border with Canada. Native lake names like Kekekabic, Ogishkemuncie, and Gabimichigami, fell easily from the tongues of Iron Rangers when they talked fishing, and the region attracted outdoor enthusiasts from around the world who wanted to experience an authentic American wilderness. North Woods décor, log buildings with dark green roofs, colorful chalk sandwich boards changed daily by dreadlocked hipsters, Will Steger mukluks, and tree stumps sculpted by chain saws into bears and eagles all helped to attract eco-vacationers who injected cash into the local economy.

North Lake Bank operated from a log building out on the main highway. It hadn't been built to appeal to the granola crowd. That was a happy accident. During the housing crisis, one of JW's best customers, a log home builder, was suddenly left with several unsellable vacation homes he had built on spec. They were pitched up like derelicts along the vast shores of North Lake. When he fell behind on his payments, rather than liquidate his business at a certain loss, JW suggested he use his unsold inventory to construct a new building for the bank, thereby saving an important customer's business and solving the bank's space problem at a bargain-basement price. The picturesque result had earned JW a feature article in *Banking* magazine and a Community Banker of the Year nomination. Since then, business was up sharply.

He pulled in, bumping up over the curb cut. A large carport supported by thick log posts and iron stanchions sheltered the drive-through lanes. The grounds were well landscaped, with a chain-saw sculpture of a leaping trout on the front strip of grass. He angled into a space marked by a small brass lawn sign that read President.

The morning's rising heat hit him hard as he stepped out. The lawn sprinkler heads hissed, wetting the sidewalk. Schmeaker's black Charger with its red NRA bumper sticker was already parked in his spot, which was marked by a similar sign that read Vice President.

With morning had come clarity. He was still the president of North Lake Bank. He could get a short-term loan to consolidate his debts. He would call Carol to apologize. It was all manageable. He pulled open the front doors, fully reinhabiting the persona of the competent and successful bank president, the man invited to speak about his successes around the Midwest. He was, truly, among the very best at what he did, and that counted for something.

Sandy smiled up at him.

"Sandy."

"Good Morning, Mr. White. Mr. Jorgenson's here to see you."

"Jorgenson?"

That was a strange bit of news. JW walked back to his office to deposit his things on his desk. He wondered what could have caused Jorgenson to make the four-hour drive and arrive by nine in the morning, when he had just seen him yesterday afternoon.

JW snugged his tie and headed for the conference room, a wood-paneled space centered by a long table. Its red surface was rich with morning light slanting in through wooden blinds. Jorgenson sat at the far end, poring over some papers.

"Frank! Is something wrong?"

Jorgenson looked up from the paperwork. His face was inscrutable.

"Close the door, John."

JW corrected course, surprised at Jorgenson's tone.

"Sure."

He closed the door and touched the button to turn the blinds down slightly, as a courtesy more than anything, and began walking between the wall of windows and the long table.

"Everything all right?"

"No, John, I'm afraid it's not." Jorgenson set the papers down and sat back as he neared. "I didn't sleep last night. I got up at four in the morning just to come and see you, so I could find out what's going on up here."

JW's heart sped up. Had he discovered the loan? "I don't understand."

Jorgenson picked up his smartphone and thrust it toward JW. The screen glowed with colors.

"Take a look at that."

JW took it and examined the image. Two men pored over a roll of blueprints spread over the hood of a truck. Behind them rose the pale ribs of a new building. He was surprised to recognize one of the men.

"That's Johnny Eagle."

"The one from your talk yesterday. And he's at the building site that Sam Schmeaker's been e-mailing me about, the one that's going up on the edge of town. Just took that this morning."

JW looked up at him. Jorgenson was clearly irritated. "What else do you know about him?" he asked.

JW put the phone down. He didn't, really. Not much more than the story in his presentation. "Moved back to the reservation after his wife died, little over a year ago."

He pulled his right cuff farther down his wrist. His white shirt and collar felt constricting under his jacket, as if they had become twisted somehow.

"Have you been keeping track of this building project?" said Jorgenson.

"There've been some grumblings about it at the Sunrise Rotary, but—" He hadn't paid any particular attention. They had just started putting it up ten days ago or so. "It's on the edge of the reservation. They haven't announced what it is yet," he said.

"Last year when he was in here, was it a tribal loan he was after?"

JW shook his head. "No, I would have approved that. It was for his house. An addition, remodel or something, and some kind of small business."

Jorgenson nodded, thinking about it. "You know he used to be a vice president at one of our competitors in Minneapolis," he said. "A real climber. They called him the Indian Obama."

JW saw the implication. He picked the phone back up and thumbed through some of the other images. "You think it's a bank."

Jorgenson looked both worried and aggressive, like a bear about to strike. "You tell me."

JW finished thumbing through the images. The struc-

ture did seem to have preparations for a drive-through canopy. "We'd lose the tribal deposits," he said, setting the phone
back on the table.

Jorgenson nodded. "Yeah, and that would probably put
this branch out of business. I bet that's his intent. Do you
know how much Capitol Bank Holdings paid for this branch?"

"No." He wanted to sit, but Jorgenson hadn't asked him
to, and he sensed that it would anger him.

"Eight million dollars. And you built it higher since."

JW suddenly realized how damaging such a development
would be to Jorgenson's CEO campaign. If a tribal bank put
Jorgenson's flagship branch out of business, they would lose millions of dollars and his entire strategy for growth near casinos
would be called into question. JW and everyone who worked
here would be out of a job, and permanently blemished by the
failure. It would be a blow to the entire community.

"You're the expert on this, John. Christ, you teach it," said
Jorgenson. "How many tribe-owned banks are there?"

"Not many. They'd need a state or federal charter to do it."

Jorgenson looked at him for a moment as if contemplating something, then nodded faintly.

"If you took a leave, do you think you could get your arms
around this thing for us?"

"A leave?" JW was shocked. "Frank, I've got my hands
full as branch president—"

"Well, actually—"

Jorgenson slid a piece of paper out from beneath the
stack of financial reports he had been reviewing and pushed
it across the table to JW.

"I've been looking into some of your loans. One in particular."

JW picked it up, noticing how the embossed recorder's

seal caught the light. He saw his signature along with the forgeries of Sam's and Sandy's as the notary public. It was the second mortgage on his home. The $100,000 figure suddenly looked staggering. He felt a wave of nausea.

"What's the problem? It's my second mortgage. That's what banks do, they improve people's lives."

"John, come on, okay? You've been waiving your payments for almost a year."

JW laughed. "You know Carol. Her redecorating—"

"Bullshit! Okay? Bullshit." Jorgenson slapped the table. "Everybody knows you've got a gambling problem, and that you and Carol are separated over it. Christ, I used to run this branch! You think I don't still have connections? I also know you're being evicted from your apartment. So let's cut the shit, and you give me some honest answers."

"Frank, it's just a little gaming."

"This is embezzling," Jorgenson said, stabbing the papers with his fingers. "Put your keys on the table. I'm going to call the FBI."

JW hesitated.

"Now!"

JW felt sick and paralyzed. The enormity of what was happening was surreal. He started to reach for his keys, but somehow he found the presence of mind to push back.

"Just, now just, wait," he said, his voice shaking. "Okay? I've made you a lot of money. I've turned this into the most profitable branch in your territory."

"That's why I was offering you a deal," said Jorgenson.

"Well, let me—" JW stared at him, but words eluded him.

"What, do you think I'm fucking around?"

JW swallowed and forced himself to focus. "No. It's just, sudden. You want me to investigate him."

"Without alerting him, yes." Jorgenson seemed to calm. "You figure out what it is and if it's a real threat." He leaned back again. "We'll tell people you're taking a leave to deal with your gambling problem. You get yourself one of those twelve-step books and you carry it around with you. Might even do you some good."

JW turned away and looked through the blinds, out at the fields behind the bank, breathing deeply in a conscious effort to get hold of himself. He looked down. Sunlight cast dark stripes across his new suit and his hands. He felt his jaw muscles bulging, and he willed them to relax.

"Okay," he said, barely audible.

"What was that? I didn't hear you."

"Okay!" JW had a sudden impulse to strangle him.

"Wise man," said Jorgenson. "Whispering Pines manages some trailer homes out on the reservation, near where this Johnny Eagle lives," he said. "Go take one. I'll cover your rent."

JW stood motionless, staring out the window. "And if it is a bank?" He turned back and presented a composed face to Jorgenson, who rose from his chair and walked toward him. He stopped and put a hand on his shoulder.

"Then I want you to stop him."

II

THE HAND

6

The sides of JW's white Caprice became caked with ocher dust as he drove. The reservation road cut through a vast landscape that alternated between trees and meadows. Stands of birch, maple, and aspen ran along high hills on the left, surrounded by sweeping tracts of Norway pine. Meadows of fall wildflowers and scrub pastures ran on the right. Scattered groupings of jack pine towered over everything, their thin trunks shooting high into the air before branching out into heads of shaggy greenery. Barbed wire sagged between ancient wooden posts pitched cockeyed in the soil. A barn collapsed into itself, its gray wood tinged with faint remnants of red paint, its blue-shingled roof folding in at crazy angles and frilled with green moss and lichens. A Model-A Ford sank into a wetland on the left.

The day was warm, but he kept his windows closed and the air conditioner on to keep his belongings from getting covered with dust. Still, the air coming in through the vents smelled like chalk, and the dashboard became coated with a fine powder. His clothes bulged in gleaming black lawn-and-leaf bags, which filled the back seat. He had once heard such bags called Indian suitcases, and now here he was, his car packed full of them, heading into Indian country. His business suits hung pressed against the doors. The front passenger seat and footwell were piled high with stuffed banker's boxes, while his briefcase rode tucked under his knees. He turned on the radio and sang along with Boz Scaggs.

The wilderness eventually crumbled into a collection of scattered prefab houses whose windows were draped with sheets and blankets. Derelict cars rusted into the yards. A trailer home stood on cinderblocks between the road and a rocky lake. Its siding was mostly stripped from its ribs, exposing a gaping hole clear through its middle. In the opening he could see the lake beyond, and inside the trailer four green-webbed lawn chairs standing in a circle around a grill with sawed-off legs. A ways farther on, a woman in office clothes pushed a sputtering lawn mower with a spindly chrome handle, its small engine spewing clouds of blue smoke. She looked at him, but didn't wave back at his gesture.

Then woods sprang up again on either side, and the houses were gone. The elevation began to climb and after a mile or so the road turned north and the forest fell away into a high oak savanna. Then it narrowed before plunging into a woodier area. He traveled through more oak interspersed with buckthorn and birch, then a wetland full of bright yellow tamarack trees standing like fire on the water. He came around a bend and slowed as he emerged into a small settlement cut into the woods.

On the right was a home with a mostly finished addition and a brown metal pole barn. On the left he found the lane the Whispering Pines rental agent had described to him over the phone. It climbed and then disappeared over a small hill. Her white Toyota pickup was parked in the tall grass beside the lane. He pulled off and parked next to it. Jorgenson had described this place as a trailer park, but when JW got out he only saw one trailer. It was a dilapidated blue one from the 1960s, and it sat under a stand of craggy burr oaks near the road.

The rental agent hopped down from the pickup. Young and blonde, she held a zippered key rack in one hand and a small tube of mace in the other. JW pretended he didn't see it.

"As I said on the phone," she said, shifting the mace to shake hands, "these are super-affordable. The nice ones are up in back, over the hill."

"Oh, so there are more of them," he said.

"Oh, yeah! The view is gorgeous! People just have a hard time finding them because this lane looks like a private driveway or something."

"I see." JW smiled.

She began to lead him up the hill into the sun, but he stopped and looked at the houses across the street, a little worried about his belongings.

"Is it okay to leave my car here?" he asked.

"Yeah, it should be fine."

"Maybe I'll just lock it to be safe. It's all my stuff."

She nodded, her expression clouding. "Okay," she said, and tucked a fine wave of her sunny blonde hair back behind an ear.

As JW returned to lock the car, he was shocked to recognize Johnny Eagle in the yard across the road. He stepped behind his car, suddenly embarrassed to be there. Jorgenson had certainly done his research, and it made JW wonder what else he had planned. Eagle was walking with a boy, and they were arguing. He put a hand on the boy's shoulder and the boy whirled away and yelled something inaudible at him. It suddenly occurred to JW that the boy resembled one of the Native kids he had seen Grossman roughing up at the convenience store. But he couldn't be sure.

The boy stormed away up to the house and Eagle sighed and followed.

"Mr. White?"

JW turned to see the rental agent waiting, a quizzical expression on her face. He glanced back at the dilapidated baby-blue trailer down near the road. There was a sun-faded, red and white For Rent sign behind one of the windows.

"Let's see this one," he said, and started toward it.

"Okay..." said the agent. Her tone implied that she thought he was a little crazy, but she walked back down the hill toward him, and the two of them headed up a short path that led to the trailer's grassy gravel parking spot.

"I don't even know if I have keys for this one," she said, opening her black zippered key rack. "Oh wait, I think I found one!"

She climbed up the two broad wooden steps—made out of some old two-by-twelves—and took out a dull pewter key shaped like a cloverleaf. She jiggled it into the stubborn lock and got it to turn, then stepped back and pulled the flimsy aluminum door open.

The interior was straight out of the 1960s. It was clean, but set up more like a camper than a house. He stepped inside and looked around. It wasn't much wider than eight feet, and maybe thirty feet long. To the right of the door was a gold-speckled, chrome-trimmed kitchen table with woven blue bench cushions on either side. A band of windows ran along the front end of the trailer, beyond the table and above the bench on the door side. The opposite wall had a small book-shelf behind the bench, and next to it, across from the door, sat a brown faux-leather sofa. To the left of the door was a galley kitchen with more gold-speckled countertop and white-enameled cabinets, and an old O'Keefe & Merritt gas stove, chrome and white porcelain. Opposite the narrow kitchenette was a small utility closet, a built-in furnace and water heater, and a tiny blue bathroom with a pull-chain light hanging over a medicine cabinet and a small porcelain sink.

He pulled the mirrored door on the medicine cabinet open. There were two rippled glass shelves and a rusty slot opening into the wall. The words Used Razor Disposal were embossed in the metal just below the slot. It reminded JW of a similar one in his childhood home, which he had always imagined as some kind of strange portal into another dimension. He swung the door shut.

Behind him was a small frosted glass window over a mismatched blue toilet and a narrow shower stall with enameled pressboard walls that were painted to look like tiles. He stepped out of the bathroom and continued on.

To his right, the kitchen aisle ended at a door to the bedroom, which was at the opposite end of the trailer from the dining table. It smelled musty and was filled by a double bed with a thin blue-striped mattress. A high bank of windows ran around the bedroom, affording some privacy, he imagined, when lying down, but letting in a porch-like light. The narrow floor space before the bed contained a dark wooden nightstand in the medieval revival style of the early 1970s, and a narrow bedroom closet with a thin bifold door on the same side of the trailer as the bathroom. He measured the wall's thinness at the edge of the doorframe. It fit easily between his thumb and fingers.

He turned and walked back into the kitchen aisle.

"I haven't been in this one," the rental agent said from the door. Her tone was apologetic. "The ones up over the hill are way nicer—"

JW looked out the kitchen sink window, and saw it

afforded a convenient view of Eagle's house and yard. He gave her a friendly smile. "This'll be fine."

She frowned and shrugged. "Why not?" She laughed and threw up her hands. "I'll go get the lease!"

Alone, he ran his hands over the cabinets, taking in the aura of cheap nostalgia. Although everything in the trailer was decades old, on closer inspection it seemed surprisingly well-cared for, with little bits of epoxy patch here and a few replaced and glued handles there, as if it had been repeatedly fixed and maintained in crafty ways.

He sat at the small table with the rental agent and completed the paperwork. Then he walked her to her truck, and she departed. She seemed in disbelief at her good fortune to have rented one of the places out here, let alone the one JW had chosen. He turned back and took a deep breath as he surveyed his new home. It was a mission, like being in the army, he told himself. This was his barracks, and all that mattered was its utility. He opened his car, grabbed two of the lawn-and-leaf bags, and carried them toward the trailer. When he went back to get his suits, he saw the boy again, leading a big chestnut horse toward a railed-in riding paddock in Eagle's side yard. The horse was planting its feet almost every step of the way. The boy, he realized, had little idea what he was doing.

He hung his suits in the tiny bedroom closet and sat on the flaccid mattress, testing it. It had a large tan water stain at the foot of the bed. Someone must have left the windows open in a driving rain. He looked out the windows to his right, over the lamp on the bedside table, and watched the horse running loose in the paddock. He watched as the boy approached and it galloped away.

JW snorted. Horses were a constant challenge, he reflected,

a mirror of one's own weaknesses. If you didn't know how to work them, they worked you. He unpacked a family photo from a banker's box and set it on the nightstand, followed by an old clock radio, which he plugged into a brown outlet protruding from the wall. Then he stood and went back into the main room to find the lawn bag that contained his bedding.

7

That night JW dreamed of his father for the first time in years. The dream had the quality of memory, for in it a flock of blue jays was attacking a cardinal in the grass. This had really happened. But in the dream his father stomped on the birds as if putting out a fire, and they flew squawking into a nearby tree. But one was left on the ground, fluttering around with a broken wing, near the dead cardinal. His father stomped on it, crushing it, and turned to JW with rabid glee.

He woke with a buck of panic, his father's baleful expression stuck in his mind. He lay in the dark, hot and sweaty, and listened to the trailer's murmurs and creaks. His heart was thumping, and a terrible lucidity came over him as he cooled and the dream faded.

He got up, his limbs stiff and dull as wood, and stumbled in to the tiny kitchen. He made a cup of chamomile tea to settle his stomach. The pot whistled as he tried to shake off the spell. As feeling returned, he sat at the tiny table and sipped in the dark. The speckled Formica glowed in the moonlight. He needed help, he realized. He had been utterly competent most of his life, but now he was in over his head—with his gambling, with Jorgenson, with his failing relationships and his enormous debts. He was coming apart on the inside. But there was no one to help him, no one who could understand, or offer aid and counsel.

He began to make a list. He would find the local Gamblers Anonymous group and he would get a Big Book. He doubted it would do any good—after all, gambling was not an addiction like alcohol—but he wrote it down. He would go to Carol and fix things with her. He would take Julie camping or shopping—whatever she wanted to do—in order to rekindle their relationship. Make more of an effort. Get over himself. He could feel a sense of normalcy and resolve returning as the list grew.

He had never before done anything like what Jorgenson was asking of him, but he tried to make a list for that, too. He would try to become Eagle's friend, he thought, and then he would search his house. The thought seemed ludicrous, like something out of a movie. He imagined breaking in, only to learn that it was all a big mistake. Eagle was probably planning to open a fast food restaurant, or something equally innocuous. He would tell Jorgenson that he had it all wrong. Jorgenson would be relieved, and he would give JW another chance. JW would put his nose to the grindstone and stay away from the casino, he would make his payments, he would be home every night for dinner, at church every Sunday; he would slowly work himself out of debt and earn back Carol's trust. Slow and steady is what he needed, just like everyone else. Conservative, clean, no more crazy risks. And no more gambling, ever again.

As JW imagined this new reality, his earlier sense of dread and anxiety began to dissipate. He had a plan in his notepad. Life was not out of control. He carried it back into the bedroom and set it on the nightstand. He lay back down, and slipped into a turgid, tentative sleep.

He woke in the late light of mid-morning, and after showering he dressed in a crisp white shirt and a nice fall suit. The ominous, unsettled feeling still lingered from the night before, but he had a plan. He stepped out of the trailer and locked the flimsy aluminum door behind him. During the ride back to town he reviewed his list, and with the mental activity the feeling began to subside.

He drove first to the county library, where he used the Internet to find the local Gamblers Anonymous chapters. One of them was meeting just before lunch in the basement of Christ Lutheran Church, an old white clapboard structure north of town. He hated the idea of joining a group like this, especially considering his stature. The whole thing seemed stupid to him, the kind of thing that he imagined urban liberals did to get in touch with their feelings. It demanded a willingness to sit among people who were not functioning at his level of accomplishment, and it would also be damaging to his reputation. He would have to find a way to redefine his identity in a way that didn't seem so broken, that allowed him to maintain more self-respect—and more importantly, the respect of others—and allowed him room for professional redemption. But first he needed the damn book. He had agreed to get one and "carry it around" with him, as Jorgenson had put it. He would have to suck it up and go to the meeting.

The church sat a few miles out of North Lake, on a two-lane ribbon of eroded blacktop that mostly served as a field-access road for local sugar-beet farmers. It was surrounded by a stand of oaks and a small cyclone-fenced cemetery with tilted headstones. JW parked behind a large four-by-four pickup—knobby tires and mud flaps the size of his car doors, bearing silver naked ladies—where his Caprice would not be seen from the road. He got out and waited for a car to pass, then followed another man into a side door and down a set of concrete steps.

In the basement a sign directed him through a service area and into a meeting room with a gray painted cement floor and walls, and joists painted white above. There was an old inlaid-wood card table bearing a stack of Big Books near the door. A hand-lettered sign on the table read, "If you need one, take one." JW took one and turned to leave, but more people were coming in behind him, so he took a seat on a metal folding chair in the back row. The room smelled of rosewater, which was probably the only digni-fied thing about it in his mind. A pale yellow plywood sign was mounted on the wall nearby, bearing the hand-paint-ed words Character Assets in shiny red letters with blue painted shadows. A long list followed in blue letters with red bullets:

> self-forgiveness • humility • self-valuation •
> promptness • straightforwardness • trust •
> forgiveness • simplicity • love • honesty •
> patience • activity • modesty • positive
> thinking • generosity • *look for the good!*

This last phrase was in a rollicking red script that dipped up and down as if it were written on the peaks and valleys of a carnival ride. JW was growing anxious to leave, but two men stood conversing in the doorway, so he remained in his chair with his legs and hands crossed, the Big Book on his lap.

Below the wooden sign was a paper one made from several pages of computer printout. There's Nothing So

Bad That Gambling Won't Make It Worse, it said, followed by four exclamation points. In the lower left corner, it bore a small image of a royal flush with a circle and a line through it.

The basement's white concrete walls had high dusty windows. A cobweb glinted in the sunlight. Hosta leaves grew thick on the other side of the glass. JW thought about the royal flush on the computer printout, imagined getting the deal in some casino poker game, and fantasized about how much he would win. ("A hundred thousand dollars!")

"Visitor, please stand," the meeting's chair was saying to him.

JW looked around. The meeting was in session and people were looking at him. He noticed that an older woman with kind eyes had sat down next to him.

"I'm sorry, I guess I wasn't paying attention," he said.

"He asked you to stand," she said with a warm smile. "Don't worry."

The chair was middle-aged, balding, and wore a navy blue plumber's uniform bearing a patch embroidered with the name "Gary."

"Thank you," JW whispered to the woman next to him. He stood and smoothed his suit jacket, realizing as he did so that he had slipped into exactly the position he wanted to avoid: junior to some well-meaning—but less intelligent and less successful—gambling addicts.

"I'm Gary L.," the man said, "and in keeping with Gamblers Anonymous tradition, we're going to start by asking you twenty questions. If you answer yes to seven or more I'm going to ask you if you think you're a compulsive gambler. All right?"

JW glanced around at the faces watching him. The farm-

er with the long brown face and fingernails. The frizzy-haired
waitress with rashy cheeks. The implement salesman with
blonde bangs combed long and low across his forehead.
The kind-looking woman in mom clothes, who wore a
home detention ankle bracelet. They seemed encouraging, but all of it was mildly disgusting. They knew nothing about him—what he did, what he knew, what he had
accomplished—or the position he had in the community.
Who were they, to judge him?

"I think you can probably skip the questions," he said,
a hand in his pocket in his best business-conference-pre-
senter persona.

"Well, it's our procedure," replied the chair.

"That's fine, but, you know, I was just going to leave,"
said JW, pointing in the direction of the door. "I just wanted to get the book and then the door was blocked. I'm sorry
to disrupt your meeting—"

"That's fine," said Gary, in a tone that struck JW as
surprisingly gentle for a plumber. He suddenly felt that it
would be rude of him to leave. He lifted an arm.

"You know what? Go ahead," he said, and smiled
around the room. "You all seem like reasonable people."

"Okay." Gary read from the Big Book. "Did you ever
lose time from work or school due to gambling?"

"No."

"Has gambling ever made your home life unhappy?"

JW let out an ironic laugh. "I don't have a home life per
se. My wife and I are separated." He was smiling as if it
were funny, he realized, and a wave of regret washed over
him. He felt his face flushing. "You know, I'm really not
that comfortable sharing personal information like this."
He looked around the room, hoping to find a sympathetic

smile. Instead, they all looked sorry for him. JW was deeply unsettled, but he clasped his hands and tried to stand in place politely.

"Did gambling ever affect your reputation?" the chair asked.

JW sighed in renewed irritation—with himself more than anything. "So I've been told." It came out clipped. He felt the blood rising in his temples.

"Have you ever felt remorse after gambling?"

"Gary, just give him a minute," said the woman beside JW.

JW shrugged. "Hasn't everyone?" Now his sarcasm was unmistakeable.

"Look," replied Gary, "you may think this is stupid, but this isn't banking. Yes, I know who you are. We're not your loan applicants. We're gambling addicts, all of us, and wherever we come from, we're all on the same level in here."

JW felt a burst of anger. "I'm sorry, I didn't realize we'd been through the twenty questions yet."

A few of the people laughed, and Gary glanced at them and banged his gavel. "That's enough," he said.

JW's mouth was dry and his feet hurt. "I'm sorry," he said. "I just don't think I'm ready for this."

"You're among friends. You can let it out."

JW looked from the chair to the others in the room and back again. He let out a small laugh and rubbed his neck.

"No," he said, "I'm not going to do that." He realized he was clenching his fists, and willed them to relax. "I'm gonna go," he said. "Thank you. I'm sorry." He began moving toward the door.

"You don't have to," said Gary.

Too late, JW realized he'd left his Big Book on the chair. He grabbed another one from the table and hurried out.

"Addiction is cunning, baffling, and powerful," he heard Gary call after him as he headed for the stairs. "It's other people that keep us sane. You can come back any time!"

He took the stairs two at a time and pushed the door open, stepping out into the fresh air and sunshine. He was angry with himself for becoming combative and sarcastic. It was shameful, really, the way he had conducted himself. Maybe there were things he could have picked up by sitting in the back of a meeting like that.

The gravel was littered with cigarette butts and withered dandelions. There were polished flecks of green glass from an old Mountain Dew bottle mixed in with the rocks near his car. He got in and closed the door. He inhaled the sweltering air. Turned the key and let the air conditioner blast dust at him. Then he pulled back out onto the highway and headed toward town.

Some ten minutes later, JW pulled up and parked in front of his house, still jangled and full of self-recrimination. It was shortly after noon. He wanted to catch Carol, and he knew that she usually tried to eat lunch at home, where she could listen to the midday program on public radio. He got out, walked up to the house, and rang the glowing round doorbell. He waited a moment. Maybe he should have stayed in that meeting. He felt as if he had made a choice between two paths without realizing it, but he also knew that he was being overly dramatic. He could always go back, as Gary had said. Any time. He rang the doorbell again. He heard the sound of a squeaking floorboard just inside, and then the door was unlocked and swung inward.

"John!" Carol smiled nervously at him. Her face was flushed and she seemed pleasantly surprised and a bit out of breath. She stepped out, pulling the door partially shut behind her. Her shoulder-length blonde hair fell in loose shaggy locks around her face. He recognized a cubic zirconium necklace around her neck, just like the one he had seen on the Home Shopping Network. It struck him as odd that she would buy something like that for herself, especially now. Still, seeing her somehow made him feel relieved and normal again.

"Hey," he said.

"You look awful." She smiled quizzically and pushed a lock from her face.

"I tried calling, a number of times."

She frowned and smiled at the same time, a mixed expression that he had always found endearing in its impenetrability. "John, you stood me up. I waited up 'til after eleven."

"I know, I'm sorry. You got time for lunch?"

"No, I don't, I have a meeting today."

"A meeting?"

"Yeah, I told you. Jim Franklin's taking me to the new agents luncheon."

He nodded. She had said that. Then he heard the squeaky floorboard inside. A flicker of insecurity darted across Carol's face, and in that instant the mirage of old times evaporated. She moved partway back through the door. Behind her in the foyer stood Jim Franklin, a blow-dried insurance agent in his early forties, whom JW had always disliked. Carol's thin brows knit together and she looked down, moving the hair back behind her ear.

"John!" Franklin said in a glad-handing tone as he shrugged into his suitcoat behind her. "How was the conference?"

JW wanted to believe that it was all a big mistake. That Jim Franklin wasn't really there, in his house, in the middle of the day, with Carol, who had been slow to answer the door. Jim Franklin, who knew about his travel schedule.

"I'm fine, Jim," he managed to get out. He turned back to Carol. "Is Julie home?"

"You know she's at school." But her voice had a little break in it as she realized why he had asked. The sky seemed to tilt in her eyes.

"It's not what you think," she said. "We have to run. We can talk later." She and Jim stepped outside. She pulled the door shut and locked it as Jim gave JW a little wave and a winking nod and headed toward his sports car, which was partially obscured by the evergreens at the corner of the house.

He nodded to Carol. "Call my cell."

"Okay."

He watched her hurry after Jim, and then the car pulled out. They both waved. He waved back. It was a fine day, and anyone watching would have thought the waves festive, the beginning of something fun.

JW walked to his car across the street, the sky beating down on him with the light of a desert. His hands were numb despite the heat, as if his arteries had been cut at the armpits. In the brilliant sunshine he could really see how filthy his car was, and that there was a rust speck forming on the lower portion of his door. He'd have to wash it, but the rust would be harder to fix.

He got in and set out for the Northland Mall. He gripped the wheel tightly. It couldn't be. It was too fast. They'd only been separated for a few months. And after all, she had said it wasn't what it looked like. He thought about their daughter Julie. In all this, it was time with her he most looked forward to, but they hadn't had much of it lately. In some ways Julie had more in common with him than she did with Carol. She was interested in things, in nature, in animals, in science.

While Carol was practical and family-oriented and tradition-bound, Julie was an impractical dreamer. He loved that about her, and he had always encouraged it.

Beyond their birthday excursions and camping trips with the Brownies, Julie and JW talked about science and the universe on trips to the grocery store, or to the Northland Mall. On one of their trips together, driving to visit his father as he was dying of cirrhosis in the hospital in Fargo, Julie read a book on evolution—which JW had bought her secretly, since Carol didn't want her reading books that openly defied the pastor's sermons. He watched the light reflect in her glasses as she read to him about the geological clock. "One hour equals about four hundred million years," she told him with awe. He watched her face fill with excitement as she pondered that sense of scale, and how so much that we think of as ancient is crowded in at the end of the eleventh hour.

"Amazing," he acknowledged, shaking his head in wonder.

She read on: "The earliest human ancestors we've discovered are about four million years old, and that's at 11:59:24. And the start of human civilization—everything we know, everything we have done since the beginning of history, all the roads and towns and cities we've built—all that has happened in the last one third of the last second, the time it takes to snap your fingers."

She looked out the car window and shook her head. "It's like an explosion."

He missed Julie with an almost palpable longing. Part of the distance that had emerged between them was her age, he knew, and the social demands of junior high. He remembered seventh grade, how brutal it was. Gone were the glasses—it was contacts and eyeliner now—and gone was the innocence.

But a big part of it, most of it, he felt certain, was everything that had happened in the year since Chris died. He missed their dates, and their car conversations, and her unguarded exuberance, in a way that made his heart ache.

Northland Mall lay on the outskirts of Virginia, a town that seemed to him like a miniature version of Duluth, some forty-five minutes down the highway from North Lake. Filled with the post-Victorian homes of mining executives and the scattered saltboxes of their minions, the city clawed its way up a giant hillside. Despite an early, five-story brick attempt at a skyscraper downtown, the tallest building to date was the water tower. Up the hill, to the north and west, the vast mall occupied as much square footage as most of the downtown. When it was built, JW had been asked to be part of a consortium of banks that provided financing, together with the Iron Range Resources and Rehabilitation Board, a government agency that was supposed to take the taconite production tax and reinvest it to stimulate the local economy. He had passed on the deal. It was too big for the area, his numbers said.

After some modest initial success, the mall had fallen on hard times during the Great Recession, making his decision look prescient. Avoiding that loss was one of the reasons North Lake Bank had become a regional leader.

He found a spot near the northeast entrance and walked across the potholed drive. Inside he could hear the sound of a distant fountain in the main concourse. He headed past the Army-Navy recruiting center, a temp agency, a sleepy Chinese restaurant, and a Goodwill, then stepped into the RadioShack. He was after something he'd seen in the store several years ago, when he was looking for an electronics project as a Christmas gift for Chris. He made his way to the back. There it was, on a bottom shelf near the door to the back room, by the old Heathkits. Dusty and forgotten, the eavesdropping hobby kit's packaging showed a twelve-year-old boy listening on headphones to his mom and dad, who were in the other room. A bug hidden behind a chair emitted lines representing radio waves. The description said it had a range of a hundred yards. JW stood, blew the dust off, and picked up some rosin-core solder and a soldering iron from the opposite shelf.

The clerk was a gregarious older man in a red RadioShack golf shirt, with silver hair in a bowl cut. More hair ran thick down his neck and arms, and poked out in a tuft from his open collar.

"You got a boy for that project?" he said jovially as he stuffed the merchandise into a small plastic shopping bag.

"No," said JW. His tone stopped the man short, but then he regretted his abruptness. "A daughter," he added. The clerk brightened immediately.

"Well, she's like my granddaughter, then! When she's old enough, she says she's going to go down the hall here and join the army and be a technoqueen. That's what I call her."

JW smiled and nodded as the man printed his receipt.

"You take care!" He handed the bag over with a big smile. JW nodded again as he took it and left.

8

The sharp smell of hot solder filled JW's nostrils as he bent over the speckled kitchen table. It was a warm afternoon, and beyond the window screens a breeze roiled the oaks in a constant sibilance, the leaves casting pale gray shadows that moved across the table like a flock of birds.

He held the soldering iron to a sprig of copper wire bent through a hole in the silver end of an electronic component and touched it with solder. The wire shifted and he moved the iron's beveled tip to better support it, then replaced the end of the solder against the wire. After a moment it emitted a soft puff of smoke and melted into a silver ball that crawled up the copper and down onto the tab. It jiggled again as he removed the soldering iron, then skinned over. A second later it had flashed into a duller gray, the tiny crystals in the metal locking into a new formation. He looked back at the pictogram in the instruction booklet, then slipped a thin green wire into the next tab.

When it was done, JW put the final screws into the receiver—a brown plug-in box with two knobs and a pair of earbuds. A small round bug sat on the table as well, together with the solder, the iron, the Gamblers Anonymous Big Book, and a large framed photo of his family in happier days.

He plugged in the receiver's cord, put the earbuds in, turned it on, and spoke into the bug like a microphone.

"Testing." It was the first thing he had said all day. He could hear it loud and clear over the receiver.

He looked out the window at Eagle's black Bronco in the drive. The sky bloomed above the trees like a Scandinavian flower. He picked up his cell phone, scrolled to Home, and pressed Call. After a moment he heard Carol's voice. "You've reached the White house, leave a message!" It was an old joke from a happier time.

"Carol, it's John. Just calling you back. Hope your lunch went well. Anyway, I'm not at the apartment anymore, I just— Call me. Please. Love you."

He hung up and stared out at the trees. The thought of Carol driving off in Jim's sports car made his chest tighten all over again, and now she wasn't calling him back. A noise drew his attention to the pole barn—the *stolpe låven*, he remembered his father calling theirs in Norwegian. They had a small one in the backyard, where they stored the lawn mower and other items—ATVs he wasn't allowed to drive or speak of, chainsaws, bicycles, once even a shiny Harley Davidson motorcycle—that would mysteriously appear and then disappear into the van of a man with long hair and a beard, after his father was laid off from the mine. "I'm selling them for a friend, but he's very embarrassed," his father explained. "Don't tell anyone." One day, the police stopped by, asking about a stolen pair of snowmobiles. But by then his father was on the road selling cell tower leases, his mother was whispering in tongues, and the stolpe låven had been empty for some time.

The large sliding doors of Eagle's pole barn opened to a cavern of shadow. Johnny Eagle and an older, stockier Indian man with a gray ponytail disappeared into the grainy murkiness, then reappeared a moment later. They each took a lawn-and-leaf bag from the bed of an old pickup truck and went back into the barn again. JW watched, wondering what they were up to. When they reemerged, the stocky man was carrying some white plastic bags. He threw them into the back of the pickup truck while Eagle pulled the big barn doors shut, and then they exchanged some money and the man with the ponytail got into the truck and rumbled off. Eagle walked back up toward the house.

JW organized the items on the table and sat back, waiting for Eagle to leave. He looked out the window again. The sun was high and the trailer was quiet. A slight breeze blew in through the screens. The lace-edged curtain turned over lazily. The buzzing of insects and the warm air soon sent him into a dozing memory. The smell of the solder and the old Formica tabletop conjured up dreaming memories of childhood times spent with similar kits, which his dad got from a RadioShack on special trips down to Duluth. You could build crystal radios, oscilloscopes, FM radios, alarm systems, a TV, or even a computer. JW looked forward to his father's homecomings partly because of these presents. His father spent most weeks and sometimes months on the road, but when he was home with a new kit JW would pester him until he came down to the basement workshop. He would carry down a six-pack in a cooler and a couple of Dorothy's root beers for JW. The two of them would work until the early hours of the morning, his dad sipping beer after beer and telling stories of his time on the road selling leases for cell phone towers, or of how the damn Indians were organizing with the crazy enviros to block them. He'd sometimes take his Motorola cell phone out and show him. "See this?" he'd say, waving the briefcase-sized device. "This is freedom. Those idiots don't know what's good for them." Later, when the beers had set in, he would hunch over the workbench. "So," he'd say, "is she driving you crazy yet? You think you can handle this?"

He was talking about JW's mother. One day during the

first summer his dad was mostly away on the road, JW's mother was at the kitchen counter, bending over some pasties on the dough board, singing her special version of an old Finnish song:

Then the aged Väinämöinen
Spoke aloud his songs of magic,
And a flower-crowned birch grew upward,
Crowned with flowers, and leaves all golden,
And its summit reached to heaven,
To the very clouds uprising.
You, my son, my Kalevala, my story of the north—

And then, mid-verse, she stopped. She had always been a little artsy, and JW loved painting the lower cupboards with her, or making chalk masterpieces on the garage floor. But he sensed that this was different. She began seeing visions, and speaking to invisible gods.

She never sang a word again, but she whispered day and night. JW thought she had gone crazy right then and there, and in a way she had. At the time there was no way to know that a small frog was growing inside her brain, extending its little webbed feet. Or that the tumor would eventually kill her when he was thirteen.

JW was charged with taking care of her when his father was on the road and she was sick with the migraines, but she just lay there whispering verses, so he spent most of his time outdoors. In truth, she frightened him. It was as if some ghost spirit from the Finnish North had taken her, and when JW was around it made her upset, so he avoided her as much as he could.

During the early stages of his mother's illness, JW whiled

away most of the time with his friends, Craig and the twins, Keith and Kevin. They were outside from dawn until dusk, with only a few short breaks for meals or snacks at each other's houses. They spent part of one summer exploring the dump, climbing into rusting cars, turning their steering wheels, the spice of dust, mold, and old tobacco smoke lifting from the seat stuffing. And they loved to play in the trees, climbing from one to another to avoid the sharks and lava below. But JW's favorite game had always been cowboys and Indians.

Craig's mother said the game was crude, and she was surprised that Keith and Kevin, who were half Ojibwe, went along with it. But the game's historical connotations never seemed to matter to the twins. In fact, JW usually played the Indian, while Keith and Kevin and Craig all pretended to be cowboys. They would share a root beer, pretend to get drunk, and then ride in a posse to hunt JW down.

JW had always admired the Indian braves in TV shows, how they hopped on horses and rode bareback while shooting arrows at their enemies at a full gallop. Some days he even put on war paint and a headdress, and bet them each fifty cents they couldn't find him before he could shoot them. They'd count to a hundred while he ran into the woods by the wetlands, where the cottonwoods and the buckthorn gave way to a green algae pond. He'd hide up in the trees and wait patiently, planning what he would do with the money.

JW woke thick-headed and woozy in the wash light of mid-afternoon. It took him a moment to remember where he was, but the musty smell of the trailer brought him back. He heard the sound of a car door slamming, and then the sound of an engine turning over. He looked out and saw Johnny Eagle backing his Bronco out of the driveway. It headed slowly around the bend, toward the reservation road.

He checked his watch. It was a little after two. The boy wouldn't be home from school for another hour and ten minutes, if the pattern of the past few days held. He stood, took the little round bug from the table, and stepped out through the flimsy aluminum door.

The wooden steps were catching a spot of sunlight. He could feel the warmth through his jeans as he stepped down onto the grassy gravel. He pushed the door shut behind him and looked around. There was no sign of life at Eagle's house, or at the white brick house farther up the hill. He looked back up the lane toward the trailer park, but no one appeared to be up that way either. It was now or never. His heart picked up speed as he stepped onto the dirt road. His fingers felt tight. He stretched them and crossed toward the riding ring and then onto Eagle's lawn. The horse stood in a makeshift stall of two-by-sixes, inside a metal lean-to. It snorted at him with an air of concern.

He crossed uphill toward the house, which had even taller trees behind it. He strolled up the white concrete walk toward the front door, trying to appear relaxed in case someone happened to be watching. Ranks of orange and green lilies stood at attention. He looked into the dark pool of a window. Everything still. He stepped onto the low front porch. His heart was pounding. A bristly brown mat in front of the door bore the word *Bendigen.* He didn't belong here. This wasn't the sort of thing he did. He pulled open the wooden screen door, knocked on the carved main door. His fingers were numb.

There was no sound. He glanced over his shoulder to see if anyone was watching. His chest felt tight. He noticed the doorbell. A glowing yellow rectangle. He pressed it and an old bell echoed inside, but there was no reaction. He looked behind him again, and up the trailer park lane across the street. From here he could see the tops of a few trailers poking over the hill.

His hand closed around the knob, feeling cold and weak. It turned. He paused, then pushed the door open and stepped inside.

"Hello? Anybody home? Mr. Eagle? Hello!"

The interior was themed in rustic wood and Native-style decor. To his right stood an unfinished room of studs and insulation. Ahead, the foyer opened into a large eating area, with a broad library table covered with piles of papers and books. The floor was wide-plank wood, marred and finished with a dull wax. To the right of the eating area was the kitchen. Despite the fact that it was only partially finished, it had massive granite countertops, a breakfast bar, a deep sink, and stainless steel appliances. To his immediate left was a corridor leading to the bedrooms.

The central air conditioning kicked on with a cool whir. JW headed down the corridor, in search of an office. His heart was pounding. On the wall was a family photo of the boy—much younger, perhaps ten—with Eagle and a woman, presumably his mother. After pausing at it briefly, JW continued, past a bathroom, to a door that stood open to a masculine, Native-themed room with a queen-sized bed. Opposite he could see into the messy cave of a teenage boy. Clothing piled in mounds. Soda bottles, chips, textbooks, and notebooks on the bed. An older laptop computer and some comic books piled atop an empty terrarium. The smell of dirty laundry and Doritos.

JW returned to the door opposite the bathroom. It was closed, but not latched. There could be someone inside, he worried, an aging grandparent or someone sleeping. He took a soft step closer, but a floorboard creaked under the carpeting, giving him away. He froze.

He had never done anything like this, and he had no idea what to expect or how to react if there was someone inside the room. He waited a moment, still, but there was no answer. He pushed the door open slowly with his shirt cuff, and saw that there was no one. He stepped into a home office. More Native décor, and the faint smell of cigar smoke. Wooden louver blinds like those at the bank hung over the windows. There was a large wooden desk, antique, 1940s design, and a black Herman Miller Aeron chair. The wall to the right was covered with a modular birch bookcase, Scandinavian style, that was divided into boxes of different sizes, with books in some places and knickknacks in others.

JW crossed to the desk. He pressed his fingertips to the paperwork on top. A pale blue report card. Jacob Eagle. *Migizi-doodem.* Cs and Ds. B+ in math. Teacher comments to the right of each grade: able but distracted; not engaged; disruptive in class.

The bookcase was filled with books about Native Americans, as well as DVDs of *Avatar, Dances with Wolves, Smoke Signals, Babel, Crash,* and *The Visitor,* a small stack of CDs—Jim Boyd, Bob Marley, Jana—and videos of pow-wows. There was also a brass eagle in flight, which JW took to be an eponymous testament to the man's inflated self-image.

He opened the center drawer. Pens and pencils, ink cartridges, a calculator. A self-help book, *Fearless Living: Live without Excuses and Love without Regret,* suggested a kind of touchy-feely vulnerability that both moved and repelled JW.

He took the bug from his pocket, wiped it clean, and

placed it in the back of the drawer. He shut the drawer and glanced out the window. The coast was still clear. Down the hill he could see his own trailer, a dirty blue robin's egg in the fine wavy grass under the oak trees.

He pulled open the desk's file drawer, again using his shirt cuff to avoid leaving any fingerprints. Neatly ordered files. He squatted and rifled through the brown tabs. They emitted a rich aroma of cigar smoke. One of the folders said Nature's Bank. He opened it and examined the contents. Motes of dust lifted off the papers like tiny hot-air balloons, sparkling in the sun.

He glanced out the window. The longer he stayed, the greater his chances of being caught. But this might be the mother lode. He scanned a page with numbers: Start-Up Capitalization. . . $3.5 Million. He closed the folder and slipped it back into the file drawer. He'd had enough. It was obviously a bank, and he was increasingly nervous. Someone could come home at any time—Eagle, the boy, or someone else. He pushed the drawer shut and glanced out the window again. He crossed to the door. But something caught his eye and he stopped. He went to the closet's bifold door and pulled it open. Inside was a safe.

He crouched and tried the handle, but it was locked. The dial had numbers every ten marks to one hundred. He tried turning it to see if it was just slightly off, but it didn't open. He stood. Glanced at the closet shelves. Office supplies. Paper. A yellow box of trash-can liners. He closed the closet door and returned to the hallway, using his shirt cuff to pull the door shut like it had been. He tiptoed quickly back down the hall and crossed to the door. He opened it a crack and looked out. The coast seemed clear. He exited into the open air of the shaded porch and eased the door shut, then gently let the screen door close. The fresh air hit him like a gasp of relief.

He stepped off the front deck and glanced at the white brick house up the road, and as he turned he saw a curtain falling back into place in a high corner window. His heart leaped in his chest. Surely whoever lived in the house knew Eagle, and would relay the story of how the white guy in the trailer had broken into his house while he was away. He had to do something. Pretending it hadn't happened was not an option. Perhaps he could still avert a catastrophe by going up and talking to whomever had been behind that curtain.

He looked both ways and then walked out into Eagle's yard, consciously adopting an aw-shucks kind of amble in his gait. He began formulating a plan: He was out looking to borrow some sugar. He wanted directions to the trading post. A dozen clichés came to mind, none of them compelling. He crossed the driveway in front of the brick house's tuck-under garage and mounted the concrete steps leading up to the front door.

It was somehow even hotter up there in the sun. The white blazed everywhere, making him feel as if he were in a solar cooker. He glanced at the tall casement windows. They all had white curtains and he couldn't see beyond them. He would improvise. Eagle's front door was set in a few feet, and he saw that it was out of view. He was just standing on the porch, he would say, making a phone call. He had wanted to greet his neighbors, what could be wrong with that? He stepped up onto the front porch.

The windows in the front of the house were all closed, but they felt watchful. He looked around in vain for a doorbell. He tried the white metal storm door, but it was locked tight. A Baltimore oriole swooped in and fluttered near a hanging feeder heaped with grape jelly, but seeing him, thought better of it and flitted away. He heard something crash deep inside the house. He knocked, but there was no response.

"Hello?" he called.

Still nothing. Now what? He stood in the blazing sun, contemplating his options. A trickle of sweat ran down between his shoulder blades. Whoever was in there had probably seen him. Perhaps they were calling the police. Or going for a shotgun. JW decided to head back to his trailer. That way at least he would have some deniability if the police did come. He could argue that the other person was crazy or just making things up, and that they were probably overly suspicious just because he was white.

He stepped off the stoop and walked back down the steps, glancing back at the home's mute windows. He thought he saw a shadow move behind a curtain. He stopped, but nothing more happened. He wondered if this was all just his imagination. He felt sullied by what he had just done, but a job was a job. He headed out the driveway and across the street, glancing back to see if he could catch anyone watching, but there was no sign of life. It suddenly occurred to him that he was a criminal now. Not technically, he reassured himself. He hadn't stolen anything. You leave your door open and sometimes neighbors wander in, that's what happens out in the country. He turned toward his trailer home, sure that he could sense someone watching him.

9

The sun had moved to the northwest and the trees no longer shaded the front half of the trailer. The metal handle was hot in his hand as he pulled the flimsy aluminum door open. It had expanded in the heat and the bottom stuck in the frame, then sprang outward with a rattling shudder.

He stepped inside. The air was spicy hot and still. He closed the door and listened to the fine ticks of the trailer's metal exterior shifting in the heat. There was no air conditioner, so he went around opening all the windows. This must be why the screens were so well maintained, he realized.

He finished with the roof vent over the galley kitchen, and then the windows in the front end around the table. A cross breeze lifted up, and he sat down on the bench, where he had a view of the white brick house through a gap in the trees. He focused a pair of binoculars on the curtained windows. They gleamed back at him in mute judgment.

JW lowered the binoculars and began formulating plausible excuses. He hadn't actually gone into Eagle's house. He had stood for some time at the door, out of view of the white house, waiting for his neighbor to return, hoping to introduce himself. You need to know your neighbors, after all. Since no one was home, he decided to say hello to his other neighbor. No answer there either, so he walked back home. Anything else was simply the result of an overly suspicious imagination, a misunderstanding.

A deep rolling build of thunder signaled a storm brewing off to the west. Here on the edge of the prairie, large anvil clouds often billowed up on hot afternoons. One could stand in the blazing sun and watch them, ten or fifteen miles distant: blue-gray rain angling down, stabs of lightning flashing inside. But this one was still a ways off, and there was no coolness or wind yet. The trees buzzed with a cacophony of insects. There was nothing to do but wait.

As the minutes ticked by and nothing happened, the warmth of the trailer grew more stifling. He put his face up to a window for some fresh air. The police still hadn't come. JW's shirt stuck to his skin, and a trickle of sweat ran down the edge of his neck. Maybe it would be all right. There'd been no phone calls, no neighbor coming out, no Eagle, no police. Maybe the neighbor wouldn't even say anything. Or maybe he had imagined the whole thing. Then again, something had crashed inside, so it was likely a person. And if the neighbor did say something, he would have to deal with Eagle directly. JW imagined him coming over with a baseball bat, or possibly even a gun. He wondered how the laws differed on a reservation, and that thought suddenly seemed to ground his thinking. He was a bank president. What he had done was crazy. He had risked everything.

His eyes fell to the Big Book. He pulled it over across the table and started leafing through it. Maybe there was something to it. A sickness was clouding his judgment, and Jorgenson had used it to make him into a tool. And yet he couldn't see a way out of the trap, and it was hard to imagine finding one in the book.

It was approaching five o'clock, and nothing had happened. The road had been unusually quiet. A single small blue Toyota with a red front fender had puttered by, slowly climbing up the lane to the trailers over the hill. Even the boy hadn't come home at his usual time.

JW was getting hungry. He headed over to the stove. He rummaged through the cabinet above and took down a battered aluminum pot and a box of mac and cheese. He ran the tap and filled the pot halfway up, then struck a farmer's match and lit the stove. He set the pot over the flame, and when crystal bubbles began to rise from its bottom, he poured in the pale tubes of dried pasta.

He looked out the window over the kitchen sink. Still nothing up at the neighbor's house, but to his right he suddenly noticed a police car creeping up the road. It slowed almost to a stop, and then, as if to surprise him, it turned sharply in and parked directly in front of his trailer. JW ducked back away from the window, his heart suddenly racing. He wondered if he, too, could pretend he wasn't at home. The car's door slammed and he peeked out to see a tribal policeman walking around the hood.

He heard the creak of the wooden steps, and then a hard knock on his flimsy door. He leaned on the counter, thinking over his options. How stupid he'd been. What was he thinking? Was this it? Would he be arrested? The knock came again. He realized that the bug receiver was still on the table.

"Just a second," he called out.

He took the receiver to the bedroom and threw it under some clothes in the laundry hamper. He swallowed and wiped his hands on his pants. Noticed his dirty shirt cuff.

He rolled up his sleeves and went to the door. There was nothing else to do. His lips felt numb. This is the way people's lives change, he thought. In quiet little moments, and there's no going back. His stomach felt jittery. He shook out his hands to get the rubberiness out. Tried to seem calm and cool. Don't assume he knows anything, or what he may or may not know. Don't incriminate yourself. He opened the door.

The tribal cop was standing on the top stair, which put him a step lower than JW. He had to shuffle sideways to avoid the out-swinging door.

"Yes sir, can I help you?" said JW.

"Mr. White?"

"Yes."

Through the fog of fear, JW noticed that the man had an expectant smile. He was waiting—for what? A confession? Maybe to see if he would give something away. JW had heard that most one-time criminals admit their crime almost immediately when confronted by the authorities. He wasn't going to be one of them.

"You don't remember me," the cop said. "Rick Fladeboe. Used to work security at the bank."

"Rick! Sorry. Of course!" replied JW.

Jesus, he thought. Fladeboe. Security guard.

"You look different in that tribal getup."

JW knew as soon as he said it that it was offensive, but he desperately wanted to keep the upper hand, so he didn't apologize—he smiled.

"Yeah, well, I heard you were staying out here now. Figured I'd stop by and say hi, welcome to the reservation and all."

"Well, thanks, Rick," replied JW noncommittally. "I appreciate that."

He saw Fladeboe notice that he was sweating.

"You doin' okay?"

JW nodded. "Just hot in here. No AC. You want to come in for a sauna?"

Fladeboe laughed. "No thanks. Say, I heard what happened, about you losing your job and so on—"

"Rick, I got some stuff on the stove—"

"I know, I know. I don't want to take your time. Just to say, listen, if you ever want, the tribe's got a gambling and addictions support group. A real nice one, we got top people, trained at UMD, the whole works. It's one of our mandates, for having the casino. We don't want anybody to get hurt."

He handed JW a business card. It bore a colorful round tribal logo, the name of the group, the Bizaaniwewin Support Group, and a phone number and web URL.

"It's a funny-sounding name, *Bizaaniwewin*," offered Fladeboe. "Means peace."

JW looked down at the card. His brow creased as he looked up from it. He felt his pulse in a vein on his neck. He wondered how word of his situation had traveled so quickly, and whether Fladeboe was acting individually, or if this was a visit some band committee had asked him to make.

"Anyway, welcome." Fladeboe gave him a curt little nod and a wave, then turned and walked back to his cruiser.

"Rick!" JW called out after him. Fladeboe stopped and looked back. "Thanks."

Fladeboe waved. As he got in his car, JW noticed for the first time that someone was sitting in the back seat. The car backed out onto the road and stopped in front of Eagle's house. Fladeboe got out and opened the back door. The boy from across the street climbed out and sloughed off toward the pole barn without so much as a word to Fladeboe, who saw JW still standing in the door, and waved before getting back into his car. He had kept the kid waiting that whole time.

JW waved back, then pulled the door shut and returned to his macaroni. He stirred it weakly, recovering from the adrenaline rush. He glanced at the business card in his left hand. Peace. The tiny crescents swam like blind fish in the roiling water. He went to the fridge and pulled out the Red Owl carton of milk. As he turned, he glanced out the window. The boy was tugging on a red lead rope, trying to drag the horse across the lawn toward the riding ring. The animal was ignoring him again. It grazed on the lawn, planting its feet against the lead rope. JW noticed how tightly wound the boy seemed. He was probably recovering from his own adrenaline rush after getting a lift home from Fladeboe. His teenage frustration wafted across the road.

"Come on!"

The horse ignored him, then finally, begrudgingly, it lifted its head and half-heartedly let the boy lead it away from the grass. The boy dragged the horse over to the riding paddock gate, unlatched it, and swung it open. He pulled with first one, then two hands, but the horse stood still, feet planted, head high, refusing to go in.

JW moved to the window, watching this little drama. Horse training was all about convincing a horse that what you wanted was what it wanted too, only more so, and JW could see that the kid had no idea what he was doing.

"Damn it, come on! Come on!" The boy pulled hard on the lead rope, stretching the horse's neck out, but the animal's feet were firm. He stormed up beside it and the horse responded by stepping backward. The boy stumbled as he tried to stay on his feet. JW heard the horse snorting.

"No!" The boy yelled. He punched the horse on the side of the neck. It threw its head and pulled hard backward, squatting on its haunches as it prepared to rear. It stood, which dragged the boy up off the ground and into its dancing front hooves.

"Hey!" he yelled at the window. Stupid kid, he thought.

The rearing horse's head could come down and break his neck, and it would trample him if it ran forward.

The boy twisted to miss the hooves and scrambled to the right, along the horse's front left flank. He's quick, I'll give him that, thought JW. Then the boy wrapped the lead rope around his wrist and kicked the horse hard in its soft underbelly. The horse screamed with a high frightened sound and tried to spin away, but the boy had leverage with the lead rope, so it reared and pulled him right back into the range of its hooves. This time the boy couldn't find his footing.

Before he knew it, JW was out the trailer door and running. The horse twisted and landed and galloped off across the lawn, dragging the boy close to its thundering hooves.

"Pride!" The boy yelled as he bumped along over the ground. "Pride, no!" His voice sounded screechy with fear.

"Let it go!" JW yelled as he ran after them.

The boy took a hard bump on a root and let go, and the horse galloped off. He lay on his stomach, the wind knocked out of him, his cheek pressed into the grass. The horse slowed to a trot and began to circle in the yard. Then it stopped at a safe distance and snorted and pawed at the lawn.

"You okay?" JW asked as he ran up. The boy was wheezing for breath and wincing back tears. He slowly got to his hands and knees. Then, ignoring JW, he headed shakily after the horse.

"Hey!"

The kid spun around. "I got it!" he yelled, then fell into a coughing fit. He was wearing jeans and a baggy Twins jersey.

"Okay. Nice to meet you," said JW. "I'm your new neighbor, by the way. Why don't you let me help."

The boy ignored him and turned back toward the horse, which trotted a few steps farther away.

"Fuck!" He stopped and stood, angry.

"You're chasing him off."

The boy's posture slumped, but he didn't turn around. He took another step toward the horse, but it jogged even farther away.

"Goddamn it!"

JW glanced back toward the trailer home. The door was standing open. He looked down at the waxy milk carton in his hand.

"Hey kid!" he said, and began marching toward the boy's back. "I got something for you."

The boy turned around. "Hold this," JW said, and shoved the milk carton into his hands. He turned toward Pride and gave him a snappy whistle. Pride snorted as he grazed, made a big sigh, then took a few steps toward the neighbor's house, still munching on the lawn.

"You're chasin' him off, old school," said the boy.

JW turned, irritated. "Go over there," he said, and pointed toward the house. "So you're not between him and the gate. Go on!"

The boy didn't move.

"You want your horse back?" JW looked at him and he looked back. "I did this for a living," said JW. The boy shook his head and walked across the yard to where JW had indicated. When he was a safe distance off, JW nodded. "Okay."

He looked down at the ground, hands in his pockets. He jangled his keys and assumed a relaxed air, not a care in the world. Just him and the horse, together and alone in a herd of two. It was like a mantra. It all came back as if it had been yesterday. If he got his mind in the right space, JW knew the horse would follow. He started whistling softly—"You Are My Sunshine"—and he grazed with his feet, swinging and poking them at the grass. He walked wide around the horse, not paying it any attention, not getting too close, just focused on the grass. I'm just doing my thing here, just leave me alone and I'll leave you alone, he thought, walking and whistling.

Pride's ears followed him like radar dishes. He stopped about fifteen or twenty feet behind the horse, between him and the house. Pride grazed, flipping his ears around, flapping his tail to scare off the flies. But JW could see from the tension in the horse's muscles that he was ready to leap, turn, and trot off down the road at a moment's notice. He stopped whistling and looked up—at Pride's chest, not his eyes. The horse snorted long and low as he grazed—a dramatic, put-upon snort.

JW took a big step toward his rear end and lifted up his arm toward him, as if he were reaching for his tail. Pride lifted his head and trotted eight or nine steps toward the gate, then went back to grazing, with a frisky air about him, light on his feet.

JW noticed the boy was studying his moves intently. He felt a sudden affection for him, rude and surly as he was. JW kept looking at the grass and whistling. He strolled wide and away and then angled back, stopping behind and to the side again, but closer. Then he took his hands out of his pockets. He kept whistling, and he walked slowly, eyes averted, toward Pride's side. The horse's ears flicked around as he grazed, but he stayed where he was.

The boy watched him, his arms crossed and a scowl on his face. JW reached out and petted the base of the horse's sweaty neck. Gentle. Relaxed. No reason to hurry. Just the two of them grazing. Then he reached down and picked up the lead rope, but left it slack. They stood there grazing for another minute, the horse munching and JW poking the grass with his toe. He examined the rope in his left hand,

pretending to be interested in its fine weave. Not a care in the
world, until he reached back wide with his right hand, toward
Pride's rear end, and whistled sharply.

"Come on."

Pride let out another long snort and then lifted his head.
He walked next to JW on a slack rope, right up to the gate.
The boy looked amazed. He began heading down toward the
paddock. JW made a kissing sound at the horse and reached
out toward his rear end again. Pride stepped into a trot and
moved into the riding ring with his head high and an eye on
JW, but without any hesitation. JW tossed the lead rope over
his neck as he went in and closed the gate behind him. Pride
snorted and circled and came to a stop, watching him atten-
tively as if waiting for the next order. It was the old magic.

The boy looked down as JW turned to him. "Can't fight
nature, son. Gotta sweet-talk her." He extended a hand to
shake. "John White, but my friends call me JW."

"Good for you," the boy said, looking right at him but not
offering his hand in return.

JW snorted at the response.

"Gimme my milk, you little punk," he said and smiled.

The boy held it out, but then began to turn the carton to
pour it out. JW snatched it out of his hand.

"Thanks," he said. "You got a weak hand there? 'Cause it
looked like you couldn't hold the milk up or something." He
turned and walked back across the street, jangling his keys in
his pocket. He laughed and shook his head as the boy walked
off toward the paddock.

"No wonder he doesn't like you," he called. "You don't
show gratitude, and you act mad all the time. Think about
it." He turned back toward his trailer, whistling "Sunshine."

As he put a foot on the first step, he remembered the

neighbor. He glanced back over his shoulder, up the hill at the white brick house, but there was still no sign of life. He stepped up into the trailer.

The macaroni was burning.

He rushed to the stove, shut the flame off, and grabbed the smoking pot by the handle, burning his thumb and fore-finger. He threw it clattering into the sink and turned on the tap. Steam filled the trailer as he sucked his burnt fingers.

10

Johnny Eagle's form leaped into focus in the oval field of JW's binoculars. He moved with a contractor through the pale ribs jutting up from the commercial building site. He looked excited, almost boyish, as he walked amid the carpenters, their air-nailers trailing pink and blue hoses. About half of the workers looked Native American. He could hear the phtt, phtt of the nailers through the open car window.

"I knew that son of a bitch was up to no good." Jorgenson was irritated. JW took the field glasses down and set them on the dash before him. The two men sat in the plush leather interior of Jorgenson's new Cadillac. JW's seat creaked and emitted an aroma of kid leather every time he moved. "I mean, what the hell, 'Nature's Bank'? How fucking pompous is that?"

The Caddy was parked diagonally in the corner of the PDQ store parking lot, facing the highway. JW took a bite from the Chuckwagon sandwich he had balanced on a paper napkin spread over his lap, and then refocused through the binoculars at the construction site across the road.

"Why the hell didn't you take the paperwork?" Jorgenson pressed him.

JW followed Eagle as he walked toward his black Bronco. He had forgotten how mercurial Jorgenson could be, and what a relief it was when he got the promotion and moved to Minneapolis. Trapped in his trailer home, in this plot of Jorgenson's,

JW had begun to wonder why he'd thought of him as a friend all these years. JW was only now coming to recognize some of his own blind spots, but Jorgenson seemed even less self-aware.

"He would have known," JW replied, setting the binoculars back on the dash. "Besides, it's not necessary. Once they file their application with the comptroller of the currency, it'll all be public. I can text you a photo."

"Don't. I gotta be hands off."

Jorgenson's cell phone rang. The display said US Treasury. He pushed the glowing green bar on the screen.

"Ted! What did you find out? Uh-huh." He cupped a hand over the phone. "It's a buddy of mine from Minneapolis, moved over to Treasury."

JW examined the building site again as he listened to Jorgenson's conversation. The canopy had a concrete footing in the middle that divided it into two drive-through stalls. It was definitely a bank.

"It's already passed preliminary approval?" Jorgenson's voice rose as if someone had insulted him. "All right. Let me know if you hear anything else." He touched the screen again and tossed the cell into the center console.

"Fuck."

JW noticed he was pale and saw he was making a fist. "They'll be doing background checks in the next phase." He glanced and pointed two fingers at JW. "You need to get back in there and find a reason for them to deny."

"You should go through his loan app from last year," countered JW. "Maybe there's an angle."

"I did. Fucker makes himself out to be Mother Teresa, which is why you need to find some dirt on him. Something Treasury won't be able to defend to an angry public. Then we can pressure them to nip this thing in the bud."

JW didn't really want to tell him about the bug, but suddenly felt like he needed to show some more progress.

"I planted a bug."

"Really? You did?" His boss brightened immediately. "Why didn't you say so?"

JW shrugged and took another bite from the Chuckwagon.

"You are a crafty bastard, JW. People underestimate you at their peril." He took a bite of his sandwich, smiling now and shaking his head. "I knew you'd come up with something. But I don't want to know any more. You pull this off, I'm telling you, you have a real chance here. Be good to have you rehabilitated."

"I may have been seen." There. He was out with it.

Jorgenson glanced at him sideways. JW knew that if he were ever caught it would cause serious legal and PR problems for the bank, but he felt he had to say something in case Jorgenson suddenly heard from the police.

"By who?"

"A neighbor. I thought I saw the curtain move. I knocked on the door, but there was no answer. I'm not positive."

"We can't have any fingerprints on this, John. I told you that."

"I know. I'll take care of it."

Jorgenson glanced out his window and saw Deputy Bob Grossman getting out of his county sheriff's cruiser nearby. Without warning, he smashed his hand against the car's big horn.

"Jesus, Frank, wait, what are you doing?"

"It's just too risky. I'm sorry, but I've had enough."

Grossman turned, his hand reflexively cupping his holster. Jorgenson yelled to him out the window.

"Bob! Frank Jorgenson. Can I have a word?"

The cop lowered his head, curious, and walked over warily. He put a hand on the roof and leaned down, looking in. His stern features softened.

"Frank, didn't recognize you!"

"New car. You like her?"

JW made eye contact with Grossman, who nodded to him. "JW."

JW nodded back. "Bob." His heart was racing.

"She's nice," Grossman said, admiring the instrument panel. "Say, how come we never see you at the Rotary anymore?" His Old Spice wafted into the car, and JW noticed a gold rear molar glinting in the sun.

"I don't get up here much, I got banks across the whole state now."

"Big shot, eh?" Grossman grinned.

"Yeah, well, what can I say?" Jorgenson shrugged nonchalantly.

"Well, I can't tell you how much the boys appreciate all the contributions you steer our way from the big dogs in Minneapolis. I think every business owner in town feels that way. You do a lot of good."

"Well, JW brings some good ones in too, I'm sure—"

"Yeah, but he's puny compared to you, Mr. Statewide." Grossman winked and grinned at JW, who shook his head in obligatory mock disgust. He and Grossman had run against each other for a city council seat several years back, and had both lost to a retired Republican environmental attorney who had moved up from Edina. The competition and shared defeat created a kind of poking friendship between them. Carol had called them "frenemies" ever since.

"Well, it's no problem," Jorgenson said. "I'm happy to help. You know that."

"Yes we do. Say, I tell you we're going to try a snowplow parade this year, like they do down in Frazee?"

"That'll be good," Jorgenson laughed. A hot wind blew through the car. "Hey, I called you over because, well, frankly I'm a little freaked out. JW just told me he broke into a house on the reservation, and I need to report it."

JW's heart sank. Jorgenson was selling him out. Grossman looked at him and the jokiness drained from his face. His eyes narrowed, and his bottom lip drooped a little. JW froze, his heart pounding in his diaphragm. The stories he had crafted raced through his mind, but they wouldn't work here.

"Frankly, I think you should arrest him," Jorgenson continued, "because he didn't take a damn thing!" Jorgenson laughed and slapped JW on the biceps. JW smiled and nodded in return, masking his fury and pained embarrassment. Finally, Grossman laughed halfheartedly, realizing he had been the brunt of the joke in some way, or at least an unwitting player. Some months back a Native American had accused Grossman of stealing a shotgun from his house while executing a search warrant. It came out only later that the man's cousin had borrowed it to go coon hunting. JW knew it was a sore spot for Grossman, and he suspected that Jorgenson had intended to make a joke that was also a subtle jab.

"You had me," he finally said, looking from Jorgenson to JW. "He's a funny guy," he said, pointing at Jorgenson. Then Grossman punched him in the shoulder and walked off.

Jorgenson looked over at JW and erupted again. "You shoulda—" he got out between laughs—"you shoulda seen the look on your face!" JW was stone-faced, but he felt his jaw muscles clenching again. "Come on," Jorgenson said and backhanded his shoulder. "We're on the same team here! Lighten up! Christ!"

JW smiled weakly and nodded. He glanced back at Eagle across the highway. He loosened his clenched fist. He briefly imagined being at the casino, playing a few hands, drinking vodka gimmies, winning real money. And then suddenly Grossman was back, leaning into JW's window this time.

"You know what I wish?" he said to them both. "I wish they'd all move. I don't mean to be racist—"

"Of course not," Jorgenson said empathetically. It was an absolution often exchanged before slamming Native Americans.

"Half my god dang time is spent chasing after their punk kids or the drunk older ones. What do you suppose they're doing over there?"

"That's exactly what we were wondering," said Jorgenson.

"I bet it's something to suck money out, right on the edge of town like that. Pawn shop or something." He breathed hard through his nose as he studied it. "Well, you take care." He rapped the top of the car door and straightened up. He hiked up his heavy belt and headed toward the convenience store.

"I'll call you," JW said to Jorgenson.

"Don't fuck this up."

JW nodded and got out.

He headed home down the narrow reservation road, kicking up a coyote tail of dust. The sides of his car—from the trim strips on down—were covered with grayish ochre again, and he found himself using the wipers to clear dust from his windshield when he passed through the thick clouds kicked up by cars heading in the opposite direction.

He traveled through various band settlements. There was a fair amount of construction underway in some places. The band was investing in tribal housing, building a number of cheap duplexes and some nicer single-family homes next to old shacks. They had begun making per-capita payments a few years back. The checks weren't very large, in contrast to those cut by some bands, whose members become millionaires on their eighteenth birthdays. But they were large enough that some members used them to begin to build new houses for themselves. A Native American at the trading post had engaged JW in conversation while he got gas, and on finding out where he lived, the man told him this was why the trailer park was mostly empty now, and why some houses were only partially completed. They were waiting for their next checks.

The construction traffic—pickups, trucks pulling Bobcat trailers, cement mixers, employee cars, and delivery trucks—had slowly pushed the gravel into waves, creating a washboard surface. JW had learned to drive the road either very slowly, in order to soften the bumps, or very fast, so his wheels skipped over the tops of the waves. He was taking the second of these approaches when a slow-moving construction van pulled out of a job site just ahead, forcing him to slow down through the teeth-rattling phase in between. His windshield was immediately covered by dust as he entered the van's wake, and he turned on the wipers. He passed the job site and noticed through the ochre haze that the workers appeared to be drinking. One of them raised a beer bottle in a salute of sorts.

JW looked away. Why the hell, he thought, did the bastards have to confirm Grossman's sweeping generalizations so perfectly? But this abrupt reaction was followed quickly by recognition of the fact that Grossman's racism, like all good lies, was rooted in truth. The simple truth was that alcoholism and drug use ran much higher on the reservation than in the rest of society, and the tribal authorities didn't seem to really do that much about it. Nor did many Native Americans seem to care much about doing away with their junk. There were collections of trashed cars, old bureaus, and sofas sitting out in their yards, and nobody seemed to care. Their dogs often slept on these sofas, or in junker cars. And then there was the story he had heard from the old Native American at the trading post: a couple he knew hung their keys on a nail high above their door when they went out drinking. That way they couldn't get back in and trash their own house while under the skull and crossbones. They slept on an old mattress on the porch until they were sober enough to climb for the key and let themselves back in.

It could be that the crew was repurposing beer bottles as water bottles, he realized as he looked over a littered yard. All that seemed to matter to these people was the utility of things, not their intended purpose or aesthetics.

The washboard had flattened somewhat and the construction van had picked up speed to about forty-five. JW caught glimpses of its blue back end when the clouds dissipated in momentary damp spots, and though he held back it was impossible to keep out of its dust stream. They had left the development behind and were traveling through an area of dry scrub pasture and tree-covered hills. He was turning his wipers back on to clear the windshield when a car veered toward him out of the cloud.

He saw that the driver was young and Native. He was reaching down for something and not paying attention. The car was full of Native boys, and it looked like the one JW had seen at the gas station. He laid on the horn, but the driver didn't look up. The other boys saw JW's car, and one in the backseat hit the driver on the shoulder. He looked up and veered at the last second, but lost control. The car's wide back end drifted over into JW's path. He cranked his steering wheel at the last instant and flew out and down into the ditch, smashing his face on something. The trees came up at him at crazy angles and his teeth banged together. Then he was up out of the ditch and crashing through the scrub pasture at what seemed like a crazy speed. The roof came down and hit him on the head and there was the sound of crunching metal.

11

JW gradually became aware of the buzzing of insects and the singing of birds. A fly landed on his lip and he tried to shoo it away, only to realize that his arm was pinned. He opened his eyes and saw an airbag slowly deflating. As it did, he noticed splatters and bursts of shining blood across the sagging surface. He became aware of a metallic taste and a feeling of pressure in his upper teeth. Something warm was spreading across his face.

He was in his car. He must have had an accident. He felt his face, and his hands came away with gouts of sticky blood. He tilted the rearview mirror down to investigate, smudging it. Blood was washing from his nose, which had a jagged gash on the upper right side of the bridge, where the broken bone had cut through the skin.

JW pushed the airbag aside and reached over to open the glove box. He pulled out a wad of fast-food napkins and gently daubed around the cut. It was puffy and red, with a tiny ribbon of maroon gelatin deep inside.

He pushed the napkins against his lower nose and mouth. The sharp swollen pain made him gasp into full awareness. He eased up and tilted his head back. The roof was intact, and none of the glass was broken. He held the wad against his nose and felt warm blood running down the back of his throat.

He sat with his head back for a moment longer, waiting for the blood to clot while he pieced together what had happened. Painful alertness slowly gave way to a deep wave of exhaustion. He needed to get home.

He reached for the ignition. The engine turned over with a great shudder before coughing to a steady run. So far so good. He lowered the wad. His face was throbbing as if a hole had been kicked in it, but the bleeding had mostly stopped. He stuffed the airbag skin through the steering wheel so he could turn the wheel, shifted into drive, and stepped on the gas. Nothing happened. He put the car in park and opened the door, leaving another sticky red smudge on the handle.

JW unbuckled his seat belt and stumbled out into the thorny weeds. He was shaky, but after a moment he steadied himself and waded out to inspect the damage. Grasshoppers transformed into butterflies and sailed away before him. Dry white blossoms of hoary alyssum bloomed all around him. Spotted with blood and soaked with sweat, his white shirt was attracting the small biting black flies that were the bane of summers up here. The car looked fine until he walked around the hood. The front wheel on the passenger side had hit an old tree stump and was resting at an angle to the car. He thought back to the car of boys, now long gone. The damn fools.

He waded back around the ticking car, then sat gingerly back into the driver's seat. His focus was returning. He pulled the door closed and tried to roll up the front window, which has somehow fallen down, but it was no use. He jiggled and tugged up on the top edge of the glass, eventually pulling it back to a nearly closed position. But then he decided it wasn't wise to leave the car running with long weeds surrounding the exhaust system, so he shut it off and rolled both front windows back down. He gingerly checked the napkin and found that his nose had finally stopped bleeding. He stuffed the reddish-brown wad into the door bin. He looked around for his cell phone and saw it lying in the passenger footwell. He leaned over and fished it up between two fingers, his nose suddenly pounding painfully and beginning to bleed again. He grabbed more napkins off the seat, pressed them to his face, and dialed Jorgenson with his other hand.

"We're sorry," a woman's voice said. "Your Verizon wireless account has been suspended. If you would like to make a payment—"

He smudged the red End button and threw the cell onto the passenger seat. He unrolled his back windows as well, and the warm breeze twisted and twirled the crucifix. There was no one in sight.

He knew from personal experience that he was lucky. It had been a little more than a year since Chris went off the road. He had been thrown from the car and killed instantly, Grossman had told JW, and the Earth fell away from under him in that instant. Each day since had been spent navigating the endless drop.

He was shaking now with a sudden chill, and with it came an unreasonable sense of loss and helplessness. How unfair it all was, this accident, that one, and the year of dissolution in between. It was too much. He jammed his hand on the horn and held it there, breathing hard and heavy, blasting it until some kind of focus and reason began to return.

Some long minutes later, he heard a car approaching from behind. His neck was stiff, but he looked in his driver's mirror and saw it was an old blue pickup with a red hood and a brown front quarter panel. He turned slowly and got out. As he stumbled toward the road the alyssum gave way to scrub grass and thistle that snagged and clawed at his suit pants. Deer flies lifted from the hot, thin grasses and buzzed around his head. He slapped and waved them away, but a handful pursued him and kept biting. Slapping at them worsened his headache. He climbed toward the road and lifted an arm. His shirt had large dark wet spots under his arms that felt the cool as he waved. A Native American man was behind the wheel and a woman was in the passenger seat. She looked frightened as they blazed on by, leaving JW standing in his bloody shirt and a cloud of yellow-gray dust.

As the air cleared, he saw a small herd of wild horses at the distant end of the scrub pasture. They were a variety of colors, and he stopped to watch, admiring their beauty in spite of his predicament. One by one, they disappeared into the forest on the far side.

There were poachers in the woods. As JW picked his way back to the wreck, he could hear their distant gunshots echoing faint and high and imagined a bloody deer crashing through the undergrowth. He eased back into the driver's seat, feeling woozy. The Jesus was spinning and swaying in a hot breeze. He turned it away and looped the beads up over the rearview mirror to stop it. His eyes fell on the Big Book on the seat near his phone. He opened it against the exploded steering wheel.

1. We admitted we were powerless over gambling—that our lives had become unmanageable.
2. We came to believe that a Power greater than ourselves could restore us to sanity . . .

The sound of tires on gravel prompted him to looked back to the road. An SUV was trailing another foxtail of dust. He got out again, his muscles aching, and trudged back toward the road. But as he neared, the SUV blew past, powdering him with dust yet again. Before he could turn back, he saw another vehicle appear over the distant ridge. He waited for it by the roadside and waved as it neared, but this one, too, left him stranded.

He considered walking home, but it was several miles away and he figured no one in their right mind would pick up a hitch-hiker covered in blood. He decided to simply stay put. Sooner or later someone had to stop. At the very least, some kind traveler would see that he was the victim of an accident and call the police. But after two more cars passed, JW began to feel both angry and desperate. He would step out more aggressively the next time, he decided, and make the car hit him or stop.

After waiting a few more minutes, he saw a new foxtail in the distance. As it approached, he could see that it was another SUV. He stepped out into the road, but as the vehicle neared it began to slow and pull over of its own accord. The windshield was dirty and he couldn't see inside. The SUV shifted into park and he could hear a Bob Marley song going. "One Love." Then it stopped. The door opened and a man stepped out. It was Johnny Eagle.

Eagle closed his door and walked slowly toward him. JW wanted to turn around. Needing help from a man he had rejected was humiliating. He watched Eagle's boots crunch on the gravel, then forced himself to look him in the face.

"Thank you for stopping," he said in his best professional tone. His tongue was dry and his lips felt swollen. "I went off the road."

Eagle looked from him to the car and back. "Yeah, I see that. Looks like you broke your nose." He was speaking too loudly, as if he thought JW might be deaf.

"Some hoodlums ran me off."

"Really." Eagle nodded, visibly unhappy.

"They took off." JW gestured in the direction they had gone. He realized that his shirttail was hanging out and began to tuck it in, then realized that such decorum was ludicrous under the circumstances.

Eagle looked at him for a long moment, then turned and whistled sharply at the SUV. The passenger door opened slowly and the boy stepped out, wearing baggy basketball shorts and a tank top. He looked as surly as usual.

"My son had those hoodlums find me, and they told me you overcompensated. Jacob here was worried about you, and he made me come look. Said we had to make sure you weren't dead or something."

JW recognized his error and his heart sank. "I appreciate that."

Eagle stood there, a hand in his pocket as if he were perturbed. Then he laughed. "You're really living in that old trailer?"

JW didn't know what to say. He shrugged. "It's cheap."

"I know! That's what I'm saying! I mean, you, of all people." Eagle half-laughed again as he gestured at him, shaking his head as if the whole thing were some sort of ridiculous miracle.

"It's a long story. Is there any chance I could, maybe, borrow your cell phone to call for a tow? Mine's . . . not working at the moment."

Eagle looked at JW's wrecked car and spoke back over his shoulder. "What do you think, Jacob? He's not dead, he can walk. Should we leave him?"

"I don't think anybody'll pick him up."

"I think you're probably right," Eagle said, looking back at JW. "Indi'ns don't like to pick up strange white guys. They can be dangerous."

JW shrugged, and Eagle gave a distasteful sigh. He nod-

ded toward the car in the field. "Why don't you get your stuff."
He turned and walked back to his SUV.

It was two hours before the tow truck finally pulled out
with the Caprice on its flatbed. Eagle and Jacob waited,
talking with him about the weather, the car, the reservation
school, and the usual Iron Range politics: who was sleeping
with whom, who was making a power play with the unions,
and the mining mafia versus the crazy enviros.

"You gonna take any of that copper money?" Eagle asked.

"They were just looking for a short-term payroll depository.
Anyway, you know how Mark Twain defined a mine, don't you?"

"No," said Eagle.

"A hole in the ground with a liar standing next to it."

Eagle snorted and nodded, and JW wondered if he had
been thinking about going for the copper money himself, if
in fact Nature's Bank was a real bank. But he knew that the
tribes didn't like the idea of the mine. The sulfate runoff
could kill the wild rice. And he didn't think even Eagle would
be that duplicitous.

When the tow truck finally pulled out, they got into the
Bronco, with Jacob sitting in back. "You sure you don't want
to go to the doctor?" Eagle asked as they buckled in. "That
nose looks pretty broken."

JW shook his head. "I don't have health insurance at the
moment."

Eagle nodded, absorbing the news.

JW had tossed his belongings in the back, but the last
item he grabbed from the Caprice was the Big Book, and
without thinking of it, he had it on his lap. He saw Eagle
glance down at the book's cover, so he casually rested his
hand over the title.

JW looked out at the place where his car had landed. A

long straight scar jutted into the pasture. Then he stared at
the passing scenery as they pulled away. It was awkward to be
getting a ride from this man, of all people, and from his angry
son. He glanced back at Jacob.

"Thank you,"

"Mmm-hmm," the boy mumbled.

"My son's getting a lot of pressure from those boys," Eagle
said, glancing at him in the rearview mirror. "I was hoping the
horse would pull him away from them."

JW looked across at Eagle. He was watching the road,
but he gave JW an appraising glance. "He said you were like
a shaman or something. Horse whisperer."

JW shook his head. He looked back out over the road. "I
grew up training them."

Eagle nodded with the air of a man playing poker. JW
wondered if Eagle was thinking through what it could mean
that he had moved in across the street from them.

"Fladeboe said you got fired from the bank," said Jacob.

JW glanced at him, but didn't answer. The scrub pasture
had given way to a pine forest as the road climbed. The rusty
red banks were thick with blueberries. They crested a ridge
and then headed down into a new valley, and the forest fell
away into fields of green and purple alfalfa, mixed with pink
balls of clover, short after the second cutting.

"He said it was a gambling problem," added Eagle.

JW glanced at him. "I suppose it doesn't help that I laid
him off at the bank."

Eagle laughed. "No, I suppose it doesn't. But to tell you
the truth, most people out here probably feel you're better off
not working for that asshole Jorgenson anyway."

"Yeah, why's that?"

"Because he's an asshole."

Eagle navigated the narrow gravel road effortlessly. Such profanity sounded unusual and strange in his stately voice. He had an air of confidence and education that seemed above it. But JW didn't disagree with his assessment.

"Aren't you married?" Eagle asked.

"No. Or, yeah. We're separated."

Eagle shook his head and smiled.

JW glanced at him. "Whatever. You got a captive audience here. Go ahead, give me all the grief you want."

"No, it's just—"

"Right. Look, I'm sorry about your loan," offered JW.

"Don't worry about it," Eagle replied. "Ancient history. So, what are you going to do now?"

JW looked back out over the road ahead. "I don't know."

"Well, if you need work, we might be able to use some help."

JW was surprised. He glanced at Eagle, who seemed to be silently kicking himself for having made the offer. He saw him look down at the speedometer.

"What, you gonna open a bank?"

Eagle laughed and glanced at him, then at his son in the rearview mirror. JW thought he saw a look pass between them. "And hire you? Gambling and all?" He laughed, then lifted a hand, catching himself. "I'm sorry, that wasn't polite. It's a wild rice business."

"Wild rice. Huh." He imagined paddies and barefoot Indians with their pants rolled up, swiping at rice with scythes. He suddenly realized what he had seen Eagle and the other man doing in the pole barn. Was it possible that's what the new building on the highway would be, too? Nature's Bank? Could it be some sort of seed bank? Or a natural food co-op? The tribes were always trying out that kind of back-to-the-Earth-type business, even though they never seemed to pan out.

"Yeah. I package and sell wild·rice," Eagle said. "What's so surprising about that?"

12

Eagle dropped JW off in front of his trailer and invited him to come over to see the operation once he got cleaned up. Bending over the tiny sink, JW gingerly daubed his nose with a white alcohol pad. He examined the jagged split in the mirror. The skin was partly open where the bone had punched through, and it was puffy and magenta on either side. Deep within the cut lurked a glistening maroon worm.

He pulled his nose down and pushed the bone back into position, crying out as he did so. He swooned with nausea and had to sit down on the toilet seat, then he gently pushed on either side with his fingertips until he was satisfied that he had gotten it right. He got up and looked into the mirror again, breathing heavily, then pulled the cut open, crying out again, to make it bleed freely. He dabbed it dry with a tissue and then pinched it shut and taped it in place with a small strip of white medical tape. He stretched another piece over the top of his nose to hold the first in place, creating a cockeyed white cross on his nose. He opened the cabinet, popped a couple ibuprofen, and drank some water. When he closed it he paused and regarded his face, struck by how different his reflection looked from his own self-image. Older, with a few graying whiskers. Gaunter, the eyes more haunted. Criminal, almost. It scared him. He pulled the light chain and walked out.

Eagle was still sitting in his SUV when JW emerged from his trailer. He could see through the trees that the driver's door was standing open and that Eagle was parked in the driveway that led toward his barn. As he crossed the road and walked up it sounded as if Eagle was on a business call of some sort. He glanced back and JW nodded.

"Okay, Jim, he's back. I gotta go," he said and hung up. "All patched up? Doctor White?"

"As patched as I'll get. Were you talking to somebody about me?"

"No. Just one of my buddies. Come on down and have a look," Eagle said, hopping down and leading JW toward the pole barn.

Jacob was in the paddock with Pride. "That horse is a pretty big project," JW said.

"Used to be some fancy show stud. White lady couldn't ride him, was gonna sell him to the rendering people," replied Eagle.

"So you're teaching him?"

"We're Indi'ns. Isn't it supposed to come natural?" Eagle said with an edgy grin.

JW laughed and shook his head

They sidled up to the paddock rail. Jacob was trying to lead the horse, but it was giving him a hard time again.

"Hey, Jacob!" Eagle called.

Jacob ignored him. Eagle whistled sharply.

"Jacob!"

"What?"

"Come on over for a sec," he said.

Jacob ignored him.

"Hey!"

"I'm busy!"

Eagle sighed and shook his head. JW could see his body stiffening. At the same time, Pride was backing up and pulling Jacob, and he began tugging hard on the rope. Anger filled the air like pollen.

"Get over here!" said Eagle, oblivious to the problems his son was having.

Jacob growled in frustration and let the rope go. It trailed in the dust as the horse trotted away and stopped some twenty feet off. He trudged toward the rail, dragging his shoes through the yellow lime.

"Got a nice horse there, son," offered JW.

Jacob looked up at him in surprise. "Yeah, when he wants to be."

"What else?" added Eagle, bearing back down on his point.

Jacob shook his head. "Thanks," he mumbled to JW, rolling his eyes, "for yesterday."

"No problem."

Apparently satisfied, Eagle started walking back toward the barn. "Come on," he said to JW, "I'll show you the operation." JW shrugged at Jacob and turned away to follow Eagle, leaving Jacob to contemplate how he would recapture the horse.

The barn had a clean, varnished concrete floor and was lined on both sides with pallet racks. On either end were large sliding doors. A large stainless steel winnowing machine with a purple conveyor feed sat in the center aisle, its clear round exhaust duct running out through a sidewall. Other equipment was scattered around the barn, including a packaging and labeling machine, a longer conveyor, an immense black cast-iron commercial scale by the front door, shining stainless work counters, and rice-packaging supplies.

An old oak desk sat close to the front, scarred and disfigured from the nicks and stains and burns of sixty years. On its top was a dirty old computer. JW took it all in, walking around with his hands in his pockets as Eagle showed him each piece of equipment with the pride of Geppetto.

"It's an amazing operation," he said as they walked toward the winnower. "But what I don't understand is why you're even up here."

Eagle stood by the machine, a hand in his pocket. "For my son," he said.

JW nodded. So maybe the whole thing was not really what they had thought. Maybe the bank was just an idea Eagle had been toying around with. Or maybe it was in fact a food co-op.

"He started getting into trouble in Minneapolis," Eagle explained, but as he was talking, JW heard yelling. He glanced up toward the paddock and saw Jacob pulling on Pride's rope. Pride reared slightly, opposing the boy and trying to get some slack. Eagle's back was to the paddock and he seemed oblivious. "I figured it's healthier for him up here," he said.

JW saw Jacob pick up a riding crop and whip the horse behind the jowl.

"Stop it! You listen to me! You stop!" he heard Jacob yell.

The horse pulled back and lurched Jacob off his feet. JW hurried up to the paddock. He ducked through the rough-hewn rails and whistled sharply at the horse.

"Whoa! Ho!" He grabbed the halter, then he grabbed the crop from Jacob's hand and threw it to the ground while the horse jerked violently at his arm and tried to pull away from him.

"Whoa, boy," he said, calmly turning him. The horse jerked a few more times, but when JW didn't get upset or hurt him, he settled.

"Why are you so dang mad at him?" he asked Jacob. "That's the second time he almost ran you over!"

Jacob glanced at him and JW noticed that one of his hands was in a fist. Then he glanced over at his dad, who was just walking up from the barn.

"He wasn't listening," Jacob replied.

"He was trying, but you were hurting him and scaring him off. Look, come here."

Jacob looked away as if the whole episode were some ridiculous exercise that JW had instigated. JW glanced over at Eagle.

"This okay with you?"

"Go for it," Eagle said from behind the rail.

"Okay. Don't be looking at your dad now. Son. Look at me. Look at me."

Eagle lifted an eyebrow and nodded toward JW. Jacob turned and looked at his chest.

"Now watch the horse. Keep your focus," said JW.

He turned sideways to face the horse, gently started petting his back and neck, and spoke to him in a low soothing murmur. He gestured to Jacob to come closer. The boy sulked over in his baggy shorts. He stepped up to JW's right, near the animal's flank, and JW nodded to him to pet the horse. Pride tried to shy away, but JW held him by the halter and turned with him, signaling Jacob to follow. He kept petting him until the horse let out a long low snort, dropped his head slightly, and allowed Jacob to pet him.

"Okay," JW said, and Jacob stopped. JW stepped back and gave his palm to the horse's muzzle, ran it softly over his leathery lips and nostrils, then reached up to scratch his cheek. Then he rolled his hand into a fist and began to rap lightly between the horse's eyes.

"What are you doing?"

"Rapping his sinuses. Calms him down."

Pride seemed to slowly become hypnotized, as if the gentle rapping were some sort of massage. Jacob glanced sideways, not wanting to be impressed. JW felt the old animal magic.

"Okay," he said. "Look." He touched Pride's side with his fingertip, running it lightly over the animal's hairs. Pride's skin flicked.

"He felt that," he said quietly to the boy. "A horse may be big, but he's sensitive. He can feel a fly on his hair. Pet him."

Jacob reached up with an open palm, and this time Pride didn't react. He ran his palm over the animal's coarse reddish hair in gentle strokes.

"He felt that," said JW. "He likes it."

Pride's eyes were getting droopy. He let out a deep sigh and dropped his head farther, sniffing and nudging at the ground, exploring for flecks of hay.

"How much you weigh?" JW asked.

"I don't know," said Jacob.

He was short and fine-boned. JW figured he was probably under a hundred pounds.

"Big guy like you," he said, "I'd say about a hundred and twenty pounds. That sound about right?" He winked at Eagle, who didn't notice. He was watching the horse, completely enthralled by what was happening.

"Maybe," said Jacob.

"Well, he weighs maybe twelve hundred. That's ten times. At a minimum. So he's gonna win every argument he wants to, right?" He wanted Jacob to see that there was no winning these fights. The boy shrugged, not wanting to give any ground.

JW petted the horse's face. "Even with me," he said. "He's too big. The only way to get him to do something is to make him want to do it. To work with his head and his heart at the same time."

Jacob started toeing the ground.

"Let me show you," offered JW. "Take the rope."

Jacob looked up, surprised. He took it, and Pride raised his head to let out a long, careworn snort.

"Okay, face forward," JW said. He stepped around the boy and out in front of the horse, so he could see them both together. "Up by his head."

Jacob stood side by side with the horse, next to his head, both facing JW. He could see the horse's tail swooshing lazily in the background.

"Good," he said. "Now scratch his cheek. Go on."

Jacob reached up to Pride's cheek. The horse shied and threw his head up, but then brought it back down, and when Jacob scratched him he wound up leaning into it.

"See, he likes that. Okay, now drop your hand."

Jacob did. The horse stood still, in a mild state of attention.

"Now take one step forward."

Jacob took a big step forward, pulling Pride along.

"Don't pull on the rope. We don't want him learning to pull all the time. He's got to decide to follow you. Right? So keep it slack."

Jacob let the rope hang and Pride stayed standing a step behind him.

"Okay," JW continued. "Now we wait. Don't look at him. Don't pull, and don't move."

Jacob stood there, fidgeting nervously, facing forward. The horse snorted and stamped once with his left foot. He nodded his head, but didn't move.

Jacob let out a frustrated pssht. "Pretty stupid training method if—"

"Watch it!" Eagle said sharply.

"All in little steps, son," JW said quietly, "all in little steps. Gotta get him to toddle before you can get him to run."

The horse bobbed his nose down and up, then finally gave in and stepped forward. Jacob let out an awkward laugh, truly surprised. "Oh my gosh! I can't believe it!"

"You see? Okay, pet his cheek so he knows he's done good. Nice! Okay, drop your hand and step again."

This time the horse followed much more quickly.

"Holy shit," said Jacob. "It's like he knows what he's supposed to do."

"He does."

"Bullshit." Jacob grinned and took another step. Pride followed. Eagle laughed and shook his head, frowning at the boy's profanity. JW grinned at him as the boy and the horse took another step, then another.

"One step at a time," said JW. He brushed his hands on his jeans and ducked back through the rough-hewn rails. He put his arm on the top rail and watched Jacob walking slowly around the ring with Pride on a loose rope.

"Kid's got an aptitude," he said. "He just doesn't know it."

"I'll be damned," said Eagle under his breath, as much to himself as to JW.

13

JW brushed his teeth over the tiny porcelain sink and banged out the brush. He could hear loud music somewhere outside. He swirled out the sink and turned off the light. The windows were open to the night and he could hear the faint sound of glass breaking, and a brilliant rise of laughter. He passed through the kitchen toward the moonlit table, curious about where the sounds were coming from. The gold-flecked Formica glowed like a pool of milk, the gray shadows of leaves rushing and dallying over its surface like fish.

The mysterious neighbor's place up on the hill was lit up like a roadhouse, its windows cranked open. The faint sound of laughter and the clink of drinking reached him over the music. Several cars were parked in the street and the driveway. He noticed a shadow moving nearby in the trees, and then a silver horse emerged and began to cross the road. It was one of the wild ones he had seen in the scrub pasture. One by one, the others followed, appearing silently and moving like spirits. Their backs shone and faded in the moonlight, their varied colors washed to shades of gray. They crossed onto Eagle's grass as if in a silent movie and walked up to the edge of the paddock, where Pride had been left to roam. JW watched him look up at the wild horses. He took another mouthful of hay, then slowly began to mosey over, his head down and trailing hay strands. When he reached the rail, he lifted his nose to sniff the intruders. Their muted muzzles rubbed and bumped in the moonlight. There was a sudden sharp whinny and Pride lifted his head over one of them. Then, pecking order established, they fell quiet and sniffed each other again. Pride turned and walked back to his hay, and the wild horses walked toward the woods beyond the pole barn and evaporated into the trees.

JW watched the charcoal leaves where the horses had been, then lifted his eyes to take in Eagle's house. The music continued from the neighbor's party. He wondered if Eagle and Jacob were over there, but then the light came on in Eagle's study. It shot a yellow glow out through the blinds, sending color out into JW's black-and-white world, and he saw the window crank shut.

He sat at the table and turned on the bug receiver. He plugged the milky-white earbuds into the jack and put them in his ears, then he tuned the knob until he heard Eagle's voice come in.

"Did you steal it?"

"No! God! Why do you always say that!?"

JW stared at the swirling shadows on the Formica. He imagined Eagle and Jacob standing in the hallway, outside the study door. Eagle had probably intercepted him, maybe had a hand on his arm.

"Then where did you get it?"

"I told you, I found it!"

"Where?"

"At the community center!"

"Where?"

"It was sitting on a bench!"

"Jacob, what are you doing?" Eagle sounded as if he were at the end of his rope. "We come up here and things only get worse. Now you got a switchblade, and you're arrested with pot—"

"Oh, like you've never smoked pot—"

"What is happening to you?" The concern again, and now anger, too.

"I hate it here! Okay? I hate everything." Jacob's voice broke with emotion. JW could almost see him turning away, putting a hand up to his nose and eyes in order to hold back tears, or at least to hide them from his father.

"I don't know what to do," Jacob said, his voice wet with mucus. "You think being here's supposed to make everything better, but it's not."

"Why?" Eagle asked, softer now.

"I don't know. Because they call me a fucking apple." Deep and hoarse.

"They're just trying to provoke you."

"I know. I miss Mom. I'm sorry."

JW heard sniffling. He hunched over the receiver in the moonlight, his fingers pressing the earbuds in. He felt dirty. He was intruding on something personal, but he had also just picked up an important clue. He took out the tiny spiral note-pad that he sometimes carried in his pocket. He flipped it open to a blank page and wrote, *Smokes pot?*

"Hey, hey. I miss her too," he heard Eagle say in a quiet tone. "But we have to make this work, just you and me. We're doing this for her, remember?"

"Yeah, right," Jacob said disdainfully. "The bank's for her, because of what her boss did. Like she'll really know or care."

The comment ran through JW like a spike. He wrote in the moonlight: *Bank's b/c of what her boss did.*

"It's the principle, son."

"Whatever."

There was a rustle of clothing and the closing of a door. JW sat, riveted, and kept listening.

* * *

IN THE HALL, Eagle watched Jacob rubbing his eye with the heel of his hand. Jacob took the knife back from Eagle's weakened hand, and Eagle let him go. He watched him head down the hall into his room and close the door, and not long after, he heard the muted sounds of *Call Of Duty IV: Modern Warfare*. His son was losing himself in bullets and fire.

He stood still in the hall's emptiness, listening to the house, then went into his study and closed the door. He sighed and leaned back against it. Things seemed to be getting worse, but he told himself that he needed to be patient. Yes, Jacob had crummy friends and bad grades, and even trouble with the law. But it was also true that the police were racist. Jacob had a good heart. He attracted troubled boys because he accepted them, and acting out was part of the grieving process.

But he also knew that it didn't have to be this way. He just couldn't seem to find a way to change the dynamic. No matter what he tried, it felt as if they were trapped in this place, in the aftermath of Wenonah's death, pulled farther and farther apart by their diverging galaxies. The apple comment was particularly concerning. Red on the outside, white on the inside. Not Indian enough meant not poor or dysfunctional enough for rez life—a sort of reverse racism. It made Eagle angry. It wasn't fair to dump five hundred years of history on a boy.

He knew he wasn't the most involved father. When Jacob was younger he had reached out to Eagle plenty of times— "Hey, Dad, let's do this"—and Eagle hadn't made the time. He always had good reasons. There was a meeting at work he had to prepare for, or a tough day he had to recover from. He would have liked to do more, he always intended to the next time Jacob asked, but the job was demanding, especially for an Indian. He was breaking barriers. It took extra energy. And banking was hyper-competitive to begin with. His coworkers didn't seem to be spending more time with their kids either, and they seemed to be just fine. Wenonah was the one who'd wanted kids anyway—and then the bottom dropped out.

After she died, Eagle realized to his surprise that living in South Minneapolis wasn't the same for Jacob as it had been when he was growing up. Jacob wasn't getting fed at friends' houses, and the friends Jacob made weren't the articulate kids of academics and professionals that Eagle had hung out with in his youth. There seemed to be more gangs, drugs, and violence. Jacob had two bikes stolen, one of them at gunpoint, and the kids he hung around with looked tougher and tougher.

It all came to a head one day in late September. Eagle had been working at the bank downtown. After a power lunch with a bunch of executives, he had put together a half-billion-dollar corporate financing package for General Mills. He came home around eight to learn that Jacob had been arrested with a friend for stealing tobacco from Lowell's drugstore.

"You should bring him home," his mother said over the phone. Eagle had banished Jacob to his room after a big fight, and then gone for a walk to cool down. He was sitting on a city bench near the rippling black water of Minnehaha Creek. Brown bats dropped from the eaves of houses, unfolded their wings, and cluttered the air. Frogs pulsed in the long grasses by the riverbank. It was two hours earlier in Los Angeles, where his parents had transferred when Jacob was five. His mom was stuck in traffic on the 405. He could hear the engines.

"At least it's tobacco," she said. "The spirits might be trying to guide him."

He pressed his cell tight to his ear and looked out at the

stone and Tudor houses on the other side of the glistening creek. Someone was having a party. He could hear the clink of glasses and laughter, the playing of a piano, and the closing of a car door. He saw a couple in evening dress walking up the sidewalk, arm in arm. He realized that part of him was secretly hoping his mother would tell him to ship the boy off to live with them in Los Angeles.

"What do you mean, bring him home?" he asked.

"To the reservation. That boy needs to get back in touch with the land," she said, "with his roots in the people, not all this wannabe gangbanger bullshit. That's a recipe for being downtrodden forever. I see the same thing here in LA. Listen to me, baby. You gotta press reset."

As a sixties-era Native rights activist and a college professor, his mom believed the land and the elders could heal Jacob, as if by osmosis. Eagle shared his white father's more skeptical views and thought her idealism naive. To him, the reservation was a place of dysfunction and squalor, not a source of spiritual rebirth. He doubted it would change anything for Jacob. The reality was that her son just wasn't cut out to be a father. He never had been.

He sat picking at the softening wood slats of the bench as she countered. "That's bullshit," she said. "Wenonah was so good at being a mom that you didn't have to build any skill. But now you have to."

"You make it sound so simple."

"It's not! It takes work. But if your father did it in his stiff-assed 'I'm a scientist, not a dad' *gichi-mookomaan* way, you sure as hell can."

Eagle laughed. "He actually said that?"

"Yeah, he said that. But I think he did an okay job with you."

Eagle sighed. He had seen the arc of his life extending forward like a shining arrow. With his gift and his ambition, he would rise to the top. As an Indian? No. As Johnny Eagle. A guy with a funny-sounding last name, who had the goods to get things done. To make progress. That was also how he was going to provide for his family, and for his son. He had a new membership at the Minneapolis Athletic Club, and with it, access to the city's financial elite. The sky was the limit.

And now he was contemplating giving it all up, just when the brass ring was within reach.

"He's your child," she said.

"I know, I know. But you're talking a career here. And I can't guarantee him anything if I leave banking." He knew how hard it would be to get back in, and that if he left, he probably never would.

It was through Wenonah, rather than his mother, that he had come to know the reservation. How ironic it was that he met her in Minneapolis. She took it upon herself to educate him about his land, his people, their history—all the things he had never wanted to hear about from his mother—and through her eyes they had always seemed mysterious and cosmic. But there were plenty of hungry young bankers nipping at his heels. Faltering for even a second was risky, much less walking away for years. He hung his head and rubbed his forehead.

"Four years on the rez. Fourteen to eighteen. Then you can send him away to the former instrument of cultural genocide, and you'll be off the hook," she said. It was her term for the University of Minnesota, Morris. "He'll be surrounded by good kids, and he'll get past this." The campus had once been an Indian boarding school where children were sent, often against their parents' will, to learn white ways and Christian religion, breaking the intergenerational chain of stories and language that had held tribes together. When the repurposed school became part of the university, it was on the condition that any Native kid who qualified could attend tuition-free.

Eagle pinched the bridge of his nose and sighed. Four years. If he could get him there. He realized he had made his decision; he was just hoping she would give him a last-minute reprieve.

And now here they were on the rez, and Jacob was having the same problems. Eagle had given it all up, apparently for nothing. In desperation, he'd bought Jacob the horse. He'd even moved next door to Wenonah's sister, though an argument over her incessant drinking had ended any hopes he had of it being a constructive relationship. What more could he do? At some point Jacob would have to start meeting him halfway. But watching him earlier in the day with the horse, seeing how excited and childlike he was, had moved Eagle almost to tears. Maybe he could steer JW toward helping Jacob more.

* * *

BACK IN HIS trailer, JW reached up to turn off the receiver. There hadn't been much sound for a while, but as he extended his hand toward the switch, he heard a strange series of clicks, followed by the squeak of a hinge. Then the crinkling of a plastic bag, and a moment later the flick of a lighter and a soft sizzle, followed by a pause, then a windy exhale. It sounded as if Eagle was smoking a pipe. A pot pipe.

JW listened in the moonlight. The table still swam with the shadows of leaves, and the music still boomed down from the neighbor's delirious party, but it was all different now. He had a grip on something that could be the answer for him.

He went to the kitchen junk drawer and pawed around until he found a small digital recorder. He held an earbud to it and pressed record. There it was again: the faint sizzling inhale, followed by a slight pause and a blowing exhale.

JW turned the receiver off. He thumbed the tiny volume dial to max and pressed rewind and then play to hear it again—sizzling inhale, blowing exhale. He pressed stop. His eyes fell to the small spiral notepad. He underlined *Smokes pot?* with two sharp strokes. The Treasury department would frown on giving a banking charter to someone who smoked pot. The fiduciary and political liabilities were simply too great. With Jesus and Lady Luck on his side, JW realized, he just may have found a way to stop Eagle and get his job back.

III

THE WAGERS

14

JW tried calling Carol on the greasy antique pay phone outside Big Al's garage. "You've reached the White house, leave a message!" He hung up, frustrated.

Inside, they hadn't even looked at his car.

"I figured you weren't coming back for her," Big Al said. This from a man, JW thought, who was always late on his loan payments.

"Why would you think that?" he asked.

Big Al shrugged. JW stood in the garage's storefront, dressed in his finest gray suit and a crisp white shirt. Cream-colored metal shelves smudged with swipes of black grease held Interstate car batteries, and stacks of Michelin tires covered the bare concrete floor, topped with cardboard cutouts of a tire man. A foggy-globed gumball machine stood by the door, full of faintly visible colored orbs. A smudged, olive-green cash register sat on the glass counter, and the air was pregnant with the smells of body odor and motor oil.

"What you drivin', anyway?" asked Big Al, peering out the window at the truck Eagle had lent him. It was hand-painted with a round Native-looking logo and lettering along the bed that read Native Organic Wild Rice.

"It belongs to a friend," JW began, then raised a hand to revise his answer. "An acquaintance. I rented it."

Big Al raised an eyebrow. He turned away to grab a shop towel for his greasy hands. "Let's take a look up under her skirt."

He walked around the counter and shoved the glass door open. A string of brass bells smashed and swayed against it as he passed. Outside, he led JW through a gate in a chain-link fence that ran around a weedy gravel yard east of the shop. It was filled with old junkers that Big Al used for spare parts.

The Caprice sat amid some weeds near the street. Big Al walked up to it, spread a dirty hand on the hood, and lowered his bulk to the ground.

"They ever catch the drunk Indian that run you down?"

"They were just kids."

Big Al grunted and stuck his head under the car.

"Well, those drunk Indian kids cost you about twelve, fifteen hundred. Hub's shot, axle's bent, maybe I can straighten it but it's probably not worth it. Steering, tie rod maybe. Boots. Who's your insurance?"

JW had dropped his collision and comprehensive coverage a few months back, when he was in the thick of the cloud. He hadn't had an accident in fifteen years, and at the time he thought he could leverage the savings into winnings that would pay the premiums for a whole year. He would double that, then repurchase them and add the rest to his nut. Looking back now, it seemed crazy. Big Al poked his head out from beneath the car to see if JW had heard him.

"I only have liability," he said.

The mechanic got to his feet, brushing his hands off on his soiled blue coveralls.

"Seriously? You got no insurance. The guy that makes me carry it on every goddamn thing just to keep my loan." He laughed bitterly, then led JW back toward the shop.

The door chimes banged around JW's head as they crossed back inside. A fat kid in a blue jumpsuit was rotating tires with an impact wrench, filling the building with harsh metallic chatter.

"Well, JW, what you gonna do?" Big Al yelled over the noise. "I said fifteen hundred to be good to you since we go back to high school. But when I get into it, it could be more. And that doesn't include the airbag. You want that done, that's another grand."

"It is what it is," JW said. "Go ahead. Except the airbag."

Big Al nodded tentatively. "Okay," he said. "I'll need cash up front."

JW looked at him. He realized he was clenching his jaw, and let it loosen before speaking. "I pushed through the loan so you could buy this place," he said just loud enough to be heard over the noise. "You didn't have the credit."

"And I appreciate that. But now I gotta pay on that loan, so I gotta have cash. I'm sure you understand." He nodded as he spoke, but his gaze was firm.

JW nodded, visibly angry. "It'll be a couple days then. Payment schedules," he said over the noise.

Big Al nodded in return. "I understand. I'll leave her sittin' there for another week or so."

"A week?"

"Two. Whatever. But I can't have it here forever. You know that."

JW nodded, then walked out without saying a word. The sun was hot. He got into the pickup and slammed the door, rattling the change that had reappeared in the handle. As he turned the ignition he became acutely aware of the feathers, the beads, and the dream catcher hanging from the rearview mirror. There was a cassette tape of Eric Clapton's *Unplugged* stuck in the player, and it played over and over. He punched it off. As he backed out, he saw Big Al take in the truck's tribal license plate, then shake his head as he turned back to the car bays.

He thought about Big Al's expression as he drove back to the rez. The entire exchange had left him feeling as if he had somehow slipped into an alternate reality, in which people like Al Bakken felt entitled to judge him—not because of his troubles, but because he was living on the reservation. He had somehow become one of Them, and there was now more to prove, more doubts to overcome. He thought he had sensed the same sort of attitude from others that morning. At the gas station, and waiting at a stoplight. No one was any less polite, but there was a coolness. Or was it all in his mind?

He turned onto the lane that ran through the trees, and then onto the barn drive that led up to Eagle's rice operation, more determined than ever to find the evidence he needed to stop him and his bank. Then he'd see about Big Al and his late loan payments.

As he pulled in by the pole barn, Eagle walked out of the big door and pulled it closed. "Where the hell've you been?" he said. "I've been waiting for you. Get in the Bronco."

* * *

WATERFOWL LAKE WAS perhaps the most aptly named lake in Minnesota. As Eagle pulled into the long grass under some trees near the shore, JW could see thousands of birds— landing and taking off, calling and arguing and eating. The lake covered some hundred and fifty acres, and the entire surface was green and tan with the wheat-like stalks of wild rice.

JW stepped out of the Bronco and looked around, dumbfounded. "More than a million waterfowl come through this lake during the fall migration," Eagle told him. The birds funneled down from vast stretches of Ontario, Manitoba, Saskatchewan, Alberta, even the Northwest Territories. The air was thick with black ducks, wood ducks, gadwalls, pintails, scaups, ringnecks, canvasbacks, redheads, mallards, mergansers, and ruddies, as well as the massive honking traffic jams of incoming Canada geese and their great white brethren, trumpeter swans. All colors and varieties of waterfowl floated and squabbled amid the rice, quacking and carping and splashing.

Groups of band members stood on the shore near canoes beached in the long grass. A group was gathered around Hal Charm, a blonde man of about forty-five who wore a floppy cloth cowboy hat and a green-netted vest.

"Hal's our biologist," Eagle told JW as they approached the group. "He's managed to double the rice harvest in the last three years."

As they neared the group, JW saw one of the Indians glance over at them in a way that was not welcoming. "Apple's got a white boy with him," he heard. "Hal, how's it looking?" Eagle asked as they entered the group.

"Well, as I was telling Black Bear here, conditions look good to me, and you can tell they look good to the ducks, too. The rice committee approved the opener for today, but we're still waiting for final word from the elders on whether it's really ready to harvest."

Just then, an elder stood up in a canoe out amid the rice stalks. He raised his two rice-knocking sticks high in the air to signal the rice opener.

"And that's it," added Hal.

The gathered groups of men, women, and children whooped with excitement. They broke up quickly and headed happily for their canoes. Eagle led JW back to the Bronco and popped the ratchet straps holding the Kevlar canoe—a Wenonah—to the racks on top.

"Come on, let's go!"

Eagle hoisted the canoe onto his shoulders, where it easily balanced, propped up by two blue foam blocks attached to an ash yoke spanning its middle.

"Grab the knockers and the life jackets," he said. He pulled a long wooden pole off the car rack and headed for the lake. JW looked around the back of the vehicle and found the vests and two three-foot-long, drumstick-like pieces of wood. They were surprisingly light. He grabbed them and followed Eagle, who already had the canoe in the water and was standing ankle-deep.

"Okay, get in."

JW walked to the stern end and began to step in.

"Hey, hold it!"

He stopped and looked back at Eagle.

"I'm not gonna let you bridge my boat! Just walk out next to it and climb in. Drain your shoes over the edge before you put your feet in."

JW looked at him.

"I'm serious! They'll dry. What, you never been canoeing?"

"Fine." JW waded out over the sandy bottom in his shoes and pants and climbed in, doing his best not to drag too much water in with him. As soon as he was settled, Eagle pushed off with the pole and they glided out into the long grasses.

"What do I do?" asked JW.

"What they're doing!"

JW took the knockers from his lap and looked around. The Indians were expertly guiding their canoes through the rice plants, each one poled by a man standing in the stern. Those in the bows used one knocker to gently bend the rice

stalks over the other and then brushed or shook the rice kernels off into the canoe. Several of them were making fast
work of it, seemingly racing.

Rice stalks glided past on either side of the translucent
yellow bow. They looked like long stalks of wheat that stood
about three feet above the surface of the water. JW tried
bending a few with the sticks, but at first he pushed too hard
and creased the stems. The heavy stalks folded over, became
waterlogged, and started to sink to the bottom. The Indians
he saw around them were incredibly fast, but they were bending the stalks more gently over the canoe with one knocker
and rubbing the other knocker over the top of them, or lightly
beating the grass.

JW tried again, and this time he got a large shower of
kernels to fall off into his lap. The rice was encased in purple-green, wheat-like coverings and was full of insects, rice
worms and spiders. He brushed some off his lap.

"Don't worry about that," Eagle said. "They won't bite you
too much."

"Easy for you to say."

"Come on, get your shit together, white boy, they're putting us to shame. This is what I'm paying you for."

JW kept at it. As the canoe began moving forward at a more
rapid pace, he developed a swiping motion, swaying the sticks
rhythmically side to side, and smoothly knocking stickful after
stickful of rice onto his lap from both sides of the canoe.

"Now you're getting it!"

Soon his feet were sprinkled with rice and his pants were
crawling with daddy longlegs and wolf spiders. He continued,
sweating, as Eagle sought out the richest patches of rice, and
then methodically poled the canoe back and forth through
them. JW found the work straining but satisfying as the level

of kernels steadily grew, first halfway up his shoes, then over and into them, and then up his ankles. The sky was mostly clear, and the carping of waterfowl filled the air. When he disturbed a merganser hiding in the rice, the sudden rush of wings made him laugh out loud.

After another hour the sky gave way to a deep crystal blue and the enriching light of September. The leaves on the trees were just beginning to turn. The ripening rice plants filled the air with a strong grassy smell, and they brushed alongside the canoe with the dry hiss of hay packing into a baler. The two men settled into an easy rhythm.

"Why do they call you 'Apple?'" JW asked. He pulled a daddy longlegs off his neck and threw it out onto the grasses.

"Trying to get to me," Eagle replied nonchalantly. "See those guys? We're gonna show them up."

JW looked over in the direction he had indicated. Two canoes were working in tandem. In the bow of one was the Indian who had made the remark about Eagle. "I'm in," he said.

Eagle picked up the pace and JW began to swipe and knock faster and faster. A wordless competition sprang up across the lake. Soon several canoes seemed to be moving faster, matching pace with Eagle and JW, as the veteran ricers worked to put the upstart and his outsider sidekick in their place.

The sun set around six thirty, and the air began to run cool down the hillsides onto the lake. Band members finally turned their heavily laden canoes for shore. JW set his knockers down in relief and rolled his burning shoulders. He had constantly pushed the rice kernels backward in order to keep the canoe from getting bow-heavy. Eagle stood shin-deep, while JW was buried up to his seated thighs. The rice smelled like a rich meadow. JW ran his tired fingers through it as the shining waters glided by.

Eagle poled them, bow-first, up onto the muddy sand bank. "Day of reckoning," he said. "Hop on out."

JW stood and purple-green kernels rained down off his jeans. He shook his legs off over the canoe one by one, still feeling many more kernels inside his shoes, then stepped out into the cool water. He stood beside the heavy canoe and pulled the bow a few more inches up onto the muddy shore.

"That's good enough," said Eagle, bracing himself before he stepped out into knee-deep water at the stern. Both men looked around at the returning canoes. None were as low in the water as theirs.

"Don't quote me on it, but I think we beat 'em," Eagle said.

JW knew enough about Indians to know that this kind of competitive thinking ran counter to the spirit some elders approached the rice harvest with, but Eagle seemed anxious to show them all up. JW, tired of being judged, was also tickled by the thought.

Several Indians walked past their canoe, heading to their cars to get plastic snow shovels and lawn-and-leaf bags. JW watched them expectantly, noting how each of them glanced into the canoe as they passed. They ignored JW, but one by one they glanced at Eagle and nodded. The man who had made the slur walked by without even looking. Eagle glanced at JW with a grin.

"I think that makes it official," he said. "Come on, let's get the bags and pack up our haul."

15

The night air was thick with insects as Eagle and JW pulled in. June bugs bumped and buzzed at the yard light high on the peak of Eagle's pole barn. Several older rez cars were already parked at odd angles on the lawn, bearing canoes that glinted in the moonlight like giant pikes.

JW got out of Eagle's black Bronco. The Indians' voices were muted. The older man whom JW had seen helping Eagle several days before was standing next to the large industrial scale by the open, lit barn. He weighed in the glistening black lawn-and-leaf bags full of wild rice, and paid the harvesters from a wad of bills he moved in and out of his pocket.

"JW, Ernie Wilkins," Eagle said, introducing them. Ernie nodded and reached for the next bag. "And this is Supersize Me," Eagle said, introducing him to a tall Indian with a ponytail who was carrying bags in to be weighed.

"Hey, man," Supersize Me said cheerfully, nodding in JW's direction.

"Over there in the barn we got Dave Caulfield" Eagle said, gesturing toward a middle-aged Indian who had the clipped mannerisms and buzzed salt-and-pepper haircut of ex-military or law enforcement. He wore cargo pants and a big gold cross on a chain that hung outside his sweat-stained olive T-shirt. He nodded at JW as he dumped a weighed-in bag onto a huge tarp that had been duct-taped to the concrete floor inside the pole barn. He took up a plastic snow shovel and spread the rice.

Trucks and cars continued to pull in, their headlights shining like miners' lamps as more harvesters came to deliver rice. JW headed out to start unloading their bags from the Bronco. The barn lights were yellow to cut down on bugs, and the open door glowed like a fireplace hearth, casting thick streaks out into the night. JW carried two heavy bags over to Ernie and the industrial scale.

"Put 'em there," mumbled Ernie. He nodded to a spot on the concrete as he weighed in other bags. JW sensed some kind of resentment, but he just nodded in return, set the bags against the wall, and went back for more.

Eagle noted the exchange, and when the Bronco was empty he clapped JW on the shoulder. "Look," he said, "that was a hell of a thing today. Who would have thought we could smoke them?"

JW smiled. "Good poler, I guess."

"Good team!" Eagle glanced at Ernie, weighing in the long line of ricers. "Why don't you go ahead and call it a night. Come on over in the morning and we'll get parching." His eyes seemed apologetic.

"Sure," said JW with a shrug. "See you then." He walked off toward his trailer, but turned back briefly. "Hey," he said. "It was a good day."

Eagle nodded with a faint smile. He waved and JW lifted a hand in return and slid out into the cool evening. The yellow barn light faded as he crossed the soft dirt road. Fingers of fog were beginning to lift off the grasses and curl around the bases of the oaks.

JW took a hot shower and came out in a towel, his hair wet and cool. From his kitchen window, he watched the

Indians continue their quiet work as he waited for the kettle to boil for a cup of tea. He could see Eagle talking with Ernie. A bluish light flickered from Jacob's window up at the house. A TV or a computer. He wondered why the boy wasn't helping.

He rolled his sore shoulders. The work was just beginning. Now that the rice season was open, Eagle had explained on the way home, band members would bring rice in from Waterfowl Lake for several more days, before expanding the harvest to dozens of other lakes, on and off the reservation. This was the world capital of Native wild rice, and while Waterfowl was the largest, many of the shallower lakes had large stands as well. The plant only grew in certain conditions, Eagle told him. The lakes had to be low in sulfates, which is why the tribes worried about copper mining. They had to be shallow as well, with a rich bottom, and the water had to be cool in the spring in order for the rice to germinate. And for this reason the band was also very concerned about climate change. It had started to affect yield as the lake temperatures rose. They were working with phenologists at the Department of Natural Resources to seed lakes farther north. The other icon of the North, the moose, had almost disappeared already.

The teapot hissed and whistled. JW poured his cup and turned off the light, then stood there in the darkness, watching the Indians as they murmured, laughed, and quietly worked into the night. When the tea was gone he turned away from the window and headed for bed.

In the morning he woke to the smell of wood smoke. He rolled out of bed and groaned. His arms and shoulders ached. He should have taken an ibuprofen. He rubbed his hair and looked out the windows. The Indians were already at it, stoking a fire in front of the pole barn.

He changed into jeans and a clean T-shirt and made the bed. After a cup of coffee and a mini-box of Frosted Flakes with milk, he put on his work boots and headed out.

"'Bout time!" said Eagle as he walked down the barn drive. "You want a coffee?"

"Just had one."

"Then let's get you trained in!" He nodded toward a wheelbarrow standing next to the tarp covered with drying rice. "See that wheelbarrow? Load it up and bring it on out to the fire."

JW stepped onto the tarp and took up the plastic shovel. He loaded the wheelbarrow and pushed it out to the fire, where they dumped it into a rectangular black pan the size of a small jon boat. The pan's steel wheels rolled on a pair of trolley rails so it could be moved easily in and out of the fire. The four men stood in the billowing smoke and turned the hissing rice with charred black canoe paddles, keeping it in motion so the kernels wouldn't burn on the bottom.

The work was demanding, but the Indians kept a steady slow pace that never let up. JW fell in with them. The sky was clear, the air was cool, and the leaves of the sugar maples around the barn were brilliant red. The smell of wood smoke made JW feel like a kid again. It rolled out from under the pan and swirled around and through the rice, infusing it along with his clothes. The blasts of warmth on his face, the intermittent sting in his eyes, the feeling of the charred wooden paddle running through the toasting kernels, the hissing over the snaps of the fire: JW was entranced. He watched the rice change from green to brown as the kernels fell from his paddle, as if in a rolling surf.

"You don't get the varied colors and smoky flavor unless you hand-parch it," Eagle explained as they rolled the batch back off the coals. "You see rice in the store that looks varied—light, dark, in-between—that's hand-parched. It's going to be much more flavorful and smoky. Plus, you can pop hand-parched wild rice. You can't pop that uniform machine-finished stuff."

"Huh," replied JW, taking it all in.

"It takes about ten minutes a pan, and we get fifteen dollars a pound instead of ten. That's a pretty good ROI."

The four men picked up aluminum snow shovels and scooped the smoking parched rice into a clean metal wheelbarrow. Then they used a straw broom to sweep the last kernels onto a shovel. Ernie led the feeding of a new batch while JW followed Eagle as he wheeled the barrowful of toasted rice into the barn.

"Our thrasher's what you might call a good example of Indi'n engineering," he said. "Supersize Me here made it."

Supersize Me walked up, pulling on leather gloves as he came. The thrasher was made from the front end of a Ford F-150 pickup truck set on wooden timbers outside the pole barn. The wheels were gone and the headlights were painted like cat eyes. Everything behind the dashboard and front windshield had been removed except the driveshaft, which ran through a three-foot hole in the barn wall and into a barrel that lay sideways on a welded metal cradle.

"Once they're parched we thrash 'em to strip off the *mazaan*," Eagle said as he wheeled the barrow up.

"Mazaan?" JW asked.

"Hulls. Beats 'em to a powder. Some people use it like flour, and others use it for insulation. You can make pancakes, fry bread, whatever. We mostly sell it for fireworks lining."

Supersize Me unlatched a small door on the top of the barrel. Inside, the truck driveshaft was connected to paddles made of old tire rubber. Two steel cables ran from the truck dash to a wooden two-by-six nailed to a couple posts near the barrel. One of them controlled the throttle and the other the clutch. Eagle ran the wheelbarrow up a small wooden ramp and dumped the parched rice into the barrel. Supersize Me clamped the door shut. He turned to JW. "You got a watch?"

JW held up his wrist.

"Cool. Tell me when we hit forty-five seconds."

Supersize Me walked outside and approached what had been the driver's side of the F-150, which had keys hanging from the steering column. It thundered up with a throaty roar. He walked back through the exhaust into the pole barn and adjusted the throttle.

"Okay," he said.

JW looked at his watch and nodded. Supersize Me revved the engine, then let the clutch out. The driveshaft kicked in and started spinning. The drum rocked and shook in its cradle, emitting a roaring hum. JW held up a hand at forty-five seconds and Supersize Me disengaged the clutch and powered down the throttle.

"Why exactly forty-five?"

"Depends on the rice."

"Waterfowl Lake rice, you go shorter and some hulls stay on," Eagle said. "Longer and you start to erode the rice."

Eagle pushed the wheelbarrow around to the other side, where there was no ramp. Supersize Me went out and killed the truck engine. "Give me a hand getting the rice into the winnower," instructed Eagle. JW unsnapped the clips on the rough metal door and lifted it off. He pulled a lever welded to the back end of the barrel to rotate it on its pivot and poured out the wild rice along with the chaff, which had been reduced to a flour-like brown powder.

When the barrel was empty, Eagle wheeled the load

over to the winnower, which sat in the barn's center aisle, back behind the big tarp where the raw rice was laid out to dry. He switched the winnower on, and its conveyor started rattling uphill, while its massive fan blew a ticking wind through the clear plastic exhaust duct. JW shoveled the thrashed rice and chaff onto the conveyor. It rode up seven feet and dumped into a chute at the top. As it fell through the machine, the blower separated the feathery mazaan dust from the heavier rice. It blew through the exhaust duct in a sudden hiss and out the sidewall of the barn, where it was collected for later packaging. Excess flour blew away in the breeze like fine smoke. And clean multi-colored rice began to pour out of the bottom chute, into a white bag that hung from a small stand.

Eagle went to get another bag, then exchanged it mid-stream for the full one, before tying it off and putting it on the scale as JW finished feeding the machine. Its rattling hiss slowly dropped off to a few ticks, then just the hollow sound of the fan. JW shut it off and came up as Eagle affixed a label with the date and weight.

"This finished product is 99.9% pure," said Eagle. "An organic foods distributor picks it up every Friday. We run these big bags through the packager and labeler to make one-pound packages whenever we have the time."

He handed JW a clipboard with a spreadsheet showing each bag's weight and number, logged with a date. JW was impressed by the efficiency of the operation.

"You keep doing what we've been doing. Keep track of the inflow and outgo, and report everything back to me. Any questions?"

"This is just so far from banking," JW observed. "Was it your wife's idea or something?"

Eagle shook his head. "She was into banking too," he said. He pulled leather gloves on and headed back out to the fire. "Used to work for your boss in Minneapolis. She knew him from when he ran the bank up here. That's how I know he's an asshole."

"Did I know her?" JW asked.

Eagle shook his head. "I don't think so." He picked up a paddle and stepped into the smoke.

* * *

JW SPENT THE rest of the week helping Ernie run the rice operation. It was mostly a silent détente. Both days, Eagle was away for hours at a time in the morning and into the early afternoon. When JW asked Ernie where Eagle might be, Ernie ignored him. When JW asked a third time, he muttered, "Meetings," and kept working.

In the late afternoons, Jacob would get home from school and ask JW to help him with Pride. One day Eagle overheard the boy asking and barked back, "Later. We're busy with the rice. Get your homework done and then maybe gichi-mookomaan will have time to show you a little more of his *moomigo-manidoo* ways."

"What does that mean?" JW asked Eagle as they turned rice on the tarp.

"What?"

"Gichi-mookomaan."

Eagle laughed, but he seemed uncomfortable. "Depends on the context," he replied.

JW turned over another shovelful and spread it out. Over by the door, Ernie was weighing in another rice delivery.

"Okay...?" he pushed.

"Means *butcher knife*," Ernie said as he plunked a bag down on the scale.

Eagle glanced at Ernie with a flash of irritation, then turned back to JW with a sigh of resignation. "Sometimes it means *butcher knife*, other times it means *white man*," he said.

JW saw Ernie smiling wryly. "*White man* is the same word as *butcher knife*?"

"I didn't make up the language," said Eagle. JW grunted and threw himself back into turning the rice.

At night he took long, hot showers in the trailer's tiny stall, trying to relax his muscles. Some nights he listened to Eagle and Jacob's conversations over the bug, a towel draped around his neck and his hair damp, but they were mostly arguments about homework. Eagle wanted to see it, because he suspected Jacob just wasn't doing it. Jacob usually said he didn't have any, or he'd already done it all, or he had forgotten it at school. Then he would go into his room, and Eagle would catch him playing online games with his old crowd in Minneapolis, and the arguments would begin again.

Other nights JW was so tired that he forgot to listen in. After a few minutes spent reading the Big Book in bed, he would turn off the light and lie back, listening to the swaying trees and the drunken howls of coyote packs until the world fell away from him.

By Sunday he was sore up and down his back and arms. Eagle had given him the day off. He lay on his mattress and fantasized about spending the day in bed reading the Big Book. He had placed it within reach on the bottom shelf of the nightstand. Reading it would be his excuse for not moving. But he had a brunch meeting scheduled with Jorgenson. He sighed and slowly swung his feet out onto the floor, bending his neck and rolling his crackling shoulders.

JW shaved and slapped on some Old Spice, then shrugged into his suit coat and ducked down to look out the kitchen window at the Indians. Seven thirty and they were already at it. For the first time in days, he didn't smell like wood smoke. He gently touched his injured nose with his fingertips. The magenta was fading, but it was still puffy and tender. He went back into the bathroom and replaced the white cross.

As he put on his tie in the bedroom, he watched the Indians in the open barn door, running last night's batch through the packager. The act of tightening the tie's knot had a powerful effect, underscoring his sense of impending return to his former world. He just wished he had his own car. He shot his cuffs and turned for the door.

16

Gethsemane Lutheran Church was within walking distance of JW and Carol's house. Built during the mining boom of the 1990s, it had high brick walls broken by vertical slices of colorful stained glass and a roof like an accordion bellows laid sideways. Pastor Rick was delivering a sermon as JW slipped in. "God said *man* had dominance over all the animals and was the steward of the Earth," he said, raising his voice, "and it is economic freedom that makes ecological stewardship available to ever greater numbers of people." JW spotted the back of Carol's blonde head and Julie's finer hair next to her near the aisle up front, but as he began to walk down to join them, several people turned to look at him disapprovingly. He slid into the back pew next to a group of Slovenian miners—squat single men with short foreheads, dressed in worn dark suits and smelling of Pinaud-Clubman—who jockeyed down the bench to make room for him. When the service ended, he was the first out the heavy oak doors and back into the sunshine.

He descended the broad staircase and walked a short distance down the sidewalk before taking up a position under one of the hickory trees that ran along the driveway to the lot. After a moment he saw the flash of satin robes as Pastor Rick stepped just outside the doors to shake hands with the exiting congregation. JW stood with his hands in his pockets and toed the sidewalk, playing with a small pebble under the tip of his shoe. He rolled it in and out of a sunny patch, then side to side and around in circles as the congregants poured down the stairs and turned past him down the walk. JW didn't like Pastor Rick. He found him to be overly solicitous toward Carol, and at the same time, judgmental toward him. "Well, you're not as observant," Carol said once when he brought it up. And as soon as she said it, JW knew that this was true. Rick could probably sense that JW wasn't under his moral authority, and if so, he likely resented it. Plus, the guy's credit was less than stellar.

Finally Carol appeared at the head of the stairs, and JW lifted himself up into an expectant stance. She was standing in the clutch with the pastor, her pale hair shining in the midmorning sun. Pastor Rick took her hand in both of his for what seemed like a long time, his satin robes hanging from his wrists. He glanced down at JW. He said something else to her and she leaned in, smiling, and nodded thankfully, then pulled away and came down the stairs with Jim Franklin, fixing her hair. Julie followed, texting on her phone.

The group stopped near the base of the stairs as other congregants flowed around them. Jim joked with another man and Julie hung back, typing something with her thumbs. Carol said something to Jim. He nodded and she started toward JW. His heart turned over at the implications of these small gestures.

"John."

"Carol—are you seeing him?"

She glanced back over her shoulder. "Jim? No! We were just walking out." Her cheeks and neck flushed red.

He nodded, his heart sinking.

"John, I'm not. Seriously." Her blue-gray eyes were open and guileless. And, he thought, just a touch haughty.

"So why aren't you taking my calls?"

"I don't know, I've been busy." Her brow drew into furrows before she recovered her composure. She tucked a strand of hair behind her ear. "Have you been leaving messages?"

"Yeah."

"Well, I don't know, I'm sorry."

Suspicion and grief mixed in an unsteady state. "I'm not gambling anymore," he said.

Jim headed over, smiling cheerfully at JW.

"Hey, John! How's it going?"

Carol waved him back tensely. People were glancing over as they walked past to their cars. It seemed obvious that their separation was a subject of gossip.

"How long?" Carol asked. Her voice was quick and desperate.

"A week." He shrugged as he said it. He knew it sounded foolish, but it was a change all the same.

"Well. That's good!" she said, as if she were congratulating a small child. He nodded, plunging a hand back into his pocket.

"Not really. But it's a start. Are you okay? Financially?" he said.

She gave a small shrug, then smiled, her eyes wisps. "I sold my first policy yesterday."

"Congratulations."

He smiled back, but it was pained. His gambling losses were the reason she had to get a job. He had always taken care of her. It's what he did. He had always managed their money, and he had been so sure that he would win far more than he would lose that it was hard to accept the current situation. Making it back was no longer a possibility. Now that he was moving past the storm he could see clearly how foolish it had been all along. He looked down, then out over the grass, toward the parked cars. It was the largest blunder of his life.

"Frank put me on leave at the bank," he said.

Her face went pale and flat. "I told Jim it wasn't true—that you would have said something." A vein pulsed in her neck.

"That's why I've been calling you." His voice was thick and throaty and it nearly broke on him. He swallowed hard and inhaled. His eyes felt thick and cloudy. He shook his head, at a loss for words. "I'm going to get it straightened out," he said, "but I can't pay the bills for a few weeks—"

She took a step back and put a hand up to her forehead the way his mother used to when fighting a migraine. "A few weeks?" Her face was white and angry, her mouth a slash. "Weeks?" She let out a few short breaths. "This can't be happening."

"Carol, it will be okay, I swear—I'm past it—"

"I can't take this. We have bills."

"I know. But you've got to believe me, it's over. Okay? It's over. I'm never going back there." He knew he had no credibility, but what else could he say? The Big Book made clear that the only way to keep from sliding back was complete and utter honesty, a fearless and searching moral inventory, and then making amends. At the time, reading the book in bed, it had all made sense. He had decided he had to tell her, if only to keep Jorgenson from outflanking him, and he had thought it would be better to get it all over with at once. But now he could see that this was a mistake. "We're working it out. Frank's just—well, you know Frank. He'll come around. Carol. It will be all right. I screwed up, okay? But I'm making it right. I love you. I never meant to hurt you."

His chest was tight with emotion. He felt naked and raw and irretrievably broken.

Her face was a moon. She shook her head and seemed to find him in her focus. "I don't know."

He nodded and smiled. "Well, I do. You're still the most beautiful girl in North Lake."

She smiled and shook her head. Her face softened, but her eyes were damp. He could feel the warmth returning, and with it a toehold of hope.

"You are! You really are. So there's just one last thing I need to tell you. To be totally honest. And Carol, I swear, this is it. You're probably going to think I'm an idiot, but . . . last year I took out a hundred-thousand-dollar second mortgage on the house." There. He'd done it. He'd told her everything. Almost.

"Oh my god—"

"Now don't overreact. Please. I promise, it'll be okay. I'm working it out with Frank right now—but he might say or do something in the next few days, and I need you to wait until we talk before you agree to anything. Okay? Honey? This is it, all of it. I love you and I'm trying."

"Trying? You are trying?"

An ocean had opened between them. "You know what I mean."

He could see her reading his lips, as if she were looking at him through a distant telescope. Jim appeared behind her and JW held up a hand. "Just a minute, Jim. Okay?" It came out sharp. Jim held his hands up like an astronaut cut loose, floating back and away.

He shook his head at Carol. "I'm sorry. I'm just trying to be completely honest here, and to make amends. It's very difficult, I mean, I'm used to being the guy in control, the man you look up to, and right now I have nothing. Carol? Are you listening? I still love you and I will make it all back. Okay? Nothing's changed, it's just that now you know. That's something that Jim here, well, I could tell you stories about him, things from his credit record—"

"Just stop!" She was pale with anger, he could see, but her tone was also pleading.

"I really need you to forgive me, to give me a little credit for the twenty years we've been together," he said, more softly now. There was a new lump in his throat, and he was trying to hold back.

She stared at him. "I see." She nodded slowly, and he nodded back.

"Please," he said. "Just give me a little more time." He saw Julie standing a dozen feet away on the lawn, still texting. He needed to reclaim some part of his dignity. He called to her. "Sunshine! Come give your daddy a hug."

Julie slipped her phone into her back pocket and came over. She hugged JW stiffly. He held her close and smelled her hair, which still had the blush of childhood. He wanted to drink her in. His baby. He held her shoulders and looked into her eyes.

"I miss you every day, you know that?" He pushed a lock of hair out of her face. His heart ached, and he knew in that moment that he would do anything not to lose her. She was small for her age, and he sometimes still thought of her as an intellectually precocious child, rather than the thirteen-year-old she had become. The smell of her fine blonde hair and the feel of her thin limbs reminded him of the times he had carried her up to bed after reading her to sleep.

"I miss you too," she said, and her cheeks flushed. It felt like the sort of obligatory greeting a teenager gives to a strange uncle.

"No, really," he said, softly. "Julie, I'm getting better, I promise." The hair fell back out, and he tucked it behind her ear again. "I am. It's me. Daddy. I love you."

"I know." She looked around for a girlfriend. "Amy! Amy, wait up!" Then she back to JW. "I gotta go."

"Wait."

She looked hurried.

"You think we could do something sometime, just you and me? Go on one of our dates? A hike or something? I still have my dichotomous key."

"I'm not really into that anymore."

"Shopping?"

She looked aghast. "With what?"

"I have a job," he said. "I can take you shopping."

"Yeah. Sure. Why not?" She looked at him as if the suggestion were completely crazy. He chose to ignore it.

"Okay. I love you."

"Me too." The pain flitted across her face like a bird. And with that she was off, flying over the lawn toward Amy. He nodded to Carol and Jim, then turned to walk back to his truck, a rolling boil in his chest.

He got to the wild rice truck and pulled open the door, exhaling deeply as he suppressed tears. He had done it. He turned back, caught Julie's eyes, and waved. She turned to Amy. He was suddenly acutely aware of how different the truck looked from most of the other vehicles in the lot. Native American organic wild rice. He got in and started the engine, then shifted into drive. He couldn't really blame Carol and Julie. But he would win them back or die trying. He pulled out, the dream catcher swaying and spinning as he headed off down the driveway.

17

The Denny's was on the north end of town, near the Curves and Hokanson's Garden Center. JW pulled the truck into the lot and parked away from the building. He checked his wallet and his pocket. He had found five dollars and twenty-seven cents in the ashtray of his car before leaving it with Big Al, and now he scavenged another four dollars and thirty-nine cents from the door handle of the truck. He got out and dumped the change into his pocket.

The restaurant was a favorite meeting place for casual business conversations, and on Sunday it was busy with the church rush. He waded through the tables, waving and nodding to local farmers and businesspeople he knew. The place smelled of coffee, bacon, eggs, and pancakes, and it rang with the hubbub of conversation. JW could hear a blender going somewhere, and the clatter of dishes from the kitchen. He found Jorgenson in a faux-wooden booth by a window, eating a large plate of pigs in a blanket.

"Coffee," JW said to the waitress as he slid into the booth, buoyed by the friendliness of the many people who had waved to him. He saw Jorgenson note his crisp white shirt and his unusually dirty fingernails. He realized he'd forgotten to scrub them.

"*Mazaan*," he said by way of explanation, then realized it provided none. "Wild rice hulls. It's like soot. Sticks to everything."

"I know. I recognized the color. Like toasted buckskin."

JW looked at him with some surprise. Jorgenson shrugged.

"What, you don't think I know anything about Indians? I used to spend time on the reservation when I first came up here, back before we took you on. Chasing squaws and doing sweats."

"You're kidding."

"Don't you remember? I used to talk to you about vision quests, all that new-age stuff."

JW remembered, flashing back briefly to some of their long talks over beers in Jorgenson's office after-hours at the bank. They had discussed meditation and the nature of the universe, and whether the solar system was really just an atom in the body of an enormous person we call God.

"Turtles all the way down," JW said.

"That's right! The old Hindu line." Jorgenson chuckled as he carved off another bite of his pigs in a blanket.

"Wrong kind of Indians, though," added JW.

"That's your problem, right there. You're too literal," Jorgenson said.

"Well, what changed?"

"Changed? Bethany."

Bethany was a divorcée who had come up for a vacation at the enormous lake home she received in the settlement. She was a born-again follower of Dr. James Dobson, and not long after she arrived on the scene, Jorgenson stopped talking about cosmic consciousness. Gone were the copies of *Be Here Now* and *A Course in Miracles*, replaced with *The Purpose Driven Life* and *The Prayer of Jabez*. The two of them went on mission trips to Haiti and Guatemala, and took in foster children from Bethany's mega-church down in Woodbury. Jorgenson embraced his new religion with the same vigor he attacked everything, telling JW of the many wealthy people he met at church on weekends down in the Cities, how he was selling more lakefront properties than the realtors up here, and spouting Bible phrases at work. His subsequent promotion was, he claimed, ordained by God. "I'm telling you, you should join the church," he had said. "In Proverbs 13.18 it says, 'Poverty and shame shall be to him that refuseth instruction.' All you have to do is look around at these Indians."

"Anyway," Jorgenson continued, "what have you found?"

"Nothing solid yet," replied JW.

Jorgenson was silent for a moment, chewing. "You called a meeting to tell me that?" he said finally, after a swallow.

The waitress was a wiry woman named Judy. She thumped a coffee mug down and poured it full from a plastic pot, which she then set on the table. "You ready to order?"

"The number three," JW said. He opened a creamer and poured it into his coffee as she left. He stirred it with a spoon, then took a sip. "Except that I think he may be smoking pot."

"Jesus! Well, that's something!" Jorgenson brightened, leaning forward. "That's definitely something. Did you see him?"

JW leaned in and picked up his butter knife. Played with it absentmindedly between his thumb and forefinger, speaking low.

"His son said something about it over the bug and I think I heard him doing it, but I'm not positive," he said. "I think he keeps it in his safe."

JW saw the light catching the edge of Jorgenson's gray whiskers as he resumed chewing, more quickly now. He could tell this was exactly the sort of evidence Jorgenson had been hoping for.

"We get him busted for drugs, the feds'll definitely reject

the charter." He stabbed a piece of sausage and shoved it in, thinking as he chewed.

"I said maybe." JW sipped his coffee and watched him.

"Well, find out! Fuck. If they're building, you know they're gonna be applying any day," said Jorgenson. "We need this. Hell, you need this." He swallowed and swigged from his cup.

JW set his coffee down and folded his hands on the table.

"First I need to work out a payment plan on my second mortgage," he said. He watched Jorgenson with the unblinking poker face he had used many times when rejecting loan applications. He had been pondering this move for some time. Jorgenson needed him and it was reasonable to seek some protection for Carol. Jorgenson stopped chewing and studied him for a moment, then nodded with the air of someone figuring out they'd just been taken in by a carnival barker.

"So that's what this is about. You called a fucking meeting because you're worried I'm going to foreclose on you." He shook his head and put another piece of sausage in his mouth. "You used to be smarter than that. You get the dope on this guy and then we'll talk." He chewed, avoiding JW's eyes.

JW took the tiny spiral notepad out of his shirt pocket and set it in a slice of sun on the table, the metal spiral curling like a silver spring. He opened to the page he had scrawled on, and noticed his hand was shaking slightly. He had confronted Frank many times over the course of their relationship, but never with stakes this high.

"Then you want to tell me what this is?"

He turned the pad around and plowed it across the table. Jorgenson read the note he had written there—*Bank's b/c of what her boss did*—then turned back to his food. JW watched him closely. He avoided eye contact, but resumed chewing.

"That's a blind alley, John. If I were you, I'd focus on the pot. Don't waste your time chasing bullshit." He finally glanced at JW and went back to eating with an air of nonchalance, leaving the notepad untouched where JW had placed it.

JW had found a soft spot, he was sure of it. He sat back, consciously controlling his face and his eyes—open, studious, unflinching. But Jorgenson wouldn't make eye contact again. JW could sense that he was hiding a weakness, some exposure that could be exploited. But what? He sought to expand the beachhead. "Is this something personal between you and him?"

Jorgenson glanced up at him and kept chewing, but then he looked around and leaned in, his eyes small and his fists balled around his fork and knife. "She worked for me in Minneapolis, okay? So the fuck what. I canned her. Worst employee I ever had. She tried to bring some equal-opportunity lawsuit. You know how they are. She was a fucking cunt."

Jorgenson stared at JW for a moment, snorting like a bull, then took another bite. JW watched Judy bring a check to the table of people behind him. He nodded, studying his adversary. "I want you to work out that payment plan," he said.

Jorgenson stopped eating. Blood rose to his face. For a second JW thought he was going to explode. He pursed his lips as if he had tasted something disgusting, then leaned in again, closer.

"Fuck you," he said, gesturing at JW with his butter knife. "What you did was illegal. I could have your ass in prison. You really want to fuck with me?" He was breathing hard and staring straight into JW's eyes. "Do you have any idea how many people I know? What kind of resources I can bring to bear against you? You are way out of line, pal, trying to threaten me over some equal-opportunity bullshit when you committed a fucking felony. I can't believe I'm hearing this, and from a fucking friend."

JW's bluff had evaporated in an instant. He looked out over the highway. He had been outplayed, regardless of whether there was anything to his hand in the first place. "I'm sorry," he said, trying to look friendly.

Jorgenson calmed. He sat back. "Look," he said. "I'm trying to do you a favor here, so quit being such a cock-sucker. You take the pot out of the safe, you put it in the desk drawer, and we call the cops. You saw him smoking. It's that simple."

JW lifted his hands in surrender. "Fine. If it's there."

Jorgenson nodded and put down his napkin. "It's there." He slid to the end of the booth as if to leave, but instead of rising he paused. "I know the mortgage is a concern. You do your job well, we'll talk. But I need leverage to justify things too, and I really don't like being threatened, John. Is that clear?"

"I wasn't threatening you, Frank. I was asking. For Carol—"

"Fuck that—"

"Look, whatever I've done in the past, I'm the one who's risking my ass, and I deserve to know the full story."

Jorgenson looked at him, shook his head, and smiled. "Well, now you do. Next time you want a fucking meeting, bring me something solid."

Jorgenson stood and left without looking back, waving and stopping to backslap or shake hands with men at the various tables he passed on his way out.

JW nodded to himself. He should have thought his approach through more carefully, and he should have had a solid fallback

position. The waitress brought him his number three as Jorgenson walked out the door.

"Did you gentlemen want your check?"

JW glanced up at her and sighed, then forced a smile.
"Sure," he said, and she went off to ring the two of them up.

18

Ernie, Caulfield, and Supersize Me were still turning rice over in the parching pan when JW got back. He could smell it as he walked to his trailer. He changed clothes and headed back out to help.

The air was warm and dry. A cloud of smoke billowed off the parching fire. He waved to Ernie and Caulfield, then entered the barn. Supersize Me was weighing in a new load that two ricers had just brought in. JW pulled a bulk bag of rice from one of the pallet racks and carried it to the packager. He had just set it down on the counter when Eagle stepped into the pole barn.

"You're back," he said, standing over JW.

"Yup."

"Why don't you let that go and come on inside for a sec. I got something to ask you about."

It was impossible to read his face with the bright light behind him, but JW sensed something in his tone that set him on edge. His mind leaped to the bug.

"In the house?"

"Yeah."

"Okay." He carried the bag back to the pallet rack and followed Eagle out of the pole barn. He noticed that Ernie was watching him with a scowl as he turned to follow Eagle up to the house. They walked in, then went down the hall to his office. JW eyed the top desk drawer as Eagle turned to look at him.

"Why do you look so nervous?" Eagle asked.

"I don't know. Do I?"

Eagle turned and opened the closet.

"I don't know. Maybe not. I keep the safe in here," he explained.

He pulled his Aeron chair over and perched on the edge of it as he leaned down to spin the dial. It clicked faintly as each number passed the set point. He spun it to zero, then looked up and saw that JW was watching.

"Actually, do me a favor and look the other way," he said. "No offense, but it's all my cash at the moment. If something happened I wouldn't want you to be the first person I think of."

"Yeah, sure. Sorry," said JW, making a mental note of the zero mark. He moved closer to the desk and looked out the window at his pale blue trailer nestled under the reddening oak leaves.

The clicks stopped and Eagle turned the lever and opened the safe. JW glanced down, but Eagle's shoulder blocked his view. Eagle reached inside for some cash. JW shifted slightly and glimpsed what looked like a baggie of marijuana on the bottom of the safe, below the shelf. His heart leaped. Eagle stuffed it farther back into the safe, in the process uncovering an old bill. Eagle pulled it out and JW looked back out the window.

"Thanks," said Eagle. "You ever seen one of these?"

JW turned and Eagle handed the bill to him as if it were an offering. He took it carefully in both hands. It was a five-dollar note with an Indian chief in full headdress on its face. It looked almost like an ancient counterfeit bill.

"What is it, a phony?"

Eagle laughed. "Oh no, it's real. It's called a Chief

Onepapa Silver Certificate, 1899. The only US bill ever to feature an Indi'n."

"I never even heard of it," said JW. "Surprised there were any."

"I was, too."

"It must mean a lot to you."

Eagle nodded. "Symbols have power for me. Same reason I keep these rice books by hand in this old ledger. Indi'ns who didn't understand money lost most of their land in this state to white traders whose most powerful weapons were the phony debts they wrote in these ledger books."

JW nodded and handed it back.

Eagle took it and put it back in the safe gingerly, then pulled out some cash. "Okay," he said, "there's two thousand dollars. Four hundred for the knockers who just delivered, three hundred for each of the guys in the barn, and you and Ernie each get five."

"I thought Ernie did the money."

"Yeah, well, I had a talk with him about that. I just think that with your skills as a banker, it makes more sense to have you handle it."

JW nodded. "Okay. Why cash?"

Eagle smiled. "Don't worry. We pay our taxes. But this isn't white America. Lot of these folks don't have bank accounts. I don't think Caulfield's ever had one, except when he was in the Army. And, no offense, but most of 'em wouldn't feel welcome going to the bank in town to cash a check."

"I see. Makes sense."

Eagle pushed the safe door shut with his cowboy boot. He reached down and spun the dial.

"Good. Now I gotta make some calls."

JW walked back through the house, taking it in differently than he had when he broke in. The home felt almost like a post-and-beam warehouse, and yet it was cozy. The expansive table in the dining area was too large for Eagle and Jacob, and it was almost completely covered by what looked like homework and house plans. Across the room, a sliding glass door stood open onto the backyard. The eating area flowed into a gorgeous kitchen with commercial-quality appliances and stone countertops, but bare sheetrock on the walls. He went back out the front door.

In the pole barn, he paid the harvesters, who had brought in two hundred pounds of green rice. He got them to sign a receipt, and then he paid the workers as Eagle had instructed. Ernie looked insulted when he handed him his money. At first JW thought he wasn't going to take the bills, but then he wordlessly grabbed the wad and stuffed it in a pocket.

"This wasn't my idea," explained JW. He counted what he had left and realized that Eagle had overpaid him. He should have had five hundred-dollar bills left for himself, but he had fifteen. He folded the bills and tucked them into his pocket, then headed back up to the house. The new role of paymaster provided him with a cover of sorts. He tiptoed up the deck stairs and eased the screen door open. He stepped inside, closed it silently behind him, and walked quietly down the carpeted hall, hoping to overhear something as he neared the office.

"But why the delay?" he heard Eagle say. "Are there any other banks you're doing this with?"

The floor creaked and JW realized he'd almost surely given himself away. He knocked lightly on the frame and stepped into the study. Eagle snapped a pencil in half. He was so engrossed in the call that it looked as if he hadn't even noticed the floorboard. He looked up as JW entered, obviously frustrated. But he quickly masked it and waved JW forward.

"Hold on, Glen. Just a minute, please." He cupped a hand over the phone and gave JW his attention.

"I think you handed me an extra thousand by mistake." JW handed the money back. Eagle looked surprised.

"Are you sure about that?"

"Johnny, I know I've had a gambling problem, but I'm not one of those white traders you were talking about. I know that was a test."

Eagle's face flushed and softened. He held up a finger, then put the phone back to his ear.

"Glen, I gotta get back to you. Okay, thanks."

He hung up, clearly upset by the call. He tossed the phone on his desk and turned to JW with an apologetic look.

"I used to give the same one to my cash tellers," JW said, "and if you're half the banker I think you are, you've got a ledger that accounts for everything down to the penny. You probably even photocopied these."

Eagle looked at him for a moment, then his poker face fell away and he opened his top drawer. JW's heart leaped, but Eagle pulled out a set of photocopies of the bills. He set them on the desk. He shrugged.

"Yeah," said JW, secretly relieved. "So don't treat me like I'm some kind of criminal. Okay?" He turned and walked out.

"Wait. I'm sorry."

JW stopped in the door. He nodded and then continued on his way.

"Look—John—stay for dinner. Please. It would mean a lot to me."

JW turned back. Eagle looked honestly apologetic. "Okay,"

he said. "But I told Jacob I'd work with him on Pride. And we gotta run down to the feed store."

"Great. When you're done."

"Okay." JW took another step, but paused again in the door and turned back. "Johnny—" he said, and then waited for Eagle to look up. "My friends call me JW."

19

JW returned to the trailer and thought over his plan. He knew Eagle zeroed out his safe dial when doing the combination. That meant if he could record it somehow, he should be able to crack it. He plugged the receiver in and listened on the earbuds to see if Eagle would open it to put the thousand dollars back, but just then he saw him step out onto the porch. He put the device away, disappointed.

As he and Jacob drove into town, JW endured a nonstop barrage of questions and observations about horses. Something had turned on inside the boy.

"When they're grazing, why is it that if you step toward their flank from behind they move away, but if you step from in front they just lift their heads?"

"Because they can't run backward. Coming from behind is running them off. From in front it's either pushing them away or saying hello."

"Can they really feel a fly?"

"Why do you think they flick their skin?"

"But—are they like people?"

"In a lot of ways," he nodded. "They're herd animals, so they're social like us. If you can manage a horse, you can manage anybody. It's all the same principles."

The kid was out there in the pen every afternoon and evening now, and JW had noticed that the horse wasn't planting his feet or pinning his ears anymore. He had heard the boy and his father arguing about how Jacob was skipping his homework in order to be with the horse, and how he was getting Ds in his classes. There was a way Eagle could check online to see the status of Jacob's homework in every class, but by the time it was posted it was always too late to do anything about it. This constant struggle was driving Eagle crazy. JW made a mental note to keep what he heard over the bug about this and other topics to himself, so he didn't give himself away. He had to focus on what he had to do.

It was nearly four by the time they pulled into the bumpy North Lake Feed Mill parking lot. The mill itself was a tall, galvanized steel building next to an old railroad spur. There was an old painted ad for Nutrena Feeds way up near the top. Around back, the tower spread out into a long, low L of garage doors into the warehouse. Across the lot was the North Lake Toro & Small Engine Repair. Together, the tower, the warehouse, and the Toro dealership made a big U around the potholed gravel lot. JW backed up to the concrete loading dock by the garage doors.

They both got out, climbed up onto the dock, and walked down to the back door of the mill. JW led the way through a back room, down a narrow hallway with offices and a small restroom on either side, and then into the store. It was full of hardware, traps, poison, hoses, cages, buckets, birdfeeders, and guns. A big window behind the counter looked over the parking lot and the truck scale outside. Manny Peltonen, the mill's owner, was a thin bachelor of about fifty-five who wore striped engineers' coveralls every day. JW grabbed a couple of Dorothy's root beers from the bait cooler and went up to the counter to order the oats. Peltonen was in a good mood, bopping around behind the dusty counter. The register dinged and he handed JW his change.

"Let's get her loaded up." Peltonen led the way back to the loading dock. But then he noticed Jacob handling the merchandise.

"Can I help you?" he said. He was polite, but JW could sense an undercurrent of suspicion.

Jacob looked up and JW saw a different boy, as if through Peltonen's eyes. His demeanor suddenly seemed surly. His court shoes, loosely tied. His baggy shorts. His loose-jointed, long-fingered movements.

"I'm okay," Jacob said without making eye contact.

Manny stood for a moment, his eyes running from Jacob to the merchandise rack and back. JW realized what was going through his mind: he didn't want to leave the suspicious Native American boy in the store unattended. "He's with me," he said.

Manny turned to look at him, his eyebrows furrowing and his face recoiling in surprise. "Him? Oh! Well, then let's go get your grain!" His face immediately softened. He grinned, but his eyes lingered briefly on Jacob as he walked past. He led JW outside onto the loading dock. He strolled over to the open garage door.

"Be right back."

Peltonen grabbed a sack dolly and disappeared. JW heard him throwing sacks, and then he reappeared, wheeling six fifty-pound bags of fourteen-percent-protein sweet feed, a mix of oats, cracked corn, pellet meal, and molasses. He parked the load behind the truck's tailgate and helped JW swing the bags into the bed. As they worked, JW noticed Jacob loitering inside the big window.

"Got yourself a stall boy, huh?"

"Something like that." JW watched as Jacob, unseen by Peltonen, stuck a pack of cigars into his shirt.

"They're good for that," Peltonen went on, his back still

turned to the boy. "Just keep 'em away from your liquor cabinet, ay?"

Peltonen winked at JW. He set a catch on the feed dolly so it wouldn't tip and they tossed the last of the bags into the pickup bed. JW nodded and smiled thinly as Jacob wandered casually out.

"Thanks," he said. Jacob came over and the two of them got in the truck and pulled out.

JW handed a Dorothy's to Jacob and opened the other. He took a long sip. The soda had been created by a woman who lived alone like some Finnish *Maderakka* on an island in the Boundary Waters. In winter, she harvested lake ice and stored it draped in sawdust. In summer, she used it to cool the brew she sold to paddlers. She had no power, no water, and no neighbors. Surrounded by two million acres, she was arguably the most isolated woman in America, a goddess of the lakes. She was gone now, but Dorothy's root beer had become an iconic drink of the Northland.

"Thanks," said Jacob, and twisted the top off.

JW thought about what had just happened as he drove down the side streets, heading for the highway, the dream catcher swaying. The cigars were faintly visible through Jacob's shirt. He pulled over and shifted into park. Jacob looked up at him.

"What's up?"

He shut the engine off. "What the hell was that all about?" he asked.

"What?" Jacob was confused and defensive.

"You like cigars?"

"No." He looked offended now, but JW could see an artery thumping in the side of his neck.

"Really."

"What are you talking about?"

"They're in your shirt. Right there."

He reached over and tapped the box through the fabric. Jacob swatted his hand away. "Don't fucking touch me." He looked away out the window, busted and humiliated. JW shook his head.

"Look, I'm not gonna waste your time tellin' you 'bout right and wrong. But I think you're stronger than that—actually, I know you're stronger than that. I've seen it."

Jacob looked down. He fumbled and almost dropped the bottle, but quickly caught it, then had to slurp up the foam from the top.

"You don't have to act out people's stereotypes," JW continued. "Those stupid kids or that asshole in there. You're smarter than them. Beat their expectation. Fight it. There are plenty of other places where people don't think like this ..."

"Like where?"

JW sighed. "Just take my word for it. Look, you do what you want. Maybe you want this kind of life. But if you want to give those cigars back, I'd be proud to stand beside you."

Jacob looked up at him, his face full of worry.

A few long moments later they stepped back into the feed store. Beyond the glass case full of hunting knives, Manny was reading a newsletter on bedding plants.

"You're back! Did you forget something?"

"No," replied JW.

He turned and saw that Jacob was petrified, with no idea what to say or how to broach the subject. He put a hand on the boy's shoulder.

"My friend Jacob here's got something to say."

Jacob set the cigars on the counter.

"Sorry," he mumbled. "It was a mistake."

Manny looked at the cigars, then back at Jacob. His wrinkled watery eyes became small and hard. "You stole those from me."

"He decided to bring them back," said JW.

Manny saw the firm expression on JW's face and registered the tone in his voice. He looked back at Jacob, his expression now somewhat cowed. "I could call the cops right now and have you arrested. They'd throw you in jail," he said.

Jacob stared at the floor. The thin wooden planks had been worn bare long ago. "I know," he said, his voice barely audible.

Manny looked back at JW. "You put him up to this."

"No sir, it was his decision. But I'd say it's a pretty honorable thing when a guy admits what he's done and owns up to it himself. Wouldn't you?"

Manny stared into his eyes for several seconds, then looked at Jacob and nodded toward the door. "Get out of here."

They drove back through the side streets in silence and turned onto the main highway. Jacob spent most of the ride picking at the label of his root beer bottle. Finally, JW reached over and shook him by the shoulder.

"Stop it!" Jacob protested, stifling a grin. Wind blew in through the open windows.

"You did a really good thing there," JW said. "I'm really proud of you. It's tough to be your own man."

"Okay, enough," said Jacob, but then he smiled and laughed awkwardly. "Come on! I mean it!"

JW smiled and took a long draught of his root beer as they drove out among the farm fields. The warm fall breeze blew in through the windows, ruffling their hair, and outside combines spewed yellow streams of grain into their wagons. He turned on Clapton, and for a brief moment, he didn't have a care in the world.

20

JW and Jacob unloaded the bags of sweet feed into the lean-to. They pulled the white cotton stitching, and the brown smell of molasses filled the air. Pride nickered his excitement. Jacob took the lids off two steel garbage cans, and they poured the sticky contents inside.

"You ever feed him wild rice?" JW asked. "It's pretty good protein."

"Oh yeah," Jacob said. "He loves it."

They put the lids back, and Jacob dumped a scoop of feed into Pride's bucket. He threw two flakes of hay in the rack. As the horse munched on the feed, Jacob went into the stall, threw a saddle blanket on him, and started to saddle him up.

"You may not want to do that while he's eating," JW said, but Pride didn't seem to mind. He kept his nose in his black rubber bucket, his eyes closed, savoring the sticky brown oats and corn. Jacob threaded the cinch strap through the buckle and pulled it tight. He selected reins and a headstall with a snaffle bit—the most gentle—and hung it on the saddle horn until Pride finished.

Out at the paddock, JW leaned on the rails and watched as Jacob rode around the ring. Earlier in the week, just getting a saddle on the horse and getting up on his back had been an accomplishment. Over the past few days it had become routine, but now it was different again. Pride started fast and kept it up. Jacob looked barely in control.

"Don't let him truck out on you," JW instructed. He could tell from the way Jacob was riding that he was nervous. The boy was squeezing with his knees and leaning forward, which made the horse trot, and then he was pulling on the reins to slow him down. Using a snaffle bit made him pull even harder than he should, craning the horse's head high and back. Pride was starting to fight and to ignore the bit, which made Jacob squeeze his knees harder.

JW knew that telling the legs to run and pulling the head back was a recipe for a horse to rear up and go over, landing on the rider. "Give him his head," he instructed. "Give him his head. Let the reins go."

Jacob loosened the reins and Pride kept up his fast trot, prancing around the perimeter. He stopped fighting the bit and lowered his head.

"That's good. Now you got him going good. Don't keep making him truck out on you. Relax those knees. Let your legs dangle. Sit back and loosen your back. If you're relaxed, he's relaxed. And keep those reins loose."

JW knew how hard this was. Making yourself relax when you were nervous was challenging. It was even harder while maintaining your balance on the back of a twelve-hundred-pound animal that was in motion and barely under control. In fact, the horse was just trying to follow Jacob's conflicting instructions, but loosening the reins and relaxing your legs seemed counterintuitive if the goal was more control.

"Put it all in your butt. Imagine you got Velcro on your seat. Stick your butt to the horse. Let your legs dangle. Your hips absorb the shock. I want to see you still from the hips up."

Jacob let the horse go and relaxed his legs. Sure enough, things slowed down in less than a length of the riding paddock.

Jacob was still stiff, but Pride slowed to a gentle trot. JW gave him a thumbs-up, and Jacob broke into a wide grin.

After the lesson, they ate barbequed ribs and corn at Eagle's great wooden table. JW reminisced about growing up in North Lake, how he had not been born into privilege but had married the town princess, and how he had applied himself, eventually becoming a bank president. Eagle held him up as an example to Jacob.

"You could do the same thing," he said. JW smiled, thinking of the bank Eagle was secretly building. Eagle probably did have that job in mind for Jacob some day in the distant future.

Outside the open screen door, the tree leaves were glowing yellow-green in the early evening light. He reached for another rib. He heard the sound of loud rap music approaching, and then a car pulled past the house. Its bass thundered and buzzed the window panes. He heard it pull into the neighboring driveway, and then the booming bass cut out. Two car doors slammed, followed by the high cymbal of a woman's laughter.

"Your neighbor sure does love to party," JW said to Eagle. He was nervous about the subject, but he also needed to know where he stood. Eagle ignored the comment and took three more ribs from the plate in the middle.

"She's my aunt," said Jacob, glancing at JW and then looking down at his food. Eagle shot him an angry glance.

"What?" Jacob asked in an innocent tone.

"We don't talk about her," Eagle replied, intending the statement more for JW.

He nodded, getting the shape of things. "Jacob's really making progress with Pride," he said, changing the subject.

"Yeah?"

"Real progress. He's a nice horse."

"JW says he's maybe worth twenty thousand!" Jacob blurted out.

"Twenty!" Eagle was shocked. "You're kidding!"

"Well, he's still a stud," said JW, "which is rare. Good bloodlines to boot. If Jacob gets him cleaned up and performing at his best, Pride has real income potential. We've financed horses like him for upwards of fifteen at the bank."

Eagle laughed. "I'll tell you what. If Jacob can sell him for twenty at the fair, he gets half and you get the other half."

"We already made a deal. He'd keep it all for college," JW replied.

"I'd split it with you," offered Jacob.

JW nodded noncommittally and took another rib. "It would rightly be yours." He saw Eagle's wry smile.

After dinner he went outside and sat on Eagle's front deck, watching the great swaths of a sweeping sunset. Purple washed into pink, to yellow and then to a deep fireball orange, like chalk in the rain. The screen door clapped shut behind him. Eagle tapped his shoulder with a wet bottle of Summit EPA. He took it and Eagle sat down next to him.

"Sure is pretty out here." JW took a sip of the amber brew. "I don't know why your people are always complaining about living on the rez."

"Which of my people are those?"

"I don't know. You know, activists."

"Maybe they're just irritated at being lumped together and told where and how to live."

JW chuckled. "Maybe. Whole country's getting angry, it seems, and everybody wants special rights. You all get gambling."

Eagle snorted. "We didn't get gambling. We always had it. These reservations are sovereign land."

"You and I know that's only true part of the time. But your point's well-taken."

"Besides," said Eagle. "Remember when white men used to get the Indi'ns drunk and take all *their* money?"

JW laughed. "Touché." He held up his bottle, and Eagle clinked it with his. "No, it wasn't anybody's fault but mine, how I screwed up my life," JW said. He looked out over the landscape, picking at the beer label. "My son died. My son died, and—" he shook his head. "I couldn't handle it. It's all I could think about. I just sort of wound up down there, passing time. All those lights. Little voices in the machines." He laughed and fluttered his fingers as if they were sparkling with fairy dust. Then he took another sip and looked out over the sunset. "It all began as a distraction. I would have grabbed at anything, I suppose." He closed his eyes, seeing it all clearly for the first time. He had been a fool, trying to control the uncontrollable, over and over, and now here he was, trapped by his own weaknesses.

"What was his name?" Eagle said softly.

JW looked at him with a start, drawn back out of his reverie. "Chris. Christopher John White. I tried to call him CJ, but it never took. He hated it." He smiled and shrugged.

"How did he die?"

"It was a car crash, just outside of town. Bob Grossman said he was high and drunk. A one-car crash, thankfully. Deer jumped out and he lost control. Totally random. The real kicker: I was supposed to help him with his brakes the night before, but because it was the end of the month, I was working overtime at the bank."

Eagle blew out air. "I'm sorry."

JW nodded and sipped his beer. Toed some sand on the sidewalk. "It doesn't matter," he said. "You just have to learn to deal with it. Or not." He chuckled painfully.

"It's hard to know what people need," said Eagle. "I wasn't there enough for my wife either."

JW glanced over at him, but Eagle just picked at his bottle label. It was clear he didn't want to say more.

JW studied his beer bottle. "I feel different now," he said. "At least when it comes to the gambling. Cured by the snake that bit me, I guess."

Eagle glanced over and saw that JW was barely hiding a smile.

"Seriously though," JW continued, "I am reading the Big Book. But being out here, I don't know. Somehow it's taking me back to my youth. Making things more bearable."

Eagle nodded. "Someday I hope we won't need casinos," he said.

JW nodded. There was a brief silence before he spoke again. "Why don't you work toward that then?" he said. His heart was racing. While the exchange had developed naturally, this was the moment he had been working toward since he first got out here. "Set up a bank," he suggested. "It's what you do. I mean, the wild rice business is nice, but you could get some economic development going. Let's face it. There's no one else up here that could do what you do."

Eagle regarded his Summit, the ochre grains on the label glowing in the long rays of the sunset. The paper was wrinkling from the moisture.

"You want to help me?" Eagle kept staring at the bottle, his expression unchanged, and with his thumb he began to peel off the label. "You probably figured that's what the new building is." He glanced at JW.

JW suddenly felt cautious. He looked away. Was this a trap?

"We just got our last bit of capital," Eagle went on.

"Treasury's been dragging their feet for some reason, but we're going to submit our national charter application on Monday."

"Jesus. You're really doing it."

The telephone rang somewhere inside the house.

"It's about time my people had a bank. You would know that better than anyone. What do you say? You want to be our token white boy? I could pay you a little more than I can for bagging rice."

JW saw that Eagle was smiling wryly. Offering friendship and a new future, free of his past, free of the things that had trapped him, perhaps, or at least free of what he had done in response to them. He took a sudden deep breath. "Wow."

Jacob burst out through the screen door. "Dad," he said. "There's a fire."

21

Eagle's bank was burning. JW could see the orange flames blossoming through the trees as the pickup lurched recklessly over the bumpy reservation road. They crunched to a stop next to an idling tribal tanker truck and scrambled out into the night.

The flames blew thirty and forty feet high, gulping and roaring with a thunderous power. The tribal firemen rushed to hook up a new hose. A breeze was blowing, feeding the flames up into great gobs that woofed up over their heads. The heat blasted them, burning their faces and the backs of their hands.

The big diesel tanker powered two massive water pumps that snapped the fire hoses taut, shooting powerful blasts into the sky. Three Indian firefighters directed water at the downwind vegetation, while two others kept their hose trained on the building. Orange reflections raced back up the giant arcs, as if the flames were fighting their way back toward the brass nozzles.

"We can't get it, Johnny, it's too big!" the fire chief yelled over the hum of the engines.

"You gotta get more water on it!"

"We got the other tanker going for another load! We gotta soak the brush to keep it from spreading or else we'll have a wildfire!"

JW looked down the slope to the county highway, where

two North Lake fire engines idled—a large pumper and a tanker—their emergency lights turning blue and yellow. City firefighters were standing on the shoulder in yellow slickers, smoking cigarettes and talking.

"What about them?" Eagle yelled.

"We canned the agreement with them when we opened our own fire department!" the chief yelled. He powered down one of the massive pumps and started working the big brass union of the slackening fire hose. Water began pouring from the coupling.

Eagle turned to JW. "I need your help!" he said. He jogged down the rocky construction access road to the highway. JW followed him down the makeshift gravel driveway and then along the shoulder, to where the North Lake volunteer firefighters had congregated with their two vehicles. Tony Amaretto, the city fire chief, was a short man with dark hair and a mustache. He stepped forward to intercept them. Eagle was yelling at him even before he stopped running.

"Can't you people see we need help?" he said, sounding outraged.

"Yes, I can." Amaretto said. He had the soft voice of an old drinker, and he lifted his hands in a gesture of helplessness. "We don't have a cooperative service agreement. We're just here to make sure it doesn't spread."

Eagle turned to JW as they stopped, full of disbelief.

"This is crazy," he said.

JW appealed to the fire chief, who was an old buddy from the local curling club. "Tony, come on. Be a neighbor, eh? What harm can it do?"

"I wish we could, JW—"

"I'll guarantee it," Eagle said, his voice desperate. "I'll guarantee your costs."

Amaretto looked genuinely upset. "I'm sorry. There's legal issues. Unless the county directs us, if we don't have a CSA, we don't have insurance. One of our guys gets hurt, he's not covered."

The trucks sat there rumbling, and JW saw the faces of the firefighters as they stood around on the shoulder or sat inside the vehicles, watching.

"This is insane," said Eagle, raising his voice. "I'm begging you."

Up at the construction site, the empty tribal tanker was backing out. Behind it, another one had arrived and was getting into position. JW could hear the beeping over the roar as it backed up.

"Take it up with the tribal council," said Amaretto. "I wish I could do more, JW. We got it straight from the city attorney."

"And don't build right on the edge of the damn town until you can provide proper fire protection!" a firefighter called out from near the cab. Amaretto held up a hand to silence him. He looked apologetically from Eagle to JW.

JW nodded. "I'm sorry, Johnny," he said.

Eagle shook his head in disbelief, then jogged back up the hill. JW turned to Amaretto.

"I gotta go help him," he said, then started after Eagle. He saw him pick up a slackened hose and connect it to the new tanker.

"Okay, go!" the tribal fire chief yelled as JW arrived at the top of the hill. The tanker driver powered up the main pump and the hose snapped stiff with water. The firefighters bore in against it, aiming its nozzle, and a blast leaped out onto the fire. But it was a containment operation now. As if to confirm this, the roof collapsed, sending out a blast of heat followed by an eighty-foot plume of sparks that dispersed like fireflies to heaven.

Eagle put his arm around Jacob and drew him close. JW stood helplessly behind in the dark, watching their glistening silhouettes as they watched Eagle's dream burn. By the time the remaining wall fell into the fire with another enormous blast of sparks, JW had a sense that something permanent had forever changed between them.

The tribal fire chief put a hand on Eagle's shoulder. He turned him toward the pickup. "There's nothing more you can do," he said, waving JW over to join them. "Don't torture yourselves." Eagle looked as if he didn't understand. Jacob tugged at his arm, and Eagle put an arm around his shoulder and the two of them began walking toward the truck. JW followed.

They drove home through a tunnel of darkness and leaves, the roar of the fire echoing in their minds, choking out other thoughts. Finally, Eagle slowed to a stop on the road in front of JW's trailer, and the roar transformed into the raging thunder of crickets. They sat there for a moment, at a loss for words. JW finally reached up and hooked two fingers around the door handle.

"Johnny," he said, "I'm so sorry."

Eagle laughed with disgust. "You know," he said, his voice hard with a bitterness JW hadn't heard before, "I find it funny that you lost your job and just happened to move in next door to me and my son. You get my son thinking you're this great guy—"

"Dad—"

Eagle raised his hand and grasped the air. He dropped his hand to his knee and looked at JW in the glow of the dashboard. His eyes were inflamed.

"What do you know about this?"

JW turned his head away and looked ahead at the yellow road, the bugs flitting in and out of the headlights, bumping blindly over and over at the glass. "Nothing solid," he said. It could have been anyone from the town, even Grossman, or it could have been oily rags. But he had a strong suspicion.

"You're working against me, aren't you," said Eagle. JW saw it from his perspective for a moment, how everything, starting with the one big coincidence of JW moving in across the street, all fell into place. He had wanted to believe. He had needed to believe.

"No," said JW. It was a lie, but it was also true in the sense that he never would have burned down the bank. "Johnny—"

"Get out before I do something I regret."

JW sat for a moment. He wanted to say something, but he couldn't think of anything that would not come out sounding like an unforgivable betrayal. He stepped out into the night and watched as Eagle pulled away and left him standing alone on the road.

He walked across the dark gravel and through the dewy grass to his shadowed trailer home, soaking his shoes and socks. A form moved in the shadows.

"John White?" a voice said.

Too late, JW saw the man as he stepped out and shoved a pale envelope into his hands.

"You've been served."

He turned and walked back into the shadows, and JW saw the outline of a dark car parked there. The glass of its door gleamed like a knife as the man got in. Then the lights came on and the engine started and the car pulled out and drove away, leaving the sulfurous stench of a new engine's exhaust hanging thick and noxious in the air.

Inside, he tossed the envelope onto the counter. He went

into the bathroom and leaned over the sink. Things had
taken a dangerous turn. This was not the kind of thing he'd
ever imagined himself doing. And yet he couldn't escape the
feeling that he was responsible for the setting of the fire, at
least in part. He took up his toothbrush and covered it with
paste. He brushed his teeth and tongue for some time, but
he couldn't get the awful taste of smoke out of his mouth. He
spit and watched the water swirl down the drain.

He sat on the edge of the thin mattress and ripped the
envelope open. Inside was a note on bank stationery, scrawled
in Jorgenson's handwriting. *Honor your commitment,* it said,
underlined twice. The note covered a formal notice of foreclosure.

JW crumpled the notice in his fist. He turned off the
light and sat there in his boxers and white T-shirt. He kicked
the flimsy wall.

His gaze rose to the family photo on the nightstand,
barely visible, like the memory of a dream. For an instant he
felt like smashing it to the floor. Chris, Julie, Carol, and him,
all in front of the house, all happy. He grunted and looked
away. The sum total of everything he had done. A middling
father in a dwindling town, teaching bankers how to rip off
Indians.

He reached into the clothes hamper and pulled out the
bug receiver. He plugged it in, tuned it, and put the earbuds
in. He felt a rush of self-loathing and almost pulled them back
out, but in the end he was in this battle to win. He had to
win.

He heard the faint sound of running water and the clack
of dishes. The dinner plates, he realized. Then the water was
shut off, and after a brief moment there was a loud smashing
clatter, as if a whole stack of plates had been dropped into the

sink. He heard the sound of breathing followed by a startling anguished cry.

The sounds were closer now. Footsteps, the door closing, a faint click, and a dim light went on in the window to Eagle's office. Then JW heard the closet door opening. His heart leaped, and he rushed into the kitchen and rummaged through the junk drawer until he found the recorder. He punched REC, set one earbud next to the microphone, and put the other in his ear. He listened to the rapid clicks as Eagle spun the safe dial to the zero mark, then recorded the quick spins of the combination.

His heart was racing. He felt as if he were lurking in the room and might somehow be caught. He had the combination! He heard the fine rustling of a plastic baggie. The pot. Eagle was getting stoned, he thought. It was getting even better. He heard the pipe being lit, and the sizzling of the pot in the bowl. He sighed, thinking again of the fire and its consequences. He balanced the earbud and went and poured himself a Dewar's. JW lifted the glass in a toast to the earbuds still lying on the mattress, and to the man getting stoned beyond them, then downed the harsh firewater in a long gulp that rushed back up and pounded him between the ears.

* * *

EAGLE HELD THE red calumet in his hand and stared at the rising band of smoke. The pipe had feathers carved into its bowl, and there were stones held to its six-inch stem with leather bindings. He put a disc in the CD player on the bookshelf—"Buffalo Soldier"—and turned the volume down.

He sat back in his Aeron chair, then slowly spun the pipe in his hand, watching the small gray stream of smoke spiral around and around in the holy way of his mother's ancestors. He looked up at the clock, and his eye fell on a book on his shelf called *The Assassination of Hole in the Day* by Anton Treuer, an Ojibwe historian and writer. Wenonah had given it to him, and one particular passage had always struck him powerfully. The book chronicled the age-old hostilities between the Dakota and Ojibwe people, fought across the battleground of Minnesota as the Ojibwe migrated west, encroaching on Dakota territory in search of the land where food grew on water. It was a feud fueled by the guns and the economic interests of French traders who wanted the gold of the age: beaver pelts. And yet, despite the often brutal hostilities, each autumn the two great warring tribes of the North would call temporary truces in order to hunt and prepare for winter. The Ojibwe word for it was *biindigodaadiwin*, which meant "to enter one another's lodges." Even in the most heated periods of conflict, biindigodaadiwin was a common practice, he remembered reading. Ojibwe and Dakota would enter one another's lodges, sleep in the same buildings, smoke the same pipes, form friendships, and even marry. Then they would be at war again the next spring, killing one another and taking the scalps home as trophies—or for bounties paid by the French, the Dutch, and the English.

For Eagle, the *biindigodaadiwin* was also over.

22

JW woke sweaty from a tangled passage of darkness. His mind lurched into the self-reproaching lucidity that had become an all-too-familiar midnight companion. He rose and paced the dark trailer, his mouth thick and dry, replaying his situation like a caged lion: a fruitless ambulation with no exit. He drank two glasses of water and took an aspirin against the hangover, a trick his father had taught him in junior high, and went back to bed. He dreamed of the wild horses. They milled around near the smoldering embers of Johnny's bank as the sun climbed past dawn, their many colors visible through the smoke.

In the morning, JW looked outside. Eagle's Bronco was gone. Ernie and the other Indians were already at work, stocking and turning. The bank fire was distressing, but the wild rice business went on. Ricers were still coming in and Johnny needed them now more than ever, he supposed.

JW sat on the edge of the bed, stiff-jointed and aching, a dull throbbing in his temples, and hardened himself to what he had to do. The fire would not stop the bank. In fact, it was stupid and unnecessary, and would only make his job worse. As sickened as he was by it, he had a larger mission, and that hadn't changed. If anything, it was more important now than ever. And for this reason, first and foremost, he had to maintain access.

A hot shower cleansed any remaining doubts from his mind. He dressed for work and stepped out into a bracing morning—a high, crystal ring to the air, the thin scent of the fire, and the smell of fall. He crossed the road and headed up the drive toward the wide-open barn as if nothing had happened. But when he neared the parching fire, Ernie stepped out of the smoke and blocked his path. The others continued working silently.

"Good morning," said JW.

"We don't need you today."

"Oh, come on, Ernie." JW went to step around him, but Ernie blocked his path again.

"Johnny says you're no longer welcome here."

His face was as hard as granite.

"Okay. Fair enough."

JW nodded, worlds shifting. His only chance to maintain access would be through Jacob. As JW passed the paddock, he saw him in the lean-to. He walked over. Jacob ignored him.

"I came to work, but Ernie says they don't need me today. You want to work on the horse?"

"I can't believe I trusted you."

JW had expected this on some level. The kid deserved an explanation, but a disavowal would have to do.

"Jacob, I had no idea that anybody was going to burn down the bank, I promise you. Okay?" And it was true. Jorgenson had hinted at it, he could see in retrospect, but at the time he couldn't have predicted it.

JW could see that Jacob wanted to believe him, but then the boy pulled away. "I'm going to sell the horse," he said.

"Don't do that," JW said, stepping forward. Firm. He took another step closer, into the lean-to. "Look, I've made some pretty bad mistakes. But two things I know for sure. One, I didn't burn down that bank. And two, you are at the begin-

ning of something really special with Pride. And I'd hate to
see you throw that away because you're mad at me. You set a
goal, and you shouldn't give up on it."

Jacob looked at him. "Fuck you."

JW stood frozen. There was nothing to say. "Maybe you're
right." He walked out of the lean-to and into the pale morning
sunlight. He saw his blue trailer in the copse across the road,
and headed for it with a growing feeling of resignation.

"Wait."

JW turned around. Jacob was standing in the lean-to
opening. JW softened his face. They stood and looked at each
other for a moment, and then Jacob said softly, "Okay, let's
train."

Jacob walked back into the lean-to and picked up a
saddle off the rack. JW stood there for a moment to let the
feeling subside. Jacob cinched up the saddle, put the bit into
the horse's mouth, and pulled the headstall up over his ears.
He led the horse into the paddock and closed the gate. He
climbed on and sat in the saddle, concentrating.

"Okay," he said. "I'm going to do everything you said."

Then he lifted the reins, and JW forgot about everything
else. Before him was not a rider and horse, but a single living
animal, smooth and reflexively intuitive. The boy just needed
to be pointed in the right direction. JW threw himself into
the task, forgetting temporarily the more unsavory aspects of
what he intended to do.

By mid-morning he and Jacob were working Pride at a
trot, practicing a more refined way of turning the horse without using the reins. Dust hung around JW's ankles as the
horse turned in the sand, over and over. Several more car-
loads of Indians arrived, and as they weighed in their fresh
rice deposits, most of them observed the unlikely pair. Ernie

and Supersize Me stretched a large blue plastic tarp out on
the lawn near the paddock to accommodate the extra volume, and soon there were six or seven hundred pounds of rice
spread out across it, drying green and purple in the sun. JW
felt like heading to his trailer for a drink of water and a break
from the sun and dust, but he saw Ernie watching him and
decided not to.

He ducked through the rail to the outside of the paddock. As he put his elbows up on the top rail he heard loud
rap music coming down the hill behind him. He turned and
saw the car full of Indian boys.

"Hey, man," one of them yelled from the front passenger
seat. "It's Tonto and the Lone Ranger!"

JW started walking toward them. "Why don't you just
leave him alone," he said. The biggest one was driving. He
looked to be eighteen or nineteen. He casually put a hand out
the window and JW saw a gun in it. He stopped in his tracks.

"Yeah, I thought so, old man," the driver said.

He aimed the gun at the tarp full of wild rice and a shot
rang out. Rice jumped and Pride leaped sideways and into a run,
frightened by the report. The boys laughed as the car sped off.

"Damn it!" yelled Jacob. His voice was scattershot with
panic. He was trying to control the racing horse, but he was
halfway down one side of the saddle, hanging onto the saddle
horn to keep from falling to the ground.

"Hold it!" replied JW. "Turn him! Pull the left rein! Turn
him around you!"

Jacob grabbed the left rein and pulled it with all his might
to turn the horse tightly around his body.

"Don't stop!" JW said. "Keep him going! Stick your heel
into his side!"

Jacob was tiring, but he kept turning Pride with the

inside rein and goading him on with his outside foot and hand, still partway out of the saddle.

"That's right! Keep him going! Use his lungs against him! Urge him into it! If he runs, he has to learn he doesn't stop until you say stop!"

The horse began to tire.

"Keep him going! Make those lungs burn!"

After another few turns, JW could see that Jacob was starting to get sloppy and might fall off.

"Okay," he said.

Jacob let up on the reins and Pride came to a stop. The horse was drenched in sweat and his breath was steaming even though the day was warm. Jacob pulled himself back up into the saddle. JW could see that his leg was shaking.

"You okay?"

Jacob nodded weakly. "Yeah, I think so."

"You hung on, that was good. So what happened?"

Jacob swallowed and exhaled. He looked as if he was going to cry. "He got scared. They were assholes."

"Forget them. You almost got dumped. That's on you."

Jacob's eyes were wet. He turned away.

"He doesn't need you, either," said Ernie, approaching the paddock.

"Fuck off, Ern!" said Jacob.

"Language," said JW gently.

"Fuck!" Jacob yelled, shedding adrenaline. He looked back at Ernie. "Just leave us alone, okay?" He rubbed the tears from his eyes on the back of his sleeve.

Ernie looked from Jacob to JW, then shook his head and headed back toward the pole barn.

"Okay, I know you're upset. Let's talk it out. What happened?"

"He shied."

"Right. With you on him. What you always gotta remember is that a horse is insecure. He's a herd animal, just like a stupid banker," JW said.

Jacob laughed through his tears. He was beginning to calm down.

"Herd's got to have a leader to keep 'em safe, right? If you're a herd of two and you don't lead, who will?"

"He will, I guess."

"That's right, but he's not as smart as you, and he's much bigger. He's not going to look out for you. So how do you lead?"

"I don't know, I was trying."

"You were hanging on. I'm talking before he shied. You gotta *lead*. That means you gotta anticipate what might happen and check him before he gets scared. Okay?"

"They shot a fricking gun, how'm I supposed to—"

"You just do! Okay? Look, out here everybody shoots guns. You could be riding anywhere and somebody'd shoot a gun. You could be hunting on horseback."

Jacob was unconvinced.

"How do you anticipate anything?" asked JW.

Jacob shrugged. "I don't know."

"You know your horse, and you know which situations might cause a problem for him. You let him know that you know, that you're in charge, and if he does what you say he'll be okay."

A breeze took up all the leaves of the nearby trees, setting them fluttering in yellows and reds. Jacob shook his head, not really understanding, but more receptive now.

"You saw them coming, right?"

"I guess."

"Okay. Now. He's going to shy at that tarp because of

what just happened. Right? Horses have long memories when it comes to danger and survival. So take him around and get him to face it. Teach him that it's not dangerous."

Jacob sighed, then took Pride back out to the rail and began circling the paddock. JW could see Jacob's leg shaking with fear as he worked Pride up toward the tarp. It was a safe bet Pride was also aware of the shaking, and it was probably eroding his confidence. "Keep his mind occupied. Ask him to side step to the left and then to the right," he said.

He watched as Jacob got Pride to take the hesitant steps. He saw the horse's legs quivering, on the verge of leaping sideways or bucking and running away again. "Okay, ask him to stop and then turn and turn back. We all need to keep our minds busy so we don't get overwhelmed by life. Same for him. Keep him busy with stuff to think about."

He watched Jacob turn the horse back, and this time he gave him a small reminder check with the reins and his left knee, just before the tarp. Pride weaved in slightly, but Jacob's knee was there already, nudging him back out. And with that little bit of anticipation and resistance, Pride stayed the course.

"Good job! He did it!"

Jacob laughed and patted Pride on the neck, his face brightening, and he looked over to see JW give him a big thumbs-up.

"Really good! A tough situation and you handled it! Okay, take him around again!"

Jacob turned the horse back toward the tarp at the far end of the paddock.

"You know that boy loves you, don't you?"

It was a woman's voice, reedy and husky. JW turned to see her walking up to the paddock fence rail next to him.

She was in her mid- to late-thirties, he guessed, and she had a rough but beautiful appearance. She had high cheekbones and wore feathers tied into her shaggy dark hair. She was wearing an olive T-shirt and skinny jeans, cheap sandals and a toe ring, and she smelled strongly of alcohol and cigarettes.

"You're the neighbor," he said.

"Yeah." A flicker of emotion flowed through her face and was gone. "Is that a problem?"

"It depends."

She nodded. "I've been watching you," she said, turning to observe Jacob. "He doesn't get like this with most people." She pulled out an American Spirit and lit up with a cheap plastic lighter, then held the pack out to him.

"I don't smoke." JW turned back to Jacob. "Okay, bring him around again!"

He turned back to her as she stuck the cigarettes back in her tiny jeans pocket. "So, do you party every night, or do you take weekends off?"

She blew smoke. "Really? That's how your mother taught you to start a conversation? 'JW, when you grow up, first thing you do is to give a woman shit'?"

"You know my name. Well, you're right, and I'm sorry."

Then to Jacob: "Again!"

And then back to the woman beside him: "I guess you saw me raiding Johnny's house for booze, then." It was a calculated risk, but one he had to take.

"Is that what it was?" She blew more smoke. "You should have asked me." She extended a hand to him. "I'm Mona." Her eyes managed to look at him and away at the same time, darting above a smile that was both coy and somehow volatile.

"I tried. You wouldn't answer the door," he said, ignoring her gesture.

She smirked and dropped her hand. She walked up to the rail and put her arms up on it. His eyes fell past the shelf of her breasts to the midriff exposed under her T-shirt. A tattoo climbed out of her jeans, a bird of some sort.

"If you were a single white woman who saw an ugly Indi'n going through your brother-in-law's house next door, would you answer your door?" She glanced at him.

"Ugly!" JW grimaced. "If it was so scary why didn't you call the police?" He turned back to watch Jacob, who was circling the horse in a smaller loop at the other end of the ring.

"I thought maybe you were a friend," she said, blowing smoke at the horse. "Obviously, that was before I came to know who you are. And then I watched my nephew fall in love with you. Don't blow it with him. I don't want to see him let down. It wouldn't be pretty."

She looked at him, then began walking toward her house. She turned back with a wry expression. "Oh and uh, nice ass. For an ugly white guy."

He sensed a kind of teasing amusement as she brushed the hair and feathers out of her face. It was strange, considering what she had just said. Especially on the reservation, where most Indians looked at him with silent resentment. She smiled, sensing his confusion, and walked away more rapidly.

23

JW watched as Mona walked toward her house, but she didn't look back. It was as if a ghost had blown in and become suddenly animate, altering everything about the situation. He refocused on Jacob and the horse.

"That's right," he said. "No matter what distractions come up, you keep him on task. Again!" He wasn't used to women being as aggressive as Mona, either. He had been so wrapped up in his own collapse over the last year that the idea he might be attractive to a woman hadn't really occurred to him.

As he stood there at the rail, he remembered the foreclosure notice in his back pocket. He pulled out the crumpled document, then refolded it and put it in his shirt pocket. He leaned on the rail and watched Jacob. He had recorded the safe clicks. The mini-recorder was in his jeans pocket. He looked toward the pole barn. The Indians were hard at work. In the paddock, Jacob was repeating the routine with Pride. JW glanced back behind him. Mona was gone now. This could be his best chance. The house was just a few short steps away. Just take the pot out of the safe and put it in the desk drawer, he thought. It wasn't stealing, and it wasn't planting anything. It was making Eagle face himself, just like he had to face himself. And it was advancing the cause of justice.

He watched Jacob make another round on the horse. If Johnny didn't wind up opening the bank, he'd still have his wild rice business. There would be no foul. It might be better, in fact. Eagle was too absorbed in the battle, forgetting in the process what was important about a boy and a horse—and about the wide river of time that flowed through our bodies with such force and speed that it took things away before we knew what was happening. If Eagle were to lose the bank, maybe he would focus on his son again. JW knew it was a rationalization, but it was also true. He would still have to find a way to deal with Jorgenson, of course, but first things first. If the Big Book was teaching him anything, it was the importance of taking life one day at a time. He looked up at Jacob, still on the horse.

"You keep working," he called to him. "I gotta run inside and use the bathroom." Jacob waved to acknowledge him, and JW headed up toward the house. He didn't notice Ernie watching him from behind the smoke of the parching fire.

JW stepped inside and closed the front door.

"Hello? Johnny?"

There was no answer. Eagle's Bronco was gone, but he needed to be sure. He had only a minute or two. In the study, he looked out the window. Jacob was still working Pride down in the paddock. The lawn was clear.

"Hello?" It was like calling into a forest. The aspen leaves fluttered, watching. He took Eagle's fancy pen off the desk and headed for the closet. He opened the door and quickly lay down on the floor in front of the safe.

He took out his little spiral notepad and set it on the carpet in front of the safe. He spun the dial to zero and pulled the digital mini-recorder out of his jeans pocket. He switched it to quarter-speed playback, thumbed the volume to max, and pressed play. He mimicked the number of clicks—one, two, three—until he got to nine, then pressed stop and wrote a nine on the notepad. He picked up the recorder and pressed play, turning the dial once again with each click, going all the way around and past nine, past zero, and then back to the number ninety-one. He pressed stop and wrote ninety-one, then pressed play one last time and turned the dial forward twenty-two clicks to thirteen.

He turned the lever and the safe opened. There was a heavy footfall outside on the deck. His heart leapt into his lungs. Too late to quit. He'd have to be quick. He stuffed the spiral notepad back into his shirt pocket and pulled the safe door open.

The screen door spring stretched and twanged outside. The front door opened. Inside the safe was the baggie of weed and an artsy pot pipe, as well as cash and files. He reached for the weed, which was on the bottom, on top of the Silver Certificate. He heard a footstep in the front foyer.

"JW?" It was Ernie's gravelly voice.

He pulled the baggie out and saw the label: Organic Indian Tobacco. He laughed silently. How stupid, he thought. He sniffed the baggie to be sure. Rich and earthy. Definitely tobacco. He stuffed it back into the safe, closed the door, and spun the dial. He quickly stepped across the hall into the bathroom and swung the door shut as Ernie stepped into the hall.

"Hey whitey."

"Are you calling me?" he said. It was possible Ernie had seen him. He looked in the mirror. The beads of sweat on his forehead glistened with the pale green of the wall tile. The door stood slightly ajar.

"Where are you?"

He heard Ernie heading down the hall, and saw him moving through the door crack in the mirror. He reached over and flushed the toilet as a ruse. He opened the bathroom door.

"Just going to the bathroom," he said, trying to sound nonchalant. He turned to the sink and ran the water. He made a show of washing his hands. Ernie stood in the hall, watching. JW glanced up at him in the mirror and caught his eye. He dried his hands and face, then turned and walked out into the hall.

"Excuse me."

Ernie grabbed his arm. Tight. Close. His breath was rich with clove chewing gum. He breathed heavily through his nose as his grip tightened.

"I don't trust you," he said.

JW looked at him. "I don't blame you," he said.

"Why are you sweating?"

"I'm not feeling well. You don't want to get what I have, believe me."

Ernie studied him, then relaxed his grip. JW passed, stepped out onto the porch, and wiped his face on his arms. A cool breeze greeted him and his skin began to contract. His shirt was sticking to his back and his pits were wet and cold. He wiped his palms on his jeans and headed back down to the riding paddock.

Then he remembered the pen. He had left it on the floor in front of the closet. He thought about what this might mean to Ernie when he saw it. He would pick it up and think of the safe. Open the closet door. Try the handle. JW had spun the dial, so it would be locked. He would walk to the window, perhaps, and look out at him through the blinds, to make sure he was walking back down to the boy. Had he left any other evidence? He patted his pocket. The spiral notepad was still there. He should be okay, except for the pen out of place, which was inconclusive. Ernie would set it back on the desk and maybe mention it to Johnny, but what would it mean? Nothing.

JW returned to the rail. Jacob was still on Pride, but he was walking him now, in the cooldown phase, the horse and boy moving as one, with ease, each footfall in the sand relaxed and steady.

"You're a good learner," JW said, feeling a sudden wave of giddiness after his narrow escape. "He's really learning to trust you."

"Thanks." Jacob smiled.

JW thought again about the tobacco, and as he did he experienced a sense of freedom he hadn't felt in years.

Jacob stopped the horse nearby. "Hey," he said, interrupting JW's thoughts.

JW looked up and saw Jacob's furrowed brow. "What's up?"

"My dad doesn't want Mona over here."

JW's lightness returned. "That's okay! I don't want her here either. She called me ugly!" He laughed. "Seriously, it's perfectly fine. I didn't invite her over, and I don't want you to get in any trouble."

"Okay, thanks. It's just that Ernie tells my dad."

JW nodded and Jacob turned away. Standing against the rail, he started running through the implications of the fact that there was no pot in the safe. He could use it to turn things around and get out from under Jorgenson's thumb. "Jacob," he said. The boy turned the horse back around. "I got an errand to run. Can you go swear at Ernie some more until he lets me use the truck?"

Jacob laughed. "Yeah, I can probably do that."

24

JW sped into the bank parking lot and pulled into the spot marked President, his strategy becoming clearer by the minute. The wild rice truck's front bumper bent the President signpost back, but he didn't care. Clapton fell quiet and the engine churned as he got out. He looked down at Sam's black car with its red NRA bumper sticker and noticed the camo and deer hunting gear inside. The deer opener wasn't for another month and a half. The guy was a nut, a survival fetishist. Schmeaker's macho fascination had always struck him as playacting, considering the man's fragile jaw, slender frame, and feathered hair.

He threw open the main door and marched inside toward his old office.

"Sandy," he said as he passed the reception desk.

"Mr. White!" She rose, alarmed, and began to follow him through the open area under the large log trusses as he headed for one of the glassed-in offices around the perimeter. "Mr. White, he's busy!"

He heard her clacking heels step off the tile and onto the carpet. "He'll make time," JW said, and kept walking.

Other employees looked up as he passed through the open area, Sandy trailing him. Through the glass wall of his former office he could see Jorgenson at his old desk, meeting with Sam Schmeaker, who stood to intercept him as he opened the door.

"John, we're in conference," Schmeaker said.

"Out of my way, Sam." He pushed the door farther open and shouldered past. He tossed the foreclosure notice and the hand-scrawled note on Jorgenson's desk.

"Seriously?" His voice was loud. Confident. For the first time in ages, it seemed, things were becoming clear to him. "This is your idea of communication and management?"

"I'm sorry, Mr. Jorgenson," Sandy said, arriving at the door, "he walked right past me—"

JW turned and raised his arms wide, herding both her and Sam out the door. "Okay, okay, thank you, you can leave now, Frank and I are now having a conference—" They looked to Jorgenson for guidance. He lifted a hand.

"It's fine. We forgot to set up a meeting this morning."

"See? Out." JW closed the door behind them and turned back to Jorgenson. Fire burned in his lungs, but he held his anger in abeyance, to see what he could learn. He regarded the man who had given him his career.

"What the hell are you thinking, coming in here like this?" Jorgenson said.

"That's what I thought you'd say. No responsibility. But I don't respond well to personal threats. You want to communicate, do it like a man."

"John, get ahold of yourself—"

"Oh, I am ahold of myself, for the first time in a long time." He put a hand on the desk and leaned in, pointing. "I told you I would check on him—"

"It's simply a legal procedure—"

"Bullshit! It's childish intimidation and it's in bad faith. Did you set that fire?"

Jorgenson glanced out his office window at the employees, who were watching the confrontation.

"It's a simple question." JW went to the window wall and closed the wooden louver blinds.

"Did you set that fire?" he asked again.

"You have no idea how much damage you're doing."

"Oh, I have a pretty good idea of what I'm doing. The problem is, there's nothing wrong with the guy!"

"You said he smokes pot."

"It's organic tobacco! And I'll tell you what else. The man doesn't do drugs, he cares about his kid, and he's trying to do right by his people. There's nothing wrong with him." He was leaning in again, high with a sense of righteousness and control he hadn't enjoyed since before Chris's death.

Jorgenson pushed back in his chair. "Well, that changes things," he said, thinking. "How do you know it's not pot?"

"Because I have the combination to his safe," said JW, waving his spiral notepad. "I found the bag, and it's organic Indian tobacco. Now you listen to me. I'm done screwing around. I understand what you're holding over me, but I am sick of living in a fucking trailer and being your personal hatchet man. And it doesn't help matters when I get this kind of threat."

"You want to quiet down, please?"

"Will you play fairly?"

"Of course."

JW took a seat. The same seat, he noted, that Johnny Eagle had once taken in this very office. But this time it was the power seat, because Jorgenson was about to start playing by his rules. "You want to stop Johnny Eagle?" he asked.

Jorgenson didn't answer, and JW figured he was probably worried it might be some kind of trap. So JW enunciated.

"I said, do you want to stop Johnny Eagle?" He sat with both arms laid wide on the chair arms.

"Of course," said Jorgenson.

"Then you have to set him up."

Jorgenson looked relieved. His jaw loosened and he leaned back. "Okay," he said, "how can we do that?"

"The only way it's going to work at this point is to plant something on him. Something incriminating. I'm the only one close enough to him to do that, and that brilliant fire has made him extremely wary, even of me. Fortunately, I still have the trust of his son."

JW knew Jorgenson would be attracted by the logic of this perspective. If there were no drugs, then framing Eagle would be the next best option and, short of killing him, possibly the only option. At the very least it would buy them time and cast doubt, which might well be enough under the circumstances. And JW was indeed the man for the job. There was no one closer. He watched Jorgenson come to the realization that he, JW, held the fate of the bank, and perhaps Jorgenson's entire career, in his hands.

"So what do you need?" Jorgenson said finally.

"Partnership."

"Partnership?"

"I'll make it simple for you. Capitol Bank Holdings gives me fifteen percent ownership of this branch, which is just half of the value I've added under my leadership, and you forgive the second mortgage—not the first—and give me five thousand now so I can pay my bills. In exchange, Johnny Eagle and his bank go away, and you get a highly motivated partner."

Jorgenson's face looked sad. "No way I could get that approved by the brass, you know that."

"Then you better think carefully about what you are going to do in your next career, because the man offered me a job.

Think about what I could do for him. What the tribe pulling their deposits out of this bank would mean to its solvency and to your bid to become CEO. I want that for you as much as you do, Frank. There is nobody who deserves to lead this bank chain more than you do, and I've been your most loyal soldier for more than twenty years. I'd like to continue that career."

Jorgenson studied him like an animal backed into a corner. JW's gambit had taken the game to an entirely new level, but this time he was the house. He held all the best cards.

"All right, you have a deal," said Jorgenson. He looked bitter and his face was ashen. "It'll take me a little while to sell it to the brass. You'll have to trust me, and you'll have to deliver."

"Oh, I'll deliver," said JW, extending a hand.

Jorgenson looked at it, then pushed back and stood.

"Save the handshake for when we close on this fucker," he said. JW withdrew his hand, feeling cautious and unfulfilled. Jorgenson walked around the desk, passed behind him, and went to the door. He opened it to reveal Sandy and Schmeaker hovering nearby.

"Sandy, be a good girl and cut a check for me to sign to Mr. White for five thousand dollars—"

"Cash," said JW.

"All right. Cash."

"Of course," said Sandy, stumbling on her high heels as she turned to head for the tellers.

Jorgenson looked at Schmeaker. "It's all right," he said. "Everything's fine. You can go back to your office." He closed the door and walked back around his desk, loosening his tie.

"You never answered my question," said JW as he made a steeple out of his fingers.

"I'm sorry," said Jorgenson as he sat back in his chair.

"You flustered me. Well played, by the way. It's a move I might have made. What was the question?" Despite his congratulatory tone, he had the air of a murderer, and JW remained cautious. Again, he enunciated very clearly and slowly.

"Did you burn down the bank?"

Jorgenson sat back in his chair and snorted as if JW had asked something so obvious as to be foolish. JW stared at him over his steepled fingers until he answered. "What? Is that a surprise? Of course I did! This isn't a fucking dinner party. You should thank me for buying you more time."

JW kept his knowing smile and nodded. Jorgenson had just admitted to a crime that was worse than embezzlement.

There was a soft knock and Sandy entered. She moved hesitantly, and had to lean in close to JW to place the stack of cash on the desk. He smelled her perfume and saw the form of her breasts moving inside her silk blouse. Jorgenson nodded and smiled reassuringly at her, and she withdrew awkwardly past JW and exited.

Jorgenson placed the money near JW, but kept his hand on it. "I trust our agreement means you'll return your focus to saving this branch," he said, holding JW with his eyes, "and forget about all this history shit."

"It's my number one priority," said JW.

Jorgenson nodded softly and sat back. He took up the crumpled foreclosure notice. "I'll ask the lawyers to hold off on this for now."

"For now? Well, in that case I'm sorry, Frank, but the deal is off." JW moved to stand. "I don't work with a gun to my head."

"Fine!" Jorgenson cut him off with a raised hand. "I'll stop the action."

JW nodded. "Good."

He stood and took the stack of cash off the desk. He hefted it before he slipped it into his suit-jacket pocket. It was a parlor trick he had perfected some years ago.

"Aren't you going to count it?" asked Jorgenson.

"I just did," he said with a smile. "Besides, we're partners." And he left the office.

Jorgenson snorted, then reached up and pressed the intercom. "Sam, come in here."

JW made his way through the silent bank, the log trusses soaring over him, feeling victorious. He pushed his way through the doors.

Outside the air was dry and warm, and he picked up the faint smell of wood smoke. He got into the pickup, reached into his shirt pocket, and took out the digital mini recorder. He looked down at it and pressed stop, then rewind and play to test the recording. He heard Jorgenson's voice and pressed stop. He had what he came for—a renegotiated deal and, more importantly, evidence to protect himself.

He slipped the recorder back into his pants pocket and backed out, leaving the President sign crooked in the grass.

25

JW sped past the billboard for Dr. Reed Orput, still promising to remake his life with a mouthful of implants. He turned right and drove four blocks down to the park that lay in front of his old house. He could see the house across the green space to his right. He circled the block of grass and Norway pines and parked across the street. He took one of the hundred-dollar bills out of the stack in his suit-jacket pocket and tucked it into his shirt pocket. He popped a breath mint and got out. The truck sputtered again as he crossed the pavement.

He and Carol had planted the twin sugar maples in the front yard when Chris was a baby. They had lost the old trees to Dutch elm disease, but the maples were tall now and brilliant red. A few leaves had begun to fall, and they skittered across the sidewalk as he approached the house. He stepped up under the portico and rang the bell. Chris had spent hours out here on his hands and knees, driving his Hot Wheels up and down the walk. JW looked out, remembering, and for the first time in a long while the thought of Chris didn't flood him with grief and a sense akin to spinning out of control on icy pavement. Bit by bit, he was putting his life back together. He heard footsteps and turned as the door shuddered inward.

"Hi," said Julie. She wore dark eyeliner and lipstick.

"Hey, Sunshine," he said. "You ready for our date?"

"Yeah, I guess."

"Okay! Gimme a sec with your mother, and then we'll hit the road!"

She seemed surprised by his energy.

"I'm excited to see you," he said, in response to her skeptical expression. She stepped back and he entered the house. White-carpeted stairs climbed straight ahead. They had a dark walnut handrail with a white-enameled balustrade, and a newel post with a carved pineapple top that was loose and lifted off. He'd saved repairing it for a project to do with Chris, but somehow they never got around to it. He ran his hand over it. He'd fix it soon.

To the left was the family room. It was the largest room in the house, a great room with a high cathedral ceiling and wood-paneled walls hung with immense brass rubbings on huge framed sheets of pale blue paper. To complement them, the ceiling was painted in a trompe l'oeil sky with powder-puff clouds, and the top of the paneling was painted with a looped chain of pale spring flowers. The room had two well-worn gray woolen sofas and a fireplace on the end wall. A large television sat in the corner. The wide bay-window bench in the front had flowered blue cushions, and the broad window's many small panes looked out on one of the maples in the front yard and to the park beyond. JW passed through the near end of the room to the back hall that ran under the stairs and led to both the basement and the kitchen. He had always loved this cut-through. It was paneled in coffee-brown wood and reminded him of a secret passage.

Carol was sitting at an ancient yellow kitchen table that had been there since before she was born, commission paperwork spread out before her. The chairs had thick red vinyl cushions and chrome legs, as if they were from an old diner. She was talking to someone on the phone, and she sounded upset as JW walked in behind her.

"But if the policy is paid," she said, "I don't understand why the commission has to wait thirty days."

JW walked around and placed the stack of cash on the table, then took a chair across from her. She glanced at him and her cheeks flushed, and for a moment it felt like old times. She shook her head and her face filled with relief. He had long ago noticed that her face was softest and most open when she was relieved, and he loved those moments with her. Something about the puffiness of her cheeks and lips made him want to kiss her.

"Okay, thank you," she said, and hung up. But then, as quickly as they had come, the joy and relief faded. Her eyes clouded and shrank, her cheeks paled, and the beauty evaporated like a mirage.

"Where did you get it?"

JW laughed. "I'm not gambling, if that's what you think. Frank finally paid me for a project I've been working on for him. I told you things would begin to work out."

She softened, glanced at the money, and then looked back at him. Color came back to her cheeks. "I'm sorry. I've just been so stressed out. I've never had a job!"

"With all due respect, I beg to differ. You have been a community volunteer for a number of important organizations, and a wonderful wife and mother. Those have been huge jobs."

She smiled gratefully. "Thank you."

He leaned forward and cupped his hand over one of hers. She still wore the large diamond wedding ring he had given her. It wobbled like a loose tooth under his palm.

"Carol, you've been so patient with me, and you've carried

such a heavy load while I—well, I just lost it. I couldn't ... Chris dying just, it was like it pulled the rug out from under me and there was no floor there. And you know the fact that I didn't help him with his brakes has weighed on me every hour of every day. It sounds like an excuse, and I don't mean to make an excuse."

She inhaled and looked at the wall.

"I put you through so much that you didn't sign up for," he told her. "I get that. But I want you to know that I'm finally recovering. Things will get better now, I promise."

"Oh, John—"

Her tone said that she had already moved on. "Carol. Look at me. Look at me. I'm not asking you to make a long-term commitment. I just need you to take one last chance with me. Just one. Because I will do anything for you and Julie, and I mean it. Anything. I have made a deal with Frank, and I will earn everything back and then some. If I do this right. Millions. You always said that family comes first. Okay?" She was frowning, troubled, and it made him think he was getting through to her. "The least we could do is to try for our daughter," he went on, "and for all the time and heartache we've already invested. Okay? Are you with me?"

He nodded toward the pile of cash. "That's just a down payment."

She smiled softly and shook her head.

"Forget the job," JW continued. "I mean, don't leave it yet, but soon. I want to take you to Europe. To Venice, and Santorini, like we always said."

"Not London?"

"London! Of course, London! How could I forget?"

Her eyes moistened and she ran her knuckles on her chin. "It's like when you got your first paycheck from the bank," she said. "Do you remember?" She smiled.

"I cashed it in and gave it all to you."

"At this very table. Why did you do that?"

JW shrugged, searching his memory. "It was ... a tribute."

She laughed, but JW could hear the sadness in it. "Why? You didn't think you were good enough?"

"Frankly, I don't know."

"I remember when I first saw you at the stable, riding and teaching riders. You seemed so sure of yourself. I liked that, I really did. When did we ever stop riding?"

JW smiled at her. "Well, we certainly can again. We can buy Olson's Stables! I've even been training a kid on the reservation, and it's been a real—well," he paused, pushing the thought and his feelings for Jacob aside. "I'm more than happy to ride with you, any time." He stood. "I'll have our daughter back by ten. Then maybe you and I can talk. That's all I want. Just to talk."

She smiled again, but her eyes communicated uncertainty. He loved her complex smiles as much as he feared them. Somehow it made her alluring, made him want to please her.

"Maybe," she said.

He kissed her, tasting her peppermint lip balm.

Julie was sitting on the blue-flowered cushion of the bay window, texting one of her friends. The incoming light cast a shade of red into her fine golden hair, and he was overcome by the desire to swoop her up into his arms as he had so many times when she was little.

"Come on, Sunshine," he said, "let's hit the road!"

They headed outside and down the walk toward the wild rice truck, and seeing it there, he was reminded of his own duplicity. But he had to reclaim his family, he told himself. And now, finally, the stakes were right. Not peanuts, but millions. He wouldn't betray Johnny for less than a fortune. He knew this was a dangerous game, but if the plan worked and he could protect himself from Frank while securing his stake, it would be some short-term pain for a very long-term gain. He would make it up to Johnny, and to Jacob. He had decided he would even offer Johnny a job, Schmeaker's job, and he would send Jacob to a college of his choosing. He imagined them working at the bank as a team, Johnny securing the tribal deposits, perhaps even dedicating a small portion of the casino deposits to a special loan fund, if the band would guarantee the loans. It would all work out. He would see to it.

The truck's front seat was covered with a wolf-like fur throw, plush and slippery in its wildness. Julie hunkered low in the thickness of it, her shoulder collapsed against the door, until they got out onto the highway. JW watched her strange posture—her long limbs folded up and pale as polished marble, her head below the window—and he suddenly realized that she was hiding. She was embarrassed to be seen in the truck. He was used to driving it by now, and he laughed and shook his head as he turned onto the highway, heading toward Northland Mall.

. "So, how's school going?" he said, trying to strike up a conversation. It was a new year in a new school, junior high, and Julie was likely swamped.

"Fine."

He asked how her classes were, and she parried with a series of monosyllabic answers, her lips small and bloodless, her thumbs pressing away at the black glass of her cell phone. He tried pointing to the trees and asking if she could identify the species, but she was obviously absorbed, and eventually he fell silent. It had recently rained on this section of highway, and the tires made a washing hiss against the underside of the truck as they drove.

"Should we listen to some music?" he said.

"Sure."

He turned on the Clapton tape, and soon they were both lost in thought. As they drove past the Many Lakes Casino he reflected on how much of his life had circled around gambling in one way or another—from his play to win Carol's affection to the risk assessments and deal structures he put in place in crafting the bank's more profitable loans. In fact, what investors and even bankers were doing in the financial markets could increasingly be described as gambling, and they all thought that they, too, could game the system. They did it with derivatives or ETFs or alternative investments, throwing large portions of the economy into danger. All of it had an element of risk and reward, of betting on an insecure outcome. Even the president spoke about Americans' "appetite for risk," as if it were a good thing. JW had shared this unexamined belief for most of his life, but now he wasn't so sure.

And it was also true, he thought, that America was particularly steeped in the idea. The American dream itself was a giant gamble, after all. It took unreasonable optimism to pack up and leave a country of origin, to risk it all based on hope for a better opportunity in a country one had never seen. That same brand of optimism had led him to believe that he could control his fate, that the world was just, that hard work paid off, and that people got what they deserved. But then a deer jumped out in front of Chris at the wrong moment.

For a long time he had wanted to believe that this terrible accident could have been prevented. But that belief had itself become a cancer—for if it could have been prevented, it was almost surely his fault. This thought was unbearable, and he suddenly realized, glancing over at Julie, that it was also unfair. To all of them.

Julie was slouched back in the seat with her feet up on the dashboard and her cell phone between her ivory knees, her painted toenails stuck with stars. He wondered what thinking he and Carol had imbued in her about risk-taking, about life and what was really important. He wondered, and worried.

"Julie? How come you don't play outside anymore?"

She shrugged at her phone. "'Cause I'm growing up?"

He tried to picture her not as a teenager, but as a young woman in her twenties. And he was somewhat shocked to find that it was suddenly possible. But what he couldn't imagine was her soul. Would she be a risk-taker, or would she be frightened after his breathtaking downhill run, frozen on the bunny hill of a smaller, safer, but ultimately less satisfying life?

Ahead lay a scenic overlook—a small gravel turn off the highway, bounded by a low limestone wall that overlooked an old mine pit. It had long since flooded and had become a favorite swimming hole in his youth. It was rumored that a mining office, a barracks, and two backhoes still stood ready under eighty feet of water, and sometimes JW had seen what he thought were their shadows far below. He and his friends would jump from the high stone bluffs, soaring like birds for forty or fifty feet—a full four- or five-second drop—before plunging into the cool water. The sense of freedom and danger combined to create a giddy, out-of-control high that was better than any drug, and it was supercharged by the sudden swoosh of cool as they arced into the depths like dolphins. Not surprisingly, the sheriff had long since put an end to it.

"Hey," he said, looking over at Julie, "instead of shopping, let's do something crazy."

Julie looked up at him from her cell phone. He saw a spark of interest.

"What?"

He pulled sharply off the highway into the turnoff. Julie sat up, looking frightened and surprised as she grabbed at the door. JW slammed on the brakes and crunched to a sudden stop in a cloud of gravel dust.

"What are you doing!?"

JW took the hundred-dollar bill out of his shirt and held it out to her. "Come on. You can spend that later with your girlfriends. Let's do something fun."

She took the bill as he got out of the truck. He stood in the open door and struggled out of his suit jacket. "Hurry up! Leave your cell phone under the seat. You can tuck the bill under it."

She frowned and laughed at the same time, then stuck them under the seat and got out. She fluffed her hair as he closed his door and came around the hood of the old truck. He reached out a hand to her.

"Have you ever been here?"

"You're taking me on a walk?"

"Oh no, it's much better than that. Come on. You'll see."

She shook her head as if to communicate how intolerably weird her dad was to anyone who might be watching—but she took his hand. They climbed over the stone wall, down a rocky path through the brush, and onto a high stone bluff that jutted out over the water. "I always imagined taking you and Chris here when you got older, but then they made it illegal," he said, kicking off his dress shoes.

Julie's expression was both scared and delighted, which is exactly what he'd hoped for. It was a flash of the old Julie, of Julie the wondrous child.

"The jump rock? You're going to fricking jump?"

"I am, and you're coming with me. We'll hold hands."

"But you're in your suit."

"I won't tell if you don't. Come on, it's fun."

He held a hand out to her. She was smiling, but she also looked unsure about the proposal.

"Trust me, Julie. You'll want to do it again, I promise."

"Are you sure?"

"I did this literally hundreds of times as a kid."

"But it's like fifty feet," she said, peering over the edge. The rocky outcropping seemed to jut out from the cliff. It fell off to either side, and junipers grew up from below the edges.

"Something like that. You just have to remember to keep your feet together so you don't get an enema."

She laughed. "You're crazy."

"That's what I was hoping you'd say. You coming?"

She looked at him and then, suddenly, she took his hand and they were running. He heard her laughing and screaming at his side as the edge came up, and then they were flying and falling, arms waving and yelling, and— and—and—whoosh! The water engulfed them in its cold clasp. They fought back toward the surface, Julie's pale limbs cutting the water above him like barkless branches.

When he broke into the air she was gasping and roaring like an animal. He gulped in air and spit water and laughed. His tie floated by his face. She looked around, treading water, and started swimming toward the rocky shore.

"You like it?"

"No!"

"No!?"

"I'm freezing, and I think you made me crap my pants!"

He laughed. "Well, tread water and rinse it out."

"I'm joking!"

They climbed out amid angular chunks of stone on the

shoreline, taking careful steps to avoid cutting their feet. Beyond the chunks lay a rocky brown path, and Julie trotted up it, hugging herself and shivering dramatically, dripping a trail of water as she headed back up to the bluff. He tried to stay with her, but she was like a mountain goat.

"Can you wait up?"

"I'm freezing!"

"Okay, go ahead, I'll meet you up top."

She scampered out of sight. He had hoped she'd want to go again, but that seemed out of the question. He laughed to himself as he followed the dark drips of her trail, recalling her incredulous reaction at the top of the bluff. But she had done it.

When he finally got to the top her sandals were gone. He picked up his shoes, his suit pants and dress shirt sticking to him like wet bedsheets. The air was warm, but he was shivering, and storm clouds were blowing in from the west. The warm truck would feel good. As he climbed up the path to the turnoff he heard a voice—and when he crested the top he realized it was the sound of a police dispatcher. Julie stood shivering next to Dan Barden's county cruiser. He was tall and well-built, in his thirties, with close-cropped, dark brown hair. Dan was Bob Grossman's colleague on the Bass County patrol. As JW stepped up to the wall, a carload of boys drove by on the highway, honking and yelling at Julie. She turned away, mortified. JW stepped over the wall and laughed.

"Hey Dan, how's it going?"

"So it is you. I didn't believe it when she told me."

JW glanced at the wild rice truck. Of course. He laughed. He stood there in his suit pants, shirt, and tie, dripping wet.

"Just showing her the jump rock."

"You know that's illegal. I could take you in for trespassing, or endangering a minor."

"Oh, for Pete's sake! How many times you jump off that rock as a kid?"

"I don't make the laws."

"Well, if you're going to do it, arrest her, not me. It was her idea."

Julie looked at him, aghast. "What? That's a lie!"

"I'm kidding!"

He shook his head and turned back to Barden. "I'm sorry, Dan, I just—" Suddenly emotion welled up in him and he couldn't explain it. "Can you let it go this time?"

Barden looked concerned, but moved. "Yeah, sure." He turned to Julie. "Just don't let me catch you doing that again, okay? Your dad has some crazy ideas lately."

Julie nodded. JW had no doubt that she would follow Barden's instructions.

"Okay," Barden said, and gestured toward the truck. Julie hurried to it and climbed inside. "She's pretty cold. You better hurry and get her home."

"She'll be okay."

Barden nodded, still skeptical, then turned back to his cruiser.

JW called after. "Hey. Sometimes you gotta do crazy things."

Barden nodded again, then got into the car.

JW was a sopping mess. He reached into his pocket for the truck keys and realized with a sudden horrible rush that the digital recorder was still in his pants pocket. He took the recorder out and looked at it, hoping he could dry it out, but saw that he had left the power switch on. The display was blank.

His heart filled with rocks. It couldn't be. He had destroyed his evidence, his insurance policy against Jorgenson. He wanted to vomit. His head was tingling. He put his hands to his forehead. Suddenly there was a loud blare and he looked up and saw Julie leaning over and honking the truck horn.

His legs were weak and the joy had left him. He shuffled to the truck and opened the door.

"Come on! I'm freezing!"

"Okay," he managed to say. "Okay." He looked up, and shook out of it. "I'm sorry," he said, getting in. "Here." He held up his suit jacket and gestured to her.

"I'll get it all wet."

"It doesn't matter."

She looked worried now, realizing that his mood had suddenly changed dramatically. She leaned forward and he draped it around her.

He pulled his door shut like a zombie and started the truck. He put the heat on max and sat for a second and closed his eyes. Then he backed out.

"I don't ever want to do that again," she said once they were out on the highway, heading back toward North Lake.

"Why not?"

The mood was suddenly pensive and brittle.

"I don't know. It scared me."

"Sometimes being scared is okay."

Neither one of them said another word the rest of the way home, but as he pulled up in front of the house and shifted into park, he turned to her.

"Julie, I'm sorry. But listen, what we did wasn't crazy. Everything good in life has a little risk to it. That's what makes living fun."

She shook her head as though she couldn't believe what he was saying. "Is that why you gamble?"

It felt like a kick to the stomach. "No, I don't think so. But I'm not gambling anymore."

"Yeah, well, we'll see how long that lasts."

She shrugged out of his suit jacket, opened the truck, and got out.

26

Carol was curled up on a sofa in the family room when he entered, the giant brass rubbings of old English tombs looming over her. The TV was blaring commercials. Julie was already upstairs, her music going in the bathroom and the shower running. His clothes were almost dry from the truck heater, except for his socks, which he peeled off by the door.

"What happened to your shoes?" Carol asked.

He went over and sat down next to her. The wool felt warm on his feet. "I took her to the jump rock."

"You did what?"

"I needed to break through to her somehow."

Carol noticed that his clothes were still damp. She shook her head, but then appeared to soften.

"It's a confusing time for her," she said.

"We still got time together. That's what counts." He looked out the bay window at the sunset. "Remember when Chris was her age? All he ever wanted to do was hang out."

She smiled. "I used to get so jealous," she said. "You got all the fun stuff."

"Work in the workshop, work in the garage. 'Hey dad, hey dad,' I couldn't get a thought in edgewise. I used to get mad at him for it. I don't know how I lost him."

She reached out and he felt her thin fingers take his cool

hand. She wrapped it in hers and rested them both on her hip. "You didn't lose him," she said. "You were a good dad."

"Thank you."

"But your hair could use a little help."

He laughed and looked down at their entwined fingers, then up at the amused smile on her face. The lamp on the table behind her cast a warm glow, backlighting her blonde hair. He leaned in to kiss her, but she put a hand gently up to his lips to stop him. She shook her head slightly.

"John," she said, searching his eyes. Her pupils were big and dark, incredibly dark. She had an air that felt almost apologetic. "You walked away from us. You weren't there." Her face went pale and she swallowed and breathed in. "I want to pursue this thing with Jim."

There was no sound. He looked into her eyes, trying to connect through the fog of adrenaline. He was suddenly two people. He was himself, and he was someone else, a viewer watching the scene as if it were a movie. His ears pulsed and it became increasingly hard to concentrate. Then he became aware of the noise from the TV again.

"Honey, this is our life—" he said.

But she was rushing forward now, almost as if this were a script she had rehearsed many times. She spoke with more passion than necessary, as if he were putting up an enormous argument. "He takes me to luncheons, he goes to church with me. He got me into a career. I'm finally taking care of myself, and Julie—"

"Honey. We've had a little bump. But we never—I mean, it's you and me. We're getting through it. I'll get you money, I told you—"

"It's not about the money, John!"

She was slipping away from him. It couldn't be happening. "No, listen—"

"You left! John! Look at me!"

He realized he was staring into space. He looked at her and saw that her cheeks were swollen and flushed. A tear ran over the soft pomegranate skin of her cheek. She reached up and held his face in her palms. "I've moved on. It's not fair to ask me to act as if the last year never happened. It's not." She searched his face.

He leaned his elbows on his knees, held his hands, looked at the coffee table. Piled newspapers and *People* magazines. Crosswords partially completed in handwriting he didn't recognize. Commercials were still playing on the TV. Such a short time had passed, and yet it contained an eternity. What did the last twenty years mean? Why had he given her his first paycheck? He had married the town beauty queen. They had been the most likely to succeed. They had a boy and a girl. And then they didn't.

"Can you tell me if you ever loved me?"

"Oh, John. Don't."

She looked away at the commercials and held her elbows as tears flowed down her cheeks.

He finally stood and headed for the door. He was shaking and weak. He stood there for a moment, his forehead pressed against the cool white enamel, listening to her cry. And then he opened the door and went out into the dusk, leaving his wet socks on the floor behind.

It began to mist heavily on the way home, and the air cooled. He turned the heat on to warm his feet. The white searchlight teepee bled out over the windshield as he neared the casino, and the neon colors throbbed and ran as he turned into the lot. He pulled over and watched the entrance, blurry in the mist. Under the portico, people surged in and out. He unrolled the window and listened. He could hear their laughter and excitement, and beyond them the faint chinking of the slot machines and their little voices of encouragement.

The wipers cycled, and he sat staring at the neon lights, bleeding out as mist re-accumulated. He listened to the old sounds of comfort and celebration, imagining the stale cigarette smoke and the savory thwacking of cards being shuffled, the soft clicks of the chips and the barks of laughter. Hit me. Hold. The song came back to him as Willie Nelson had sung it: clear, soulful, and thin as an old hillbilly psalm. *The other night dear, as I lay sleeping, I dreamed I held you in my arms. When I awoke dear, I was mistaken, So I hung my head and I cried.*

He sat and listened for a while longer, then started the truck and shifted into drive. He sat idling with his foot on the brake, trying to empty his mind. The windshield was washed a rusty indigo, and it flashed him back momentarily to the deep acidic water of the old mine. He took his foot off the brake. The truck crept forward. He turned the wheel and gave it a little gas so he didn't block the person turning into the drive behind him. Then he turned onto the highway and slowly, slowly, ran the truck up to speed, feeling the pull of gravity where his bones had once been.

It was cold and damp as he neared home. The reservation road sank into pools of fog so thick he slowed to a milky creep. He rolled up the windows and turned the heater back on, filling the cab with the sharp musty odor of mouse turds. The road swam and the trees ran alongside in a black tunnel. The wipers left concentric arcs of water, blurring everything. He drove hunched forward and squinting like an old man.

Twenty minutes later, he parked near the paddock and turned the engine off. Outside, frogs and crickets sang in a resounding chorus. He stepped out into the racket and walked to the lean-to, where he hung the keys on a nail inside the door. As it had been the night after the fire, everything was wet with dew. Pride was in his stall. The rice tarps had been taken in and the pole-barn doors were closed tight against the mist. The houses on the hill were dark. The yard lamp on the peak of the *stolpe låven*'s gable was surrounded by a fuzzy halo of water.

JW walked across the gravel road, his shadow running long and jerky before him in the mist. His head throbbed on the sides and behind his eyes as he turned onto the grassy drive that led up to his trailer.

The wooden steps were black and soft with water. He saw a wavy paper note taped to his door. The blue ink was blurred, but he could still make out the lettering in the faint light. *Stay away from my family.*

He took it down and went in, pulling the thin metal door shut behind him. He turned on the overhead light in the kitchen and saw that he had left the windows open, soaking everything within six inches of them. He went around and closed them. The warmth of early September was disappearing, and for the first time he could feel the deep cold of the coming winter.

The trailer had a propane furnace in a metal-faced cabinet next to the bathroom. It had a pale grill speckled with small spots of rust. He had never tried to use it, but now he lifted the grill off its pegs and set it aside. He held the tiny silver pilot knob down and heard the faint hiss of propane. He bloodied his knuckles in the small sharp spaces and burned his fingertips with match after match, but he couldn't get it lit. He finally gave up and turned off the pilot. The air was pregnant with gas. He crawled into bed in his damp office clothes, but began to feel like he was smothering. He cracked a window even though it let in the cold and damp, got back into bed, and drew the blankets around him.

If he just lay still, part of him thought, maybe the world would change, and this would have all been an illusion, a bad dream, an alternate reality. If he stayed like this, shivering and still, maybe he could hold off the compulsion of the casino that was again washing over him. He felt the blankets around him, pilled and comforting as a musty childhood teddy bear. He had almost forgotten the craving, the incessant gnawing to avoid the bad feeling, to stave off the depression. His family, his job, his home, his identity—gone.

A shiver came over him and he pulled the blankets tighter. The mattress above his pillow felt cold and wet.

IV

THE PLAY

27

Jacob lay on his bed playing *World of Warcraft,* but he couldn't stop thinking about his mom. For a long time after she died it had seemed natural to want to call or text her, or to ask for her advice on the various challenges associated with being an Indi'n kid in mostly white society. The habit of her presence lingered, as if she were just away at a powwow: hard to reach, but due back soon.

It wasn't so much letting go of her presence as it was the habit of her, the placeholder, that was hardest, because it left a hole where nothing fit, a hole that stayed open and sore and reminded him over and over that she was gone, and that she wasn't ever coming back. It was this void that drove him to do stupid things. He was sure of that because he hadn't done them when she was around, at least not as much. She had corralled him, set up the sidewalls to his paddock, and kept him facing his tarps and moving forward. Now there was nothing, and sometimes he forgot.

These days random memories would intrude and he would have to stop the game lest he be killed. He set it aside, lay back on his pillow, and stared at the ceiling. She had worked the early shift at the bank so she could be there the second he got off the bus. He remembered their afternoon snacks together, and how she made sure he did his homework and practiced the piano. Somehow her pushing made the drudgery that accompanied these tasks tolerable, even satisfying.

"You know how much I love you?" she would say.

"A lot," he would reply.

"No, not that much. Just more than anything else."

Her laughter had always been an invitation to joy. She had dimples, and her teeth gleamed broad and flat in the sun. He could feel her hands on him, pulling his tight shirt over his head, mussing his hair, smearing it flat with spit, wiping his chin, pulling his ear, sending him out to school, grabbing his biceps tightly when she raised her voice and told him no.

They had a game when he was little. "Are you a red boy or a blue boy?" she'd ask.

"Blue!" he would yell.

"Are you a fast boy or a slow boy?"

"Fast!" he would yell.

The choices defined him: blue, fast, smart, hungry, musical, surprising, jumping.

"Do you want to go to bed before your bath or after?"

"After!"

She took him to his lessons, to his haircuts and his appointments. She made him get braces and then made sure he brushed his teeth around them in order to avoid polka dots in the enamel. She checked his toothbrush to make sure it was freshly wet. She argued with him and made him do chores, and she yelled at him when he sloughed off responsibility.

His afternoons were always busy, and as they drove to piano or did homework over cookies, she would ask him about his day. How did he feel about what had happened? How interesting was the latest assignment? How would he deal with the latest boring worksheet? Then she would tell him about his father. He was going to be a little late, but it was because he was doing great things. Everybody at the bank looked up to him with pride, and Jacob was lucky to have such a great dad.

It had been two years since she died, but it felt like a
lifetime to Jacob. His afternoons had become void and gray.
Everything was flat and lifeless. Piano no longer held any interest, and doing homework made him feel as if he were ban-
ishing her memory with each stroke of the pen. How could
anyone simply go on alone, he wondered? Life shouldn't be
normal after something like this. We should go crazy. We
should go into the woods and tear off our clothes, and scrub
our skin with sticks, never to return.

After the funeral, after grandma and grandpa went back
to California, after *Papa Mooshum* left, he was alone. When
the school day was finished, he would spend long hours playing video games, until his dad came home with take-out, or
picked him up to go get sushi or Mexican. Then they would
sit and his dad would ask, "So, how was your day?"

"Okay," he'd say.

"You get your homework done?"

"Yeah."

But he wouldn't check.

The next spring Papa Mooshum died. Jacob's grandfather
had been sending him weekly cassette tapes since his mom's
funeral, his grainy voice telling stories about her as a little
girl, coughing through his emphysema in some echoey room.
Jacob initially loved listening to them, but with time his voice
grew more and more distant. And then when he died, the last
vestiges of her presence in Jacob's daily life came to an end,
leaving a gaping hole where the placeholder had been.

He wound up in detention, where he met other kids who
had empty placeholders in their lives. In their shared broken-
ness, they had a common language, and they found that they
could understand one another without talking. He began hanging out with them more often after school, filling the abandon-

ment with spray cans and baseball bats, with baggy shorts and more fighting. And then he started skipping school altogether.

Jacob felt the void even more acutely now. It had weakened in some ways over time, but recently he had been feeling more out of sorts. Uncomfortable. He got up and went down to the lean-to to brush Pride. It was calming. Here and here and here, he ran his hands over the immense creature in the salty dimness. This is where you put your foot, your hand, your butt. He pressed his ear against the horse's broad neck and felt the warmth of him on his cheek. He wrapped his arms around him, and Pride stood still while he did. You keep your mind inside the animal, he thought. You lose yourself and become one, that's what JW had said. He stood with his eyes closed and imagined.

The oneness fed him as he went back to brushing, almost as much as the structure and the guidance he'd always found in his lessons. He missed those lessons. It had been three days now since he and his father had had their latest big fight. When his father told him JW was no longer allowed to be around him, he had pushed him, almost knocking him over. He had been grounded ever since, and he had begun to drift. Pride's skin flicked at the brush.

The air inside the lean-to was warm and humid and smelled of horse. Outside it had turned cool and crisp after the mist blew away with the dawn, and the leaves were colored brightly beneath the fiercely blue sky. He wanted to get out in them with the horse. And now JW was gone. He had banged on the trailer door, but there was no answer. He had gone around the windows, but the curtains were closed and the heater was not on, and he found that he was angry, in a way that made him even angrier, because there was no name for it.

Jacob put a halter on Pride and clipped on a lead rope. He

unhitched the stall gate and led the horse out nickering to the paddock. As Jacob turned back to get him some hay, he heard the rez kids' car thumping down the hill past his aunt Mona's. He pulled two flakes of alfalfa from the open bale and heard the music stop. As he walked back out, carrying the hay, he saw Hayhoe getting out from behind the wheel.

"Hey," he said, walking toward Jacob with his hands in his pockets. He was tall and languid, and wearing a thread-bare army jacket.

Jacob threw the hay over the railing to Pride and turned to face him, ready for anything.

"Yeah, what?"

"We heard somebody torched your dad's bank and the town fire department just watched it burn," Hayhoe said.

There was no hint of teasing in his voice, which Jacob found surprising. "Yeah," he said.

Hayhoe held a cigarette between his thumb and fingers and pointed it at Jacob as he talked. "You may be an apple, but we gotta stick together on this."

"I don't know what you're talking about."

"Okay," said Hayhoe. He leaned on the rail to watch Pride. "I'm sorry we scared him."

"It's all right."

"You think that's right, what they did?"

"No."

"You think anybody's ever gonna fuckin' pay?" He looked at Jacob, his elbows still on the rail. He looked upset, as if he had been robbed.

"There's some law. There wasn't anything they could do."

"You believe that? There's a law that says the fire department can't put out a fire?"

Jacob shrugged.

Hayhoe took another drag and shook his head. One of the other kids in the car honked the horn, and he turned and yelled, "Fuck you, just give me a minute!"

He stomped his cigarette out and walked over closer to Jacob. "Come on, you're one of us now, and there's only so much shit we can take. Know what I'm sayin'?"

"I guess."

"So let's do somethin' back. It's called standing up for your rights. Okay?"

"Okay."

"Yeah."

Hayhoe held up a fist to Jacob, and he touched it with his own. Then he followed Hayhoe over to the car and got in the back, next to one of the others. He immediately noticed the smell of pot smoke.

"Gentlemen, meet Jacob. Jacob, this is Jeremy and Cheese Whiz."

Hayhoe stepped on the gas and the Maverick shot off down the road, scattering a sweep of heart-shaped yellow aspen leaves in its wake.

* * *

THE SOUND OF the car reached JW in his trailer, where he lay in the same fetal position he had assumed three nights before. Aside from going to the bathroom, drinking water, pulling off his tie, and eating a couple saltine crackers, he hadn't moved. He'd just lain there, staring at the wall. He wore the same wrinkled suit pants and dress shirt. He was razor-stubbled and mussy-haired, and the blanket was pulled to his chin. He was folded inside himself like the old collapsed barn on the side of the reservation road. Carol was gone. Chris was gone. Julie was a gulf away. He imagined Carol in their bed with Jim, and Jim with his hand on Julie's shoulder. It tied his intestines in knots.

28

The boys got drunk in the woods with four cans of Pit Bull
that Jeremy stole from the back of his aunt Lena's fridge at the
bait shop near the public access to North Lake. Jacob watched
him over the pile of old stones they called grandfathers and
sipped on his beer, the bubbly bitterness filling his head with
cotton batting. Jeremy was lanky and tall, and though it was a
brisk day he wore only a jean jacket over his bare chest, which
was tattooed with crossed tomahawks. Jeremy had told them
about how his uncle Goose sometimes drifted back into town,
and when he did, he always had a case of Pit Bull in the back
of the fridge so he could deal with Lena's nagging. But nobody
had seen Goose in over two months, and some people were
saying that he had gotten himself arrested in Duluth. Jeremy
figured that by the time he came back he might have forgotten
how many beers he had in there, so he said they should stop
by and nab some of them. He distracted Lena by introducing her to Jacob while Hayhoe and Cheese Whiz raided the
fridge and stuck the beers in Cheese Whiz's school backpack.
They all looked at the minnows and suckers for a minute, and
argued over the best places to catch sturgeon, then piled back
out into the car.

Now they sat in the remnants of a sweat lodge Goose
had held with his cousin Cocoa Butter when he was on
vacation from his job at the DNR. People called him Cocoa
Butter because he was always putting sunscreen on. The

two men had said they wanted to initiate the younger guys, so they made Jeremy and Hayhoe and Cheese Whiz dig up and carry grandfathers all day. The boys had to ask each rock if it wanted to come, "and some of those fuckers were heavy," said Hayhoe. The birch branches from their deer-hide wigwam stood around them like an empty rib cage as they sipped on their twenty-four-ounce gold cans.

"It was a big deal and the grandmas were all smiley about it for like a week," Hayhoe said. They laughed and pried at the pile of grandfathers with sticks. He threw one of the rocks at Cheese Whiz, who was reading an ACT practice book.

"Hey, Harvard, don't worry about it so much."

Cheese Whiz toed the rock back into the pile. "Chill out, dude. If I don't get into Harvard my uncle said he's gonna disown me." Jacob could see that he was writing a lot of math symbols in the margins.

"His uncle's a big lawyer in Minneapolis, represents the band," explained Hayhoe. "Lotta pressure for such a little brain."

"So what's it like living in the city?" Jeremy asked, turning to Jacob.

"I don't know. It can be pretty tough, but in different ways."

"Gangbangers and bullshit," said Jeremy.

Jacob shrugged, and Hayhoe spoke up again. "I lived there for a while with my dad. It can be tough. That Little Earth."

"I didn't go around there too much," Jacob said.

The sky glowed big and deep azure as the sun began to set, and they made a fire and threw on some sweet grass, which Hayhoe told Jacob was holy. Then they set up the empty beer cans on a log and Hayhoe showed them how to shoot them with his gun. He had stolen it from a hobo he'd found sleeping in the train yard down by the feedlot in Saint Paul.

"You got to lock your elbow," Hayhoe said to Jacob, adjusting his arm. The gun was heavy. "It's all about force and acceleration, right Cheesy? Otherwise the shot'll go wild. Give it a try."

Jacob squeezed and the gun recoiled like a throw baler. The can fell to the ground and Hayhoe clapped Jacob on the back, his beer-drenched breath washing over him. "You're a good shot! Kid's good!"

They went through half a box of his cousin TV Boy's ammo, setting the cans up and slowly peppering them with holes. The Indians up here all had nicknames like that, Jacob had learned. TV Boy, Cocoa Butter, Cheese Whiz. Almost no one was referred to by their real name, except when their grandmothers were mad or if somebody wanted to make some kind of point, and it was hard to keep them all straight. They stopped at Jeremy's grandmother's house, where they all ate fry bread and listened to her old stories about all the sex people used to have. The powdered sugar made Jacob's dirty fingers sticky and brown. They raided her garden shed for the gas cans Jeremy said she kept there, then drove in to North Lake.

* * *

JACOB SAT IN the back seat, his head buzzing from the sugar and the beer. They all laughed most of the way, the headlights coming at them like reverse beacons, and Jacob suddenly realized they were under the yellow glow of the big metal canopy at the Food 'n' Fuel. They piled out of the car, and the cool air washed him into a clearer attention.

"Is your grandma a sex fiend?" he asked Jeremy.

"She's always talkin' like that," he shrugged.

"I think she'd hump a tree if it wasn't stuck in the ground," said Hayhoe. He took the two rusty gas cans out of the trunk. They pulled off the cork-gasketed lids and started pumping vaporous green gas into them. "Man, those cans are old school," noted Cheese Whiz as they watched the vapors pour out of their wide mouths and run down over the concrete.

"Poboy alert," said Jeremy. They all turned and watched Grossman's car fly by on the highway.

"He can stop us all he wants," shrugged Hayhoe. "We ain't got nothing, just gettin' ready to cut some grass for our grandmothers, be upstanding citizens."

"Make your grandmother's place look citified," said Cheese Whiz.

"You boys need to make certain the yards on the reservation look as clean and upstanding as our yards do here in town," said Jeremy in his best uptight white-alderman voice. They all laughed, and then Hayhoe clicked the pump off.

Hayhoe ditched the car in a wooded path off a damp gravel road. They took turns carrying the heavy gas cans through the cut wheat field that lay between the woods and the back of the bank. They set them on the lawn between the building and the back drive, stretched their tired arms, and Hayhoe unscrewed the top of the first can.

"This is for your dad, man," he said, looking at Jacob. "You're both part of us now. We stick together, Indi'n to Indi'n." He hoisted the can and poured the green liquid over the log siding, darkening it in the moonlight. Jacob could smell the thick stench of it. Jeremy and Cheese Whiz took turns pouring from the other can as Hayhoe handed his can to Jacob. "Okay, little bro, your turn. Don't get it on your shoes or they'll know who did it."

Jacob's hand closed around the old wooden handle. He lifted it and felt the gas sloshing back and forth inside. He splashed some out onto the log walls just as Cheese Whiz struck a light.

The flame leaped toward Jacob in a sudden giant woof of yellow heat. "Holy shit!" yelled Jeremy.

Hayhoe yanked Jacob back by the collar. They stumbled backward and fell to the pavement, the gas can draining on its side beside them.

"Fuckin' assholes, you almost burnt us!" said Hayhoe.

"The gas can!" said Jacob.

The fire quickly took hold. Hayhoe scrambled for the can and ran it into the field. The boys followed, then turned and looked at the blaze in frightened wonder.

"Jesus," said Cheese Whiz.

"We gotta go!" said Jeremy. He began screwing on a gas cap. Hayhoe found the other cap on the edge of the grass, and they hoisted and lugged the cans back through the field, running and looking behind them as the fire continued to grow.

"Jesus, it's going fast, huh?" observed Hayhoe.

A powerful fear rose in Jacob as he ran through the sharp bristle. He thought of Grossman, who had roughed him up when he had arrested him before, and he thought of how mad his dad would be if he got caught again, especially over the bank. JW's old bank. "I can't be caught doing this," he said.

"Don't worry," said Hayhoe as he and Jeremy carried the cans back through the field. "We stick together."

Just then, Cheese Whiz yelled, "Cops!"

They saw a sheriff's cruiser racing along the highway toward the bank, its blue and red cherries turning. It pounded up over the curb cut and shot into the bank parking lot, its searchlight cutting out the night.

"Go with him, go!" Hayhoe said to Jacob. "We'll meet you at the car!" He nodded toward Cheese Whiz and Jacob split off with him, the sharp wheat stubble stabbing at his ankles as they angled away into the night.

* * *

GROSSMAN MADE OUT the silhouettes of two people running with gas cans as he finished calling in the fire. He blurped his siren and flipped on his PA. "You there!" he yelled into the mike. "Stop. Put your hands up! Now!" But the figures just kept running deeper into the cut wheat, so he floored it and drove the cruiser out after them. It thumped and yawed and fishtailed in the soft earth, and he heard a rooster tail of mud spraying his wheel wells, then a sick wet thump as the car bottomed out and got stuck in a tractor rut. He shifted into reverse, but the cruiser didn't move.

"Shit!"

He aimed the searchlight at the fleeing forms and got out to give chase, unholstering his service pistol. He had called in the fire as soon as he saw it, and by now he could hear the North Lake Fire Department sirens in the distance.

"You're not gonna get away," he yelled at their backs. "You're only making it worse."

Then one of the two figures stopped while the other kept running. Good, he thought. He could get this one to ID the other.

"Smart move," he yelled, and then there was the flash and bark of a gunshot.

He wasn't knocked out, but it felt as if he had been, even though he was fully aware of the passage of time—every split second of it. Lying on his back in the wheat stubble, Grossman focused on the burning pain in his shoulder. He reached up to touch it, and his world went white with fear when his hand came away hot and sticky with blood. He rolled over in the stubble.

"Oh my god, oh my god," he muttered, and then he threw up into the moist black dirt.

For a few minutes that felt like a lifetime, Grossman lay there on his back, his shoulder throbbing. He imagined other shots whizzing overhead, between him and the flickering sky. There were northern lights. He could hear nothing, but he was certain that if he lifted his head it would be shot off. His heart pounding, he gingerly felt the shoulder with his right hand. The bullet had cut the skin and muscle above his left collar bone, but it was just a flesh wound. He could hear the fire engine arriving, the voices of the firefighters as they hooked up and began battling the fire. And then he heard Dan Barden's voice, calling out to him from near his car. He wanted to answer, but his voice was lost in his chest. Finally, after some effort, he rolled onto his knees, got slowly to his feet, and tottered back over the rutted field.

"My god, Bob, you're hit!" said Barden when he saw him approaching. Beyond him a fire engine stood in the lot. The firefighters trained a hose on the blaze, sending out a cloud of steam that rose white and billowy through the truck's lights and into the night.

"I'm not feeling so well," Grossman replied, and lay back on the hood of his cruiser.

The fire was doused quickly. The damage to the thick logs was minimal, Grossman heard the captain say, as a paramedic daubed his wound with white gauze. "Thanks to your quick action, Bob," he added with a respectful nod.

Against Grossman's better judgment, he let Barden drive him to the North Lake hospital, where he spent three hours getting stitches and a bandage, and then down to County, where he filed a report and called his boss, Big Bill Donovan, at home.

His wife Margie came to pick him up, her face white with fear. She drove him home while Barden went up with a tow truck to retrieve his cruiser.

The days that followed held small rooms and coffee. County deputies and agents from the FBI and the BIA questioned him ad nauseam. Officers canvassed the reservation, the school, the gas stations, and the trading post. They hung out at the Pit Stop, at the Tamarack Restaurant and the Many Lakes Casino, asking questions about who had started the fire, and who had shot Deputy Grossman. It was a full-court press, but the Native Americans weren't talking. Nobody knew anything. Or at least they said they didn't. But Grossman knew they hung together.

Despite searching extensively, the police didn't find the bullet that had hit him. Big Bill actually asked Dan Barden to check Grossman's service pistol to make certain he hadn't inflicted the wound himself, a line of inquiry Grossman found both insulting and laughable.

Big Bill offered him paid leave per union rules, but Grossman insisted on going back on duty the next day, as if nothing had happened. "You fall off a horse, you get back on," he said. It was important to make a statement to the Native kids that they couldn't intimidate him, and it was good PR for his image with the public. Still, for safety's sake, Big Bill reassigned him to the south territory until the investigation was finished.

As he drove up and down the highways around Virginia and Hibbing, Grossman couldn't stop thinking about the shooting. He began to wonder if the bullet hadn't borne some kind of old evil Indian magic curse, infecting him in a spiritual sense. It was irrational, he knew, but over the coming days this conviction took hold.

29

It was on the morning of the third day that JW finally swam
back from the darkness. A metallic smashing and scraping
slowly clarified, eventually taking shape as the clattering
and sizzling of a pan on the stove. He smelled bacon and
heard an egg crack. He turned over, his head dry and thick,
and saw a woman in his galley kitchen.

"Carol?"

"You had no bacon, no eggs, what the hell do you eat
around here?" It was Mona. She had a cigarette going, and
blew smoke into his bedroom.

He turned back to the wall, feeling exhausted in spite of
the fact that he had been in bed for days.

"I like what you've done to the place, though. This one
used to be mine, before we started getting the casino payments."

"Please go away," he said to the wall.

"Go away? I just got here. I tried calling you out with beer
last night, but you wouldn't answer. I figured you were dead or
something, figured I better get down here with some food so
we could all celebrate. There goes another ugly white man."

"Why are you doing this?"

"Because you got a boy out there who needs you. Not that
you noticed. Not that his dad noticed either, he's so damn
fired up about getting that damn bank going. Why don't you
get cleaned up, you look like shit."

JW stared at the wall and listened to her jabbing the bacon around. "I'm serious! Get your ass out of bed!"

He sighed and turned over. After a moment he swung his dead legs slowly down to the floor. He sat still for a moment—a wave of dizziness—then got up and stumbled into the bathroom, clearing his dry throat.

"Don't just take a pee and brush your teeth," he heard her say outside the cardboard-thin door. "I expect a man to be showered and shaved and nicely dressed when I cook him breakfast."

JW flushed the toilet and made it so.

When he stepped back into the kitchen he saw she had found a tablecloth that he didn't even know he had, a bright yellow tourist map of Minnesota, with lumberjacks in the northeast, the Mississippi headwaters in the northwest, and a jumping trout in the center near Brainerd. Laid out on it were plates of purple-brown *mazaan* pancakes, bacon, eggs over easy, coffee, Many Lakes Ojibwe maple syrup, and orange juice. A plastic trash can by the door served as a basket for the unused foodstuffs and cooking utensils she had brought. She seemed happy.

"Move! Sit!"

He slipped onto the bench by the door. The morning was warmer than the last few had been, which he took as a good omen. There were deep half-moons under his eyes that the shower hadn't cured, and his hands were shaky from low blood sugar. A fecund, cool breeze wafted in through the windows and over the tablecloth, smelling of earth, oak bark and leaves.

Mona's shaggy hair hung around her face in the cool morning light. He watched the shifting seas of her eyes as she chewed her bacon, holding a half piece between her fingers.

Indians could have light eyes and even blonde hair, he knew, but her eyes were striking. They had fine dark rims around the irises that gave her a slightly wild quality. JW set down his fork and swallowed.

"Thank you."

"Mmm Hmm. So what are you so depressed about?" She picked up her mug of coffee and held it between her hands, warming them the same way Carol did.

JW laughed painfully and poked at his pancakes with his fork. "Well. I lost my son, my job, my reputation, my house, and all my money. And now I've lost what was left of my family."

"I heard you had a gambling problem. But you're not gambling. You're lying in bed."

JW sighed. "I guess I just decided to feel bad, and that's the safest place to do it."

"Decided to feel bad. Kinda weird."

"Instead of going and gambling it away, which is what I've been doing. I was sitting there in the casino parking lot, and I thought, 'I don't want to go back into the avalanche. I can just sit here and feel this shitty feeling,' you know, 'for one minute. That's doable. Then re-evaluate.' And the minutes have sort of strung together. I'm hoping it'll run out, but I would feel guilty if it did." He shrugged. It sounded stupid.

"Actually, that's sort of profound," she said, then nodded as if that confirmed something, and looked out at the trees. "Although judging from the condition I found you in, I don't know if it's the best long-term strategy."

He snorted and nodded, and they went back to their breakfast.

"I have a question for you," he said finally, and finished swallowing. "How did Jacob's mom die?"

She looked back down at her food. He sensed a sudden

momentousness, as if she didn't want to get into it. She took up her knife and cut off another piece of pancake.

"She OD'd." Her mouth drew into a thin line. She crammed the pancake in and began chewing.

JW nodded slowly. "Did she always do drugs?"

"No. That was my problem." She stared at him defiantly as she stuffed another piece in her mouth. The feathers in her hair hung by her cheek. He could tell that she was ready for a fight, but he had never felt less judgmental. He nodded.

She shook her head and began to pick at her food with the tip of her fork. "She was on the straight and narrow."

"Why did she start?"

"Look, I don't know what he's told you, but it wasn't my fault, okay?"

"I didn't mean that. I don't know anything about it." His voice was gentle. He reached for a way to make her understand, some gift of intimacy. "I used to be real close to my son. I mean, we were"—he shook his head and held up two fingers—"like that. But as he got older, he kinda got away from me. I don't know how. I think I was just too busy. And he just fell in with some rough kids. But maybe it wasn't even that, maybe it was just bad luck. He tried to miss a deer on the highway just east of town, and he crashed. Gone, just like that. After the funeral I … I thought I was fine. You know: the strong husband, man of the family, wife and daughter grieving uncontrollably, but I was okay. And then I just started spending more time at the casino. I don't even know how it happened. I guess it was just a little shot of hope. Or sometimes I think maybe I was just try-ing to fight back against chance, against the fucking bad luck that killed him and ruined my life. And you know what? I have no fucking idea, and it doesn't matter. Things don't always have to make sense."

She nodded slightly, then looked down at her plate. "Her boss at the bank, he used to run the branch up here. He hired her out of high school to come work in Minneapolis."

JW thought he vaguely remembered her, but he couldn't be sure.

"He was really nice to her, told her how smart she was. He kept promoting her, and we all thought, 'God she's really made it.' But then one day she calls me and says she just talked to her boss on her cell. He was back up here, and he called her down in Minneapolis and said that there was a discrepancy in the books, that somebody had reported her. He said he was going to call the FBI. She was totally freaking out. I mean, this girl was valedictorian, okay? Johnny was her dream. Building this bank was her dream. There's no way she would put all that in jeopardy by stealing."

Mona's righteous anger was rising. JW frowned and shook his head in agreement.

"She drove all the way up here to show him proof, but she was nervous." Mona swallowed, and looked out at the leaves, her chin on the butt of her hand and her wild eyes shining. "She got careless. Fucking girl just got careless."

"What do you mean?" JW asked. He felt certain he was on the cusp of something.

She sighed deeply. Rather than look at him, she told the story to the trees. "Her boss was in a room at the casino hotel. He didn't want proof. At first she thought she didn't have any choice. I mean, what woman would put herself in that situation, right? She must have deserved it somehow. But then she told him no. She said 'No!' And he raped her."

JW closed his eyes. "I uh, I ..." He shook his head, fumbling for a new hold on things. "Why didn't she press charges?"

Mona looked back at him. "JW." She spoke to him in the tone of a disappointed mother. Even in her anguish, she was obviously disgusted by the question. "Tribes can't prosecute white people. Don't you know that? And state laws don't apply the same way on reservations. And then he had whatever bullshit 'evidence.' Jorgenson's like you. He works the loopholes."

He looked at her, instantly ashamed. "Like me?"

Mona continued, disregarding his objection. "She bought a morning-after pill and she came here. She wanted to get high and forget all about it before she went home to her man and her baby, and I was—" she froze and her voice broke "—fucking stupid enough to let her." She wept at the trees for a moment, then looked directly back at JW. "Johnny's never forgiven me. And I guess I haven't either."

He sat, frozen, and listened to her quiet sobbing. The sun in the birches' yellow leaves spoke of fall, of vulnerability and decomposition.

30

When the doorbell rang, Jacob was thinking about the fire's aftermath and stabbing his knee with a compass. It was something he had begun doing lately, without knowing why. He sat on the toilet and pushed the sharp end of the compass into the soft skin on the side of his kneecap until it bled. The pain somehow brought focus and some fleeting measure of absolution from his gnawing fear and guilt.

He was at loose ends, his mind shuffling and disjointed. He and Cheese Whiz had split from Hayhoe and Jeremy at the bank and run in a different direction. They heard the gunshot and kept running, afraid that one of the other two had been shot by Grossman. They hid in the trees, afraid to move or make a sound. When the fire was put out, they circled back, only to find that the car was gone. They waited for half an hour, wondering if Hayhoe or Jeremy would come back for them, and then they decided to walk onto the reservation, so no one would know they had been in town. They stayed in the ditches along the highway and cut through the fields to the reservation road, and then Cheese Whiz called his uncle Smokestack, who picked them up from the old sweat-lodge site, where they had been drinking beer earlier in the day. Eagle was angry when he learned that Jacob had left in spite of the fact that he was grounded, but then Jacob told him how they had been at Jeremy's grandmother's, eating fry bread and listening to her stories, and then how Cheese Whiz had shown him how to do a sweat, how they build the lodge out of birch branches and deer hides, but how his uncle Smokestack just uses tarps, why worry about deer hides, but the fire tender would still use a deer antler to carry the hot grandfathers one by one from the fire into the lodge, and then how they would throw sweet grass and water on the hot stones, swatting themselves with fresh branches as they asked the spirits in, Jacob saw his father's face soften. He rushed through the story, making the account so detailed and enthusiastic that his dad finally raised a hand to cut him off. Instead of punishing Jacob, he just sent him to his room with a warning not to do it again.

It wasn't until the next morning that Cheese Whiz called to tell Jacob that it was Grossman who had been shot. Hayhoe and Jeremy had gone to visit relatives in Montana. They agreed to say that Cheese Whiz had spent the evening teaching Jacob about sweats as a way to welcome him into the band.

In the days since, Jacob had lived in terror of someone discovering his role in the bank episode. In hindsight, he realized that he had put everything—their lives here, his father's mission, their relationship—at risk in one stupid moment, and now he was trapped in its looming shadow.

When the doorbell rang, his heart leaped. His dad wasn't home, and the police had been everywhere asking questions. He wiped the blood from his knee with a wad of toilet paper, then tiptoed silently to the front door and peeked through the peephole. It was JW. Jacob stood deliberating for a long moment, then pulled the door open, relieved and angry at the same time.

"Jacob," said JW. His eyes were rimmed with red, as if he

had been crying. "I just learned what happened to your mom. I don't know what to say."

Jacob felt an impulse to slam the door in his face, but another part of him wanted him to apologize. "Where have you even been?" he said.

JW sensed his anger. "I just took a few days off," he said. "I'm sorry. I'm back now."

"And I'm supposed to be happy."

"I thought maybe we could work on the horse."

"Are you fucking kidding me?" How could he tell JW that everything had changed? That he had tried to burn the town bank down? That he was living in terror? That he hated JW for abandoning him? He looked away, at the unfinished living room.

"Okay," replied JW.

"Wait." Jacob didn't know what to say. "Fuck you."

JW nodded and turned away. Panic reared up in Jacob. "Wait."

JW paused. "I'm sorry," Jacob said, floundering in confusion.

"Hey," said JW. "It all just fucking sucks," and Jacob knew he understood.

* * *

JACOB RODE PRIDE bareback. He was still angry, but it felt good to be focused on something outside of himself. Maybe he could just forget about what had happened. Red boy, blue boy, meld with the horse.

He felt in charge around JW, as if he could see things that he forgot about otherwise. Who he was. How he was. What mattered. The feeling slowly started to counter crazy out-of-control fear and guilt he'd been swimming in since the shooting. He knew Ernie would tell his dad that he was working with JW again, and he knew his dad would be angry, but he didn't care. He needed this like water. This was the one thing he was doing that wasn't wrecking things, and his dad would just have to deal with it. He walked the horse around JW, who stood in the center of the paddock. "Okay," said JW, his hands in his jean pockets, "let's bring him up to a trot. What you got?"

Jacob shifted his balance forward and gave a slight squeeze with his knees, prompting Pride to step up into a trot.

"Good job! Nice transition!" JW called after him. "Keep him in the same circle now, don't let him wind out."

Jacob smiled in spite of himself. JW knew what he had just accomplished, even if it was lost on everyone else: the intricate details, the subtle communication, the shifts of balance that took hours of practice and concentration and only made things look invisible and natural to everyone else. He went around again for another dose of praise, focused intently on the circle—the perfect circle, at a fast trot, with loose reins. He shifted his weight to face slightly into the circle he wanted Pride to create, their minds becoming one.

"That's right!" cheered JW.

Jacob kept Pride turning at a steady trot, raising dust that lifted into a yellow cloud. Around and around and around.

"Good!" JW bellowed at him through the dust. "Bareback is all about balance and connection. As your discipline improves, so does his!"

The rhythmic motion and the fur and the sweat and the reins in his hands, the thumping hoofbeats and JW's shouted encouragement, all grounded Jacob and brought him back from the cloud of anxiety he'd been caught up in. He vowed he would never go back to his bad ways. He felt Pride's spine becoming one with his tailbone, the two of them fusing into one animal, one nervous system, one brain, one ocean of emotions.

"This happens because he tests you, and again and again he finds he can trust you," JW bellowed through the dust. "Discipline, consistency, trust." *Red boy. Blue boy. Red boy. Blue boy.* It went through his mind like a drumbeat. *One animal. One animal. One animal. One.*

"With these three things, your horse becomes more than just an animal. He moves beyond just doing the job in spite of his emotions. He learns to discipline the emotions themselves."

Jacob's thighs were wet with Pride's sweat. He leaned forward imperceptibly, and Pride stepped into a perfect rolling canter.

* * *

THE TRIBAL COUNCIL met informally in the chair's second-floor office in the new community center. The three men and two women who could make it sat around a large oak table, surrounded by a four-foot-high wainscoting of quarter-sawn oak. The tribal chair's imposing carved-oak desk sat diagonally in a far corner, flanked by the flags of the United States, the State of Minnesota, the POW-MIA, and the Many Lakes Band of Ojibwe.

They were meeting as an ad hoc property committee on a special question relating to a new tribal bank. Johnny Eagle sat by himself on one wide side of the table, and they sat on the other, the windows to their backs. On the left near the chair was Betty Two Horse, an old Native woman with frizzy hair who was slowly sinking back into the earth, her spine bending between her shoulders, the folds of her ears and neck adorned with Native-made jewelry. Jeremiah Wilson sat next to her. His labored breathing and oxygen hose were a palpable force in the room, filling it with the sucking regularity of his respiration. Sidra Wilkes was next to him. She was in her late thirties, and her face had a sort of elfin beauty. She smiled encouragingly at Johnny. Next to her was Jim Hole-In-The-Sky, nearly fifty, and a respected scholar who wrote Ojibwe histories and taught college in Virginia. Tribal chair Ed Bishop sat to Eagle's left at the head of the table, wearing a sporty black racing jacket with beer logos. Bishop was a former lobbyist for the band's casino enterprise, and at forty-five he was energetic, entrepreneurial, and aggressive as a tribal chair: wound tight, but politically smooth and good at building consensus among council members and elders, who, in many other bands, were constantly at odds with one another. He had overseen the drive at the state capitol to secure matching funds to build the new community center they were sitting in. That had earned him a decade of goodwill and a reputation as a visionary, which he was determined to utilize in order to push through more changes. He opposed expanded state gambling and managed the band's touchy political tap dance on the issue of copper mining. Johnny's vision of a Native-owned bank appealed to his sense of legacy.

"Okay then," Bishop said. "Are we ready?"

Bishop looked around the room. The other council members all nodded, except Hole-In-The-Sky. "You know the town of North Lake's all over this," Hole-In-The-Sky said.

"I know, believe me," Bishop said. "I was just talking to Mayor Knutson this morning."

"And?"

"I told him we support full prosecution of any individuals found to be guilty of arson."

"We just don't want them thinking that these events are in any way connected, or that we somehow condone what happened."

"Connected?" said Bishop.

"They already are," replied Wilkes. "We've had fourteen cars with slashed tires and three more arsons of our own since. White teens are thinking it's a sport to drive through the reservation housing developments at night. I'm worried that someone else is going to get hurt."

"Look," said Eagle. "Maybe we should table this. I don't want to put you in hot water. That wouldn't do any of us any good."

Getting help from the band was something he had avoided previously. He was a newcomer, and a suspect one at that. He also wasn't good at politics, and getting embroiled in a larger controversy over the arson in town was the last thing he wanted. But Bishop had paid him a visit soon after his fledgling bank burned. He brought Wilkes and Hole-In-The-Sky with him, and the four of them had sat in Eagle's small office and discussed what he was trying to do, and how he was trying to honor Wenonah's vision. They decided to help him, but now that they were on board, it suddenly seemed as if things were infinitely more complicated, especially after the North Lake Bank arson, which had created problems for everyone.

Bishop leaned forward. "We're elected to get stuff done," he said. "I'll call the motion. All those in favor of providing Nature's Bank with free space in the southeast corner of the community center in exchange for the prescribed equity share in the enterprise?"

Several members said "Aye."

"Opposed?"

Silence. The council members began to smile at Eagle.

"Motion carries."

He banged his gavel.

Eagle was stunned. "Did that really just happen?" he said.

"It really just happened," replied Bishop. "We've got ourselves a new tribal bank!"

The councilors broke into grins and pushed back their chairs, reaching over the table to shake hands and congratulate Eagle. Even Wilson struggled to his feet and extended a frail hand. Eagle couldn't quite believe it. These people had regarded him as an interloper just a year ago, and now they were backing him despite the risk. He laughed and shook their hands, overcome with gratitude.

* * *

BRUSHING THE HORSE, Jacob felt satisfied. The fear and guilt and anxiety had subsided, and he could almost recall what it was like to feel normal. JW had taught him from the beginning that brushing was a critical part of both training and riding, and now he did it religiously and meditatively, extending his connection with Pride. Dirt and sweat combined with pressure points on the saddle to make hot spots. Brushing Pride after rides got some of the dirt and sweat out, and stimulated his skin to prevent sores. As Jacob brushed, Pride hung his head lower and lower, closing his eyes, and Jacob moved more and more slowly, losing himself in the musky smell of horse sweat and dander.

JW walked in to help with the stall duty. He took some of the wild rice greens and fed them to Pride over the stall half-wall as Jacob finished brushing him. Despite Jacob's performance in the ring and his generally good mood, he was quieter than usual. No rapid-fire stream of questions. None of the usual jabs and insults.

"You doin' okay?" JW asked as he flopped the unused saddle back onto its wood stand.

"Yeah."

"You just had a great ride out there. You seem kinda quiet."

"No. A little bit. I'll be all right."

He couldn't tell JW about the fire or the shooting, or the compass stabbing, even though he trusted him. He was too ashamed. He took Pride's feed bucket out and gave him a scoop of sweet feed.

"My dad's getting an eagle feather tonight," he said, walking over to the hay stacked on pallets in the corner. "I'm supposed to be in the ceremony." He flipped open his switchblade and cut the twine strands to pop open a new bale, then slipped it back in his shirt pocket.

"It's the highest honor Native people give," he said, opening the bale. "He's getting it because of the bank."

He carried two flakes of hay over to Pride's stall.

"You wanna come?" Jacob shrugged, and emotion welled up in him unexpectedly. He quickly turned away and stuffed the flakes in Pride's hayrack.

JW nodded when Jacob glanced back at him, signaling acknowledgment but not agreement. He glanced out at the guys working in the pole barn. JW knew they were keeping an eye on them. "Your dad wouldn't want me there," he said. "At least not until I've talked to him."

"He won't be back before then," said Jacob. "Ernie's driving me. Please? I just need ..." but then he stopped. "Fuck it, it's stupid, never mind." He began restacking the tipping haybales.

"You really want me to go?"

Jacob turned and wiped his face on the back of his hand. "No, it's okay. It's bullshit anyway."

JW nodded and stood there watching him.

"I'd need to take the truck," he finally said. He nodded to where the keys hung on the nail.

"Yeah, sure." Jacob glanced back from his stacking. "But only if you want to."

* * *

BOB GROSSMAN WOKE in the middle of the night with pain shooting down his left arm. His chest felt like it was being squeezed by an iron band, and he was in a cold sweat. He rolled over and woke Margie, and after trying to persuade him for a half and hour, she drove him to the hospital in Virginia. The cardiologist, it turned out, was an old classmate from high school in Cloquet, named Knut Kneevold.

"I think it's post-traumatic stress disorder," Margie told him.

"It's not PTSD," Grossman said. "I told you, it was my fucking heart. Sorry. It's probably my diet, okay, or sitting on my ass in the car all day."

"Well, these tests," Kneevold said, leaning in, "aren't really indicative of a heart attack, Bob, or really any kind of arrhythmic event. Your levels are all well within the normal range, which is good news, and when we put you on the treadmill, you look quite healthy." He nodded with an upbeat hopefulness that Grossman didn't find at all hopeful.

Margie smiled in relief. "That's what I told him."

Kneevold's raised eyebrows wrinkled his forehead as he nodded at Margie.

"But I'm a cop," Grossman said. "PTSD, I deal with shit all the time. It's not PTSD."

"Look," Kneevold said, "anxiety is—"

"It's not anxiety."

Kneevold looked at him and nodded. "Let's monitor it, okay? We'll keep an eye out for other things it could be, and we'll have you come back in another month, and we'll run the test again. In the meantime, as a precaution, I want you to try taking a baby aspirin a day. Fair enough?"

Grossman cast a sour but resigned look at Kneevold, then sighed and nodded. "Fine. Whatever."

"We'll get you back in top form one way or the other," added Kneevold.

Grossman drove home. Margie finally broke the silence.

"You know that Panamanián cruise you were always talking about?" she asked.

"Margie, I can't. We gotta find this guy. Otherwise our credibility is shot."

"But you don't have to be the one, Bobby."

"Look!" he exclaimed, more sharply than he'd intended. "I can't have this, Margie. I get a mental dock on my record, PTSD, anxiety, whatever bullshit they want to call it, I can just kiss my chances of running for sheriff goodbye."

She waved dismissively. "Big Bill would still endorse you." Big Bill Donovan had been elected seven times, and he was widely considered to be a kingmaker.

"Big Bill won't be able to do anything. The public doesn't want a cop running around with mental problems, okay? We have guns. You get it? So please, I know you mean well, but just lay off the PTSD, okay?"

Margie folded her hands in her lap. She looked out the windshield.

"I'm worried about you."

"Don't be, I'll be fine."

She was nonplussed. He glanced over and saw her pensive stare. He hated it when she got like this. He sighed.

"Look, I'm going to reach out to the Native American community and try and make some inroads on this. If it is panic attacks or whatever you want to call it then that should make it go away, okay? We've been on bad terms lately, and if I can get some of them working with me so that we solve this thing, it will all go back to normal. Okay?"

Margie's face lightened and she nodded, feeling more hopeful. "Okay." At least it was a constructive approach, something she had been telling him he ought to do for the past two or three years.

31

The night was warm and dark. *Oshkagoojin 'aw dibiki-giizis*,
Mona had called it, a new moon. The eagle-feather ceremony
was set for this night because it symbolized a new beginning.
Mona told JW this when he asked if she would come along.
Apparently the event had been publicized in announcements
on and off the reservation, even in the *Mesabi Daily Mining
Advocate*, though JW hadn't seen any of it. He knew Eagle
wouldn't approve of either of them being there, so when he
heard her car thundering in he figured what the hell, and
trudged up and caught her. He had half-expected her to be
drunk, but she was just returning with a few bags of groceries. He needed a guide and companion, he said. He had
no idea where the tribal community center was, much less
what to expect when he got there. To his surprise, she smiled
softly, put a hand on his shoulder, kissed his cheek, and said,
"I'd be honored."

It was dark when he fired up the wild rice truck and she
came down from her house, and he felt almost as if he were
going on a date in high school.

"Hi," she said as she got into the truck. She had on a
beaded leather jacket, and she wore boots over her skinny
jeans. Her diamond stud earrings glittered in the dashboard lights. She gave him a smile and swiped her hair off
her cheek. "You ready for this?" She raised an eyebrow—
she was wearing dark eyeliner—and her smile was skepti-

cal, as if she thought he was in for something that he might not be able to handle.

"Yeah," he said, shifting into reverse. "New experience."

"You've been getting a lot of them lately." She turned the Clapton on and cranked up the volume. "Let's rock it white-man style," she said, holding up two fists and snapping her fingers.

"You think that's white-man style?"

"Oh love," she sang along with Clapton, but even more sentimentally.

"Shut up," he said, and turned it off. "You're spoiling it."

She laughed and clapped her hands in delight. He knew how to be teased. She was ready for a fun evening. JW followed Mona's instructions and headed up over the hill past her house, a direction he'd taken only once before.

Ten miles down the dark winding road, the community center sat on a hill overlooking Waterfowl Lake. He parked the truck in a close-cropped field just east of the center. As they stepped out of the truck, JW looked up to see stars so thick and a sky so black that his balance left him and he grabbed the truck bed for support. The whole field seemed to lose its earth and sail like a ship through the heavens. He felt sewn into things, a part of the firmament. He passed the tailgate, came together with Mona, and felt her warm dry hand slip into his.

"It's pretty awesome, huh?" She said.

"Yeah."

They flowed together through the ether. Stars had always had the power to do that to him, but tonight, out here with Mona, the effect was somehow enhanced. A warm breeze lifted his hair and washed his cheeks. Beat-up old Toyotas and Buicks rumbled and bumped into the hayfield, their headlights casting yellow beams that bobbed around them as if they were at a drive-in movie.

The building looked like a giant spaceship from a science fiction double feature, or a sculpture of some sort in Minneapolis. Ground-set floodlights lit a long architectural wing of stacked flagstone and glass that shot northward like an arrow toward Waterfowl Lake. On the south end was a large round structure in the shape of a gigantic drum. Jutting out from it was a corner of stone and glass that reached toward a wetland and the distant tribal fire station a hundred yards beyond. JW recognized the fire truck and tanker from a week ago, glowing in the yellow light that emanated from open garage doors.

The entry reached out toward them with a long thick wood portico and a walkway of enormous stone tiles. As they walked in through the new glass doors to a sweeping atrium, JW could hear drums. The room had high clerestory windows that glistened with stars. Hidden lights wrapped gently over the red-hued wooden posts and beams, and the blue and maroon and ochre of the artwork. Stacked gray flagstones made up some of the walls, and he felt as though he were a frog on the bottom of a great pond.

They turned down a smaller hallway that was lined with wide walls of wood panels hung with the tanned pelts of moose and deer and wolf. Old black-and-white photos of Indians were interspersed among the pelts, and display cases contained beaded leather jackets and feathered memorabilia. A well-lit wall farther down was completely covered with hundreds of framed eight-by-ten photos of tribal members who had served in the various branches of the United States Armed Forces since World War II. JW looked at the names, but there was no apparent order.

"People are encouraged to move them around," Mona said. "They put them by other relatives. The whole wall slowly organizes itself according to our living clans. That way we can see how we are all connected, and we don't forget the ones who died or are missing."

JW nodded and she led him on. The drums were louder here, and people were passing them from behind. They turned a corner and she pulled him toward double doors opening into a loud and crowded gymnasium.

The bleachers were full and buzzing. The yellow painted concrete block wall was emblazoned with a single word in blue letters: Perseverance. Near the center of the room, four men beat a traditional moose-hide drum that was about three feet in diameter. They wore ribbon shirts, which looked like Western-style golf shirts with ribbons hanging from the shoulder yokes and buttons that only went down partway. The drumhead was held taut with leather thongs. Four leather pouches, equally spaced around the drum, held four staffs that faced the four directions, each dangling an eagle feather.

JW and Mona made their way across the gym floor, to an open spot on the far bleachers. As they picked their way up through the crowd there were points and giggles. *Zaagizi'*, JW heard someone say. Mona blushed and squeezed his hand, pulling him onward.

"What are they saying?"

"They think you're my boyfriend," she replied.

As they sat, other men stepped up to the drummers and began to sing a Grand Entry song. Some of them wore ribbon shirts and jeans, others wore street clothes. One wore a suit and others wore traditional garb in the old style, one with horn-rimmed glasses. A few of them began to dance clockwise around the drum. The men's mixed clothing reminded JW of their yards: he could discern no rules of order. Mona leaned in and lifted a finger toward them as she talked warm and humid by his cheek.

"Those are some elders and tribal council members and other leaders."

He nodded. The music suddenly stopped and the dancers filed off and sat down. The room quieted. It was hot, and smelled of bodies and sweetgrass. JW looked around for Eagle and Jacob, but couldn't see them.

"Where are they?"

"Somewhere in the crowd."

An elder stood and made his way toward the drum, holding an eagle feather that trailed a red horsehair tie. He waved it to the east. "*Wabanung!*"

He turned to the south. "*Zhouwanoong!*"

He turned west and waved it there. "*Ningabianoong!*"

Finally he waved it in the general direction of JW and Mona. "*Giwedinoong!*"

Mona leaned in close and put a hand on JW's forearm. "Wow, they're really going all out. This is like a powwow."

"*Migizi!*" the elder called out to the crowd, and after a moment a man stood. It was Johnny Eagle. There was smoke in the air, a fine scrim of it. He was wearing a ribbon shirt, with jeans and fancy cowboy boots.

The elder began to speak in Ojibwe. "It is not every day," he said, "that we honor one of our sons or daughters with a bald eagle feather."

Mona leaned in close and translated. Her breath smelled of spruce gum. He could feel the warmth of her forearm against his, and the curve of her breast where it pressed against his biceps.

"It is illegal for anyone in the United States to possess these feathers except in this rare honor," the elder said in

English for the benefit of the children and the few non-Native visitors he saw in the audience. His high reedy voice carried clearly across the gymnasium.

"Our brother Johnny Eagle is being given this highest honor for his selfless efforts on behalf of the band," the elder continued, "from his wild rice business, which has offered a livelihood to many, to the new bank, whereby we may support ourselves and take care of our own people with our own businesses. This is a good vision! And it is a vision not just for those of us in this room, but for our children and our children's children, on down through seven or more generations."

Eagle looked awkward and uncomfortable in the ribbon shirt, yet regal in presence and bearing, as if he were somehow above these strange Ojibwe ways, but was humoring them and humbling himself nonetheless. He towered over the people seated around him in the audience. The elder moved next to the drum and then motioned Eagle in with a wave.

The drummers began beating the drum and a singer stepped up next to them to sing a traditional eagle-feather honor song.

Eagle stepped off the last bleacher and down onto the gym floor. He seemed to hesitate for a moment, and then he stepped into a dance, moving slowly over the painted court stripes toward the center of the gym floor, dancing clockwise, or sunwise, around the drum, tall and awkward in his cowboy boots. When he passed the elder, the elder handed the eagle feather to him. Eagle took it and kept dancing clockwise around the drum, and then the whole drum group joined the singing, taking the whole thing very seriously despite Eagle's lack of grace.

Eagle made another clockwise circle, dancing around the singing drummers and holding the eagle feather aloft to the four directions. Then Jacob stood up in the bleachers. JW saw that he, too, was wearing a ribbon shirt, and he looked even more awkward and stiff than his father. JW shifted in his seat, suppressing an urge to wave to him.

Jacob looked at the bleacher steps, and began taking them one by one down onto the floor. He glanced toward JW without making eye contact, then started dancing.

"God, I feel bad for him," JW said.

Mona squeezed his arm. "Don't."

Jacob danced his way in and followed his father around the singing dancers. As he did, people began to stand. By the time he had made a circuit, the whole crowd was up and moving with the rhythm of the drums, dancing down onto the gym floor.

"Come on," Mona said, pulling at his hand.

The people already on the floor began following Jacob and Johnny in a huge clockwise wake around the drum, dancing to the beat. People were flowing around JW and Mona from upper levels of the bleachers, and hopping down onto the floor. She pulled harder.

"Come on!" she said.

He followed her down onto the floor. He did a little one-legged hop, trying to dance, but now it was his turn to feel horribly awkward and self-conscious. People laughed and some pointed, enjoying his white gawkiness. Mona leaned in and yelled to him.

"If Jacob can do it alone, you can do it in a crowd!"

She turned away and danced on, keeping hold of his hand. It felt more awkward for JW to walk, so eventually he tried first one step, then another, and pretty soon he was dancing, trying to keep up with her, and then he was just a part of the dance, and the whole room was heaving and circling in a shaggy mass.

The music ended with four powerful drumbeats, and the

room fell mostly quiet. People were sweating and smiling. JW found himself grinning at strangers.

Johnny Eagle mounted a short dais so he could be seen. He held the eagle feather aloft and the crowd began to applaud.

"Good evening, *Anishinaabeg!*" he said in a booming voice, and the crowd went wild.

"Thank you so very much. Thank you!" His powerful voice echoed over the sustained roar.

"Thank you! Thank you." Still, the applause continued. "Thank you." He held up a hand again and the room finally grew quiet. He laughed.

"You guys are great," he said, and they applauded again. He stood, taking it in, and JW had the sense that he was watching some sort of transformation. When the crowd finally began to settle, Eagle began in a speaking tone and they quieted to hear him.

"What is a bank?" He looked around at them with confidence. "To its shareholders, it's a way to make money off your money. To its depositors, it's a safe place to store *their* money. But to its borrowers—to them it's a precious resource, allowing them to attain the American dream of home ownership and a college education, or even a basic car with four wheels that are all the same size and color." The audience laughed and he took in their response for a moment before becoming serious again. He used his hand, his fist, and he pointed for emphasis, but always with passion and a smile, as if he had been speaking for years.

"That resource is called opportunity. Opportunity. A bank is where we can come together as a community in order to pool our resources, to help one another prosper in good times and get by in bad. But too often we see credit denied, not on the basis of risk, but by greedy profiteering, masked as concerns over tribal sovereignty. This happens to our brothers and sisters all across this great country, denying them the opportunities others in our shared nation take for granted. Now, we cannot blame our white brethren."

Here there were scattered boos from a few young men, but Eagle held a hand up to quiet them, shaking his head.

"No, we can't. No, we can't. It is too easy to chalk this all up to race. Especially in times like these, when tensions run high. Both whites and Indi'ns do it. We are both trapped by the sins of our fathers, all those poisoned waters, all those hard feelings and justifiable suspicions that make the present and the future so hard to see. But if we are truthful, we must admit that we all have a share of the responsibility. We cannot expect a white banker in North Lake, Minnesota to lend to a homeowner on a reservation if he cannot secure the loan. And we cannot blame a white banker in Detroit Lakes for worrying about stable property values in Native areas, where addiction and crime run at higher than normal rates. These are just the economic realities. And even if we could blame them, where would it get us?

"But neither, neither can we accept the lack of capital that helps create that poverty in the first place. If we can't borrow from the white man, then we must open our own banks, with our own money, and create our own opportunities!"

The crowd thundered with applause. Mona leaned over. "We don't normally clap like this," she yelled.

"Now," Eagle continued, "we all know what happened down at the construction site. Maybe it was an accident, and maybe it wasn't. But what I can tell you for sure is that it's not going to slow us down."

The crowd applauded again and some of the young men whooped.

"Let me be clear. I do not condone the kind of cowardly

act that resulted in someone trying to set fire to the North Lake Bank, nor shooting at a good police officer. That may not have been one of us, we don't know, but the deputy says he saw Indians running away from the scene of the crime. I like to think we are better than that, and I hope those involved are brought swiftly to justice."

More applause, led mostly by women, with a few men joining in. JW noticed Jacob was looking at the floor.

"Today I met with the tribal council, and they voted to dedicate part of this gorgeous new community center to house our new bank. It's not as close to North Lake, but it's still on a main road, and it has one great advantage I hadn't considered: it's next door to the tribal fire department."

The crowd laughed and applauded again.

"So. What is a bank? A bank is community. A bank is all of us pulling together, and becoming more that the sum of our parts. A bank is hope, and a vision for a brighter, more prosperous tomorrow. Thank you for this great honor. It means more to me than you can imagine. Thank you Anishinaabeg!"

Eagle waved and stepped back as the crowd gave him a huge ovation. JW glanced at Mona as they applauded. He was stunned by the sense of greatness in Eagle's transformation, the effortlessness of it, and the sense of unity and vision he had created in the audience. He felt the hair standing on his neck. The gym was getting hot and stuffy. People were gathering around Eagle in a big crush, seeking to congratulate him.

"Do you want to stay?" Mona shouted over the din.

JW shook his head.

"I don't want to spoil his night."

She laughed. "You wouldn't. There's a rule that everyone has to leave animosity outside when they enter a pow-wow."

But JW shook his head. Rule or no rule, he was too inti-mately connected with everything Eagle had spoken about. And then there was the fact that he still had to find a way to stop him, or he would lose everything. Congratulating him now would only make it harder. "We can talk to him later," he said.

As they walked back through the great entry hall, the col-ors of the artwork seemed even more vivid, the piled flagstone walls even more palpable and the soaring wood columns even richer. JW wanted to run his hands over everything. He won-dered at his heightened senses. Some white people he had known sought this sort of thing out. They clothed themselves in Native traditions like spiritual outfits, traveling to pow-wows and sweat lodges and pipe ceremonies as if they were horse shows, with more dedication than many Indians. JW had always thought of this as a sort of cultural gentrifica-tion, and he found it annoying. People should just be who they were, and he knew that most Indians didn't like such skinwalkers either. But there was something about the sense of connectedness he felt after dancing with everyone, and nobody really caring or judging him, that was undeniable. He felt light, which was making everything more difficult.

They pushed out through the glass doors into the warm dark night and Mona slipped her small hand into his. The sky pulsed down at them, fat stars throbbing with the beat of the drums echoing in his mind. Mona gave his hand a little squeeze at the tailgate and they parted and walked up either side of the truck to their respective doors.

32

JW drove back along the dirt road to Mona's house. She slid over next to him on the fur and stubbed out her cigarette, leaving only the peach and tobacco smell of her hair behind.

"Thank you," she said.

"For what?"

"I don't know. Just bringing me. Being a good sport with our Indi'n ways."

"I should be thanking you. Imagine me trying to dance alone."

She laughed. "It was good to see him honored," she said. Her face and dark hair were lit softly by the dashboard. "People haven't been too accepting of him until now," she said.

"Well, it looks like he's overcome that."

She nodded. "Johnny is a force of nature. He always has been."

She tilted her head onto his shoulder and put a hand on his knee. Her hair licked at his face, then fell away in the buffeting breeze from the window. He suddenly realized how long it had been since he'd had anybody put a head on his shoulder, or a hand on his knee, and the scents drew a well of emotion up inside him. He turned his face into her hair for a brief moment, letting the smell and the feel of her feed him.

After a moment, Mona spoke again. "I've been thinking

about what you said. About feeling bad instead of trying to make the feeling go away. I haven't had a drink since we talked. I want you to know that's major progress for me."

"I know it is," he replied, a little taken aback. "Congratulations."

"I feel like I've known you for a long time."

He squeezed her hand and they drove on in silence, the road leaping forward into the headlights, then falling away, frogs and crickets singing in their wake. He remembered a night camping with Julie, when they had hiked to a precipice in the Boundary Waters and lain there looking up. "What if the world is upside down," she had asked, "and we could fall off into the sky?"

As he and Mona topped the ridge and came down from the heavens, he saw a car turn on its lights as it emerged from the trailer park lane. It turned and headed away down the road toward the highway.

It was a dark night for someone to have driven down that hill and forgotten to turn on their lights, he thought. And then he suddenly realized that it must have been someone coming out of his parking area. As the car neared the curve, his headlights picked up a small hint of red on its back bumper. A vague sense of recognition shot through him, and then the other car turned the corner and drove out of sight. That spot of color was in the same place as the NRA bumper sticker on the back of Sam Schmeaker's car. And the car was dark and sporty, with a slightly elevated back end, just like Sam's.

He slowed the truck, turned into Eagle's barn drive, and came to a stop near the paddock. He could see Pride standing and looking at them, black and white in the throwaway light. Mona rose from his shoulder. He sat there for a moment, thinking, the green dash lights glowing on him. Should he back out and give chase? If that was Schmeaker, Jorgenson was likely behind it, and that meant he was being outflanked somehow. Mona turned to look at him. She wiped a strand of hair out of her face, tucked it behind her right ear.

"Come up," she said. Her lips were full and inviting, as if she had just awakened from a nap.

JW turned the engine off and sat there in the dark, thinking again. What could Schmeaker possibly be doing here?

"I should check my house," he said.

Mona looked at him, trying to understand. "Can I come with?"

It occurred to him that she thought he was rejecting her. "Sure," he said.

They got out and walked to the lean-to. JW hung the keys on the nail by feel, and saw them glint in the starlight as his eyes adjusted to the dark.

"Come here," he said. He slipped his hand into hers and they walked together along the faintly visible paddock fence. Pride let out a long low nicker as they passed.

"It's okay," said JW. "It's just us."

They crossed the road, the stars pounding down on them, and walked up the drive to JW's trailer.

"How come so few people live up there?" JW pointed over the hill to the rest of the trailers. He wondered if the other car could have been from one of them.

"The band built better housing over by the community center," Mona replied.

He didn't see any letter or notice outside his trailer, and there was no one lurking in the trees. He climbed the steps and slipped his key into the lock. "You probably want to step back," he said.

Mona gave him a strange look, but did as he'd suggested.

"I thought I recognized that car," he explained. "But it was probably nothing."

She looked around, concerned. He pulled the door open slowly, then stepped in.

The floor creaked as Mona followed him in. The door had been locked, but he was still suspicious. He turned on the light and looked around quickly for anything that was out of order. But everything looked just as it had when he left. Then his thoughts leaped to the bug receiver.

"Give me a second, okay?"

She nodded and he stepped into his bedroom and partially closed the door, leaving just a narrow crack. He sat on the bed in the starlight and drew the clothes hamper between his legs. He plunged his arm into the clothing and felt the plastic box, then the cord. It was still there. He sat in the twilight, staring at the door. He pushed the clothes hamper away and got on the floor. He moved to the bedside table and reached under the mattress. His notepad was gone.

He tried to think back. This was definitely where he had been hiding it, but it was also true that he had been pretty disoriented the last time he had it out, when he returned from seeing Carol.

Could he have left it in the truck? Was he being paranoid?

The bedroom door edged open and Mona stepped in.

"Are you okay?"

"Yeah, I'm sorry."

She sat down and slipped an arm around him, then tentatively kissed his jawline, sending a current down both sides of his chest.

"Come up to my place. Please."

He glanced out the window up toward her house. It was much closer to Eagle's than his trailer was. If something happened, he would be in a better position up there with her. He nodded.

She took his hand and opened the door wide. He stood to follow and she led him back through the kitchen and then out under the stars. He flipped off the light and pushed the trailer door shut, and they strolled across the dark, foggy lane, the trees heaving and lurching overhead. The air had grown warmer.

"Just a sec," he said. "I just want to make sure I didn't forget something in the truck."

She followed him back to the pickup. He opened the door and checked the seat by the dome light. He looked on the floor and felt in the crack between the seat and the back, but the notepad wasn't there.

"What are you looking for?" she asked.

"Nothing," he said. "Just a note I had written to myself. No big deal." He closed the door. It would have to wait until morning.

Her fingers felt small as she led him up her flagstone steps. She stepped up onto her front porch, pushed open the front door, and led him inside.

Despite its pristine outer appearance, the inside of the house was only partly finished, not unlike Eagle's, but her work areas were lived in. The living room, to the left, was two-by-sixes and bare insulation. Beer bottles, tree stumps, rugs, and a stereo with huge speakers suggested that this was where the party sounds had emanated from.

Mona saw him looking at it. She leaned back against a foyer wall, lifting her ankles to pull off her tall boots.

"I know, it's a pit," she said.

"No, no, it's not that. It's just, I thought it would all be finished."

"I ran out of money," she said. "And anyway, we Indi'ns do things in stages."

He nodded.

"It's also more like a rubber room that way," she said with a smile. With her boots off, she was about two inches shorter. He looked down at her bare feet and she took his hand. "Come with me. You'll like this better."

She led him up a short carpeted hallway and opened the door into a clean bedroom that filled the end of the house nearest Eagle's. In contrast to the debauchery of the living room, it was serene in here.

"See? This is more to your taste, right?"

"I'm sorry," he said. "I'm not one to judge."

"You're the only guy that's made it past that door."

He looked at her, not sure if she was serious. "Really?" he asked.

"Stop fucking this up." She put her arms around his waist, her cheek on his shoulder. "We're both assholes, but we try. Now let's stop thinking so much for a little while."

He held her as she pressed herself to him. He felt himself growing hard against her, but his eyes were still drawn to the corner windows facing the street.

He pulled her tighter, his mind racing.

"I'll be right back," she said, and then walked into the master bathroom.

JW turned and looked out the window. Down over the paddock and through the swaying branches, he could just make out his trailer. What could Schmeaker have been up to? he wondered.

"Hey."

He turned. She was wearing a blue-flowered negligee, and her bare feet melded into the plush carpet as she walked, her breasts moving freely under the silky fabric.

She hung her arms around his neck, and wove her fingers into his hair at the back of his scalp. "Do any Indi'ns ever call you whitey?" she asked. "Besides me?"

"Sometimes. Ernie does."

"I like it," she said. She kissed him. Her lips were warm and her breath was piney. "I think you should own it." She kissed him again. "I'm usually attracted to losers and bad guys. Which one are you?" she asked him, her lips plush against his as she talked. He could feel her breasts on his chest.

He grunted. "Both. But I'm trying not to be."

She put her lips to his neck. "Good," she said into his ear, "'cause I could use a change." She bit his lobe and then stepped back slightly into the starlight. She unbuttoned his shirt and pushed it off, kissing his shoulder. Then she stood back, opened her silky robe, and let it fall. Her wild-rimmed eyes seemed strangely vulnerable, and she stepped in to hold him, skin on skin.

She slid a hand into his jeans and he felt himself respond. The jerky unhitching of a button, the freedom of a zipper coming open, the fumbling out of denim. These awkward acts held a sort of immutable grace. The softness and wetness and entwining of limbs seemed natural and preordained.

When it was over he lay with her hair strewn over him and fell into the wilds of the universe. In his dreams he was a young man again, training horses, with his whole life before him.

33

From somewhere in the deep forests he returned. The dreams fell away and the stark clarity of everything he had done washed back over him. He looked at the clock radio next to Mona's bed. Four thirty in the morning. He turned over and tried to go back to sleep, but closing his eyes cast his mind into a state of hyper-caffeinated brilliance. He thought back to the car and the swatch of red on its back bumper, the angle and elevation of its back end as it disappeared into the night.

The only thing missing was his notepad. He remembered waving it in Jorgenson's office. He had told him that it contained the combination to Eagle's safe, and that the only solution was to plant something incriminating on him. His heart raced. If the car he saw last night was Schmeaker's, this was the only possible explanation. In which case Eagle was in danger.

JW considered going down and waking Eagle up. But then he would have to tell Eagle how he came to have his combination, and everything would come out. There would be nothing to stop Eagle from calling the police, nothing to protect what was left of his life. Mona stirred next to him, but didn't wake.

Another option occurred to him. He could go check out the safe himself, while everyone was asleep. The thought made his heart race anew. And as he mulled this possible step, it became increasingly clear that if he was going to do it, he would have to act immediately, before the sun was up. He turned over and looked at the clock. Ten to five. He lay back and imagined the police coming, the safe opening, drugs inside, Eagle being arrested.

He rolled quietly out of bed. Mona turned over and he froze, but she fell back to sleep. He felt around on the floor for his pants, and pulled them on. He couldn't find the rest of his clothes. He would have to risk it. In and out. Grab whatever was there and hide it, or bring it back here.

He tiptoed barefoot from the room and down the hall. He could see light coming in through a back door. He made his way to it and out onto a small concrete patio. He gently closed the back door, then crossed the patio and stepped out into the backyard.

The grass was dry beneath his feet, and the air was cool on his bare chest and arms. He ran to the end of Mona's house and stopped. He looked around the corner toward Eagle's house, fifty or sixty feet away. There were no lights. He ran to the back of the house and up to the sliding glass door. It was completely dark inside. He climbed onto the small deck and tiptoed to the door. The handle was unlocked. He hesitated a moment, thinking of how dangerous this gambit was. He could still just go back. Then he slid the door open.

JW saw the eagle feather on the dining room table. It fluttered in the disturbed air. He stepped inside and could hear Eagle's heavy breathing. He listened, then tiptoed to the corner of the hall and peered around it. Both bedroom doors stood ajar. Other than Eagle's breathing, he couldn't hear a sound. He stepped quietly into full view and nothing happened. He tiptoed down the carpeted hall toward the office door. He could feel the nylon strands under his bare feet, and he remembered to avoid the squeaky spot. He was shaking. They would wake soon. And if some sort of bust were planned, that would happen soon as well.

In the office, he stepped to the closet door and put a hand on the edge to quiet it. He slowly pulled it open, and then he got down on his knees and recalled the combination. Nine, ninety-one, thirteen. He began slowly turning the safe dial, cupping a hand over it to muffle the clicks, and stopping to listen every several clicks to make sure Eagle or Jacob weren't shifting in bed. Nothing. He cranked the lever down and the safe door popped open.

Bundles of cash spilled out onto the carpet. With a lurch of panic he shoved his hands under the cascade, but when it stopped, there was nothing but more heavy breathing down the hall. He let the cash down gently. Bundles of fives, tens, twenties, fifties, hundreds. It suddenly occurred to him that the money could be Eagle's. Perhaps it was part of the capital to start the new bank, or even an investment from the band.

He would live with it. He looked around for something to contain the cash. There was a box of Glad trash can liners on the shelf above. He pulled one out, quietly spread the bag open, and started stuffing it with bundles. He listened to Eagle and Jacob's breathing. He was sweating now, and he felt almost nauseous from his racing heart. He flipped the safe door shut, turned the lever and spun the dial, and pushed the closet door closed.

JW grabbed the bulging white trash can liner and, tiptoeing on the balls of his feet, carried it to the door. He paused and looked around the corner toward the bedrooms. It seemed as if they were still sleeping, but the breathing had become quieter. Had they heard something? He stepped out into the hall and tiptoed around the corner, where he felt cool air settling in through the open sliding glass door.   ·

He stepped out and turned to close the door, but as he did so, he heard the toilet flush inside. His hands and arms suddenly cramped and he felt as if he were choking. He slid the door shut under the flushing sound and leaped off the deck. He crouched and steadied himself with one hand in the rubbery grass. He swallowed and tried to breathe. His mouth and throat were dry, and his heart was pounding in his ears. He stayed hunched under the edge of the deck, listening. Finally, after what must have been five minutes, he decided to dare it. Squatting low, he ran through the grass, keeping below the level of the deck. He made the corner of the house and paused. He had to get the bag of cash to his trailer: down the hill, past the paddock, and across the road. He decided to try for the cover of the truck first.

He hoisted the bag and ran for it, feeling his pulse in his neck. He half-expected Eagle to raise an alarm, or call out to him to stop. But he reached the truck and ducked down behind it without incident. His lungs were heaving, his fingers splayed into the dusty gravel of the barn drive to steady himself, the plastic sack of money on the ground beside him. He was lathered in sweat despite the morning's coolness. The sky was warming into a pinkish-yellow dawn.

He swallowed and looked around the front of the truck, gathering himself for the dash to the trailer. But just then a dark blue sedan flew past and came to a stop in front of Eagle's house. Its disc brakes hissed quietly and tires crunched on the gravel. It was followed by a county cruiser and a tribal police car. Two men in jackets marked FBI got out of the sedan. Bob Grossman and Dan Barden exited the county cruiser, and Fladeboe stepped out of the tribal car. They lifted their door handles and pushed the doors closed quietly with their other hands. Jesus, JW thought. He had been right.

He ducked back behind the truck. There was no way he could make it to his trailer now. He looked again and saw Grossman nod at Barden and wave a finger in a circle. Barden nodded his understanding and started heading around the back of the house. The others moved up the walk toward the front door. He heard them knock. Jacob's confused voice answered with something unintelligible.

"Can I help you?" Eagle's voice carried out into the dawn.

"Mr. Eagle, I'm Deputy Sheriff Grossman with the Bass County Sheriff's Department, and these gentlemen are Agents Richardson and Olson from the FBI. You know Officer Fladeboe. Sir, is there anyone else in the house?"

"Just my son," replied Eagle, his distant voice hoarse with sleep.

When JW looked again, he saw Fladeboe walking down the hill toward the paddock. Now he would surely be exposed. He glanced behind him. The lean-to was ten feet away. He picked up the bag and lugged it over to the lean-to, noticing in the process that the plastic was stretched thin, the bills almost poking through the membrane. The dusty soles of his feet felt cool on the brown earth of the lean-to. He looked out from among the halters and lead ropes, and saw Fladeboe pass the truck and duck through the rails into the paddock. Puzzled, JW strained his neck and watched Fladeboe bend over, jam his hand into a zippered plastic bag, and pick up a handful of horse manure, closing the bag around it.

* * *

EAGLE WAITED ON the porch with Jacob and Grossman while the two FBI agents entered the house. He saw Deputy Barden step in from the back sliding glass door in back.

"I don't understand," he said.

"It's in the warrant," Grossman replied. Eagle noticed that he was sweating, and he kept looking out at the trees.

Eagle looked over the warrant as Fladeboe came up the walk, carrying a sealed plastic bag filled with—of all things— some of Pride's manure. The two computer-printed pages said the court had found probable cause that he was involved in a burglary of North Lake Bank the evening before, and authorized the officers to search for cash, horse manure, and other evidence of the crime.

"Horse manure?"

Fladeboe stepped up with the bag. "They found some on the carpet of the bank and outside the back door, and it had red horsehair and wild rice hulls in it."

Eagle was indignant. "That's ridiculous," he said.

"Tell it to the judge, Johnny."

Fladeboe had dated Wenonah in high school, and Eagle had disliked him since learning that. He was too much of a pleaser, a wannabe white boy, and here he was, going out of his way to help them screw over a fellow Indian. Deputy Barden stepped out onto the porch.

"Mr. Eagle?"

He turned. The deputy's forehead jutted forward to form an officious shelf above his eyes. "We need you to step inside."

"Okay." Eagle couldn't think of what they could have possibly found, and he began to wonder if they had planted some sort of evidence. He turned to Jacob, suddenly wanting a witness. "Come on, son."

Jacob began to follow, but Grossman held up a hand.

"You stay here."

Eagle looked into Grossman's eyes and grew concerned. The man had unbuttoned his shirt collar.

"Why?" Eagle asked.

"Sir, inside. Now!" said Barden.

Grossman shot Eagle an edgy grin and shook his head, as if they were old friends and Eagle was being ridiculous. "He'll be fine."

* * *

JW THOUGHT ABOUT hiding out in the lean-to until they left, but realized the plan was too dangerous. If the money had been planted, the police would be looking for it, and if they didn't find it in the house they would search the vehicles and the outbuildings. He had to get it to his trailer. He glanced out again and lifted the stretching bag of cash. Everyone had gone inside now except Jacob and Bob Grossman, who were talking to someone he couldn't see.

JW ran for it. He crossed the road with the bulging sack and ran through the low brush on the far side, then in under the oak trees. Sharp sticks, rocks, and thistle barbs jabbed at his feet. His lungs burned with an uncontrollable urgency as he raced over the grassy gravel and up the wooden steps to his trailer, thankful for the partial cover of the oak trees. He opened the door, lifted the heaving bag in through it, and slipped inside, turning quickly to whip the door quietly shut. His arms and hands felt numb. He doubled over, heaving and sweating, trying to catch his breath.

He felt dizzy, and his vision broke up into swimming pixels. He swallowed and leaned over to look out the eating area window, to see if he'd been spotted. They were all still looking toward the house, and Eagle was nowhere in sight. He grabbed a dish towel and wiped his face, then leaned on the counter in front of the sink, catching his breath. Out in the middle of the road, he saw a bundle of cash fluttering in the wind.

He was at the trash can liner in two steps, and he immediately saw where the plastic had stretched and torn. He dropped the liner and looked out the window. He would have to retrieve the bundle. He glanced up at Eagle's front porch and saw Grossman step away from the house and look out over the yard and the road.

* * *

BOB GROSSMAN WAS trying to get his heart to stop racing. The guys inside had found Eagle's safe and had asked him to open it, while he was stuck outside with the kid. He turned and scanned the trees. Some Indian could be aiming a deer rifle at him right now, he thought. They had a grapevine. He noted how thick the trees were here, with an undergrowth of buckthorn and red sumac. A shooter would be virtually invisible. He shouldn't have taken this assignment, he realized. Margie was right, it was too soon. But he was trying to impress Barden and Big Bill, to show them he wasn't the paralyzed babbler that Barden had found lying in the wheat field, with nothing but a small flesh wound.

He turned back to the kid. It was the young ones who were the most dangerous. They had access to firearms, but they lacked judgment, and he was sure they had tried to gun him down once already. This one, Jacob Eagle, was a pot smoker and a thief, a living example of the kind of miscreant that had made his life miserable. The kaleidoscope of his mind shifted, and a new interpretation of recent events suddenly fell into place with shocking clarity—with this kid as the key.

"What's your role in this?" he asked, his heart speeding with anticipation.

"We didn't do anything," Jacob replied.

Grossman examined his expression for any sign of guilt. "We've got a tip that says otherwise. Somebody saw your dad's vehicle. Now how 'bout we back up and you tell me who set the town bank on fire?"

He took a step toward Jacob, studying him menacingly.

"I don't know what you're talking about," Jacob said. But Grossman could sense a falter in his answer, a lack of conviction that suggested he was lying.

"Did you take a shot at me?" He stepped in close and loomed over Jacob.

"No!"

"First you tried to burn the bank down, then you took a shot at me, and then you robbed it—"

"My dad got an eagle feather last night—"

Grossman poked him in the chest. "Bullshit. I don't want to hear about it. Tell me about that bank fire."

"I said I don't know what you're talking about!" The kid's voice broke. He was sounding less convincing each time he spoke.

Grossman sensed that he was onto something, that he was nearing a moment when all the truth would come out into the open and order and peace could be restored. He worked to expand the beachhead. "I know your dad's a bunker, and his bank caught fire. You two must be feeling pretty angry about that. So you figured you'd take it out on the good guys."

"No!" Jacob said, his voice still shaking.

"Town bank's just trying to keep people's money safe, they keep your tribal money safe, and you, you little fucking punk—"

"Bob!"

Grossman looked up and saw Barden inside the screen door. Barden shook his head and Grossman was suddenly aware of how he had the kid pushed up against the house with a hand against his shoulder. He nodded to Barden and backed off. "We'll get you," he said to the kid, and glanced out over the yard. "We'll get you."

He wanted the kid to know he was onto him. That he was going to watch him like a hawk. And he wanted to see what the kid would do, now that he was rattled. He turned back to him. "If you had anything to do with that fire, your ass is mine. You so much as shit outside this house and we'll get you. We're talking to people all over this reservation."

He popped another stick of gum in his mouth and turned back to the trees.

The sumac leaves fluttered red as blood cells in the morning sunshine. But suddenly his eyes were drawn to something more urgent: a greenish-gray bundle in the middle of the road. His heart began to race again. He took a step away from Jacob, and a bite of recognition ran through him. He reached for the radio mike on his shoulder. "Dan, I need you to cover the kid for a minute."

"Now what?"

"Just do it."

"Ten-four."

Barden appeared behind the screen door and Grossman stepped off the porch. He headed toward the road, his hand resting casually on his holster in case there really was somebody out there in the trees. He could do this, he thought with increasing confidence.

* * *

EAGLE HAD DONE the combination on the safe at their request, but when he was finished Olson told him to step away and not turn the lever. He backed up and got to his feet, and Olson knelt down and stretched on a pair of latex gloves.

"Sir," he said, "is there anything I should know about the safe? Any trip mechanisms, or any firearms in there?"

"No, it's just my papers and some cash—for the business."

Olson glanced up at Richardson and placed his hand on the lever. Eagle watched him pause, close his eyes for a moment, and pull the safe door open. He inspected the inside, then looked up at Richardson and Fladeboe.

"Only papers, like he said. No cash though."

This struck Eagle as wrong. He was sure he had put eight hundred dollars in there to pay the ricers. He wondered if he had left it in his jeans in his rush to get ready for the ceremony.

"What's in the baggie?" Richardson asked.

Olson pulled the baggie out and sniffed it. "Tobacco. It says organic Indian tobacco on the label."

Eagle looked at Richardson and lifted his hands in an expression of incredulity.

"Why's it in the safe?" asked Richardson.

"It's sacred. I'm a pipe carrier."

Richardson nodded, skeptically turning over a tiny piece of gum in his cheek.

Fladeboe lifted the Ziploc bag. "There's wild rice in the

horse manure," he said. Richardson stepped up to examine it. He squeezed the bottom.

"Keep searching," he said. "The money's here somewhere."

Fladeboe nodded and lowered the sack. Agent Olson stood.

Eagle spoke up again. "Can I just ask you gentlemen how horse manure equals probable cause?"

Richardson looked at him as if he might be offended, but his face was inscrutable. Then he inhaled and seemed to come to a sudden decision. "Last night someone broke into the North Lake Bank. Same bank, you might remember, that just had a fire. The officer out on the porch was shot by a fleeing suspect after that incident."

Eagle swallowed. He knew this was dangerous territory. Law enforcement had spent the better part of the week trying to get information out of anybody and everybody on the reservation. He had never seen them so on edge.

"Whoever it was couldn't crack the main safe, but they cut the night depository open and got away with a hundred and seventeen thousand dollars in a bank cash transfer," Richardson continued. "Fortunately, they all had recorded serial numbers." He seemed to be studying Eagle's reaction to this.

"But what could I have possibly had to do with that?" Eagle asked.

"We got a phone tip. Someone saw your vehicle. A wild rice truck."

Eagle's mind leaped to JW. "Who saw it?" he asked.

"That's not important at this point."

"John White? Was that your tipster? The banker with the gambling problem?" Eagle could imagine JW stealing the money and trying to pin it on him.

"I can't say," said Richardson, but the name seemed like new information to him.

Eagle pressed his advantage. "Last night he could have been driving that vehicle without my permission. I was at a public ceremony in front of hundreds of people, being honored by the whole community, and then I was here at home with my son. When did this burglary happen?"

Jacob was shoved into the room by Grossman, who followed with Barden.

"Quit pushing me!"

"Shut it," Grossman said, pointing toward him aggressively.

"Deputy, what's going on?" Agent Richardson asked, his voice filled with irritation.

"This kid has a long history of trouble."

"Now just a minute," objected Eagle, but Grossman held up a hand to silence him, and with the other he held up a bundle of twenty-dollar bills. "I found this in front of the house."

"It wasn't in front of the house, it was out on the road!" Jacob yelled.

"The road in front of the house," Grossman clarified, but his tone was patronizing and his teeth were clenching his gum.

Richardson took the money. He glanced at Olson, and Eagle saw Olson step closer to him.

"Look, I didn't have anything to do with this," Eagle said.

He saw Barden nod to Grossman, and Grossman step over to block the door, legs wide, chewing his gum. "Oh, come on! I'm telling you, I have no idea where that came from, and if somebody actually saw the vehicle as you claim it would have been John White who was driving it."

Richardson took out a list of serial numbers from his shirt pocket. He glanced at Eagle, then scanned the list against the top bill in the packet. He looked up at Barden.

"Arrest him."

"This is bullshit!" Jacob yelled. "He didn't do anything!"

Grossman and Barden moved in on Eagle, crowding him toward the desk. "I've never seen that money," he said. "I've never seen it!" He pointed at Grossman. "For all we know, he could have dropped it there! He harasses our community all the time, and he has it in for my son!"

Grossman stepped up behind Eagle, enveloping him in a cloud of body odor. He exhaled through his nose, and Eagle could smell his spearmint gum over the acridity as Grossman wrenched his arms firmly behind him and closed a pair of cool metal handcuffs around his wrists, clicking them a notch tighter than necessary. "You know what they say," he said low in Eagle's ear. "Nut doesn't fall far from the tree."

Deputy Barden stepped up in front of him. "Look at me, Mr. Eagle," he said. "You have the right to remain silent—"

"It's all right, son," Eagle said to Jacob, wanting to protect him from the idea that his father might have done something this wrong. "This is all a mistake. We'll figure it out. I want you to go tell your aunt—"

Grossman snugged the handcuffs even tighter and wrenched Eagle's arms painfully together behind him. "Listen to the man," he said. Then Eagle felt him step back as Barden finished reading him his rights.

But as he did Grossman leaned over his desk and looked out through the blinds. "Hang on, Dan," he said. And then, "What the hell?"

Richardson moved in front of Eagle and looked out as

well. Eagle stepped back to make room, nearly tripping on Grossman, and looked out through the blinds. Smoke was billowing out of the windows of JW's old blue trailer home, rising in gray tufts through the orange leaves.

34

Green and yellow flames shot high from all four stove-top burners, sending up smoke and sparks. The trailer was filling with a noxious cloud from the blackening curls of cash. JW stripped bands off the bundles in his hand and crumpled more bills to fuel the fire. He had opened the windows and the roof vent to let the smoke out and attract attention.

He reached into the trash can liner and pulled out two more handfuls of cash bundles and threw them full onto the flames like small logs. He coughed at the dappled cloud of smoke and ash that rose up and spread across the ceiling. He ducked to look up at Eagle's porch from the window over the kitchen sink, catching a breath of fresh air. He wondered how long it would take before they noticed. He grabbed the dish towel and ran it under the tap as the cash burned hot and crackling next to him, then wrung it out and held it over his face.

* * *

GROSSMAN FOLLOWED RICHARDSON and the other officers onto the porch. Barden stepped out with Eagle.

"That's John White's place," said Fladeboe.

"Who?" said Richardson, seeming surprised.

"John White. He's the president of the bank," replied Grossman.

"Well, get the hell down there!" Richardson ordered. "What the hell's the bank president doing in the trailer?" What else have I not been told?"

Grossman began jogging down the walk. Smoke was pouring from the trailer's open windows and a vent on the roof. He wondered if JW was really inside. Fladeboe jogged up beside him. They ran across the grass and up to the trailer home. Grossman stepped up the wooden stairs, his bravado returning, and pounded on the aluminum door.

"JW, you in there?" There was no answer, but they could hear someone coughing and choking.

"This isn't right," he said. "You sure this is John White's place, not some fucking meth lab?"

"Yeah," said Fladeboe, his face red. "I've been here before."

Grossman was still skeptical, but he pounded again. "JW! We know you're in there! Come on out!"

They could hear flames crackling just inside, and more coughing. Grossman unsnapped his holster and drew his gun. He thumbed the safety catch off and stood beside the door, his back to the trailer wall and his gun pointing at the sky. His heart was racing.

"You'll have to come get me," they heard from inside, followed by more hacking.

Grossman nodded to Fladeboe, who also drew his gun. He took a breath as if preparing to jump into a lake, feeling suddenly shaky with adrenaline, then he whipped the door open.

A cloud of hot smoke engulfed him. Grossman stepped up into the hot interior, and through the smoke he saw JW covering his face with a towel and feeding bundles of cash onto a fire on the stove top.

"Hold it!" he yelled, his gun aimed at JW.

JW glanced at him and kept going. Grossman rushed him and they crashed onto the floor, the bundles scattering across the floor around them. Grossman was on top of him in the smoke, and JW was pawing at him like a wild animal. Grossman was choking, his eyes burning. He raised his gun and hit JW in the head with the side of the barrel.

JW yelled in pain and his arms bent up over his face to protect himself. "All right!" he barked, coughing desperately. "Get off me!"

Grossman saw that he had opened a gash over JW's left eyebrow. "God damn it, JW, what the fuck—" he yelled, but then smoke filled his lungs and he started to cough and choke as he gasped in even more. His head was spinning.

JW seemed to recognize that Grossman was in trouble. "Get out, I'll follow!" he said.

Grossman nodded, his eyes burning. He crawled off JW and headed for the door, his arms shaking, his eyes raining. Somehow he managed to look back and make sure JW was following.

* * *

JACOB STOOD ON the porch with his dad, Olson, Barden, and Richardson.

"Stay here, son," Eagle said, eyeing the trailer.

They watched as Grossman, coughing, fell out of it. A moment later, JW followed, then stumbled shakily to his feet, holding a sagging dish towel. Fladeboe trained his gun on him and he raised his hands in submission.

Jacob was dumbfounded. This was impossible. JW had made him return the cigars. He was his friend. Something was wrong.

Grossman stumbled to his feet, lost his balance, then stood again. He put his hands on his knees for a moment, and hacked deeply, silver bands of snot and saliva streaming from his nose and mouth. Fladeboe got JW to place his hands on the trailer wall, then holstered his gun and began to frisk him. Barden's handheld squawked and Grossman's voice came raspy over the radio.

"We got it! We got the money!" he gasped.

A sense of confusion and betrayal rose in Jacob. He had seen JW come out of the trailer with his own eyes. JW had stolen the money.

"—whole bag of it," rasped Grossman. "He was burning it on the stove." He wiped a stream of snot from his face.

"Ten-four," said Richardson. He was standing beside Jacob. "Is it still burning?"

"Just what's on the stove. I gotta go back in and put it out," replied Grossman, turning back to the door. But then Fladeboe said something to him and Grossman nodded and went to handcuff JW, while Fladeboe took a deep breath and stepped up into the trailer. Then Jacob heard the hollow metal whoosh of a fire extinguisher and the smoke began to slow.

"The son of a bitch," said Eagle, his hands still cuffed behind his back. He looked at Jacob. "I'm sorry I exposed you to him, son. I should have known better."

"But he was at the eagle feather ceremony, with Aunt Mona—"

"They found the money in his trailer, son. This whole thing was his doing."

"I guess the FBI had it wrong," said Deputy Barden. He glanced at Richardson, who nodded in reply.

Barden stepped up behind Eagle and hiked his arms up. Jacob saw tears come to his father's eyes, then heard the cuffs fall away with a dull clink. His father brought his hands around in front of himself, rubbing the angry purple rings on his wrists.

Jacob looked at him with concern. "Are you okay?"

Eagle nodded.

* * *

"OKAY, JW." GROSSMAN was wheezing as they stood by one of the cars, but otherwise seemed to have recovered from the smoke inhalation. "I'm gonna read you your rights. You have the right to remain silent. Anything you say can and will be used against you in a court of law. You have the right to an attorney. If you cannot afford an attorney, one will be provided for you—"

JW looked up at Eagle and Jacob and the agents on the front deck. A flock of mergansers flew overhead, carping and squabbling. The sky was teakettle blue. He could see Eagle's intense stare and feel his hatred radiating down at him. There was nothing he could say.

Jacob toed the ground, no doubt feeling betrayed. He saw Fladeboe intercept Mona as she rushed down the road.

"What's wrong? Why are you arresting him?"

JW caught her eye and shook his head, attempting to convey that she should not say a thing. He saw the worry and confusion on her face, her feathers flashing in the morning sun.

"Just stay back, Mona," instructed Fladeboe, holding up his hands to bar her way. "She's the local drunk," he said to Grossman. She slapped him, prompting Fladeboe to grab her wrists. "Settle down, Mona," he said, and walked her backward.

JW breathed heavily through his nose, but he said nothing and looked away.

* * *

ON THE DECK, Jacob was filled with an undirected rage. His heart told him something was wrong. "Dad, it can't be—"

Eagle raised a hand to silence him.

"You need to listen to me!" Jacob said, trying again. But Eagle was focused on Richardson.

"It looks like we may have had a bad tip," said the agent. "I apologize."

Eagle nodded curtly, then watched as the agents and Deputy Barden began walking down to the cars.

"Dad," Jacob said, but Eagle cut him off again.

"Not now," he said. Then he raised his voice, addressing the agents. "If he was your tipster, he was probably going to plant that up here. He was trying to stop us." Richardson stopped and turned back.

"That's interesting," he said. "Why do you say that?"

"I'm opening a new tribal bank. You might have heard that it, too, was set on fire, but mine burned down. We were going ahead anyway. You think this is a coincidence? He came out here and got a job working for me. He was trying to destroy us."

Jacob was boiling inside. He had had enough. "You're wrong!" he yelled. He shoved his dad and stepped off the porch.

"Jacob!" Eagle called out after him, but Jacob was heading down the hill. He needed to explain that JW had been out with them last night. And he needed to know what was really going on.

He heard Grossman talking to JW as he opened the back

door of the cruiser. "You had it all, and you threw it away. And for what? A lousy roll of the dice?"

JW looked at him, but said nothing.

"Listen to me!" Jacob said, racing up to the car. "You're making a mistake! He was with us last night!"

Grossman pointed at him.

"Back the fuck off." He called to Barden on his radio. "Dan, can you get me a fucking perimeter?"

"Ten-four," barked the radio, and Barden started walking down to the cars.

"Stay back or I'm going to fuck you up." He pointed at Jacob, then turned back to JW and put a hand on his shoulder. "Watch your head," he said.

Jacob grabbed his arm. "Just listen to me!"

The blow came fast as Grossman spun and backhanded him hard. Jacob stumbled backward and fell onto the gravel. His knife flew out of his shirt pocket and sprung open.

"Weapon!" yelled Grossman.

Jacob scrambled to his feet, his face burning and his eyes blind with rage. He let out a roar of frustration and rushed Grossman.

The blow had sound, a blast that hit Jacob in the chest and blew him backward with an otherworldly force. He stumbled, but stayed on his feet. He put a hand to his chest and felt a sticky warmth and an aching. His hands came away greasy red.

Grossman's Ruger was smoking and his chest was heaving. The painful ring of the shot filled his ears.

He heard Eagle screaming, and turned to see him running toward them.

His Aunt Mona was crying and fighting to get out of Fladeboe's grasp, but she was making no sound at all.

"Goddamn you, Bob, he's just a kid!" he heard JW yelling from somewhere. "Call a fucking ambulance!" It sounded like tinkles.

There was a rushing and then he was in his dad's arms on the gravel. His lungs wouldn't lift. His heart pounded in his chest. He felt the warmth on his back and it was somehow comforting. He let out an involuntary, burbly cough and felt the hot, coppery-tin taste of blood in his mouth. He struggled to wipe his dry lips, and his hand came away with a pink-tinged froth.

"Jacob!" His dad's face loomed before him, but the sound of his voice came from a mile away. "Jacob! Can you breathe?"

His dad pulled his own T-shirt off and pressed it into him. He shook his head. He tried to speak. His breath was weak and came bubbled and dark, and he struggled and grappled with an unspeakable urgency. His dad leaned down and put his ear close. "I'm sorry," he managed to whisper, and then the darkness rushed over him.

* * *

JW RODE IN the back of Fladeboe's car, destined for booking at the Bass County Government Center. A metallic bitter taste filled his mouth, and his clothes and hair reeked of smoke. The blood from the gash over his swollen left eye had coagulated and was sealing his eye shut. He could feel it, dry and scabby, on his cheek. The ambulance rushed and bumped on ahead of them on the dusty reservation road, leaving them in a cloud of dust so thick that Fladeboe had to work his wipers.

"Can you turn on the emergency radio in case they say anything about him?" asked JW.

"It is on," said Fladeboe.

But there was only a dead silence, cut by periodic snippets of barely intelligible communication from other towns in the far twilight of radio range.

They pulled out onto the highway, past Eagle's burned bank. He stared at the tag hanging and spinning from Fladeboe's rearview mirror: a picture of four Indian chiefs in traditional headdresses. The caption read, Homeland Security: Fighting Terrorism Since 1492.

* * *

THE AMBULANCE DOORS opened outward at North Lake Hospital's emergency entrance. The EMT with Eagle and Jacob hit a lever as he got out, and the gurney's legs scissored down onto the asphalt as the driver came around to take the other end. Jacob was unconscious, with an oxygen mask on his face and tubes running into his arms, but they had managed to restore a faint pulse that ran through him like a tiny serpent. Eagle followed as they wheeled the gurney toward the sliding doors, bags of plasma and saline swinging violently from the chrome rack.

As they rushed down the wide hallway, Eagle became aware of a woman in hospital blues at his side, saying something about insurance. Two RNs ran up to join the gurney, and the EMTs filled them in as they hurried forward. Jacob was pale and pasty as lard.

"Sir?"

The woman's hand was on his arm. Eagle reached into his back pocket.

"Here's my wallet," he said, hurrying after the gurney. "It's all in there."

"Thank you, but I need you to come with me. You can't be with him in surgery anyway. Please, sir."

One of the RNs looked up at him and nodded, and in that

moment he felt Jacob's soul slipping away from him. The force of his will could not keep Jacob alive. He was in the hands of others, who neither knew nor cared for him. As he stopped his forward rush, Eagle felt he was somehow finally giving up, and a sickening knot swelled in his heart as he watched the EMTs and the RNs wheel his son away around a corner.

"Sir?"

He turned to the woman and nodded, and she led him into a maze of glass-walled offices.

"You may want to wash up a bit," she said as they stepped into her office. He suddenly realized that he was shirtless and streaked with his son's blood. She pushed a folded hospital gown at him and nodded toward a back corridor. "Men's room is the second door on the left."

Eagle elbowed the door open and turned on the faucet, leaving sticky smudges on the handles. There was only one sink and toilet, and the door locked from the inside. He flipped the lock with his elbow, then went back to the sink and began washing the blood from his hands. Red rivers swirled around the white porcelain and ran down the drain. He pulled his hands out of the water and stared at the mirror.

"My God," he said, "what have I done?"

V

THE PAYOUT

35

In describing prison to Julie, JW observed that to Midwest Lutherans and hardened criminals alike, beauty has a palliative effect. In fact, he continued, beauty is as essential to the soul as air is to the body. The state prison in Stillwater was a post-Victorian example of this principle, and he described it in letters the way he once told her of the organelles of cells and the gill pouches of pharyngulas embryos from whence fish and people both spring.

Built in 1914 on the upper bluffs of the Saint Croix River, which separates Minnesota from Wisconsin, the prison's tall brick façades had enormous windows and decorative flourishes that would be deemed impractical and unnecessary today. Its population of murderers, thieves, and drug dealers spent their lives in a twenty-acre square that was surrounded by guard towers and a high brick wall erected by the inmates themselves. There were buildings for the administration along the river side of the square, a hospital, a counseling center, special disciplinary housing (otherwise known as solitary), three industrial manufacturing buildings, and three very large cell houses.

The interior walls were finished with light blonde bricks, and the bars, gates, and railings were of blue-gray painted steel, a contrast that gave the building a light, airy feeling. The floors were made of a faintly pinkish stone that was polished to a reflective shine, and the corridor floors had a slight dip, worn thinner in the center by the daily traffic of a hundred years.

There were two main cell houses, each containing a detached, completely enclosed cell block—four tiers of blue-gray painted steel bars, cells, and catwalks—that sailed like a battleship inside in its own private, bounded ocean, never touching the outside walls. The other house, D block, had five tiers.

But what really characterized the prison was its enormous windows, which let in a wash of high milky light of the kind that would suitable for a painter's studio. This was especially true in the cell houses, whose exterior walls were three-quarters glass. In fair weather, these steel-framed window walls could be operated with levers to completely open the cell blocks to the breeze. The effect was of soaring freedom, which was sometimes a torture, but more often a balm.

The catwalks of JW's cell block had a catwalk that led along the cells like the gunwales of a battleship. During open hours, prisoners who were not at work stood on the walkways and leaned over the jointed pipe railings, talking or staring out the windows at the world beyond the walls. Otherwise they congregated by the telephones and exercise equipment that stood under the vast window walls in the wide stone aisle of the first floor.

Yet despite the beauty of the windows, and of the pipe-jointed railings and the pink floors, the cells themselves were instruments of torture. Numbered with black stencils, each was a mere six feet wide by nine deep, its front wall of bars the perfect receptacle for the guards' night sticks. The cell offered neither space nor privacy, nor room to think too far beyond the mundane and the daily, and JW hadn't anticipated this closing of his mental world. Each cell held a single metal bunk rack hung from the wall with two solid steel brackets, a tiny sink, an attached metal desk with a built-in stainless stool, a bookcase, and a stainless toilet without seat or lid, which sat in full view of inmates and guards, and of escorted visitors and administrators of both genders. All showers were on the first floor, at the far ends of each cell house, and afforded a similar lack of privacy.

At some point, in light of these conditions, modesty inevitably gave way to a sense of indifference, as if the men there were little more than cattle. Over time, JW had come to share this immodest apathy, with one notable exception—he still closely guarded one last important secret: that he was, in fact, innocent, at least of the crime he had confessed to. He couldn't stop wondering if the space he bought Johnny Eagle had even been capitalized on in the wake of the events on the reservation.

It was a warm September day again, a little over a year after his arrest, and the windows in his cell block stood open to let in the breeze. Moving air lifted things and blew away the smells of defeat that sometimes seemed to emanate from the steel itself. He lay on the bunk in his first-tier cell, reading a copy of *The Economist* from the library and listening to the radio on low. Radios and TVs were supplied for good behavior, and came in clear plastic housings so inmates couldn't hide contraband in them. Cell phones, tablets, and computers were forbidden, and all communication with "the streets," as the guards called the world outside the prison wall, went through monitored channels.

JW had tried several times to find news of Jacob and Johnny Eagle since his arrest, but he hadn't turned up anything reliable. Carol and Julie had visited shortly after he was incarcerated, and JW asked them what they knew. Sitting opposite him in the visiting room, separated by a five-foot sea of blue carpet, Carol looked disconcerted. "Honey," she said, "I guess I just don't understand any of this."

"I don't expect you to," he said. Then he asked if they knew whether Jacob had survived the shooting. They said they thought he had, but that they'd heard he was in a long-term care facility. When his subsequent questions went un-answered, he eventually stopped asking.

Then he heard of a new Ojibwe inmate from northern Minnesota, and he hunted the man down in woodshop. The inmate told him he'd heard about the shooting, and that the boy had died. JW was not permitted to make unsolicited telephone calls, so he sent letters to Eagle and to Mona, apologizing and begging for forgiveness. These, too, went unanswered.

Over the following months, his world had slowly contracted to what could be found within the prison walls. No one came to visit him. No one wrote or called. And as a result, JW turned increasingly inward. He became wiry and jaded and focused on the job at hand. But in idle moments he would think back to the events leading up to his arrest, shifting and re-shifting them until patterns of meaning that had seemed entirely clear grew murky and confused. His greatest source of comfort was a clear sense that he had behaved honorably, even if no one outside knew it. And yet—

Jacob.

He spent days mulling over minute details of the entire last year of his free life, building vast gossamer webs of cause and effect, and then tearing them to shreds, forcing himself to stick only to the known facts, and to abandon any thoughts of happy endings, of karma and people getting what they deserved. That way lead to the unending dry road of depression and loneliness. He was beyond that now.

In the end, he told himself, life was not joy but catastrophe. There was no way around it, and so he needn't feel so bad. We all lose everything in the end. For him it was just a little sooner, and he had at least done it for a cause.

And yet there was the boy.

It burned at him, even though he couldn't imagine having done anything differently. His mistake was that he had acted too late, resisted Jorgenson too late, and been too slow on the uptake. In short, his were defects of speed and intelligence, perhaps, but not of character.

And yet.

He probably never should have gotten involved with Jacob. Had he not made him care, then at least the shooting wouldn't have happened. But then he doubled back yet again. Given the circumstances, the racism, the shackling arms of the past reaching forward, guiding everybody into ignorance of the past—could it have gone any other way? Given Grossman, could it have gone any other way? Was it even responsible to contemplate? Had he acted with the necessary kid gloves? Was it not his duty to first do no harm? Had he always been a prisoner of circumstance? Was he a killer, just the same?

In the end, he always concluded, he was who he was. Just as Eagle and Jacob were who they were, and Grossman was who he was. People had their roles in the play, and sometimes bad deeds led to good endings, and good deeds led to bad ones. It was all a big gamble, really, and thinking one could predict the outcome was hubris. Nature did not have a human morality, and chance led down strange alleyways. Why did he get that jack of hearts? The odds were totally

against it. Everything would have been different. Why did a
deer jump out in front of Chris when it did?

Chance.

The men played poker on the floor of the cell block, all
day long, every day. Penny hands. He could hear them now.

Lady Gaga sang low over his small radio. *Baby, I was born
this way.* *The Economist* was three months old, but it had
an interesting article on the reinvention of America for the
new global economy, and how this was happening because
of innovation and increased corporate competitiveness, particularly in the manufacturing and financial-services sec-
tors. The future was bright for the companies that knew
how to capitalize in this new environment. He couldn't help
but think of Eagle and Jorgenson and the seminars he used
to teach. He turned the page. Full-page ad for Las Vegas.
What happens there stays there. Pretty blonde in low-slung
white satin, boobs hanging half out (come hither, they call),
laughing and gripping a guy's arm, five o'clock shadow, collar
open, perfect white teeth, young and rich and happy with
their gorgeousness. This is how we see luck.

He set the magazine down. The steel wall above his bunk
had a twenty-seven-inch square that was painted a darker
gray. Charcoal, not the pleasing blue-gray of the rest of the
steel in the cell block. It was the one place where personal
effects could be displayed, according to the prison fire code.
Taped in the square was a Valentine's Day card from seven
months ago. He reached up and took it down—rough paper,
faux-torn edges—and opened it for the umpteenth time. It
bore a photo of Julie behind rubber bars in a funhouse jail
cell, crossing her eyes. *I miss you, Daddy. Love, Julie,* was
written beneath it. He smiled.

Something had changed with Julie in recent months. She

was writing him letters, and she was opening up in ways he hadn't seen since the old days. Perhaps his absence made him the perfect listener: a grateful recipient of any observation, no matter how mundane. But whatever the cause, the change was a source of great joy for JW. On low days, he would pull her letters out and reread accounts of boy troubles and the brutal competition between eighth-grade girls, of her science homework and the trees she had identified. She wanted to explore the oceans, she wrote, and was thinking of becoming a marine biologist. After all, ninety percent of life on Earth happened below the surface.

The song ended and the station went to a commercial break. He stuck the card back up on the wall and turned back to the magazine, propping himself up on his elbow. Copper mining in Alaska, thirty-one tribes up in arms, more water troubles, Tiffany CEO opposed, arbitrage and currency trades, Goldman Sachs and SolarCity, Tesla electric cars charging forward, gold and palladium market moves on the dollar, sockeye salmon spawning, the rebirth of Ford and GM, auto sales up worldwide, China as the future. His thoughts drifted to banking and corporate competition, currency manipulation and microlending, and then suddenly he realized that this line of thinking had been prompted subliminally: a radio commercial was blathering on about some new bank with a variant of an irritating jingle he had heard so many times before. "New home? New car? New business?" Something about the announcer's voice was familiar. "Get the lowest rates online at Nature's Bank, the cold country's best source for hot cash!"

36

Nature's Bank was hung with a vinyl banner proclaiming its *Grand Opening*! A new drive-through canopy jutted out from the southeast corner of the community center. The window faced southeast to the wetlands and the fire station beyond. Finished in the stacked flagstone-and-wood style of the community center, it looked as if it had always been there, as if the drive-through were simply a bluff rising from the wetlands and water. Eagle admired it with satisfaction.

The place was packed. Cars filled the community-center lot and the overflow field beyond, lined up for the grand opening of what his employees were calling Nature's drive-through.

Rick Fladeboe stood on the main highway directing traffic, but he was of little use because of the backup. Eagle walked up and down the row of cars that had made it into the driveway, handing out flyers, joking, and shaking hands. When he had embarked on this journey in the dark months after Wenonah's passing, he never could have imagined this. It was always about the drive forward, the push against the odds, the power of will to make it happen or die trying. It was a means to flush his anger and his guilt, his grief and shame and fundamental distrust of life. More importantly, he could see only now, it was about being a good father, making a meaningful contribution, and surviving without sacrificing everything that he hoped to become.

Then, just as suddenly, a new goal had emerged: to be not just an Indian bank, but *the* bank. And here he was, thanking and greeting Indians and townsfolk alike.

The band had gone all out. Ceremonial drummers drummed and sang near the stone entry waterfall as people flowed in for a sip of hot apple cider and an oatmeal *muzuun* raisin cookie, and to open a new account and get a chance to win the new Tesla that was roped off and gleaming in the lot. Others came simply to see the new bank and to experience a bit of history.

"It's a great day!" a woman yelled to Eagle. He bubbled up with a bright smile.

"Yes, it is!" he replied joyfully. He looked over to Rick Fladeboe, who was gesturing to get his attention.

"I let her jump the curb," he yelled. "Now everybody wants to do it!"

He pointed to Eagle's black SUV, which was parked in the lot. Mona hopped down from the driver's side and a second later Jacob got out of the passenger seat.

He still looked weak and pale, Eagle noted, but he was alive, and that's all that mattered. He headed over to greet them.

"I thought you were supposed to be in school," he called to Jacob as he approached.

"Are you kidding? I was dying to get here." He played it deadpan and Eagle grimaced, drew him in roughly for a quick neck hug, and then shoved a handful of flyers at him.

"Just hand 'em out?" Jacob asked.

"Meet all our friends," Eagle replied.

Mona stepped up as Jacob moved off with the flyers, and Eagle smelled the aura of tobacco that always seemed to surround her. "I can take some too," she offered.

He split the rest of his stack and gave her half.

"Jacob told me you're still telling people JW's responsible for his getting shot," she said as she took them.

Eagle hated her constant tirades on this subject, and his face became hard as stone. He and Mona had gone around on the topic so many times over the course of Jacob's recovery that the exchange had long been chiseled into predetermined paths. Eagle was tired of the anger that resulted from it. She had helped save Jacob's life, it was true, and she had been loyal in the sense that, in order to build a new relationship with Eagle and Jacob, she followed through on her promise never to communicate with JW. But when she brought it up repeatedly at times like this, he couldn't help but be irritated.

"Mona—" His voice came out high and complaining.

"What?"

"He framed us. We've been over this."

"He didn't."

"He was a typical white boy, and he was doing everything in his power to stop this very bank. From day one. Now stop it. Please."

He looked around for the next car to greet, but Mona stepped in front of him.

"'White boy?' When did you get all racist, Mister Half-White Boy? He was good for your son, and you should stop saying that. You were nicer when he was around."

"Good for him? He got him shot! Your nephew—"

"I remember that speech of yours the night before—"

"Look. I don't want to argue with you, especially not today," he said. "Let's just forget about the whole thing. You have your opinions, I have mine. It's over. At least for now." He laughed painfully at his own compromise offer. "Okay?"

After a moment she nodded.

"You guys cover the drive and the lot. I'll walk the highway," he said, trudging off in an effort to shake the bad spirits, and to get away from her.

Vehicles idled on the two-lane highway, waiting to turn left into the lot. Eagle waved to Fladeboe and then worked his way down the row of cars and trucks, chatting up the drivers and their passengers, handing out flyers and raffle tickets, thanking them for coming.

As he worked his way along the row he noticed a Cadillac a few cars ahead. The driver was engrossed in an animated phone conversation, and as he got closer he saw that it was Frank Jorgenson. He handed a flyer to the car in front of him and moved forward, his heart ticking up. Jorgenson's window was down and he could hear a voice over the car's audio system.

"They're all pulling their money out," he heard the caller on the other end saying in an alarmed tone. "Even the white people—"

"I can see that!" Jorgenson barked at the dashboard.

"What should I do?" Eagle heard the voice say, and he recognized it as Sam Schmeaker's.

He rapped on Jorgenson's hood, making him jump in his seat, his face washed white with panic.

Eagle laughed. "Mr. Jorgenson," he said.

"You stay the fuck away from me." Jorgenson fumbled at his arm rest and his window began to close. He tried to pull out onto the shoulder, but he was completely boxed in.

Eagle laughed again and shook his head. "You don't have to worry about that," he said. "Just wanted to welcome you to the new bank." Then he leaned in close to make sure Jorgenson could hear him through the glass. "Wenonah's bank," he said.

"It was her dream." He stared in at Jorgenson's pale face and saw his chin tremble.

The cars ahead moved forward a notch and traffic loosened momentarily. Jorgenson cranked the wheel of the Cadillac onto the gravel shoulder and sped away, kicking up a cloud of dust that settled over the other cars.

A horn honked and he turned to see one of the women from the tribal council grinning in the next car. "Give me a damn flyer!" she said. He grinned and resumed walking the line, feeling relieved.

The three of them—Eagle, Jacob, and Mona—spent the rest of the afternoon in a state of suspended joy, a lofted floating sensation that Eagle could only liken to what he had felt at his wedding to Wenonah, wrapped in the well-wishes of nearly everyone they knew, plus a hundred new friends. But this day also had a somewhat bittersweet quality, because of the circumstances surrounding its inception.

At four o'clock, Mona gave him the keys to the Bronco and the three of them piled in. The next big wave of customers consisted of people stopping by after work, but Eagle was confident the staff could handle it. They had been training for this day for a month. He had something important to do before it got too late.

The cemetery was a quarter mile from Waterfowl Lake. Interspersed in the tall grasses were a haphazard mixture of spirit houses, crooked whitewashed crosses, and homemade tombstones hung with wreaths. The graves were set at odd angles to one another, placed on the edges of hillsides or tucked in stands of birch trees. The stones and crosses bore the names of his people. Stella Two Bulls. Eddie Musher Arnason. George Bigwolf.

The spirit houses were the spookiest for him—low-slung

mausoleums with shingled or birchbark roofs, moss-covered and creepy. Their wooden-slat walls covered the aboveground bodies and possessions of the dead, all of which were visible through the slats. The glimpses of clothing and hair still gave him the willies. Feathers hung from nearby trees.

Wenonah's grave had a conventional tombstone; he had seen to that. She had never expressed a wish one way or another—death had always seemed to be decades away—but he knew he would not be able to handle the thought of her rotting there on the ground in the wind. Her grave was on a hill with a view of the lake, just as she would have liked. He remembered her joy in leading Jacob by the hand along its watershed when he was a little boy. They would wind along the edges of the wetlands, following the scat trails of animals and the tracks of pheasants, and she would point to the different kinds of dung and tell him stories about the deer and the fox, the rabbit and the bear.

The gravesite had a view of a corner of the community center, far in the distance. It wasn't the corner with the bank, but that didn't matter. She had a piece of it just the same. And the bank was named after her greatest passion.

He stood by while Jacob approached the grave, carrying a fall bouquet of purple asters and green hydrangea blossoms that glowed with a pale aquatic light in the long afternoon sun. This was Eagle's first time back here with him since the funeral, and he saw that the boy's face was puffy around the eyes. He squatted down and placed the bouquet in a short metal holder that Eagle had put there for that purpose in the first weeks following her burial, when neighbors and friends in Minneapolis were still bringing them meals or taking Jacob for the weekend. He would drive up and spend Saturday afternoons with Wenonah, bringing her fresh bouquets of purple hyacinths and daisies. He would sit next to her in the seedling grasses and look out over the lake, wondering what to do now that all his shortcomings were clarified in the sharp inner mirror of anger and grief.

Now the grass was long and dotted with yellow dandelions, clover, and the curled violet remnants of alfalfa blossoms. Jacob knelt in them and put a hand on the headstone as if it were her shoulder. He leaned in close and Eagle heard him whisper, "I love you, Mom." Eagle knew how much he needed this.

Mona had been to the grave many times herself. At first Eagle would see her in passing, or hovering on weekends, but more recently she had taken to coming during the week, while he worked. He would find her flowers and other offerings when he came up. Now, when Jacob stood away from the headstone, she moved in and squatted next to it. She unbuttoned her top and took something shiny from around her neck. It spun in the sun on a blue silken ribbon. She draped it over the rounded stone and walked away without looking back. When Eagle knelt close he saw that it was her one-year Alcoholics Anonymous medallion.

He kissed the headstone. He ran his hand over it and felt its cool granite smoothness. He thought of her skin, of her warbled laugh, of lying next to her cool naked body and running a hand over her hips as she told him stories of the Anishinaabeg and their search for the land where food grew on water, reconnecting him to a past he had never known and a future he was eager to explore. He thought of her fiery eyes, too quick to anger, and even quicker to laugh. How could he not have moved back up here? he wondered. How could he not have left his life in Minneapolis, with all its compromises and lost moments? And before that, how could he have spent so much time away from her and their son?

He stood then, feeling right in this place for the first time. Then he brushed the dirt off his hands and they walked away.

37

It was ricing time. Eagle looked up from the winnowing machine and saw Mona struggling to lift a large black lawn-and-leaf bag onto the industrial scale.

"I can get that," offered Jacob.

"Thank you," she replied.

Jacob recorded the weight in a notepad and paid the ricer. They shook hands and the man headed to his car, past Ernie and Supersize Me, who were turning rice in the smoke of the parching fire.

Watching Jacob, Eagle felt a sudden blossoming of pride. His boy was becoming a young man.

The rice committee had declared the season open unusually late this year. Many of the migratory waterfowl had already spent a few days bobbing around amid the rice stalks, but finding them green, they lifted off and flew south without eating much. Then an Alberta clipper blew in, the great northwest wind that heralds the onslaught of winter in the Northland. The waves lashed at the rice stalks in a cold fury, swamping them and sending them to the lake bed. When the surviving stalks were finally ready to harvest, the crop was half what it had been. The biologist told Eagle that it was only on account of the long cool spring and summer that some of the rice was still green and strong enough to withstand the storm.

Ernie and Supersize Me were back for the season, but

Shawn Lawrence Otto

Caulfield's Guard unit had been called up for duty in Afghanistan, so Mona and Jacob pitched in to fill the gap. Jacob was fifteen now, and Eagle noticed his developing muscles and emerging confidence, though he still had an air of fragility.

Supersize Me had taken Jacob under his wing. He was teaching him how to navigate the finicky moods of the thrasher, a special responsibility that was the next best thing to driving. Jacob assumed the role with careful attention to detail, monitoring the revolutions per minute in the dashboard tachometer and timing the operation for exactly forty-five seconds, unless they were running harder-hulled rice from farther north. He even volunteered to change the engine oil as the season got underway, and Supersize Me assisted, handing him box wrenches, oil-filter wrenches, and shop towels.

Eagle pulled a full white woven poly bag of clean rice out from the winnower chute. He tied it off and replaced it with an empty bag, then got the winnower going again, its frenetic conveyor squeaking and clacking over the pneumatic howl of the blower. Last year so much had revolved around JW in one way or another, and he was glad to have him gone. They had kept the horse; Jacob still rode him daily and was worlds beyond where he had come with JW. Over the summer, they had taken Pride to horse shows nearly every weekend, and they had begun accumulating blue ribbons and nine-hundred-dollar stud fees.

Mona came over as he finished shoveling a last load of rice from the wheelbarrow into the winnower. "I need to take a break and cover my tomatoes. It's supposed to frost tonight." She wiped the sweat off her face with her upper arm.

"That's fine," he said. "I need to enter today's deliveries in the ledger anyway." He left the guys to continue spreading and parching, and walked with her back up toward the house.

In the spring, he had finally finished the living room. But he didn't yet have any furniture for it, except for a large flat-screen TV and a Playstation that he and Jacob used to play games. Two controllers lay on the floor near a pair of bean-bag chairs. He washed his hands in the kitchen, filled a glass with water, and headed down the hall to his office, where he counted his remaining cash and put it back in the safe.

The safe and house had stood open for days in the commotion following the visit by the FBI, and somehow the Chief Onepapa note had disappeared. He took a moment and searched through the safe for the fourth or fifth time, still unable to accept its loss. One of the police officers or perhaps even one of his own employees must have taken it; when he came home from the hospital, the safe was still open and the bill was gone. He had heard that Grossman was suspected of stealing a shotgun from another house on the reservation, but after all the statements and trauma he was too tired and bitter to pursue a complaint that seemed minor in comparison to what had happened.

He closed the safe door, sat at his desk, and pulled out his ledger book. The wooden blinds cast dark stripes over its wide pages, enriching them in an old-world fashion. He still kept the wild rice books by hand as a symbolic act, recalling the nearly half of Minnesota that his people had sold and never really gotten paid for. He took a notepad and several signed scraps of paper out of his pocket and picked up his special fountain pen, in order to record the weights of raw rice deliveries and the monies paid for them.

Ed Two Horses had brought in thirty-five pounds and Springer Watson fifteen. As he wrote down the entries, his special pen ran dry. He shook it and tried again, but the ink was gone. He unscrewed the back and pulled out the cartridge, then opened the top desk drawer and began to rummage around inside for a replacement. He couldn't find one initially, so he slid the chair back and pulled the drawer wide open, reaching all the way to the back, where his hand fumbled over an unfamiliar round object.

The thought of what it appeared to be seemed absurd and disturbing. He set it on the desktop and continued rummaging around until he found the remaining ink cartridge. He scribbled on the cartridge package until the ink flowed blue, and finished making his entries.

When he was done, Eagle picked the bug back up. He had bought a kit like that himself once, intending to give it to Jacob back when he was ten or eleven and obsessed with pretending to be a spy. Eagle remembered Jacob poking mirrors taped to sticks around corners, a single eye wavering in them. But then Eagle had gotten busy at work, and somehow time had gotten away from him. He had figured that the kit was tossed when they moved up here from Minneapolis, but maybe it hadn't been. Maybe Jacob had found it and assembled the bug on his own.

Eagle sat back, his fingers toying with the plastic device. The thought was ridiculous. Jacob was fifteen. He wasn't interested in electronics projects or in spying around the house, and he doubted he even had the patience to make one of these things. All he ever wanted to do was to ride horses, to cruise with his friends, or to play *World of Warcraft*. Then, with a sudden jolt, Eagle's eyes lifted to the window, and to the abandoned blue trailer in the copse of old oak trees below.

He went down to the barn and dug around in the toolbox until he found a pry bar. He passed Jacob in the hissing smoke of the rice, his charred canoe paddle floating light in his hands as he turned it in a rolling cascade.

"What are you doing?" asked Jacob.

"Just checking on something."

Eagle crossed the street, pry bar in hand. He toed the bark and leaves off the wooden stairs in front of the trailer home. A tattered remnant of yellow crime-scene tape flapped from a weathered piece of duct tape near the door. He lifted the pry bar to the door crack in order to pop it open, and was surprised to find that there was already a dent of a similar size. Apparently he wasn't the first. He inserted the pry bar in the dent and levered the door open with a pneumatic gasp.

Inside, it was damp and bone-chillingly cold. The windows were covered with a fine patina of dust and ash. The air reeked of dead smoke and chemicals. The plywood subfloor groaned underfoot against the trailer's metal frame. The place felt like a mausoleum.

The stove top, the counter, and the floor were littered with tiny bits of charred money and the dried white powder from the fire extinguisher. The cabinets and walls were charred black around the stove, and soot clung to the cabinet doors and ceiling. Old dishes moldered in the sink, the food long dried to them.

Eagle was surprised to see all the tiny flecks of cash. He had a vision of meticulous FBI scientists tweezing evidence into sterile bags, but maybe they didn't need to. After all, JW had confessed. Seeing his clothes and possessions still lying about collapsed time. Suddenly it was a year ago, and Eagle's feelings of outrage and betrayal rushed back with a surprising force.

He opened the kitchen drawers, looking for the bug receiver. There had been no testimony about a bug in the confession or at the sentencing hearing, but it made sense that JW would use such a device if he had been planning to frame him. He dislodged books, plastic dishware, and old groceries. Not finding anything in the main section of the trailer, he went on to the bedroom. He looked in the bedside table and through the banker's boxes in the closet, but there was nothing.

Eagle sat on the flaccid mattress, thinking. Maybe he was wrong. Maybe his anger over JW's betrayal had blinded him to other possibilities. The eavesdropper could be one of the guys in the shop, or possibly even Mona. Or perhaps it was whoever had taken his Chief Onepapa bill in the days when the house and the safe had stood open.

He saw JW's dirty laundry in the clothes hamper outside the closet. He pulled it over. A spicy mildewy smell mingled with the smoky dampness as he dumped out the year-old unwashed clothes. And there, in the pile, he saw an electric cord.

He pulled at it and found a rectangular plastic box and some attached dangling earbuds. He fished them out from the shirts and pushed the pile of clothes away with his foot. He plugged the cord into the outlet by the nightstand and held one of the buds up to his ear and said, "Testing."

It came through loud and clear.

He turned the box off and unplugged it. He sat in the cold and looked out the bedroom door at the still trailer stretching out before him. He finally had evidence that JW had been spying on him. But what did it matter?

He tried to see the world through JW's eyes. He had been working for Jorgenson, trying to undermine the creation of Nature's Bank. That much was clear. He had bugged Eagle to get information. That was why he had rented Mona's old trailer in the first place. Eagle glanced out the window and noted the view it afforded of his own home. He felt like a fool

for having offered JW a job, and for letting him work with
Jacob and the horse. He had believed that it could be different, that times had changed, and that the past didn't need to
determine the present.

But why, then, did JW start burning the money at the
worst possible minute? If the plan was to frame him and it
had gone wrong, why draw attention to himself? The panic
scenario had always bothered him. JW wasn't the kind of
guy to panic, and if he had been working with Jorgenson, the
cops wouldn't have been looking for him. There was also the
question of how a bundle of cash wound up in the road. His
first theory was that Grossman had planted it. He was friends
with JW and Jorgenson, and he hated Indians. But after JW
was arrested these questions had nagged at Eagle, until he
eventually moved on.

He stared at the charred flecks of burnt money on the
floor in front of the stove. A new theory began to emerge in
his mind. What if he and Mona were both right? What if JW
had been spying, but hadn't planted the money? Could it have
been Jorgenson? Was it possible that JW and Jorgenson had
some falling out, and then that JW got up early and took the
money out of his house? Or could that have been his plan all
along? He remembered how he had been drawn from sleep
that morning with a sense of urgency, and thought he had
heard the sliding door opening.

He sat up with a bolt of insight. There was a way
to test this theory. He fell to his hands and knees and
crawled into the kitchen, scanning the scattered bits of
money, fleck by fleck, moving methodically across the floor
as if he were a chopper pilot on some mountain search and
rescue. And then he found it, as different from the rest
as one snowflake from another. The tone of the ink, the

particular curvature of the engraved filigree, the quality of the paper—he had memorized these details over many years. It was the last remnant of his 1899 Chief Onepapa Silver Certificate.

There was only one possible explanation. JW had somehow been in his safe. Mona had always said that when she woke at dawn, he was gone. He must have broken into the safe, removed the cash, and taken it to his trailer, mixing the eight hundred and the silver certificate in with all the rest. But why?

If the getting-fired-for-gambling story was real, it would have been to double-cross Jorgenson. To get a new start somewhere with the money, or maybe even to go gambling again, either of which seemed true to his low character. But he had made a mistake. He had dropped a bundle in the road.

But then why had he started burning the rest, when everything else he had done was thought through so carefully? Why bring such terrible consequences down on himself, when the FBI would have arrested Eagle for the theft? Why would he have thrown it all away? And gone to prison, no less?

He stared at the remnant, turning the question over and over. None of it made any sense. He sighed and looked up through the dusty window. He saw Jacob turning the rice in the smoke, and in that moment, Eagle understood.

38

The three-story metal shop had very few workers, and JW was able to spend most of his time there with a sense of freedom that was not available elsewhere in the prison. Metal carts and racks of steel sheets and tubing were stored in the broad open expanses of the first floor, between the concrete columns. The exterior walls were of white painted bricks, the top edges of which were covered with the dust of decades, and banks of enormous old frosted-glass windows shot the space through with angles of white light. The broad open expanses were filled with the scraping sparks of grinders, the high whines of drills, the screeching zuzzing of diamond saws, the clanging of metal tubes, and the crackling flashes of arc welders.

JW enjoyed the creation process, absorbing himself so deeply that he could forget about the intricate bars of the inner prison he had fashioned for himself. He was paid seventy-five cents an hour, a premium over the fifty-cent starting wage. The Department of Corrections took half of this to offset part of the cost of his incarceration, and he put the rest in a college fund for Julie. As he worked, he often found himself thinking of Jacob and Pride, of ricing with Eagle, and of the night with Mona, when he felt he was being reborn. His body warmed and loosened as he imagined her smoky peach hair and her feathers, but he now felt sure he would never see her again.

His mentor was a master welder named Jimmy Johnson,

a weary black man in his early forties who had long ago been caught selling an ounce of marijuana to an undercover cop. Johnson would soon be leaving and JW hoped to take his place. And so today he was being tested.

His task was to weld together a series of cut square tubes, making base frames for snowplow brackets. The parts broke frequently from the force of plowing snow, and the Minnesota Department of Transportation relied on MINNCOR, the prison's business enterprise, to make new ones. He stood in a twenty-by-twenty-foot work area that was cordoned off by thick sheets of translucent red plastic strung between the columns. The purpose of the sheets was to protect workers outside from the blinding light of the welders, but they created a defined space that he thought of as his own. A large steel table sat in the center of his work area. A grounding clamp was clipped to one corner of the table; its thick black cable ran to a red arc welder that emitted a hollow humming sound where it sat by a heavy outlet. There were a couple of metal scrap barrels beside it, and a set of acetylene tanks.

Johnson watched as he arranged the tube pieces, squaring them like building blocks, then clamping them. He lowered his mask and touched them with the welding stick. He removed the clamps and started laying in a reasonably smooth bead along the first joint.

As he worked, a guard ducked in through a flap in the plastic, holding a clipboard up to shield his eyes. He spoke to Johnson as JW completed another spray of blue sizzling sparks and the smell of ozone filled the air.

"White!" Johnson yelled over the noise.

JW lifted his face shield and the guard became visible, waving.

"Looks like you're gonna get an ass-whooping," yelled Johnson. "But nice job on the weld."

JW took off his gloves and headed over to the guard.

"I guess they've been paging you," said the guard over the screeching of a diamond saw next door.

He nodded toward the flap in the red plastic. JW ducked through it and stepped out into the main corridor, removing his earplugs and tucking them into a pocket in his coveralls. He walked ahead of the guard, past men grinding steel and cutting parts, shooting out long pheasant tails of yellow sparks.

It was sunny outside, but cool and autumnal. The guard followed him through the pitted asphalt yard, toward a fifteen-foot-tall chain-link fence topped with razor wire. There was a gate at the open door of a small control house. He entered the house and walked along a narrow corridor, between barred windows on the left and a long counter on the right, then stepped through the metal detector. He stopped with his feet on the red marks and extended his arms while a guard patted him down, searching for shop-made shivs, tools, and contraband. He signed out on the clipboard, then exited on the other side of the tall fence, followed by the guard.

They headed across more worn asphalt, with pavers showing here and there beneath. The yard door of the main housing complex was a little ways northeast of the fence. He climbed the four stone steps worn into a progression of spoons and waited. The guard reached past him to press the intercom button and the door buzzed. He pulled it open and stepped inside.

The corridor was wide—twenty feet across—and on the far side stood a guard desk. To his left the cafeteria rotunda rose high behind gray-blue bars, slanted with misty shafts of light. To his right the corridor ran several hundred yards past the cell houses to the administration building and the only gate in or out of the prison.

"Hey, Chaz," he said to the desk guard.

"Hey, JW. Got any new bank deals hopping?"

JW smiled as he signed back in. "No, but I heard about one on the radio. Nature's Bank. You should check it out. Best rates around. You can set up an account online."

"You're not fixin' to rob it, are you?"

JW handed the clipboard back.

"I didn't steal anything the first time."

The guard laughed. "Yeah, you and all the other guys in here."

He headed down the pink stone floor, toward the administration building and the visitors' center at the far end. The walls here were sandstone-colored tile, the windows huge contraptions of metal and frosted glass, and the gray-blue bars segregated everything into discrete sections. The gates were all open.

"It's not an 'ass-whooping,' by the way," the guard said as he ambled along beside JW. "You got a couple visitors. Totally unscheduled. They got the Warden to let 'em in. Couldn't fucking believe it."

They walked past the door to D-block on the right. The entrance to the visiting room was ahead, just before the corridor ended at the main entrance. Most inmates initially expected to get a lot of visitors, but only a few had any at all. Carol and Julie had visited twice, but Carol knew you couldn't just show up unannounced and expect to get a visit, unless something urgent dictated it. He hoped nothing serious had happened.

The last time he had seen them was in the early summer. What he remembered most was sitting across from them, five feet away, and wishing he could hold Julie. He looked forward to seeing her again.

He waited in front of the steel door that led to the visiting room. It buzzed and opened and he headed through another metal detector, then stood for another pat-down. He turned left down a smaller corridor and was buzzed through another locked door and into the visiting room.

Johnny and Jacob Eagle were waiting for him. His heart was suddenly racing. Jacob shot up a hand in a sort of wave. JW glanced at the guard, who motioned him in. He felt his knees and hands shaking as he sat down opposite them. He cupped his hands together and leaned forward, elbows on his knees. He didn't know where to begin, what to say. He breathed and smiled and rocked up and down on his toes.

"I didn't expect it to be you two," he finally got out. He laughed and wiped his eyes on a sleeve.

Eagle shook his head, frowning and smiling at the same time. Jacob showed his teeth as if the whole scene were funny, but then JW realized that his eyes were watering.

"How are you?" he asked Jacob.

Jacob ducked his head to wipe his eyes. He nodded. "Fine."

JW nodded back. He felt powerfully moved but also awkward, intimate and yet a distant stranger. Time had passed and things had changed, and there was more flowing between them than could be put into words.

"I'm so sorry," JW said, and a wave of grief washed up in him.

Eagle leaned in. "We want to go back to the FBI."

"Don't," barked JW, before he could even think out his

reply. Guards shifted off the wall and began to watch him. The Native inmate next to him glanced over, then at Eagle.

JW softened his tone. "It won't turn out well." He met Eagle's gaze. "They'll assume you were in it with me, and they'll come after you as an accessory, or as an accessory after the fact. Frank's got a lot of friends. That's the last thing you need right now."

"But we know you didn't do it," said Jacob.

"There's no way to prove that."

Eagle met his gaze, then looked at the floor. "I hadn't considered that possibility," he said. He leaned in, obviously set back. Then he forced a smile, trying to soften the mood again. "Well, shit."

"I'm stuck, my friend," said JW. He looked at Eagle, then at Jacob. "I do appreciate the thought though, I really do. But I knew what I was in for." His voice broke a little. "It just means so much to me knowing that you know, and that you are both all right."

Jacob looked at him and shook his head. "It's not right."

"Life isn't fair. You of all people, know that. And look at you! You must be a half a foot taller! You ever sell that horse?"

"No. I couldn't. I show him."

JW smiled and nodded.

"I'm sorry we didn't let you know we were coming," said Eagle. "We wanted it to be a surprise, but I didn't realize they can't accommodate that very well here, and they said the paging system doesn't work well in—"

"Metal shop."

"I'm sorry we didn't answer your letters. It took me a long time to see past things."

JW nodded. "It's okay."

A black female corrections officer walked down the row

behind the prisoners, distributing inspected visitor gifts from a gray plastic mail cart. She handed a manila envelope to the Indian next to JW and a white one to JW, and then she laughed. "You like this?" she said. "We got a red man with a red envelope, and we got a white guy with a white envelope. Now we just need a few black envelopes for all the black dudes in here and we be all set."

"Open it!" Jacob commanded.

JW turned the envelope over in his hands. It glowed white in a shaft of milky light that had begun to fall across him from the high windows.

Eagle leaned in close, his elbows on his knees and his hands clasped. "I want you to know that we bought the North Lake Bank assets for three million. We haven't got the final audit yet, but I'm guessing that means Jorgenson lost at least four."

JW looked at him. "Five," he said, not breaking his gaze. "At a minimum. They bought the bank for eight, and it was worth over twelve before all this."

Eagle nodded. "And they fired him."

JW felt a thud and a release. He frowned and laughed and wiped his eyes on his shoulders, then smiled at Jacob, who nodded at the envelope. "Open it."

He reached inside and found a thick piece of paper. He pulled it out and unfolded it. It was his hundred-thousand-dollar second mortgage, stamped PAID in big blue letters across the top. He looked up sharply.

"Anything you need—for you, your daughter, her college—you just let me know," said Eagle. "We owe you so much more than that."

JW frowned and nodded. "Thank you." His breath shook as he inhaled.

"There's more," said Jacob.

JW finished unfolding the document as if it were a holy relic, and a bald eagle feather fell out onto his lap. He caught it by its red horsehair tie.

"The band had a little ceremony for you," explained Eagle.

Attached to the end of the horsehair was a business card: John White, Tribal Adoptee; Honorary President, Nature's National Bank.

"Hold up, hold up," the female corrections officer said. "It looks like the censors got stuff back in the wrong envelopes."

JW turned the items over in the milky light.

"No," he said. "They got it right."

ACKNOWLEDGMENTS

This novel owes its life to many voices. It is impossible for me to list every helpful influence and contributor, but there are a few people to whom I owe very large debts of gratitude. Daniel Slager, my editor and publisher, was an incredibly thoughtful, incisive, and helpful partner as I shaped and polished the marble, as was his amazing team at Milkweed Editions. Friend and mentor RD Zimmerman gave generously of his time and insight as a novelist. Sidra Starkovich and Rose Berens, each in their own ways, helped me to take my stumbling grasp of the truth and shape it into a truer depiction of Ojibwe culture and the struggles Native people still face in many places around the world, but especially in Minnesota. Terry Janis generously read and commented on an early draft for similar purposes. Cathy Chavers spent two long afternoons with me, teaching me how to hand-process wild rice (it really is the best), while the excellent Fed Gazette provided (believe it or not) key inspiration. My brilliant literary agent, Joy Tutela, and everyone at the David Black Agency were extremely supportive and creative in helping me find the right partners. My mother Lilly, an immigrant American, brought me up in a house full of foreign students and instilled in me the perspective of the outsider, together with the conviction that communicating across cultural divides is not only wonderful and enriching and family-making, but absolutely essential to success in our shrinking world. My father Allan read like a monster throughout my childhood and instilled in me a love of books. The He-men book club laid the foundation for a beautiful partnership. The members of the Loft Literary Center have provided years of support and friendship. And my amazing wife, Rebecca Otto, encouraged me to write this novel until I finally listened to her. There are many others, and I am grateful to you all.

SHAWN LAWRENCE OTTO is the award-winning writer and co-producer of the Oscar-nominated film, *House of Sand and Fog*. He also writes for film and television's top studios, including DreamWorks, Lions Gate, and Starz. An award-winning science advocate, and humanitarian who co-founded and co-produced the US presidential science debates, his nonfiction book Fool Me Twice was honored with the Minnesota Book Award. He lives in Marine on Saint Croix, Minnesota. *Sins of Our Fathers* is his first novel.

Design & typesetting by Mary Austin Speaker

Typeset in Fairfield Light